In the Kingdom of Mists

Also by Jane Jakeman

DEATH IN THE SOUTH OF FRANCE

In The Kingdom of Mists

JANE JAKEMAN

Doubleday

LONDON · NEW YORK · TORONTO · SYDNEY · AUCKLAND

TRANSWORLD PUBLISHERS
61–63 Uxbridge Road, London W5 5SA
a division of The Random House Group Ltd

RANDOM HOUSE AUSTRALIA (PTY) LTD
20 Alfred Street, Milsons Point, Sydney,
New South Wales 2061, Australia

RANDOM HOUSE NEW ZEALAND LTD
18 Poland Road, Glenfield, Auckland 10, New Zealand

RANDOM HOUSE SOUTH AFRICA (PTY) LTD
Endulini, 5a Jubilee Road, Parktown 2193, South Africa

Published 2002 by Doubleday
a division of Transworld Publishers

A catalogue record for this book is available from the British Library.
ISBNs 0385 603703 (cased)
0385 605021 (tpb)

Typeset in 10½/15pt Stempel Garamond by Falcon Oast Graphic Art Ltd.

Printed in Great Britain by
Mackays of Chatham, Chatham, Kent

1 3 5 7 9 10 8 6 4 2

For J.M. as always
and dedicated to the memory of Camille Monet

Contents

Author's Note   9

In the Kingdom of Mists   11

Historical Note   419

Acknowledgements   421

Claude Monet: Chronology   423

Picture Credits   427

Author's Note

It is a matter of historical record that Monet experienced extraordinary difficulties during his painting campaigns in London in the years 1899–1901. These were, no doubt, due in part to the ever-changing mists and fog which hung over the Thames. But there is an unexplained factor which evidently lay deeper than this. He described himself as being in a state of complete despair and unable to finish the paintings. Clearly he was experiencing a profound crisis.

Prologue

PARIS, 1927

QUITE SUDDENLY, HE GLIMPSED THE PAINTING ON THE opposite wall, the water-lilies, white and crocus-gold, floating in their long pool of misty blue and lilacs.

It was with surprise that he felt his stomach knot with anxiety: so many years had passed since he had last experienced this sensation. And it seemed absurd that the picture should provoke it, so that at first there was puzzlement as well.

Then a woman's voice, from somewhere further down the oval sweep of the gallery, was coming closer. 'Darling, you must come and look at this! Oliver? Oliver!'

'I'm sorry, my dear.' Stand perfectly still, don't try to speak, only let the breath regulate itself, the life continue.

'What is it? You look ill!'

In another moment you will be able to speak. 'So hot in here. This damned collar!'

Breath coming back. Normality. Life resumed.

He ran his finger round the inside of his stiff wing-collar.

Old-fashioned, he thought. No, dammit, I'm just becoming old. Too old to change my ways. Wish I hadn't seen it, though, there, on the other wall, after all this time.

He turned his head away to leave the gallery, but the press of people made it difficult to move, and now Clemenceau was making a speech. 'Glory of the French nation . . . his recent death a fearful blow to France . . .' The old man was very frail, and his weak voice could barely be heard. But the crowd was still for a few minutes, and then when the tired voice fell silent it started to agitate again, following the long curves of the walls, as if it were ambulating round a shrine. A young woman brushed up against Oliver, her glass of white wine tilting, a thin blue frock clinging to her body. She was pursued by a flushed and excited youth who forced an arm through the crowd and pulled her away.

The girl gave Oliver a little smile, a tiny twist of the mouth, no more, and let herself be pulled off in the direction of a painting. He might have responded to that half-smile, in another life, before this moment.

Other bodies closed up the gap. People jostled him, continually nudging against his back, his arms, his thighs, the men in light jackets, the women in pastel dresses. His own body was all firmly encased in wool tailoring.

It was still only May, but the heat was becoming unbearable.

As his eyes wandered across the gallery he felt cut off from the babble. The murmur of French voices was occasionally pierced by high-pitched English ones, but for a few moments he seemed unable to understand any words at all. Then came his wife's voice again. 'What is it, Oliver? Would you like to sit down?'

She had taken his arm, and, yes, he did feel dizzy suddenly.

He put his hand to his forehead and felt a cold perspiration. He fumbled at his breast-pocket for a handkerchief, his fingers thick and clumsy as they groped for the smooth stiff folds: time seemed suspended even as he stood there, his arm across his chest.

He closed his eyes for a moment, hearing a rushing and sighing, like the sound made by a woman's skirt, but then he recalled the present and realized that it could not have been so: women no longer wore such dresses, those long skirts that had swept along floors.

'Do you want to go home?'

He heard the question but could not answer. The crowd parted for a few moments and again he saw the picture across the room suddenly, saw it fully now without any intervention or relief. There was no excuse for turning his head away, even. The woman, holding on to his elbow, turned her head and followed the direction of his intense stare.

'It's an interesting painting, of course,' she was saying. 'We can come back and look another time, if you like,' she said gently, 'when there aren't so many people.'

He moved towards the white expanse of wall, with the patches of browns and greys and purple-blue glistening along it, the long, thick streaks of oil shining wetly.

'So fast.'

His wife looked at him uncomprehendingly. Into his mind had sprung the vision of an old man leaping around a room where the walls were lined with canvases. He was picking up first one picture and then the next, slashing paint frantically, peering out at the river almost like a crazy creature, shaking his head in despair as the light failed. The room grew darker, even as Craston watched the scene replayed within his mind's eye.

And that other room, the room remembered, was now more real than the one in which he stood, where the human press jostled against him and there were egg-white slicks of wet light on eyes, on collars, on sweating cheeks, as heads turned towards him. He was perceiving it, not in the present cool Parisian light filtering from the ceiling, but dimly, as through the gloom, the remembered darkness, of London long ago.

'Oliver?'

Craston turned and saw a woman at his side, a brown-haired, middle-aged woman with a little hat on top of her head, dressed in white stuff with frills round her neck. She stepped back as though alarmed, and he looked down and saw pale stockings gleaming over flesh, thin calves and ankles.

Recognition came back suddenly. 'I beg your pardon, my dear. Quite all right now.'

She was looking uncertainly at him. He felt her hand on his arm and it seemed to be pulling, hanging like the weight of a dead bird, weighing on him and warm through his jacket.

His wife was looking across the room now, following the direction in which he had gazed so intently. 'I've never noticed it before,' she said, 'but there are red streaks in that picture – in the water. Really crimson . . . I suppose it's the reflection of the sunset.'

Yes, thought Craston, perhaps it was that. The sun on some of those London winter afternoons had been a great red glowing ball, the colour of the inside of a blood-orange, shooting across the soft muddy-brown of the river for a few moments at dusk. He remembered seeing the sudden track of light on the water.

But that was not all there had been to see. It depended how you looked at things, of course – no, that wasn't right. What you looked *for*, perhaps that was better. What the painter had looked for, whatever impalpable hazes he had been searching to capture, had not been all there was to see. At least, not all that he, Oliver Craston, had seen.

He felt ill again, and very tired.

A woman with dyed yellow hair and bright rouged lips came towards them, pushing through the knots of people, offering a wide smile, her teeth white and sharp.

'My dear Sir Oliver ... Lady Craston ... So good to welcome you ... We are most honoured to have the representation of your country at this occasion ...'

'Ah, madame ... quel honneur ...' He took her hand and bent over it. That would be enough. He knew her, he was certain, but he couldn't remember the damned woman's name. Sufficient years of diplomatic experience meant he gave nothing of this away.

As he pressed his mouth to the outstretched hand, seeing its shit-yellow freckles of age as his eyes came close to the skin, he dimly recalled that this woman was now the owner of an art gallery, and fled inside his impenetrable armour of politeness.

She led him down the long room, and all along the walls the colours danced – blue and lilac and yellow, ochre and frothing white and ultramarine – as the crowds parted and re-formed, parted and merged again, and glimpses of the pictures came in jigsaw pieces. There were the soft round shapes of pale lilies, with curving streaks in the dividing calyx engorged with dark clitoral crimson and scarlet, or dashes of bright paint forming tiny curved buds like reddened and bitten points of flesh. He had never noticed these things before, in these pictures.

Did the old man *know*, then, in some way? he found

himself thinking. Did he sense the cruelty that had lain so close to him? And look at it and discard it? Just take what he wanted, and nothing else?

The woman continued to talk and he murmured responses. Who was she? There was something about her that he had known in a previous existence, something that had once excited him, but was now forgotten, like a game left somewhere in his student days, abandoned, unfinished.

She introduced him to people from time to time as they swept or crept towards her. 'Sir Oliver Craston . . . You have heard of the Craston Collection? Yes, Sir Oliver is of course an honoured guest, a lover of art . . . He knew Monsieur Monet in London . . .' And his own voice, responding, 'Yes, well, that was a great privilege . . . all rather a long time ago. No, I don't recall very much, I'm afraid.'

Liar, he said to himself. Moments in the past sometimes seemed so clear to him now. The truth was surely that he recalled some things exactly. His youth and the Thames in winter.

1

LONDON, 1900

IN A ROOM HIGH UP BY THE RIVER, AN OLD MAN WAS carrying a painting. He had come through the tall glass doors leading from the balcony overlooking the swirling dark water, and set the canvas carefully on an easel, where its wet oils gleamed so that it seemed to move in the light as if it were a living thing.

It showed a familiar sight, yet made almost monstrous: a bridge across the Thames, portrayed as the artist's eye had caught it. A dark, arched shape loomed across the canvas, and the rippling waters beneath glistened lilac and purple beneath a thick mist. Low on the right was a fiery pool of scarlet and crimson where the dying sun had briefly caught the surface of the water, and within this were darker shadows: a boat, perhaps, with tiny gesticulating figures, or perhaps a piece of driftwood, something strangely shaped, sweeping towards the bridge in the last burning light of day.

The painter's thick body moved steadily about the room as he rubbed the stiff joints in his hands, discarded a heavy cape,

17

poured himself a glass of wine, and finally seated himself at a desk beside a window. But still, though he took up his pen, he did not settle entirely to writing but glanced out every few moments at the satiny gleam of the icy Thames flowing alongside the Embankment below. So oppressively low and close seemed the sky that it was almost as if a sheet had been partly draped over the window of the room, though an occasional glow of light in the west indicated a dying sun hidden behind heavy cloud.

Within the shadows of the room, he tugged at his great spade-shaped beard, and began his letter. He wrote with a certain clumsiness, the pen spluttering occasionally in his hand. 'Alice, my dear darling,' he scratched heavily across the page, 'I may have to break off at any moment and go back to my canvas. The effects of light in this climate will not wait!'

But, looking up from the desk yet again, he had to acknowledge that the day had finally gone. It was dusk outside. 'We have had some brilliantly clear mornings,' he wrote, 'then one by one the fires are lit and the smoke and fog return. I find myself like a soldier on watch, waiting moment by moment.'

He looked up again and out through the balcony doors to the river. There were sketchy human presences discernible on jetties and in boats, disturbing the heavy viscous surface of the river, breaking up the mists with thin bony shapes and sketchy outlines. Through the haze he saw the masts, the boats and oars that dipped in and out of the mist and the water, the black and bruised-purple masses of the sacks and bundles with which the frail cockleshell craft were loaded. And every minute, every second, the prospect changed in front of his eyes with the whole fluid movement of drift and current, of heavy clouds rich with chemicals, aniline purples, chromes, viridians.

'What I want is the moment itself,' said the old man to himself, searching out with his tired eyes the very instant of change, the mystery of those fleeting seconds of dawn or dusk. What he sought in the end would be the solitary presences of water and light dashed on the canvas, with scarcely any regard to those living specks going unknowingly about their business, wrapped within nacreous or indigo shadows.

He turned his head and looked towards the bridge downriver. Now the sun had vanished, and there were points of light from carriage lamps moving above the brownish-black water, their long, swelling reflections slipping across the Thames. He abandoned the letter, laying it aside for completion the next day.

The following morning, he rose while it was still dark. Having wrapped himself in layers of jersey, he moved the painting and the easel out on to the balcony. He went back inside and collected his tools and cape before returning outside. The thick cold air poured down into his lungs as he settled the canvas on the easel, under an awning that was too flimsy to keep off the elements entirely.

A flurry of snowflakes blew into his face as he squinted into the half-light of dawn over the river, and from the water below came the muffled sounds of shouts and splashes, the lapping of the tide that takes all the flotsam and jetsam of London swirling inexorably away. But in spite of the cold his right hand was dashing from the palette to the canvas like a spider, swift and purposeful. His eyes peered towards the east and took in one effect of dawn after another, now one oily streak of orange falling across the bridge, now a tender rose-red burning up the iron hull of some small tramp steamer labouring on its long course downriver. The last flakes of snow whirled down towards the water. Finally, a pale golden sunshine bathed Waterloo Bridge and the chimneys and hulks beyond that lined its banks for all the long and ancient stretch towards the open sea.

Here, where the building commanded the great sweeping curve of the Thames from west to east, the rooms overlooking the river were flooded with the clean light of early morning. But a terrible urgency overtook the painter as the light began to change. There would be only this short time to capture the sun rising over London before the normal darkness of a wintry day took over. As dawn faded, the sky became paradoxically greyer. The grimy-eyed workers scurrying to the factories began their shifts. The tall chimneys would send their great black and yellow banners of smoke across the sky, from the soap factories, the dye factories, the spurting red dust of the brickworks. In the houses of the rich, sleepy servants would be hurrying up backstairs with heavy scuttles and kneeling in front of warm ashy grates. From the myriad huddled streets would rise a forest of slender grey smoke-plumes, and all eventually would form their choking blankets layered against the sunlight.

Soon, too, Michel would arrive, and the old man knew his son would be gently urging him, with all his well-intentioned affectionate persuasion, to come inside.

'Papa, you will get pleurisy! It is dreadfully cold.'

What else had he said, a day or two ago? 'What a terrible city this is. The kingdom of mists!'

The patriarch of the Monet family had been startled, taken suddenly back to a time when he was young and callow and unsuccessful. Those were the very words the young man's mother had spoken, thirty years ago, in another room less than a mile away in this same city. And yet Michel had never known his mother, who had died soon after his birth, so that for the old Monet it was like an act of witchcraft almost, of conjuration, to hear those words from his son's mouth.

It was a troubling thought, one that disturbed his work, which he had conducted relentlessly, day in, day out, for so many years. This place, London herself, was surely the witch, the mystery, conjuring up things he had long forgotten, which came drifting and swirling through the mist as he tried to paint.

Now, this very moment, as he studied the luminous nature of the dawn in sky and water, he perceived the outline of a prow, some little skiff cocking about feebly on the currents of the Thames. It brought to his mind another image, which came between him and the view along the river. There had been another boat then, in the blue and lilac light over the Seine. And on the other bank of the river a country church, sketchy in the distance, its white stones looking almost like things of nature, like cliffs and outcrops of chalk. And the faint grey ghost of that other boat upon the water. Long ago. Years before.

The son came in, a tall figure walking through the shadows at the edge of the room, and put his hand on his father's shoulder. 'Did you finish your letter?'

'No, no, I'll finish it tonight. Somehow, I found myself thinking of your mother, as she was when we were young. I painted her on the bank of the Seine at a little village, a place called Bennecourt, long before you were born.'

Michel Monet was puzzled. It was unlike his father to talk about the past. The huge energies within his tough, stocky body seemed always directed to the future. But the old man went on, hardly aware of his son's presence, or so it appeared from the way he was staring down at the river. 'She was sitting under a tree, on a day when the water was absolutely still and clear, with the white reflection of the inn across the water. She was wearing a striped blouse – I can remember that clearly – and a hat with a blue ribbon was lying on the grass beside her. But she had her head turned away, looking out towards the water. I couldn't see her face.'

'Papa,' began Michel, alarmed by the strange despairing note in his father's voice.

'Oh, I don't mean to worry you. In this city, this blasted black inferno of soot and smoke, I'm not sure of things, that's all. But I loved her, you know, and here sometimes I remember her. It can't be helped.' The old man drew a handkerchief and rubbed at his eyes. 'It is this damned country, where the fog and mist rule. They play tricks with the sight.'

Michel said gently, 'Father, it's so dark, I must put on the light,' and the expensive electric chandelier, of the type proudly fitted by the management in every room of the Savoy Hotel, blazed out, banishing the recollections of that dappled sunshine of a long-distant summer.

Outside, the river ran its course as dawn swept slowly along it, from the sweet meadows of the upper reaches to the filthy effluent that disgorged into the salt waters, and the men and women who lived alongside it prepared for the day.

2

OLIVER CRASTON SHIFTED UNCOMFORTABLY IN THE PARLOUR of the house in Barnes, but he knew nothing would stop his mother in full flow. She was playing hostess to her Reading Circle; he had been summoned to greet her friends and was hovering on the edge of the group.

The maid had brought in the telegram as his mother was pouring tea. The heavy brown velvet curtains at the windows looking out on to the river were looped back to allow a little sunshine to cast its beams through the lace, and Oliver watched his sister's face, caught in its rays. She, Maggie, was holding a thin hand up against the sun to shield her bird-like bright brown eyes. 'Boot-buttons,' he had teased her, when they were small. 'Your eyes are like boot-buttons – all round and brown and shiny. Just like Nedward's.' Maggie had upset their mother when she said one day, 'I don't like Nedward. He looks all stupid.'

For some reason that long-forgotten moment of honesty and an image of his much beloved toy animal crossed Oliver's mind in the hushed silence that followed the entry of the maid with the telegram. The salver was held out to Oliver, and not, as everyone clearly expected, to his mother. He opened the folded buff paper, stared down at it and then passed it to Mrs Craston, who relished the moment and held the slip of paper at arm's length, peering at it through her lorgnette. The faces around the tea-table were watchful, the eyes trying to gauge her reaction before anyone spoke.

The arrival of such a missive, possibly bearing news of catastrophe, entailed both the ceremonious moment of silence with which the Reading Ladies greeted its appearance and Oliver's own subsequent embarrassment at the tameness, the lack of drama, in his telegram.

'Oh, splendid news! Oliver has been accepted for the Foreign Office! What do you think? We'll have an ambassador in the family!'

Mrs Craston rattled the silver teaspoon against her cup with satisfaction, and Maggie jumped up and put her arms about his shoulders. 'Oh, we're so proud of you, dear Olly – but we knew it would be all right!' She smiled her thin-cheeked, toothy smile rather defiantly around the group, knowing what had been passing beneath the surface, reading his thoughts, as usual. Her skin was dry, papery, but now flushed with a little pink of excitement and pride.

He put up a grateful hand and held her warm fingers in his. There were murmurs of congratulation from the assembled company, but he had sensed a moment of near-disappointment in the unheroic contents of the telegram. It should have offered an army commission, or an order to join one of the regiments leaving for South Africa.

Young Craston had not joined up: that was the thought in the ladies' minds, Oliver was sure. There was some embarrassment, yet at the same time he was beginning to feel a touch of defiance, such that even he was slightly surprised. Just down from Oxford, he still knew little about himself, but among the few things of which he was sure was his distaste for soldiering. It seemed to him the most boring and stupid of activities, involving much red-faced shouting. And for once his family was in agreement: his father valued intellectual achievements far above military enterprises; his mother desired above all things to shield him from danger.

Such sentiments went unspoken, of course. There were certain things often left unsaid in that tall, dark mansion where his father seemed to have perpetual indigestion, stirring glasses of greyish powdery water which he tossed down his throat with a rictus of distaste, his lips drawn back from his teeth. In fact, Oliver rarely saw his father and scarcely recognized any paternal physical inheritance within himself, save perhaps for the deep-set eyes and long, slouching physique. But since he had never seen his father unclothed he could not be certain what physical attributes they shared beneath the clothing.

Other seeming unspeakables beneath the Craston roof included Oliver's position as only son, and the genteel financial precariousness in which he had been reared. The younger children were all girls, and it was understood that it would be Oliver's task eventually to support them if they had not found suitable husbands. Oliver's sudden death in battle – however gallant – might be a disaster for them.

So he had not volunteered for the Army, currently embattled against the Boers in South Africa. His mother never reproached him with that, of course, for she would never have wished him into danger, but he knew that her friends made remarks sometimes. 'My son, Toby, you know, with the regiment . . .,' someone would say, and perhaps his mother merely imagined the pursed mouth, the sideways look, understanding the meaning, the imputation of cowardice cast upon her son. It distressed Mrs Craston, perhaps even cost some of her fragile friendships. Of course, she did not say so, but he sensed it on her behalf. Sometimes he wondered if he were, indeed, a coward.

On this occasion, as on many others, he made his apologies and slipped out of the room and into the cold peace outside. A few minutes' walk brought him to the Thames.

He loved this stretch of the river. The Thames still ran clear here; it had come down from its source through willows and pastures. It was the river he had grown up with, listening to its sounds as he lay in bed at night, and, on hot sunny afternoons, splashing about and catching small glistening fish in a net that he swept up, sparkling, out of the water with a rush. He had known this river at Oxford, bathed in it, cooling his skin on hot May evenings. He had not really known it could be anything else till he went to work in London and saw the dark torrent that ran towards what he thought of as the ancient terrible places of London – Wapping, Deptford, mere names to him. He could scarcely believe it was the same river. The slums beside it lower down its course were as foreign to him as another country, places whose inhabitants lay in festering warrens alongside the quays where Oliver and his like would never venture.

Now, on this winter's afternoon, a slight mist hung over the water in the otherwise relatively healthful air of Barnes. He contemplated walking the few miles to Richmond, or Kew, perhaps. A constitutional at a steady pace along the bank under the overhanging willows would help him, as always, to get his thoughts in order.

3

ONCE HE HAD EMBARKED ON HIS EMPLOYMENT AT THE Foreign Office, Oliver kept his private views about the Boer War to himself. He was ambitious enough for such caution, though sufficiently principled not to be blackmailed into volunteering for what had come to seem a futile argument. He was convinced that the Boers would not be overcome with the ease implied by government propaganda.

So he worked quietly and obediently at the small mahogany desk that had been assigned him, and to which he made his way each morning after his initial briefing. Out of the window he had a view of St James's Park, and liked to look at the birds on the lake. It was now frozen in places, so that the ducks skated comically as they tried to land. Peering at shifting shadows on the surface of the water, he wondered if they were patches of ice or sluggish, drifting water, achingly cold shallows.

Oliver did not hope for the Diplomatic side of the service,

since his family were unable to guarantee him an income sufficient to support the life-style required of embassy staff, but he could reasonably hope to rise in Whitehall, and he was industrious. Day by day, Britain grew more and more isolated. The foreign press became increasingly agitated in its criticism of the Boer War, and Oliver was to take special notes of these attacks and to prepare summaries for his superiors. What happened to his reports, so laboriously compiled, he never knew: they vanished into some leather-bound folders, ferried discreetly from room to room, never to be seen again by their originator.

Sometimes as he sat at his desk he heard the clacking of type-writing machines, and daily, on his way in, he bade good morning to the two ladies who operated them, sitting very upright, both with pince-nez glittering on their noses, in an outer office.

They wore dresses with thick plush cuffs that rubbed against their desks as they typed and little stiff collars that came up scratchily under their chins. These were two sisters, Miss Elcho and Miss Julia Elcho, who must have been almost of a birth, so twin-like were they. But they had different birthdays: he knew that because two small collections were made annually and gifts of chocolate or pastries purchased. Miss Elcho and Miss Julia each reminded the staff of the other's birthday, and it happened that Miss Julia's birthday fell soon after Oliver's arrival, so that it made an occasion of some small talk. He was grateful, since these were practically the first words anyone had spoken to him other than to instruct him in his duties.

'Have to chip in,' said Madigan, who sat at the other desk in Oliver's room. Madigan had sleek black hair and eyes and had been a blue at Oxford. His big-muscled legs drummed beneath his desk as he reached into his pocket and produced a couple of florins.

Oliver didn't have Madigan's gift for chaffing with the lady typists or the other clerks, and anyway, as the war progressed, he began to feel that he had best keep to himself. He wondered how anyone could miss the signs of looming disaster, but seemed entirely alone in this. Every day in the newspapers, in spite of the bombast, there were advertisements for more horses to be bought for the war and desperate charitable appeals from hospitals flooded with the sick and wounded. Even the fashionable London hotels had been persuaded to give up suites for occupation by wounded officers. All you had to do was to look at the front page of any newspaper. The war was not going Britain's way.

'The enemy has apparently been bombarding Ladysmith all day.' Madigan was reading out a headline from *The Times*.

What will happen there? thought Oliver. No victory, surely.

In one way, things were easier than he had thought. His initial fear had been that his failure to join the Army in the Transvaal might have been noted and considered a suspicious lack of patriotism. It had not taken him long to realize that safety lay in the FO's overweening opinion of itself, which was that no-one within its portals could conceive of any higher duty than being in its service. If the question had ever arisen, the reasoning would have surely been that he believed he was of far more use to the nation here in London than in pursuing any foolishly quixotic notions of offering his services on the field of battle.

Even in the space of a few weeks, Oliver's life had fallen into a routine. He did not mind this – indeed, he found it comforting – but he found that he grew more and more restless at home. There were intermittent battles between his father and Maggie. Oliver had a natural feeling for tactics, and understood that while he lived beneath his father's roof he was in no position to lend any real support to his sister, though passing the Foreign Office entry examination, notoriously difficult, had given him some advancement.

One evening, Oliver went home to find Maggie and his father in open conflict. For the first time, he consciously realized that his quiet-mannered father was a tyrant.

'What is it, Mags?' Oliver hoped to break up the tension between the other two, who were facing each other like combatants.

'The London School of Medicine!'

Maggie's words conveyed little to Oliver, though he did recall seeing something about it in the papers.

'It's a school of medicine especially for women – where they may study all the courses needed and get properly qualified. There are women teachers, as well as students.'

Their father's voice thundered out in rage. 'I care not how many silly women are there! My daughter will not be one of them. It is not a suitable occupation for a woman and that's the end of it.'

'But, Father, there are so many of us who have proved it to be so, now.'

'It is a waste of time to teach them! The truth is that they may learn like parrots, but they will have no real understanding of science! What scientific discovery was ever advanced by a female brain?'

'There never will be any, as long as men deny us the right to make them!'

'I've said no, Maggie! Do you seriously believe I shall revise my opinions?'

30

Maggie flung herself out of the room and they heard her footsteps running up the stairs. Oliver looked across at his father. He was his own flesh and blood: they both had the long flat fingers, for instance, the thin body, the deep-set grey eyes.

In later life, Oliver suddenly foresaw, he would hunch over like his father. Yet there seemed no communication between them: his father's opinions were completely at odds with his own. Craston Senior was himself a biologist, lecturing at University College to an audience that probably included a few women, yet he took no pleasure in his own daughter's love of science. Oliver took her side, both through natural affection and because he recognized that Maggie had an extraordinarily quick brain, one much better suited to scientific work than his own.

While he was a student still, there had been nothing he could do, except sometimes to obtain textbooks for her in Blackwell's and, quite ridiculously, he felt, to smuggle them home in his trunk at the end of each term. But later the chance of helping Maggie became a great spur to working hard for his final examinations and he found himself determined that one day he would be able to persuade his father in her favour. The Foreign Office offered Oliver this possibility, because it gave him a greater degree of independence. He was now a man among men, earning a salary, however meagre.

It changed his standing within the family in another way: he was free from his mother's curiosity, because he simply told her he could not talk about his work, and she could not question him. In the past, she had always wanted to know about his friends, his schoolfellows, their families. It was loving, he knew, tinged all the while with a mixture of anxiety and hope. 'Now, don't go and forget your parents!' she had admonished him, after he had told her of the luxuries of Abbington Magna, the stately family home of a fellow Oxford student. Yet she had also said, when Oliver described the imposing study of the paterfamilias, 'Well, if he's that important, perhaps he can do something for you! Tell me more about them.' Always, he had had to describe to her, account to her, until now.

She turned his obligation of secrecy into a virtue, of course. 'Now, don't any of you ask Oliver what he does, because he can't tell you! He's just not allowed to talk about his work at all. It's important government business, you see, and even his father and I know nothing about it!'

This, said at dinner a few weeks after he had commenced his Foreign Office employment, seemed a good moment to bring up the subject of a change in his life. He knew it had to come and wanted it, was grateful to the new status in the household which his employment had brought about.

'Mother, I think I should move out. Into bachelor's chambers – something of the sort. There are some good sets near the Embankment – and I can afford it now.'

His mother's shocked features demanded an explanation, and Maggie had fallen silent too, a shadow of anxiety in her eyes.

'Sir Howard has arranged for some important meetings and I may be needed at short notice, you see. If I am closer at hand they can easily summon me at need after hours.' The explanation was a kindness, offered as an afterthought.

Mrs Craston's dismayed face, which he had loved so much when he was a small child, now evoked in him the familiar sense of guilt from which he had suffered for many years where she was concerned, but he had some new strength to deal with it. He had a job, a profession, now there was some expectation of his ultimately fulfilling the role of supporting his sisters or at least being of social assistance in the matter of marrying them off.

'People will think you are unhappy at home! What will they say?'

'It doesn't much matter what they say.'

But this, he knew, was cruel. He saw it in his mother's face: her thin eyebrows arched and her mouth trembled a little. There were her Reading Ladies, there were her gossiping, chatting acquaintances. At the prospect of his mother's genuinely suffering from what she believed others to be saying about her, Oliver softened.

'I will be able to see you frequently, Mother, I'm sure. I expect I can come to your Reading Circle teas quite often, you know. It'll be all right – we'll just tell everybody it's something to do with my job.'

Two weeks later Oliver left his rooms on the south bank, crossed Waterloo Bridge and strode along the Victoria Embankment. This had become his regular walk to Whitehall, passing Cleopatra's Needle as it loomed up out of the mist. Often the fog was so thick that he almost banged into the wrought-iron benches with their foolish decorative sphinxes gazing out hopelessly in the direction of the water. Sometimes he even fantasized that beyond these creatures, somewhere in the mist, lay the Nile, a world of light green and golden yellow which he had seen in paintings, a world teeming with fish and birds.

Across the water came muffled creaks and scraps of other sounds, of voices, rattling chains and the lapping of water. The boats manoeuvred blindly on the river in the fog. Their lamps were shorn of all radiating light, mere circles of grey and yellow, as if they drifted along behind sheets, and he listened for the sounds, trying to work out their directions. Upriver or down? Ferry-boats? Tugs? Lighters? He knew nothing about water traffic. It was like a shadow-play going on behind a screen, whose plot and rules of composition he had to guess from fragments glimpsed and heard.

A factory hooter on the opposite bank, a long, mournful cry, broke into his train of thought. Irritation built up as Oliver increased the pace of his walk in a vain attempt to keep out the damp and cold, for his overcoat and long scarf seemed to offer no protection this morning; they merely gave off a dog-like smell of damp wool, with which he would have to live all day. At least if he'd gone to Africa, he wouldn't have to endure this appalling climate. It had snowed earlier on, and the morning sunlight would not last long.

His task this morning was to wait upon a Swedish diplomat who was staying at the Savoy, and to ferry some documents thence back to Whitehall. 'A glorified courier,' he told himself, increasing his dislike of the day. 'A messenger boy!'

Glancing up at the riverside façade of the hotel, he was distracted by something that had intrigued him every morning that week – a figure who had been out on one of the higher balconies no matter what the weather. A man with a big beard and heavy, thick build, sometimes with a rug or heavy shawl round his shoulders against the wind, and, before him, the leggy rectangle of an artist's easel. Sometimes the man was working at the canvas, sometimes peering straight ahead, into the fogs and mists, as if he saw things there within them.

There was the figure once again.

Oliver turned sharply up the steep narrow street that led from the river to the Savoy.

UNDER THE THIN LAYER OF ICE DISTURBED AND FRACTURED by viscous ripples, her face was a pale floating oval, the strands of fair hair caught in frosted crystals at the surface of the dark water.

The men who had been walking to work at Bly's Wharf, near Waterloo Bridge, waded into the shallows and, cursing at the cold, lifted her out. The woman was fully clothed, and under a dark dress her body was obscenely and ridiculously encased in a pink whalebone corset. Through the stout pink lacing and the steel eyelets pressed a black and muddy ooze that clung to the skin. With its pathetic suggestion of sexual frivolity, a thin frill of sodden lace edged the top of the corset.

'Better to deal with these things early in the morning,' Clyde Gulliver said, as he approached the slab in the morgue. 'They're over and done with then. Cold night, last night – we had some snow, didn't we?'

A few rays of sun still came through the windows at the top of the morgue walls. Gulliver was constantly complaining there was not enough natural light here, and the sulphurous gas-mantles that would be lit later on did not much assist his work. He scheduled his post-mortems for as soon after dawn as possible. As well as the light, it gave some privacy to the work. There was less chance of any gawping urchins or other unauthorized spectators attempting to snatch a glimpse of what went on. Sometimes they tried to climb up to the windows on teetering piles of crates or barrels. 'I've asked for frosted glass,' he said to Inspector Garrety, by way of conversation. 'There are some damned odd people who hang around morgues.'

He selected a surgical knife and began to cut at the matted pink knots: the dress, of some woollen stuff, had already been slit off and lay on a side table. Garrety jerked his mind away from the soft sounds but did not turn his head away as the torso, released from its constriction, spread and settled on the slab. The corset was handed over to Gulliver's assistant, Martin Hallard, who stood ready at the side.

'She hasn't been in long. Six or eight hours, I'd guess. The water's been close to freezing – in fact, I hear in shallow places it has frozen over – so that would have prevented the onset of decay. You'll observe, Inspector' – Gulliver held up an arm, extending the hand – 'that the skin is still unwrinkled.'

Garrety was familiar with the condition known as 'washerwoman's hand', where the skin became thick and corrugated after a body had been in the water, and had some idea of the stages of the process.

'But then look at this, down here.'

Garrety was unsure what was meant. The skin of the legs and torso seemed to have a mottled and bumpy surface, like the appearance of a plucked bird.

'*Cutis anserina*,' said the pathologist. 'Goose-bumps to

you. Goose-bumps to me, unless I'm trying to impress. Important thing is what it means. Means she was warm when she went into the water. But it doesn't mean she was alive. In fact, she could have gone in soon after death.' Gulliver opened the mouth and ran a finger inside. 'Not much in the way of mud or gravel – not the amount of river muck you'd expect—'

' "One more unfortunate"?'

The hackneyed words of this trite poetic phrase had become common parlance between policeman and pathologist. 'One more unfortunate/Weary of breath,/Rashly importunate,/Gone to her death!' The cruder terms, 'jumper', 'floater', were left unsaid, for there was a mutual acknowledgement between the two men of a hint of feeling that survived the fearful experience of their work. Often women taken out of the river were pregnant, servant girls turned out of their employment; occasionally they were respectable spinsters unable to face the expense or the social disgrace of an illegitimate child. At some time in the early hours of the morning, often with the aid of a bottle of gin, they would decide that life was no longer bearable, and the only solution lay in the dark waters of the river flowing beneath their feet.

The pathologist was wiping ooze away with a cloth. Garrety moved to the head of the table and looked down at the face.

'There's no sign of froth in the mouth,' said Gulliver. 'Drowning in fresh water normally causes a very persistent foam. I've observed it as long as a week after immersion.'

Garrety recalled seeing it on other drowned faces, like a tongue of ectoplasm emerging from the jaws.

'I think', said the pathologist, standing back and staring down, 'that we have an exception to the rule. First of all, she's a bit older than usual – I'd say she's in her mid-thirties, so she's not some young girl who's been led astray.'

He reached for a scalpel. 'I'll take out the organs, of course, and tell you more when I've examined them, but this one probably didn't die of drowning. I'll lay odds there's not that much water inside her, and the lungs won't be sodden. It's much more likely *that* was the cause of death.' He gestured towards the chest.

Garrety leaned over and saw what Gulliver meant. There was a small, gaping, lipless black mouth, less than two inches across, under the breastbone and to the left. The breasts were full and heavy, tipping outwards away from the wound.

'Probably went straight into the heart. It looks as if that's what killed her.'

'Self-inflicted?'

'Unlikely. She could have done it herself with a sharp kitchen knife – something as ordinary as that. Provided, of course, she knew exactly where to do it – and that's not so easily taken for granted. I'd think we're most probably not looking at a self-inflicted wound.'

Garrety moved closer. He lifted up the left hand of the corpse and rubbed with his fingers at a ring, disclosing the gleam of gold. 'Married – that's not usual, either.' The face was still covered with slime, and the pathologist took a clean gauze, leaned forward and wiped some of the mud away. The eyes stared up.

The woman had delicate features, a small nose, a mouth that, though it now hung open and exposed a lolling tongue, must once have been like a round bud.

'Well nourished. The teeth are good.' As he spoke, the pathologist leaned forward and wiped again. 'Let's get her washed down. No, wait a moment!' He stretched out an arm, signalling to Hallard, who held the corset up.

There was the slit on the woman's body that had drained the life blood out of her heart, but there was no corresponding slit in the front of the stained pink corset.

Garrety said nothing, but lifted the dress and slid his hand down inside the neck. Water dripped down on to the green-tiled floor. There was no cut in the dress, either.

'It appears someone went to the trouble of putting her corset and her dress back on,' said Gulliver. 'After she was stabbed. No stockings or petticoat, though – maybe they were too much trouble. And then she was dropped down.'

'I'll get my sergeant to ask round locally, see whether anyone recognizes a description.' Suicide was looking less and less likely but Garrety didn't want to go down the other road. His mind shied away from the implications of it.

Gulliver turned away and went to a trolley where a set of implements – saws, knives, serrated razors – was laid out ready in an open case. 'She could have been pregnant. Looks a bit distended – I mean, more than one would expect after immersion. I'll let you have a full report.'

'Doesn't seem to have been much on her – no jewellery, apart from the ring; no purse in the pockets. Someone got her clothes back on and put her in the water, but whoever it was made sure there wasn't any way to identify her.'

'Often it's the father,' said Gulliver. His voice always had a throaty, rasping undertone; in the morgue the carbolic fumes scoured his throat like sandpaper, and he smoked harsh little cigars whenever he could. 'Wanting to get shot of them both. Probably glad to see the back of the poor bitch.'

Gulliver pulled a thin orange-red rubber hose that was attached to a tap over the body and began to sluice off the remaining mud: gradually it slid out of the lines and folds of flesh, and the muck that still clung to the lower part of the torso was washed off. There appeared a white belly and hips, the skin disclosing the bluish-silvery gleam of decay, and matted pubic hair.

Garrety looked away as Gulliver pulled the body further down the dissection table so that the buttocks were at the edge, and opened the legs. As the dirt poured off, running brown through the channels around the slab, both men started.

Neither of them spoke as they gazed at the crazy mass of punctures and scratches.

Murder was a word that hung in the mouth like the smell of the river.

5

A WEEK LATER, AND ON A VERY SIMILAR MORNING, GARRETY walked through Lambeth and to the spot near Waterloo Bridge where the woman's body had been pulled from the water.

Had death occurred close to where she had been found? If not, the body would have had to be brought to the river, and that would probably have been the murderer's greatest risk of discovery. It would have had to be at a time when there were few people around – no idlers, no trolleybuses ferrying their sleepy loads to work or home again. No-one in the vicinity of Bly's Wharf had reported seeing anything unusual, but, given the freezing fog and the endemic local distrust of authority, that meant nothing.

The murderer would have needed some light – enough to see that the coast was clear. At night the street-lamps' glow barely penetrated the river mists.

And if there was a killer, did he perform his work at night? Not necessarily. It could have been done even in the full light of noon – if there were no eyes to see it.

Garrety found that it needed a strong effort of thought to wrestle with this idea. The Ripper's killings had made all murders seem deeds of darkness. Yet it was worse, he found, to think of this as being done in the light. That some man had actually gazed at a woman, seeing everything, seeing her face, the terror on it, watched the colour of her blood as it started to spurt – had looked at all that and not relented ... The pitilessness of killing in daylight was a terrible thought to Garrety.

The grey bulk of Waterloo Station loomed before him in the snow shower. He paused briefly on his way to the river, and saw the long sheds stretching down the track, the rails glistening. The hot odours of steam and coal, thick in his throat as the smell of wet gabardine, reached everywhere, even here where he was standing a little way outside the station, on the first springing arch of the bridge. The bright winter's daylight would soon be overtaken by smoke. This was an interlude only, before the city began its dirty, noisy stirring and bustle. Garrety looked up at the sky and shivered, then gazed upriver to where the streak of Charing Cross Bridge spanned the Thames, the criss-cross of its iron struts gleaming sharp-edged in the sun.

Now, with no progress made in the case, he watched the embankments and bridges. For what, he scarcely knew, save that perhaps some pattern of movement would emerge – or else some break in a pattern. He saw the cold morning sun slowly filling the sky downriver. He could make out a few shapes, scurrying along the Victoria Embankment on the opposite side of the river, mostly scattered figures in grey and black, their heads down at an angle, tucking their chins into scarves and mufflers. From the way they moved, he could tell the direction of the wind blowing along the north bank and out into the water. Here, he was protected from it by the great sheltering bulk of the station.

His eye picked out one of the shapes as a figure that had recently become familiar, its particular gawky fast walk now more recognizable than its appearance, and he began crossing the bridge, feeling the force of the wind as he moved out.

He could see him now, coming along the Embankment. Tall, with his head up, not conceding anything to the weather, and pushing forward at a good pace, a straight-backed young man, moving exactly as he had done for the last two days. Or possibly for longer: it was only two days ago that Garrety had noted down his movements, only four days since he had started keeping this systematic watch and observed this man.

He had singled him out as part of the daily pattern of activity that moved along the embankments. The crowds criss-crossed the river, going from home to work and then back again, from the wealth of the north side to the squalor of the south. Each day they made their way, moving out over the currents that flowed in ancient tides and ripples, pattering across the bridges over the rippling dark water. This was such a curious little rectangle on the map of the city, thought Garrety, this half-mile or so, bounded by the riverside slums of south London on one side of the Thames and the precincts of the Savoy Hotel on the other. It was slung between the railway stations of Charing Cross and Waterloo, so that the human antheap was constantly in turmoil around these epicentres, churning in and out and back and forth.

On this particular morning the young man turned away from the river and made in the direction of the Strand, rather than for Whitehall as on previous days. He was nearly there now, at the entrance to the little street that led up the side of the Savoy Hotel, and Garrety himself was almost across

Waterloo Bridge. Watching from the end of the parapet, not over the water but over the frosty pavement of the Embankment, Garrety saw the young man making his way up the steep alleyway alongside the Savoy Hotel, heading for the Strand. He did not break his step: he carried on without a pause and turned right at the top of the alleyway.

Putting on a spurt, Garrety was in time to see him turn into the courtyard of the hotel and walk confidently into the lobby. The commissionaire, magnificent, gold-braided, staring into space, held the door open for him.

Crossing the Savoy courtyard Garrety followed his quarry, but he had to push open the doors for himself. The commissionaire was berating the driver of a baker's van who had the temerity to deliver rolls to the guests' entrance instead of to the kitchens. The smell of warm bread drifted across the courtyard and Garrety remembered how hungry he was.

The foyer seemed enormous, like a tennis court, and his feet sank soundlessly into the red and gold carpet set amid a black and white marble floor. Opposite the entrance, shallow stairs led down to a long vista of palm trees, mirrors and tables, where smells of bacon and kippers arose as waiters moved discreetly between the breakfasting guests. There was a distant gentle murmur of voices, the well-bred slight scraping sounds of knives and the tinkling of coffee-spoons.

Across the foyer came two men, one an elderly fellow who somehow seemed at odds with his surroundings, a squarely built man of about sixty, with a thick white beard in which there was yet a deep streak of black. He planted his feet solidly on the ground as he strode towards the doors. His companion was a much younger man, thin with a hollow face, who, in spite of his youth, gave much less of an impression of strength than the older man. Both were dressed for walking, in soft tweed overcoats and heavy scarves.

The younger man turned towards the reception desk and called out in a strong French accent, 'We are just going for a morning walk. My father will want breakfast in his room when we return.'

'Very good, sir.' Behind the great mahogany desk, the clerk turned to speak to the young man whom Garrety had followed; the policeman moved close enough to catch the end of the conversation despite their muffled voices.

'Fourth floor, sir, room 427. His Excellency's staff are expecting you, if you would like to go to the lift. And how is sir this morning?'

The young fellow seemed to find this unctuous remark as irritating as did Garrety, for he gave only a brief nod before heading towards the lifts. The indicators glowed like fireflies in a row.

The clerk turned his head towards the newcomer. 'Yes, sir?'

Before Garrety had even spoken, the desk clerk had taken in his shoes, his ulster, his rough shave, and all the humble details of his person were voicelessly recognized in the intonation of the clerk's greeting. 'I can afford to be rude to this man,' it said. 'Not too rude, for he may be respectable enough, may even have some little authority. But one thing is certain – he will never be a guest in this hotel.'

Garrety leaned on the mahogany expanse. 'That ... that gentleman. The one who has just gone upstairs.'

'Yes?' The clerk was definitely hostile now. If there was one thing the guests of the Savoy expected, it was discretion. That went without saying, amid the plush and the hushed voices, the doors that slid soundlessly open, the dishes that gloved hands served from silver trays.

Garrety produced his card.

The other held it up and peered at it. He leaned over the counter. 'Superintendent ... Garrety. Ah, a policeman.' This was said in a whisper, though none of the pampered guests was around to be appalled at such a vulgar eventuality.

'Yes,' said Garrety, more harshly than he intended. There was no point in beating round the bush, though. 'I need to know that young gentleman's name.'

There was a scraping cough. 'Our guests and their visitors enjoy complete privacy while they are in this hotel, Superintendent.'

Garrety restrained himself. In some places, his word carried power. In others, and this was one of them, it did not. There were highly placed people here, people who could have him sacked with one click of their fingers, he had no doubt. Even if his face had fitted, even without the Northern Irish accent and his own damned stubbornness, he had no security for a moment. To the likes of him, the Savoy was a foreign country, with its own rules and regulations that protected the golden bugs within its luxurious hive from any withering breath of cold air.

'I would be grateful ...' Damn it, why grovel? Garrety drew himself upright, taking his elbow off the counter. He was not going to be patronized by this squib. 'I wish to speak to the house detective.'

It was usual for big hotels to have such people on the staff, though their tasks were normally confined to guarding the valuables and getting the guests out of scrapes.

'I doubt if he will be free at this hour.'

'Oh, don't be so damned pompous, man. Tell him I want to speak to him and I don't care if he's shaved or not. I'll wait here.'

He felt better as he turned on his heel and settled himself into a huge red leather armchair. The clerk was picking up a black telephone, winding the handle with angry energy. The deep carpet and plush curtains seemed to swallow up all sound and he heard only the murmur of the clerk's voice drifting across the great empty space.

Then the clerk beckoned Garrety over. 'You can go up. Room 521. And the gentleman's name is Craston.'

Garrety made towards the lift, and the clerk called out pityingly, 'Fifth floor!'

The lift rose soundlessly, a great well of empty space rising heavenwards amid the sleeping rich, and the policeman saw his pale face reflected in the ghostly etched glass of the floating box.

THE ROOM STINKS. I KNOW THAT CARPET HERE SOAKS everything up. The smell.

Things not remembered?

Oh yes, but they hover round the mind, don't they?

Get the damned window open. That's it, blast of fresh air. River air. Restores myself. Resurrects myself.

The wind hurling past my head, and it's still snowing, damn it. Night's going, though. Some light downriver. I can see the white streaks of daylight and some boats making eastwards.

Reminds me of that other boat, the one we went out on, the SS *Briton*, bound from Tilbury to Cape Town with the Scots regiment we took on board at Dublin. The bagpipes were sounding out over the water, all wrong somehow, howling pitifully like animals as we slipped away further and further from their home.

It was Calmont who pressed me into going – Archie Calmont.

I hadn't seen him since we were students. Now I recall

when I first saw him, at some lecture or other, and I wonder to myself, how can we ever know? Who would have thought that chance 'friend', to whom I had spoken no more than a few dozen words in my life, would seal my fate, perhaps? The war changed me, what I saw there.

I met him outside Guy's, as I was coming away from another of those damned Boards. Of course, he took it I was volunteering.

'I'm going out myself in a month's time,' he said, with an eager face. 'The old man's raised a private medical corps – got funds for it from all his well-heeled patients. They adore him, you know. "Dear Sir Gregory, what a wonderful man! I don't think I'd ever trust another doctor – not with *my* heart!"'

Young Archie was doing quite a good imitation of a squeaking, adoring female. The Calmonts were one of those old medical families – grandfather had been a trusted Edinburgh physician, father a distinguished surgeon. Now young Archie seemed to be making a fair bid as Medical Corps star. Not for the Calmonts, of course, the vulgarities of the usual route – the Royal Army Medical Corps – oh no! This was a private unit that would go out to succour our troops in South Africa, all equipment purchased, all salaries paid, by Sir Gregory's fund.

Well, why not? It suddenly seemed obvious when I saw the idea reflected in Archie's friendly face, almost the minute it had popped into my head. He spoke before I did, with no need for me even to drop him a hint. 'Come with us! No problems with the old man – I'll tell him you're a friend from student days! That is, unless you've got something better to do?'

But this was mere politeness. Even Archie Calmont, not the most observant of men, must have noticed the shabbiness of my coat, the roughness of my shoes.

Sometimes I can't remember how I first got to this room; was it after I was invalided out? At any rate, I come back to it every night, and sometimes there are things I am carrying.

It's when I wake up that I start being frightened. 'Terrified' is more the word: I was frightened in the Army most of the time, of course. Although, naturally, I was never at the front, just behind the lines waiting for the stretchers, but, still, it was bad enough: the dirt and heat and flies, those useless orderlies, the screaming.

That's the thing about working in tents: no sound is muffled; not the grinding of the saws, nor the shouts. 'Hold him down, there!' and then the yelling. The thudding into the zinc bucket of bits and pieces that were parts of men, had once been the limbs of children. That was a terrible thought – you couldn't bear that, if you thought about it.

Sometimes there was chloroform: not always. Supplies took a long time to ship out. They can have no idea, the people waiting their turn for civilized butchery in the London hospitals, no idea of what it is like in a field tent. If they knew, no-one would ever go to war again.

You can't imagine the thirst we felt there, on that dry, stony ground with the vultures ready overhead and the shrubby little clumps of bushes and hills. And at Bloemfontein and Klokfontein and every damned Fontein, where there is in reality only parching dry heat and the very names torment the poor devils in their burning hells. At Enslin, there were men lying down on their stomachs and lapping like dogs – it was not even water, just thin red mud fouled by mules. It was smeared all over a man's mouth and tunic when he got up at last and walked away, frightened, shamefaced, each man alone. When the men are thirsty like that, you cannot bring water near them; they will run to it regardless, knock one another down, tip the cart over. Eventually, the regiments stopped bringing water carts on to the battlefields. There was never enough anyway.

I have a brandy now when I think about it, and for a while I don't need another. Some days I can go without a drink altogether. At other times, after just a single one I feel good, a warmth starts flowing over my body and then the memories are better, they are ones I can feed off.

Because the truth is that I wasn't horrified and appalled all the time. Of course not. You couldn't carry on working if you were. I was indifferent, professional, damn it, I was a surgeon with more experience after a couple of months there at the age of thirty-three than most hospital surgeons get in a lifetime. Only of men, though, as I had told them at that interview board, just before I met Archie. They suggested an army hospital might suit me better.

It was a piece of luck meeting young Archie, with his plans for the Calmont Medical Unit. Luck as most men account it, anyway. It's quite beautiful there in the cool season, the veldt stretching away, the rivers a kind of steel-blue, and the farm-houses little patches of white with groves of grey-green eucalyptus round them.

Close my eyes for a few moments now and think of that.

Need a drink, this morning. Now. Should be in my great-coat pocket.

Pull myself up. Bad evening, last night. My legs feel swollen.

Coat on the bed. The rough wool, my hand diving into the pocket. Christ, Christ! Don't say it's not there – please, sweet Jesus, let it be there . . .

Cold feel of the bottle in my hand. I straighten up and I can hear my own breathing slowing with relief as I pour out the brandy into the glass at the side of the bed. 'Don't need to take it straight from the neck, young fellow!' Oh no, not me!

Sit down on the bed. The hot spirit flowing down into my stomach. The wonderful *mercy* of brandy, the speed with which it flows through the body, hammering into the veins and the heart.

7

GARRETY FOUND HIMSELF IN A CORRIDOR THAT SEEMED endless. It was carpeted with an even deeper plush than that of the lobby and gilded wall-lights gleamed between the solid numbered doors that seemed an infinite distance apart. A maid in black and white was carrying a pile of towels and scurried past the policeman with a little bob of a curtsy.

'Where's five-two-one?'

She pointed ahead.

The door had ivory numbers on it as did the others, but in addition there was a peep-hole let into it, and it looked as if it had a few scuffs and scratches. It opened almost as he knocked.

The man who opened it was outlined against the light. 'They telephoned up. I'm Castleton, the house detective.'

Garrety was waved into a room, large but plainly furnished and, he thought, probably like a doss-house compared with the guests' rooms. The man was an employee, after all.

Wouldn't do for the paid servants to have anything that might compete with the titles and tiaras.

He walked to the window, drawn by the strangeness of seeing the city from this height. The chimneys on the south bank were smoking now, the factories sending their yellow and black plumes streaming across the bluish air. Garrety stood, fascinated. From here he could see the heavy smoke sinking down and feathering out over the river. It reminded him of a souvenir an aunt had once brought back for him from the Isle of Wight, of graduated layers of different coloured sand, sliding and slipping in a glass tube, one on top of another, smoky grey, yellow, buff, brown. He would have gone on watching, but Castleton pushed forward an armchair and Garrety took it, while the house detective sat opposite.

'Shall I send for some coffee?' asked Castleton.

'No, thanks. Won't take more than a few minutes.'

He wanted coffee badly, but decided to wait, and took a long look at Castleton. He was just right, thought Garrety, for a job like this. He was extraordinarily good-looking in a well-bred way, fair-haired with a neat, glinting moustache, and tall and slim with a long, bony face. He wore a fine wool dressing-gown of dark green. On the bed behind him lay a suit, waistcoat, shirt and tie that looked immaculate. This man could definitely pass among any aristocratic gathering as one of their own – he would not have looked out of place at Ascot or the House of Lords. He could have followed a duchess – or a pickpocket.

'I was just getting dressed. I suppose you've come about the Frenchman. I thought someone would. "They'll be keeping an eye on him," I said to myself.' The voice had a neutral, unidentifiable accent.

Garrety said nothing and Castleton carried on: ''Course,

that sort of thing's right out of my province. I help them out a bit, sometimes, with the foreign gentry, if you know what I mean. But usually it's diplomats or politicians of one sort or another – never seen anything like this before. Strange cove. But what would you expect? The man's an artist.'

'You been keeping an eye on him yourself?' Garrety was in the dark, but he had clearly stumbled on something interesting.

'Well, to tell you the truth, I thought there might be something in it.' He made a clicking gesture with his fingers, as if counting coins. 'And, our *monsieur* being a French artist, I thought there might be something else as well – know what I mean? Wouldn't mind a peep through the keyhole.' One of the elegant arched eyebrows dived down in a sudden wink.

'But would the management allow that sort of thing . . . ?'

'What, painting nude models? Oh, they can do anything they like when they're safely in their suites, as long as they don't cause a scandal in the street. There's all sorts goes on here.'

Castleton gave an odd smile. Garrety watched him carefully as he went on talking.

'And plenty with the boysies, too. You'd think they'd be more careful after poor old Oscar copped it, wouldn't you? Seems to have just put a bit more spice up the arse for some of them. Made it more tasty – sense of danger and all that, with your lads on the look-out waving your ruddy great truncheons!'

Castleton's hips under the brocade dressing-gown gave a wriggle that was almost, yet not quite, parodic and he laughed a little before continuing. 'But there's nothing like that with the old French cove – no time for bloody sex at all. He's filled the rooms with pictures all half-painted, and he gets up at the crack of dawn – before, in fact – in all weathers. Then at midday off he goes, and back at dusk – the day's over for him, really. He does have a few pals come round sometimes and they jabber away in French, but they're mostly old blokes like him. No anarchists, I reckon, if that's what they're scared of! That why they sent you? Worried in case he's mixing with the politicos? They're on the side of the damned Boers, the French. It was in *The Times*. Got to keep up with what they read here, y'know. That what's interesting you?'

All Garrety had to do to keep this man talking was to nod.

'I do speak a bit of the lingo myself. Had to, for this job – we get a lot of fashionable types over from Paris so I got a little lady's maid to teach me a bit . . . She taught me a bit more than how to speak it, as well . . . Anyway, I don't reckon there's anything to it. He's got a son who comes sometimes, writes a letter to the wife in France just about every day. I get them to let me have a look at the envelopes. Reckon she's got him on a tight leash – there's a photograph of her in his room. Terrifying old bat, if you ask me. Sure you won't have some coffee? I'm going to order some for myself.' Castleton reached for a bell-pull.

'Sure, thanks. Well, that's all very useful, thank you.'

'What's your patch?'

'Lambeth.'

Castleton whistled, and came out with a laugh, and his accent changed suddenly to real London Pride – although, having been in London for only six months or so, Garrety couldn't have said if it was true cockney, from the area reached by the sound of Bow Bells.

'Well, well, Lambeth, my old home town! I had to learn different when I came this side of the river. Don't suppose you'll run into any of the Savoy guests round there— Hang on, Waterloo on your manor?'

'Yes.'

'Ah, well, some of our toffs might find themselves in trouble round there, getting mixed up with shady ladies or having their pockets picked or whatever . . . Do me a favour, give us a call if they end up coming to your nick. There's some very shifty types hanging about Waterloo Station!'

He rose, went to a card case on a table beside the bed, and presented Garrety with a stiff piece of white pasteboard.

J. D. Castleton, Esq.
The Savoy Hotel, London

and then beneath in flowing copperplate:

*Private Investigations. Absolute
Discretion Assured*

'Very nice.'

'Cost me a few bob to have them done. Bit of moonlighting, really. Still, the management don't mind as long as it keeps the lords and ladies happy.'

Garrety put the card in his breast-pocket. He got up to go and Castleton again made the clicking gesture with his hand, sliding it meaningfully towards an imaginary pocket.

Garrety deliberately ignored the movement, hurried to the door and, as he was on the point of going, turned back. 'By the way, a young fellow called Craston. Know anything about him?'

Castleton turned his eyes up to the ceiling and considered, as if running through an invisible inventory of the hotel's guests. 'Calls by occasionally when there's some big foreign politico here. In the FO, I think, but not very high up. Hang on, I'll see if they know anything downstairs.'

He walked across the room and picked up a wall-mounted black telephone. His south London accent slid easily away. 'Cynthia? Now, tell Uncle Jonathan, there is a certain young gentleman called Craston ... Well, any little snippet, my dearest girl.' He looked slyly across at Garrety. 'See you on the floor – we'll have a twirl, eh? Thanks, darling bud.' He returned the piece to the cradle.

Did he have something? Garrety would never get at it if he didn't play this vain devil's game. Not giving anything away, he waited patiently as Castleton stroked his silky little golden streak of a moustache.

'Nothing that signifies, Inspector. He's officially visiting the Norwegian trade representative. Only he asked about something else as well – our Monsieur Monet, if you must know. Cultured little ponce! Or is he?'

8

HERE, ABOVE THE RIVER, I CAN SEE DOWNSTREAM, TOWARDS the Pool of London. There is a barge moving slowly, her lights making dim-glowing circles on the rippling water. I've closed the balcony doors behind me not only to keep out the January air – it is a freezing day and I mustn't let my patients suffer – but also because I cannot bear to hear them any longer.

It was my father who pushed me towards medicine. He was a doctor and so was his father. But my father and I shared nothing in common, except our straight dark-red hair.

'Of course you'll be a doctor – no question about it! My son will study medicine as I did – and your brother was the most brilliant student of his day, don't forget. You won't measure up to him – can't be expected – but you'll plough along. It'll all be well enough.'

That room in which I was beaten so often, hated him so often, the rows of dull-spined medical books under the glass of the bookcases. The pictures where the pages fell apart, grotesque and horrible beyond dreams, the grey photography of the newer books. It made them worse, because there was no defence against it – these were real images, real people, their limbs bulging and twisted. There was an old man with his testicles hanging down to the ground; a live child, her eyes crawling with larvae. *Tropical Diseases. Gray's Anatomy.*

'If you're going to be a doctor, you can't be so much of a woman! Look, damn it!'

His hand on the back of my neck. The photograph of an emaciated creature lying on a bunk, a woman with her eyes just black shadows, long hair framing her face and a sharp white edge of bone sticking through the flesh of her leg. *Advanced tubercular ulceration observed on the west coast of Ireland.* I've never forgotten the picture or the caption.

He knew how I hated it.

'But I want to go straight into the Army, Father.'

'You'll do your medical training first. My son won't let me down. You'll get used to it.'

You do get used to it, mostly. But I can't get used to the sounds.

The terrible thing about the sick and maimed is that there are always noises haunting the night. Sometimes the wounded men, who try so hard during the hours of daylight to keep back their cries, find release in their sleep. They will scream in their dreams, unashamed. Sometimes there are the farcical noises and stinks of the sick-bed, which turn into the vile accompaniments of dysentery as a man's guts explode in a welter of green faeces and water. The smell of that illness is like no other – it is as if nature herself were issuing a reeking warning: 'Get hence – infection!' Any animal would run as far as it could. But the Army won't let us obey our instincts: under pain of court martial, we all stand our ground – the men in their filthy encampments, the orderlies running up and down with bedpans.

And we doctors, of course.

I saw so much of it in South Africa that it scarcely troubles me, and of course the cases that have returned to England are much easier to deal with here. The wounded officers have everything they could require, and clean linen is the order of the day. But, still, at night I prefer to forget it when I can, and shut the doors behind me when I emerge to contemplate the river for a while. It is my habit to do this every evening, to clear my lungs. And my mind, so far as I can.

This morning they were talking round the table where I sat earlier, a group of patients who are convalescent, sitting about, a couple of them leaning over *The Times*, ranting on about the French. 'Frightful lot – completely on the side of the Boers.' And then another John Bull joined in with braying accent, reading out from the paper for the benefit of his fellows. ' "They fancy they serve the Boers by denouncing England, which they imagine to be destroyed because she has lost a few thousand men killed, wounded or captured." '

'Disgraceful. Cowards, the lot of them,' growled another.

These men, crippled, maimed for their country, are mad against the French – against the rest of the world, if the truth be known. Britain stands almost alone in her attempt to crush the Boers. Yet these men know from their own experience, for they themselves are the maimed and wounded from that conflict – they are the victims of the map-makers and the generals.

The newspapers perpetuate the lies, with just an occasional hint – very discreet, nothing to frighten them back home – of how disastrous the war with the Boers is proving to be. There's a letter – anonymous, of course – in the correspondence columns, complaining that the War Office maps are hopelessly inaccurate. The generals have no idea of the lie of the land out there.

Well, I could have told them that already. How, I ask myself as the patriotic indignation rises like helium in the rooms behind me, is it impossible for them to ignore the self-evident truth and believe something conjured up out of their own minds? What is the trick of it? How have these grown men deceived themselves?

These officers here, wounds healing beneath my care, have been told nothing since their schoolroom days but tales of the glory of England, sung songs about the splendour of fighting for her. What men have believed in for so long is not given up easily. I suppose they cannot encompass the terrible possibility that all they fought for should prove to be worthless – their gallant leaders are liars, the Queen Empress at Windsor just a foolish old woman. No, they cling to these old nursery fables like children in the dark. Oh, I know what I am, but truth is sometimes even in our mouths, whispered by the tongues of the damned.

This morning I read one ominous line of newsprint: 'The number of cases of dysentery and fever is increasing.' And I see in my mind's eye those rows of feverish bodies in the stinking tents, the puddles of filth seeping from the beds to sink into the African earth. The memory of it makes me despair – the real sense of despair that blackens the world and all the damned fools within it.

So then I turn inwards, into myself. Outwardly, I function: I sit in a chair, I dress for dinner. But I feel there's no-one inside my clothes: there is a body that moves, fingers that turn the doorknob. Something will happen, later on.

Go back in. Walk through the rooms, smiling, nodding.

Like a real person. And they'll speak to me as if I were. I can feel my outer skin, my lips moving, hear my voice replying to them.

'Good evening, Doctor!'

'Evening, Sminton. Almost time for the plaster to come off, I think!'

'Oh, hello there, sawbones! Fancy a jar?'

And here I am, answering, in a perfectly ordinary sort of way, as if I were just like everyone else. 'No. Not just at the moment, thanks. Ah, Captain Cheriton, how's that new dressing? Good man!'

It's so easy; just move your limbs and your mouth: they see what they want to see, hear what they want to hear.

9

THE OLD MAN WAS DRESSING FOR DINNER, METICULOUSLY inserting links into his deep cuffs. On the dressing-table stood a silver-framed photograph of four small children, the soft velvet of their clothing reproduced in sepia folds, their white arms graceful, their plump legs encased in long socks cut across at the ankles by the straps of their little slippers. The large mirror in his dressing-room reflected the glimmering of his shirt-front, the big room with its blue and green satin counterpane, and the thin figure of Michel Monet, who was holding a bow-tie ready to pass to his father.

'What time are they expected?'

'They'll call for you at seven, Papa. And then we're all going to have dinner in the grill-room.'

'Plenty of time, then.'

There was a pause. Michel held out the tie, but his father turned and stared at his son's face. Several long moments passed.

'I think I see something of it.'

'Of what, Father?' Michel was perplexed. For the first time, he realized how they all depended on his father's strength. Alice, of course, nourished them all, ran the household, but it was the father who supported the entire enterprise of the huge family. Eight children – but Michel then remembered, with deep pain, that Suzanne was gone . . .

'Tell me, Michel, have I ever made any distinction between you and Jean and the rest?'

'Why, no, Father. What's wrong?'

'And yet, you and Jean, you are *my* children. My sons. If I were a farmer, you would be taking on the land.' The old man laughed, and looked down at the gold cuff-link in his hand. 'Before you came along, when your mother and I . . . when Jean was born, things were very different. You look at the river out there, but you don't know anything of what it means. How could you? But I don't blame you, Michel. You're being brought up as a rich man's son – cigars and good wine and motor cars!' He sat down heavily on the side of the great bed. 'When Jean was born, I threw myself into the river.'

Michel looked at his father in stunned silence. That this man, that absolute rock of their lives . . . that he at some time should have felt such despair seemed to shake the young man to the foundations of his being. It was as if all the life at Giverny – the garden, the hothouses – all rested on such unstable ground that it could be swept away in a torrent.

'Sit down,' said his father. 'There are things you should know. Things I haven't thought about in years.'

Michel obeyed. His legs felt unsteady.

'You can't imagine what it was like. Your mother and I – well, we were not even married at that stage. She was in Paris. I didn't even have the money to stay in Paris with her; I had to go home and stay with the family at Saint-Adresse.'

There was a pause. The old man had bowed his head.

'Father, don't distress yourself, I beg you. Forget these old memories . . .'

The massive old head was raised up slowly. 'No, I must be more honest. It wasn't just the lack of money. I didn't have any interest in the child – didn't want it, and that's the truth.'

Michel was astonished. His father, the head of the huge tribe at Giverny, the patriarch among artists, how could he not want his first-born child?

'I didn't realize then how I felt about him, or about your mother. But when I got to Paris and saw them – how she had managed in that horrible place, how brave she had been, then I had such a great rush of emotion . . .' The old man touched his breast. 'You know, she didn't even have enough to eat? And I, what did I do? I felt in such despair at first. I could afford nothing for them, couldn't support them – I wished truly that we were all dead. The sense of being such a failure I couldn't even provide for my son, that was so terrible! I have never known such blackness as when I sat there and thought I could not even buy candles to light the room and see his face. And then there was the river, and it looked . . . as if it would swallow me up and be an end to all my troubles. It was August, such a hot summer night in Paris, you couldn't breathe, and the rooms smelt so! I went down to the Seine; there was a breeze and the water was like a stream of silver in the moonlight, and I knew I had only to disappear beneath that surface for my troubles to be ended.'

Michel did not dare to speak. His father's face seemed to be staring into the mirror.

'So I jumped.'

'Oh my God, Father—'

'And it was cold, wonderful, and I sank down and down . . .

through the scum and through the weeds – you know, the water was so alive under the surface, so full of things that stir and pull at you. We think there's nothing there, but if you go down and down, through the layers, the stalks, the leaves, the ooze . . . But my body was fighting it. Not I, myself, but my lungs, and my arms, my limbs – they struggled and tore at the things that wound round me . . . So, somehow, I came to the surface, got to the side and climbed out. And I tore off my dripping shirt and stood there, waving it like a crazy creature in the moonlight – I don't know why – as if I were signalling something.'

Michel reached out and took his father's hands. 'You've never said anything like that . . . Sometimes, I've felt—'

'Perhaps there is something that we share, you and your brother and I. You and Jean are different from the other children, but Alice and I, we never speak of your mother. I never told anyone about that time in the river, except when I wrote to poor Bazille and blamed him for not sending me more money. I used his studio at one time. And he was killed in the war with Prussia, so there has been no other living soul who knew of it.'

Michel was silent, his head bowed, struggling to cope with this new image of his father as a desperate young man. Then he looked up and said, 'You haven't painted their portraits.' He gestured at the photograph of the children.

The old man understood his son. 'Not their faces, not really looking at them, as I did Jean, when he was a baby, lying in his cradle. I painted him asleep. He was so solid, you know, his head such a strong shape. You'd think a baby would be fragile, but he wasn't, not at all. He was as hard and real as that old wooden doll – maybe you remember it? He fell asleep clutching hold of it, with its round head just like his!

And the striped shadows in the folds of his little gown – and his face looked so sad! He'd cried himself to sleep that night, and then the moonlight fell on him through the window: he was all black and silver, with the only colour in the flush of his cheeks.'

Outside there rose the sounds of London at night, mounting up to their eyrie on the fifth floor; the clopping of hoofs, the whistling of engines.

'So then I knew I wanted the child. He was flesh of my flesh and blood of my blood. But the thing is, what is so strange, I didn't know that till I painted that picture of him. That was how I understood it.'

10

GARRETY WAS TIRED, DRAGGING HIS FEET IN THE HEAVY BOOTS as he plodded along Lower Marsh, just beyond the south end of Waterloo Bridge, where the street market had closed now. The stalls and awnings had been taken down, and there was only the soft debris of some rotting carrots and sprouts in a gutter to show for the activities of the day. That, and a woman sitting in a chair outside a public house, in spite of the weather, a shawl muffled round her neck and chin. Her head lolled; her arm was stretched out. Presumably the market stall had had a good day's trading or otherwise she would have been on her feet still, trying to get a bloke up against the wall, if she hadn't made a few bob selling onions. Her eyes focused as Garrety passed, however, and she broke into the great beaming smile of the happy drunk.

'Ah, I love a bit of red hair, my darlin'! Nothing like a red-headed man for a bit of heat in bed!'

He laughed good-naturedly and side-stepped the out-stretched arm neatly. 'Good night, Lolo!'

'G'night, darlin'!'

The little incident had amused him, but now as he turned left towards the neat row of houses in Westminster Bridge Road and saw that a light was burning in their bedroom window anxiety gripped him again. He had started to think of it as he had been walking home, had found himself counting off the days. He almost couldn't bear it another time, though he had thought that every time, and he had stuck with it. He thought of Aline's face turned up towards him, the tears in her eyes again, and hoped against all expectation that things would be different.

He let himself into their little hall, took off his greatcoat and hung it on the varnished hall-stand. He called up the stairs, then ran up as he heard her answering cry.

She was lying on the couch and the room smelt of eau-de-Cologne and the salts that she used: a small green bottle was lying on the table beside her.

'Is it . . . ?'

'Oh, Will! It's always the same! I'm not a normal woman.' Her hands were rubbing her body in an unconscious movement, as if feeling anxiously for something that wasn't there after all. 'Other women do it, they drop them like animals; they have babies when they don't even want them!'

'I'll make you some tea. Has it . . . has it started?'

She nodded, and he sighed as he went downstairs.

It had been destroying her over this last year, as he watched helplessly. He had come to dread the spottings of blood in their bed, the brown streaks on her linen, that appeared remorselessly, month after month. And every time the signs drove them further and further apart in her evident sorrow at not being able to conceive, and his inability to tell her that he too was stricken and grieving. Unspoken between them was

always the suspicion that at the root of it was the con-
demnation to this life in London, the fogs, the sulphuric air.
The rest of the world took this for the natural state of affairs.
Their neighbours, his colleagues, Lolo and the other market
stallholders, they had all been born into it and knew nothing
else.

In the kitchen he pulled the thin chain, tipping down the
bar under the gaslight mantle with a tiny click, and the yellow
glare sprang up, harshly shadowing the corners of the room.
The kettle needed refilling: afterwards, he turned on the gas
burner, struck a match and heard the popping noise as the
blue flames caught hold. He made the tea and poured it out
into a breakfast cup, not one of the dainty teacups that were
too small for his big-jointed fingers and didn't hold enough
for Aline anyway.

'We couldn't go back?' It was a question, but not a hopeful
one. She knew the answer. Garrety remembered from evening
classes the definition of a rhetorical question: 'a question that
does not expect an answer'. Well, this was a question expecting the answer 'no', and he must give it.

Sitting at the end of the bed, he did so, and she was quiet.
He knew that she believed their marriage to be cursed, not
just by the division of their friends and families, as any union
must be that had bridged the Protestant–Catholic divide back
in Belfast, but by her barrenness as well. He stroked her
shoulder, and she gradually became less agitated. His touch
still had the power to soothe her.

After a while, she said she felt well enough to get up.

'I have to go out again,' he said.

'What, on a night like this? You can barely see your hand in
front of your face. We never had anything like these terrible
fogs coming down at home!'

He despaired too sometimes, at the opaque nature of vision here and how obscured it was, and longed for the far clean distances of Northern Ireland. Yet, as it was not always foggy even in London, so it was not always like this with Aline: often, she was gay and laughing and brought back flowers to their tiny house, which was then a radiant well of warmth and light in the midst of the river darkness. It'll be like that again, he thought. She'll be all right.

'I'll have something to eat first,' he said.

It was Friday. She usually went to the fish-stall in the mornings.

She managed to smile. 'Yes, I've got some herrings in the pantry. Shall we have them grilled?'

'Sure, you're a wonderful griller of the herring itself!' and she laughed at his exaggerated accent and got up from the couch.

After the meal, she said hesitantly, 'Will, Mrs Salmon says they pulled someone out of the river.'

'Silly old trout!'

But she didn't join in their usual amusement about the owner of the fish-stall.

'Don't you go worrying, my darling.'

But it wasn't lost on Aline, the usual reason why a girl should jump into the freezing and filthy water. Will saw the thought pass through her mind and winced.

Neither of them spoke for a long while, as the night cleaned away the smoke and fumes that London had given out during the day, and brought down its own pall of fog over the city.

11

OLIVER REMAINED IN THE OUTER ROOMS OF THE NORWEGIAN minister's suite at the Savoy till midday, awaiting an urgent response to the documents he had brought. The proposed trade agreements were not, it appeared, sufficiently in Norway's favour. The Norwegians were claiming separate consular representation from Sweden, and predicted that dissolution from Stockholm was imminent. So the young man sat in an antechamber while from within came stray words – *storting, fylker, Pomerania* – of which he dutifully tried to make sense in case there should be anything useful to report, but the language seemed impenetrable.

From time to time he glanced through his copy of *The Times*, only partly registering the headlines, PROGRESS OF THE WAR, FENIANS ARRESTED, all remote from his world. It was rather hard to concentrate, he found, as he sank into an armchair deeply upholstered in crimson velvet and contemplated an arrangement of hothouse lilies in a crystal vase through which shone rainbow flashes of light. A life of idleness at mid-morning, of thick carpets and sweet scents, seemed to him quite delightfully strange.

He had accepted a small glass of some fiery liquor, which seemed quite unsuitable at this hour of the day, and then more gratefully the coffee that was provided while he cooled his heels. Rarely entrusted with a mission outside the office, he was anxious to do his best.

At one o'clock, the doors of the inner Viking sanctum were flung open and he was entrusted with the communication he was to take back to the Foreign Office. By this time hunger was intervening and, coming down to earth, he lunched at a chop-house in the Strand, reasoning that all his seniors would now be doing the same in their clubs in St James's and Pall Mall. Then an hour or two at his desk with his French newspapers, paying attention especially to the political columns in *Le Figaro*, and his European tasks for the day were completed. He was free to leave, and there was still half an hour or so of daylight, though the sun was low and casting a reddish light from downriver as he walked over Westminster Bridge and turned along the south side of the Embankment, past St Thomas's Hospital.

Walking along the waterside he saw the flotsam and jetsam slapping at the banks, the faces of the tugmen who coasted near the shore, the loads and rigging of the boats, the black tarpaulins, the old coiled ropes and fenders. A jetty, its planks old and slimy-looking, stretched down to the water. At the end of the jetty there were two small children and a woman with a checked dress and a shawl. The children leaned over, poking with sticks down into the water.

Out in the river, but closer to the far side, a small steamboat was chugging along, tarpaulins pulled over a heavy load, two long furrows of water rippling in its wake. Seagulls screamed somewhere overhead. Upstream, the Houses of Parliament were glowing a deep red in the dying sun.

Nothing notable. An unremarkable day.

And then suddenly there was a commotion on the steamer: the helmsman was shouting something indistinct and the sound of the engines changed to an irregular phutter and then cut out. Two more men appeared on deck, calling out to each other, made for the stern and peered down into the water. Then one of them went and got a long pole and thrust and prodded round the froth of the propeller, making awkward pushing movements till something seemed to snake free. There were more shouts on the deck of the little vessel, and a log-like shape just below the surface seemed to roll and drift with a current that swept across. The engine started up again. The men were yelling, pointing to the shore, screaming at the children on the jetty. Something dark in the water continued its long roll towards the shore.

The woman, who had been leaning above the water with the children, suddenly cried out and pulled the two small figures away from the edge. She ran up the jetty towards Oliver, her arms stretched out behind pulling the two boys after her, and her mouth was open in a great scream that choked into words as she came near Oliver. 'Down there! In the water!'

Fearful of what he would see, he forced himself to hurry over the slimy wooden planks to the place where she had been standing and looked down. He saw something white trailing slightly like a fleshy stalk just below the surface and near to the piles of the jetty. The thin brown water washed back and forth and the white curving cusped parts above the stalk moved with it, so that they seemed to be opening and closing like petals.

His eyes were reluctant, but his brain insisted on identifying what he saw. It was the lower part of a human arm, below the elbow, with a hand that flopped and trailed as the river water slid between the dead fingers, opening and closing them softly. The rest of the body was just under the surface, bobbing, a long shape, folds of cloth billowing out.

Even then, he could scarcely bear to believe it. Looking back up the jetty, he saw there were two men at the top carrying a coil of rope: he ran towards them and one of them came and looked over his shoulder, and then raced back, calling for help. Things started to happen. The steamboat headed for a nearby pier, where it moored in deeper water, and the men on board stared blankly towards the jetty. As they secured the boat, one of them yelled towards a fellow on the bank and his words reached Oliver through the cries of the seagulls. 'Propeller clean cut it! Went through the rope!'

A passing barge was hailed and its boathooks prodded and thrust into the bubbling mud beneath the landing-stage at the end of the jetty, where the water seemed churned into muddy shallows. At last, a great string of something seemed to be pulled clear, and a long, dripping tangle came up on the end of the pole and was deposited, with a deft twisting of the hook, on to the wooden planks. Even through the weeds that clung to it, Oliver knew what he was looking at: he knew, rather than analytically observed, that the hook had torn off part of a scalp with a long tress of hair clinging to it.

One of the men was speaking to him. 'Ah, we find them, sir, all the time. The rest of the poor thing won't be far away. Will you stay here for a minute, while I get what we need? We have to keep those bairns away.'

Oliver thus found himself with a scrap that had once been part of a human being, and some primitive feeling made him think that he must stay with it, that he owed it something, though he could not think what, except this dreadful sort of watch-duty that kept him by the stinking river. The men on the barge were shouting exchanges, but he did not know what they were saying: their dialect might well have been another language altogether. The beshawled woman standing at the shore end of the landing stage stared goggle-eyed towards the river. She clasped the smaller boy, pulled him round and pressed his face into her dirty checked skirt. The gesture made Oliver feel more lonely than ever, standing at the far end of the jetty over the little heap of hair and flesh as though he were its last guardian. His time there seemed an eternity. And he stared upriver at the setting sun, which seemed to be sinking with horrible speed into the dusky waters of the river.

'Look at it,' he told himself. 'Look!' And though he desperately wanted to turn away, even to run and bury his face in the woman's skirt alongside the child, he forced his head to turn towards the scraps that had fallen off the boathook. He obliged his eyes to open again upon them, like a lonely sentry.

Then he became aware that there was a knot of men hurrying towards him along the landing-stage. They carried something that looked like a stretcher – yes, he was sure it was a stretcher – and set it down at the end of the jetty. There were swirls in the water again, and, with a long clumsy pole that had a horrible comedy about it, something was steered to land. It was still all below the surface, but there was a call from one of the men, who was reaching over the side. 'Got it – there, hang on!' Another fellow reached down. And, in a gross parody of two butcher-boys dragging a leg of an animal carcass apiece, they pulled up two white human legs that stuck out of a great swathe of dark cloth, and hauled the long shape awkwardly on to the slats of the jetty, where it oozed and settled beside the detached piece of scalp and hair that Oliver guarded. He moved back.

The wooden planks reverberated as men in uniform now came pounding down from the road and hid the body from sight as they grouped around it. At last one of the policemen, a man with silver buttons and a high collar, detached himself from the others.

The uniformed man put a hand on Oliver's shoulder. He felt the hand striking through him, warm, powerfully human and alive, and a current of gratitude towards the other poured through Oliver. He was relieved of his duties, said the gesture, the touch of humanity on his shoulder. There was no need for him to continue his self-appointed vigil, no need to look at the thing any longer. He turned round to face his rescuer.

He saw a big red-headed man, with bristly grey pushing among the red, and pouches under tired eyes. 'The propeller caught the side of her head. Nasty mess.'

Oliver felt a terrible wave of nausea.

'Garrety, sir. Inspector William Garrety.' The other was introducing himself, and he became aware that a card was being pushed under his face, but didn't bother to look down. Suddenly he felt a wave of hot liquid rising in his throat and the hand on his shoulder moved to support him as he swayed his head out over the edge of the planks. The brown gush from his stomach poured into the waters of the river, and he saw it floating there for a moment. There was a swirl of bubbles and bits of bacon fat and kidney, evenly diced by his teeth. He found a handkerchief.

The other paused for a few minutes, allowing Oliver to regain some composure.

'I'll need your name and address, sir, if you don't mind.

Then we can get you a cab and you can go home.'

Oliver automatically, without thinking, gave the Barnes address. Then he said, 'I'll walk a little. Need some fresh air.'

The policeman looked at him gravely, with a certain obser-vation that Oliver registered only obliquely, wondering why the grey eyes suddenly seemed so sharp, and supposing he himself must be a pretty despicable object, puking his guts out like a schoolboy.

'I shouldn't walk far, sir, if I were you. You've had a nasty shock. It'll be a while before you get over it. Let me take you up to the top there and find a cab for you.'

'No, it's all right, thank you, I can make it. It's not far . . .' He gestured in the direction of the road at the top of the jetty, where traffic was moving back and forth, and the world was going about its normal business, while down here, where death had made this stupefying appearance, time stood still.

But they were already walking along and he was grateful for the sense of a strong presence at his side. He didn't expect Garrety to say anything, but he heard a deep voice beside him, surely an Irish brogue.

'It's a terrible thing, sir. Death, I mean. It takes us all savagely, somehow, one way or another, even those that don't show anything.'

Oliver cleared his throat. 'Have you . . . have you seen a lot of it, Inspector?'

'Yes, sir. And I still feel sick to the pit of my stomach. Every time, Mr Craston, every time. For the stomach, have a brandy straight away, sir, is my advice. But I won't tell you to forget what you've seen. You'll find it does go away, though. With time.'

Their footsteps clumping sullenly on the sodden wood, they reached the top of the jetty.

12

IT WAS THIS EPISODE OF THE WOMAN IN THE RIVER, HORRIFIC as it was for Oliver, that led to experiences that would always distinguish him from his fellows. Many years later, they would keep alive for him even into old age an inner life that they had long forgotten.

What he had seen in the water had in a way shocked him out of all social nervousness. It was so elemental, somehow, so much the basic thing, such an encounter with the ultimate reduction of flesh and blood, that it swept away all his sense of the conventional. Oliver Craston the schoolboy, a gentle, trusting child, had perforce adapted to the customs and the crudeness of his small society, and Craston the young man had continued this process, feeling his routine enclose him every morning as the stiff white collar daily enclosed his neck. He had expected, without giving it conscious thought, that this carapace would remain for the rest of his life. But he was still too young, his defences too thin, and now on the Thames jetty they fell from him with each step he took, so that he felt weak, even tearful.

When he reached the road with Inspector Garrety, he felt his legs giving way. But he was able to walk with the older man into a roadside tavern – a shack, really – the sort of place he had never been to in his life and probably, but for this incident, never would. He found he could ignore the stares from the knot of roughly dressed watermen at the end of the bar and walk behind the broad shoulders up to the counter. A woman – he took in some straggling fair hair piled on top of her head, a shawl pinned round her shoulders – raised an enquiring face to the newcomers. It was quite a young face, yet shrewd. 'She realizes something has happened,' went through his mind, and he thought then in terms of something having happened to him, to Oliver Craston, of the suffering that he himself had undergone with the finding of the body, not of the horror of the death itself.

'A brandy. Make it a big one, my love.' Garrety put some coins down on the counter.

She reached for a bottle and poured a brown liquid into a glass, looked at Oliver's face and put in another splash. Garrety slid the glass along the counter and Oliver picked it up, gripping it tightly so his hand wouldn't shake, and drained it in a single gulp, feeling a fiery burning in his stomach. Crude stuff, but he had scarcely begun to drink brandy anyway: he was still a downy-necked hatchling among the club bores who circulated after-dinner bottles, and this stuff served its purpose. He felt warmth flowing through his veins and he gasped a sigh of relief as his taut, hunched shoulders relaxed. The nausea left him, though he was still uncertain of his voice.

'Aren't you having a drink?' he said cautiously.

'I'm on duty. But you looked as if you needed one.'

Garrety led Oliver to a table at the side of the little room.

The windows were small and the panes dirty, but by the dusty light that filtered through them Oliver now began to take in the group of drinkers clustered at the bar, mostly men with unshaven faces in heavy clothes and thigh-boots.

The woman was looking curiously at them.

Oliver stared down, away from her gaze, seeing the pale ring-marks through the reddish varnish.

The weak daylight was striking on Garrety's shoulders and one of the men nudged another, as if they had just recognized the uniform.

'Bad, was it?' said the woman.

Garrety merely nodded. No-one said anything, but the woman sighed softly as she poured something out of a black bottle for one of the men.

Oliver realized that this drinking-den was a small refuge for those who lived alongside the river, labouring sometimes up to their thighs in its dirty mud, knowing its moods, watching its tides and currents, the driftwood, even the bodies of the drowned. There was a window looking out over the water, from which they had probably observed the proceedings on the pier.

He nodded.

'First one?' The woman was talking to Oliver now.

The group of drinkers looked at him, with neither pity nor hostility. And he looked back at them, gazing directly, fully, perhaps for the first time in his life.

'Been in long, had it?'

This was one of the men, wiping his black moustache on a kerchief. Oliver had little idea of his age: the eyes were young, at any rate, but the face was mostly in shadow.

'I don't know . . .' Oliver's voice trailed off. 'It hadn't . . . floated far, I don't think. There was a cord . . .' He swallowed, then found his voice again. 'Couldn't she have come from anywhere – anywhere upriver?'

'There's a cross-current there. Could have come cater-wise 'cross the river, even. But if her were weighed down, her wouldn't have moved far.'

And another voice, older: 'Ay, there's pits down in the mud round the footings of that bridge – she might've stayed down in one of them till the rope rotted. Reckon the paddle-steamers churned it up.'

Another voice broke in: 'Nay, it's the cold snap. There's currents that change when the ice starts to come. Powerful, some of 'em. Could move a body, even if her were weighted.'

'Poor soul.' This was from the barmaid.

Garrety had said nothing, but there was something in his manner that discouraged conversation, and the others fell silent, then began talking among themselves about the loading of some coal barge at Whitechapel Steps.

Garrety looked across the table at Oliver and said, quietly, yet in a voice that had a kind of inexorability about it, 'Mr Craston, you are a resident of Barnes, I believe you said.'

'Er, no, that is where my family live, Inspector. I gave the address out of habit. I have only just moved quarters, you see. I am in a set of rooms near the Embankment.'

'Oh?' It was as if a fox had scented something. 'Tell me, why did you find it necessary to leave the family home?' As he spoke, Garrety passed a pocket handkerchief across the table, adding, 'Your collar, sir,' so that as Oliver rubbed the place that the policeman indicated, finding some unpleasant traces of yellow froth, he felt like a shamed schoolboy.

'Well, you see, Inspector, I left for reasons that are ... are to do with ... I cannot tell you entirely – that is, I am engaged in diplomatic work and it is easier for me to fulfil my duties ... I may need to work at odd times, you see.' He thought he had made it sound as if he were engaged in important activities.

Oliver looked across the table and saw the grey eyes fixed on his, the arms folded, waiting. He took another swig of the brandy. He was more aware now, as his stomach recovered somewhat, of its harsh cheap taste.

'So the information you gave me at first was not correct.' There was a long pause. 'This is a very serious incident, sir.'

Oliver briefly considered the possibilities. He didn't want to go on, he wanted to get straight back home, but he guessed what would happen if he walked out and left this policeman. A message sent to the FO requesting confirmation of his claims, the matter reported back, young Craston known for his involvement in what looked like a particularly sordid death ...

He imagined himself standing in front of that formidable desk. 'Yes, but I was merely *there* – when the body was found. I was an entirely innocent instrument. I could not refuse ...'

'Unlucky, Craston, unlucky. You were noticed anyway. You won't be much use to us, not if you are known to the police force.' He could hear the last words in his mind, spoken in rolling, contemptuous tones. It would mean the end of his real career prospects, of that he was in no doubt.

Oliver looked across and was disconcerted to realize that the big man still had his grey eyes fixed across the table. The smells of stale beer and cheap alcohol came wafting from the bar. The other drinkers were all studiously ignoring the two newcomers and backs were turned in an apparently animated private conversation.

'But perhaps you can tell me why you were near the jetty.

Since you have taken to living on your own near the river. Sir.'
The last word was added with such irony that it was almost a
threat.

Oliver made a quick decision. 'Very well, Inspector. I do
assure you that I came to be here merely by chance. I was
walking back to my rooms. It has no connection with . . . my
mode of employment.' His voice echoed thinly into the
shanty and he was aware of what a pompous young fool he
probably sounded.

'Can you give me the names of some persons who could
support what you say?'

'I would really rather not, Inspector . . .'

'If you please, sir.' Garrety did, however, hold out some
hope to the unhappy youngster. 'It may not, of course, be
necessary to contact these gentlemen.'

'Very well.' But Craston, looking over at the bar, saw that
one or two of the men were watching covertly, and he had the
impression they might be able to hear the conversation. He
pulled his card-case from his pocket, turned over one of the
slips of engraved pasteboard still bearing the Barnes address,
and scribbled two names upon it, and his new address.

'These gentlemen, Inspector. At the Foreign Office.'

There was a pause. He held out the card, which Garrety
took in his big, red-knuckled paw.

'Well-known names, sir. Well, I see no reason to trouble
these personages. If you can make your own way home from
here . . . Then I'll be off. Goodbye, Mr Craston, and thank
you for your help. We will ask you to make a statement concerning the finding of the body. Someone will call on you.'

Garrety slipped the card into a pocket, rose and walked
away, nodding in the direction of the barmaid and the knot of
drinkers.

Oliver was overcome by relief. He was on his own, he could just get up and leave, if his legs would stand it. He tried, tentatively, and found they seemed to be in better working order than when he had entered the place. The policeman's departure had caused a little stir in the group at the bar, who were now looking at Oliver. 'Well, I think perhaps I'll be off,' he said in their general direction.

There was a long silence, during which Oliver felt it incumbent upon himself to make a gesture of some sort, but he did not know what was expected of him, how to extricate himself. Finally, he got up, saying awkwardly, 'Will you all have a drink?' and, putting a crown piece on the bar, turned to the door. The men said nothing, but one of them nodded his thanks in Oliver's direction and held out his mug for the barmaid.

Outside there was still a trace of the sunset, though Oliver felt that aeons of time had passed, and the street-lamps were already glowing. He looked about him, to see the name of the place, but the shack was so flimsy, so fragile a container and protector of the battered humanity inside it, that it did not even merit a sign.

As he stood irresolutely and still confused in the road, a carriage rolled by him, causing him to step back in shock, and he was aware of a face gazing out. The carriage passed on but suddenly a window was pulled down and a voice called to the cabby to stop; he pulled up a few yards beyond Oliver and a figure stepped out.

'Sir! Are you unwell?'

The accent was French, and Oliver saw a thin, dark young man stepping towards him. He advanced with an expression of concern, and Oliver suddenly realized that he himself must be looking alarmed. He would have slipped away rather than suffer to be observed in this state, but the young man had already come up to him and, peering at him closely, put an arm round his shoulder.

'Let us take you back with us,' said the young man, helping him towards the carriage.

Oliver was awkwardly aware that he must smell of cheap brandy. 'Thank you for your kindness . . . I must explain – there was a terrible . . .' Not knowing how to describe what had occurred, he settled for a word that did not begin to convey the horror of it, yet was the only one that sprang to his lips: 'There's been an accident. A dead . . . a dead woman in the river . . .'

The young man paused as he began to understand the predicament. 'And you – did you find her?'

Oliver nodded.

A rapid exchange in French, of which he was able to pick up the gist, followed between the young man and someone in the depths of the carriage.

'Papa, this young man . . . something awful has happened. I recognize him from the foyer of the hotel this morning. We can't leave him here.'

'Get him inside, then. We'll take him back to the hotel, and call a doctor if necessary.'

Within the carriage a massive bearded head was turned towards him, and a pair of dark eyes gazed in his direction. Again for Oliver on this fateful day, the normal protective casing of his soul was shattered. The eyes peered fixedly at his face. He felt the gaze as something that he had never before experienced, almost as a physical event, and it seemed interminable, searching, leaving him with a sense of nakedness.

It was the old man he had seen on the balcony. Oliver turned, almost seeking refuge, towards the young man, who responded quickly to this unspoken appeal, perhaps understood its cause.

'Ah, monsieur, excuse me, I have forgotten my manners. This is not a time to wait for polite introductions. I am Michel Monet, and this is my father—'

'Yes, yes,' Oliver felt bound to say. 'Of course, I have heard of you, sir. My name is Craston – Oliver Craston.'

The formalities seemed as much as the occasion would sustain.

The carriage jogged over Waterloo Bridge and turned into the Savoy courtyard.

13

'WON'T YOU COME TO OUR SUITE AND LET ME SEND FOR SOME tea, perhaps? Are you recovering from your experience? I'm afraid you still look very pale.'

Oliver ever afterwards thought of that day as apocalyptic: his first taste of death, his first taste of cheap drink. And perhaps a first brush with other strong experiences, feelings harsh and powerful, that had been present, he scarcely knew whether in himself or in others, inside the little shack on the jetty.

'My father crosses the river to catch the afternoon light from the other bank. The hospital along there – St Thomas's – has let him have a room, quite high up. He usually stops painting when the light goes, but today we were returning a little early. We are expecting a visitor. But my father is reluctant to leave his work. That is all that interests him here, you see. He paints Westminster, with the setting sun falling on it. Oh, the effect is quite spectacular, I assure you. Nothing you would see in nature! During the day he can hardly be persuaded to stop work; the time is so short in winter – the sun almost vanishes at midday! My father works too hard, but we cannot prevent him.'

Craston understood. The old man had followed dawn and dusk along the river, crossing from one bank to the other to gain the best vantage points.

He thanked his rescuers again, and found himself being swept along with them.

'Please come and rest a little, and then take tea with us. We were rather concerned – you looked so very pale when you came into our carriage. Are you sure you don't want me to call a doctor? Well, if you really would rather not ... Oh, we have two suites, 541 and 542. My father uses one as a studio.'

In the room occupied by the painter as a studio, unframed canvases stood propped round the walls, stacked in layers, and the smells of oil-paint, linseed and turpentine were harsh, yet somehow cleansing, almost like some scouring dis-infectant fumes. Oliver had somehow expected chaos where an artist was concerned, but he saw that clean trestle tables had been set up, bearing boxes with carefully aligned tubes of paint in fat immaculate rows, and jars containing forests of brushes. This was a picture of order, yet out of the darkness at the edges of the room sprang shapes and colours from the shadowy pictures lining the walls: the black outline of a bridge, the orange tracks of a glowing, dying sun.

Oliver found himself mesmerized by what he saw, for the paintings seemed the climax to a crazy day. They looked care-less, almost mad, violent with great streaks of paint that glistened wetly. The room was lit now by electric light, though only the wall-lights were on, and the heavy velvet curtains were undrawn so that he could see lights on the river below. The window to the balcony had been shut, and a chair, a rug and an easel brought just inside the window embrasure.

On the easel stood a picture that threatened to overwhelm him. As he looked, his mouth seemed to fill with the taste of the fog that hung above the river. He could recognize the grey-brown structure of Waterloo Bridge, the dark colours of coke and carbon. There was the roadway running across, with thick encrustations, a kind of monstrous furry growth like mould or lichen clinging upon it that must represent the outlines of creatures scurrying back and forth across the river. Creatures like himself.

Oliver drew back, frightened at the implications of the picture, at the littleness of humanity and the darkness of the river.

He was relieved when young Michel Monet led him through a connecting door into the next room, which was furnished as an ordinary sitting-room. Michel seemed to be laughing at him a little. 'Oh, yes, I suppose you are not used to modern art, to Impressionists. There are still not so many people in Paris who take my father's work seriously. You'll understand it better if you get to know us, but it's a shock at first. Papa, I'll ring for tea while you take off your coat.'

Then he was aware of Michel catching his elbow and saying, 'I think you'd better lie down,' and he was being steered through into a bedroom and lowered on to a wide bed. He sank gratefully into the soft depths.

'Close your eyes and rest.' Michel's voice seemed distant.

When he awoke, some time – an hour or so – seemed to have passed, and he started up in embarrassment. His shoes had been removed and placed beside the bed. Catching sight of his rumpled hair in a mirror, he hastily used a silver-backed comb lying on a tallboy to make himself more presentable.

Horrified at his behaviour and unfamiliar with the consequences of shock, he attributed it, with a sense of shame, to the cheap brandy.

Going into the sitting-room, he found the Monets talking quietly. They looked up at him with concern as he came into the room and he was relieved, thinking of his own father's likely reaction to such an episode, that their faces did not appear in the least censorious; rather, they were concerned for his well-being. He thanked them again for taking him into their carriage and the conversation drifted into French. After a moment or two, M. Monet excused himself and went to wash his hands.

'I ordered tea while you were asleep,' said Michel. 'I hope you feel like taking a little to eat, also.'

There was a discreet knock at the door and a waiter wheeled a trolley into the room. A white cloth was removed to reveal plates of sandwiches, small cakes dusted with icing sugar, a teapot and a spirit-kettle, as well as thin gilt-edged cups and saucers. Michel walked over to the door and switched on an electric chandelier that hung over the table.

Oliver was expecting the young man to pour the tea, or perhaps to ask the waiter to do so, but the door opened and another person entered the room. Oliver had assumed for a moment that it was the old man come back, but he remembered the visitor Michel had mentioned, and found himself looking at a young woman who hovered in the heavy dark doorway like a white butterfly shaking itself out. She was wearing a pale dress with falls of ribbon and her hair was fair. He could not see her face clearly in the side light and found himself longing for her to move forward so that he could see what she looked like. So intensely did he feel this that it became a matter of inward desperation for him over the next few moments.

'Oh, allow me to introduce you,' said Michel. 'Rosaline, this is Mr Oliver Craston.'

Oliver edged towards her – surely she would step forward? – but she remained a pale spectre against the darkness of the doorway.

'Mr Craston, this is Miss Darby. I lodge with her family, you know, in Bromfield Road. I am here to learn English, you see, so it is better for me to stay with a family than with Papa. In any case, I would interfere with his work if I lived here in the Savoy with him.'

'It might interfere with your amusements, Michel!' A soft voice, with an English accent, maybe a hint of something else, not French, came out of the shadows.

'No, Rosa, you betray me!'

Oh, please, please, Rosaline Darby, let me see your face, thought Oliver, and did not yet know why he longed so much to see it.

'He has been skating almost every day, Mr Craston, for the last week, since this freezing weather came.'

She stepped into the room at last and he saw large diamond-shaped blue eyes, full of brilliance and gaiety. They were somehow exactly what he had expected and yet the fulfilment of his expectations and desires seemed to be in itself a cause of dread.

'But we are all really very glad of it,' she continued, and for a moment he had lost the thread of the conversation. 'Although I tease him, Michel has not been at all well recently – in fact, his health has been causing some concern, has it not?'

'Oh, please, I am really very well!'

Michel Monet turned to Oliver. 'Rosa is over-anxious – and so are the Darbys – because my sister Suzanne died quite recently. Her health was frail, but it was still a cause of great distress.'

'I'm so very sorry to hear it.'

'Thank you. But it is my father who is most affected. He still hasn't recovered from the news.'

'Though it is rather unusual, is it not, that he should feel it so much?' broke in Rosaline. 'You see, Monsieur Monet was not Suzanne's father.' But there was no time to ask her anything about this, for the old man came back into the room and as he took his place at the table Oliver could see his face clearly for the first time, the powerful eyes and great, flowing, spade-shaped beard, still with a lot of black in it.

He felt that he must say something. 'You may not see much of London – I'm afraid that the weather is very foggy at present,' he offered dismally, conscious that this line would scarcely do service even at his mother's reading-bee teas. But there was an extraordinary and excited response.

'Oh, that is good news!' The old man beamed round. 'I am longing for a real *brouillard* – I have come here expressly to paint the fog and mists, you see, or rather to paint the light as it falls upon them, and through them . . .'

Oliver absorbed the conversation and his surroundings, content to take the cup that Rosaline passed him and to sit with this extraordinary family. Michel entertained the company and indeed did not give a great deal of opportunity to the others. At first, Oliver was merely grateful, since it exonerated him from saying much. He was unused to the openness of his host and the questions were not the kind that his mother's friends asked. Thankfully, no-one seemed to want to know where he worked, and neither did anyone ask him which university he had been to. Gaining confidence, he began to recount the story of the boarding-house in Paris where he had briefly lodged, with a landlady who made her lodgers recite Victor Hugo every evening, and this seemed popular with his audience. But he was aware all the time that, beside Michel Monet, he must cut a dreary figure. He imagined Michel in Paris, with a group of friends round a table at Maxim's, perhaps, or walking along the sunlit boulevards with some elegant woman. Oliver's Paris, his brown-painted boarding-house, his earnest circle of student friends, was a different world altogether.

14

OLIVER THOUGHT THAT FIRST EVENING WITH ROSA WOULD
stay in his mind for the rest of his life: the shadows in the
corners of the room; the white cloth over the table, on which
fell overlapping pools of light from overhead; the faces of the
others round the table.

The old man leaned back, heavy, relaxed now that his work
was over and the light of day entirely gone. For the most part
he said little, looking keenly across the table at Rosaline's face
from time to time, but in a curious, assessing way. If she felt
the strangeness of his look, she showed no reaction: perhaps
she was accustomed to it. Oliver had never known this before,
a young woman at whom a man was openly staring remaining unabashed, indeed, in utter self-possession. It was against
all he knew about how young ladies were supposed to behave,
and he imagined how his mothers' friends would have
reproved such a lack of modesty in their own daughters. Her
face was an oval floating above the insubstantial white wraith
of her dress; her eyes seemed huge, the sockets shadowed by

the harsh light above. But this general ghostliness was offset by the vitality of her behaviour, the bold part she played in the conversation, even the gusto with which she bit into the thin sandwiches and demolished them swiftly. He found himself watching her mouth, observing tiny crumbs of white bread on the red lips. If her face was pale, her lips seemed a brilliant colour, the effect enhanced by electric light.

'My father wants to paint all day long. He works outside, on the balcony, but I must say your weather makes me ill!'

'Oh, Michel, you are always complaining about your health!' said Rosaline impatiently. 'I'm sure Mr Craston doesn't want to hear about it!'

Oliver was embarrassed. 'Oh, I'm sure – that is . . .' His voice trailed off, but the older Monet rescued him unexpectedly.

'Never have I seen such extraordinary effects as that of the light filtering through the fogs as it touches the river. There are a hundred colours in your atmosphere here – and it is such a terrible task to capture them!'

'Yes, Papa,' said Michel, 'but remember it is February! To paint outside all day, exposed to the freezing fog and the dirty air as you do, from dawn to dusk – you are not a young man, remember!'

Unexpectedly, it was Rosaline who provided the rejoinder. 'Yes, but to suffer for what one achieves, to take risks for it, isn't that what the artist has to do?'

'I don't consider it like that,' said the old man slowly. 'For me, it is not a matter of choice. It is what I must do.'

'No, indeed, Papa, it is like some compulsion that drives you to the limits!' said Michel.

He turned to Oliver. 'Mr Craston, my father is nearly sixty years of age, yet I have seen him painting in every kind of weather – even while his clothes were becoming stiff with frost!'

'But there is something I must tell Mr Craston,' said Michel's father. 'After what you have experienced today – it will help you to absorb it, to live with the memory of it.'

Oliver was deeply surprised. Somehow, he had not expected the artist really to have paid much attention to what had happened to his unexpected guest, or to have given thought to the future consequences to Oliver himself of finding that poor, rotting creature. The old man did not live in a world of his own entirely, then, he thought.

'Mr Craston, to understand things, you must always look beyond appearances. That is what I am trying to do with my paintings of the river. You have looked into the depths, Mr Craston, and it is very ugly down there, is it not? But one must see the things that lie beneath the surface. That is what I am struggling to do with my painting. That's why I cannot rest.'

Michel moved forward abruptly, and his father laughed. 'For Michel, things are different! He has no struggles! My son likes an easy life, Mr Craston.'

Oliver had never thought that there was more to the work of an artist than dabbing paint upon a canvas. He understood now that there was something about the nature of art which he had never before encountered. That this might involve some pain or turmoil, that they might be out of doors in the depths of winter, braving the elements, that there was some kind of battle in which they might be engaged – these were new ideas for him.

It is hard, then, it must be a stubborn thing, he thought to himself, but then abruptly Claude Monet, as though his son had not spoken, suddenly looked at the watch on his chain and rose from his place at the table, saying, 'I must apologize to our guest, but I find I have forgotten the time and I have an appointment for dinner. Will you excuse me, sir? I have to go and dress.'

'Who are you seeing for dinner, Papa?'

'The painter Mr Sargent. He comes here for me and we will go to dine, I believe, at a grill-room with some of his friends.'

Craston took a few moments to recognize the English name, for Monet had pronounced it in the French way, but was then duly impressed. Sargent had been talked about even in the Craston circle. He was the kind of artist who was so rich and well connected that he could scarcely be the subject of prejudice, even though he was of American descent and Italian birth. Sargent moved in the best society – painted its members, commemorated their triumphant moments. Oliver had the fleeting impression that there was a kind of pride in the mention of his name even here, in the presence of the most famous living French artist.

Claude Monet merely gestured vaguely and withdrew from the room into the inner mysteries of the suite. Oliver stood up hastily, murmuring apologies and feeling that perhaps he had outstayed his welcome, but Michel said quickly, 'Oh, please, Mr Craston, don't apologize! But, as a matter of fact, we should be returning to Bromfield Road, shouldn't we, Rosa? We will be expected for dinner there.'

Oliver surprised himself by the strength of the annoyance he felt at this comment. He was even more surprised when Rosa laughed, and said, 'Michel, you cannot always speak for me! How do you know I haven't something better to do than to ride home with you?'

Michel said nothing in reply, merely laughing as he rose and fetched a heavy cloak for Rosa and a thick overcoat for himself.

Did Rosa often speak to him in that bold way? Oliver felt that he had blundered into a group whose private talk carried its own codes. Their very looks, their gestures, were read differently from those in his own limited social experience. Clearest of all was that the relationship between Rosa Darby and Michel Monet was not that which convention imposed between a lodger and the landlord's daughter. The easy way in which Michel helped her into the great dark-blue velvet cloak, which flowed and swung around her body, somehow suggested a familiarity that made Oliver wince inside. The cloak was as much part of the absurdity of the whole occasion, its strangeness, as anything else – such a garment would never have been seen in Barnes.

Rosa shrugged away from Michel and held out her hand to Oliver. 'Goodbye, Mr Craston, but we'll meet again!' Her hand pressed his with surprising strength.

As Michel showed him out, he said, 'Mr Craston, I hope we can count on you to call on us again. To be frank, my father does not see many English people and I myself need some new company.'

For the second time that day Oliver produced his new address and Michel noted it carefully, adding, 'So we'll definitely meet again, I hope, Mr Craston!'

Oliver found he was unable to look away from Rosaline until he realized she was looking at him questioningly, when he tore his gaze away and stared down at the yellow laurel crowns woven into the blue of the Savoy carpet till he thought they would be imprinted on his brain.

As he stepped into the lift, he thought he heard something – a distant cry, perhaps, almost a shriek – ringing down the shaft. Even though it was faint, it seemed shocking in those discreet surroundings. The lift attendant heard it, too. 'It's the sixth floor, sir. They fitted it up to nurse wounded officers – I think it were one of the princesses arranged it all. They cries out sometimes, poor fellows. Can't help it, you see.'

He pulled the door across the lift shaft, shutting out all sounds.

15

I WATCH THEM CAREFULLY. SOMETIMES I STAND MIDWAY along a bridge and let them scurry past me as they move oblivious of the dangers of the dirty waters, the hidden currents. Not for me the mindless wandering in the streets, the sudden lunge and rapid obscure performance upon some unknown and nameless creature, the spending of energy in darkness.

That's what it is, of course. Energy. Its most pure and creative form, to be experienced as godlike.

That's why it's too important to be wasted on some toothless prostitute. After all, I'm not demented: I don't go out and give way to my urges just as I wish. I am not an animal: I have instincts, but I control them. So with each one: I do not confront them at random.

I know the lie of the land. I look down from my balcony and I see the human shapes crossing and criss-crossing the embankments and the bridges, their sketchy outlines through the fog, the women in their skirts and bustles, their little boots.

And, later on, when I have made my dispositions, when I have picked out one of the herd, I hear her.

I hear her feet pattering through the darkness, but there are sounds that muffle the footsteps.

Sometimes I go out into the endless corridor and all I hear echoing along it are the howls and wailing of the damned – at least one would think so, but I can tell you by experience, by hard and sad experience, that they are the cries of wounded men. Padded and muffled by thick walls and carpets and by more than that, by the flesh of men who bite their own hands so as not to cry out, who will keep the shame of their pain silent as long as they can. Now they are facing the imagined hells of their futures or of their memories, coming to terms with stumps that will always ache, legs that will always drag. Their loving mammas and sisters have fluttered round, but must leave them to their 'convalescence', as the process of journeying back to this country of the living, of crossing the bridge back into this preposterous world of safety and politeness, is known. There is this period when they must shed their roughness, hide the truths that their wounds have made known, and become once more fit for civilized society.

And so I endure my own 'convalescence', and when I can bear to do so I contemplate the future. I know in the lucid intervals that further degeneration is the only possible outcome. I have studied myself, you see, or, rather, those like me. I knew when I saw the landmarks on my way, each time it happened.

Of course, I didn't know when I was a child. Not then; I loved the dog. Only later, when *he* came, after that, I understood. When I thought the devil was in the dog, in its red mouth, his saliva drooling out. And, even then, I did not know *what* I was. Not until I came to study it.

After the war is over, there'll be no more need of my services. And I cannot expect another position in civilian practice, except perhaps for a workhouse or an asylum, eking out a miserable existence by tending to those barely a rung below me in the scale of wretchedness. The thing I cling to, the thing that makes me feel I have some chance of sanity left, is my hope to perform some scientific experiments, following the cool manipulations of logic, rather than hanging always to the bedsides of the sick and dying. Yesterday I walked alongside St Thomas's, where it stretches along the south embankment, the yellow lights burning in the long cold wards, here and there a figure moving through the rows of beds. It reminded me of the days when I was doing my training, the time when I studied at night between being summoned to the wards below.

Nothing was said in public, of course – in fact, I'm pretty sure nothing was ever put down on paper. It would have looked so bad for the place – and the nurse was a drunkard who should have been dismissed long before. And, anyway, they had no real proof. 'Loath to accuse a physician of such an act!' That was old Sir Harrington Bailey, damned fool. There was a portrait of him hanging in the entrance, near the statue of the Nightingale.

It would be quite wrong to think that I hated all my medical studies. I was not such a stupid brute – I was brutalized, perhaps, yet still capable of learning and of delighting in study, when it was safely remote from humanity. The examination of patients, cultivation of the 'bedside manner', the taking of a case history: all these things were distasteful to me. God, how some of them stank! The sores, the gangrenous wounds, the rashes and blisters.

I hate to use the stethoscope – the sound of the heartbeat is an obscene testimonial to the power of the vital force. Surgery is of more interest – at least, it was at medical school and in the teaching hospitals, where the patient was chloroformed and obedient, scarcely to be distinguished from the dead, the limbs marvellously flaccid, the body unaware, the mind unknowing. In South Africa, these things became mechanical. At Spion Kop, the field labourers pressed into service as bearers stretchered the wounded down, those they could reach, who were not left screaming out their thirst on the battlefield. We worked on men with their faces blistered by the heat, their blue army shirts stiff with blood, and as we worked the hyenas devoured those of their comrades who had been left to die in the trenches. And at Colenso you could see from miles away the lines of ambulance wagons drawn by goaded oxen as they came rocking across the veldt towards the field hospitals. The hospital tents were in a circle around the operating tent, but the wounded overflowed the tents on to the ground outside. The earth itself was covered with the dying.

If these things were written now, would any paper publish them? In any case, no jingoistic idiot who swaggers in the London streets would believe them. The men on stretchers shrouded with tarpaulins – that was all we had, in the end. The blood-stained grass. The amputees who tried to crawl out of the tents for fear of being shelled. The sun, like fire, burning through the canvas. The operating table, with an orderly removing the limbs as if they were butchers' chops, as fast as I amputated and sutured, and throwing them into a bucket beneath the table. The living awaited their turn on the floor underneath the operating table. If they were still conscious, so much the worse for them, as the severed limbs were flung into the buckets beside them. And still the endless processions of wagons rolling across the plains, each surrounded by its black buzzing cloud, and attended in the air by the hovering lines of vultures. All my training, the innocent surgical studies of the medical student, with room for ghoulish jokes – this was its ultimate use in the service of their country.

But there were some things I had studied that I find wonderful still, now I have returned and can take them up again – how could one not? The worlds under the microscope, for instance, those visions of pure line, shade and colour, in which I can lose myself. I ordered a Zeiss with dark-ground illumination, all particles, cells and veins rendered bright against the background. I have a microscope fitted with a chamber for the examination of fluids, and in it I observe movement without life, the material of which human beings are made without humanity. I set my eyes to those cold rubber cups and enter a world sealed and remote, untouched by love or hate.

By the time I returned from South Africa, I knew the course of my life was set and the time remaining to me is short. But I have a little money left from the sum my mother made over to me. I can set up my own practice.

Across the bridge. Not here. It might be cause for question on this, the fashionable side of the river. Rich people know too much, they have no *desperation* in them.

I saw something the other day that made me pause. It was just an ordinary scene such as one might glimpse in any good hotel – a quiet domestic moment glimpsed through a doorway. A maid, standing in the laundry-room looking at a folded pile of linen, absorbed in her task.

Of counting the sheets.

I have found a room on the other side of the Thames. A surgery.

16

JONATHAN CASTLETON SAT IN HIS ROOM AT THE SAVOY HOTEL, stretched out comfortably in the big armchair nearest the window. In his left hand was a new morocco wallet bearing his initials in gilt, and in his right a neat sheaf of white banknotes which he had just extracted from the tight clean folds of the wallet itself.

On top of the banknotes was a slip of stiff white writing-paper bearing a brief message written with a heavy nib. He read the words again: 'This should make all quits.'

He wondered for a few moments whether to keep the slip of paper, but decided it was not worth the trouble. It bore no identifying marks – he held it up to the light hopefully, just to check, but there was not even a watermark, much less a crest discreetly laid into the paper.

He's been damned careful, thought Castleton. Not signed, not even with initials. There was nothing to identify the writer of the note, except five words written in a perfectly ordinary hand, with, if Castleton was not mistaken, a common nib such as might be found anywhere. No, there was nothing in that direction – no point in keeping the note for future purposes. If the hotel detective were ever to produce the message in public, its author would undoubtedly disown it, probably with a laugh and a jeer. 'My hand in this note! Gentlemen, let us not descend to absurdities! Will you believe the claims of a hotel employee? Why, this could be the work of anyone in this room! It means absolutely nothing – perhaps someone paying off a gambling debt, that is all. Some young scamp who didn't want his pater to know he came to grief – something of that kind, I dare say. Let's hear no more about it!'

And the room would ring with male laughter, the cigar-smoke wreathing over the dining-table, and the author of the note would be quite safe.

Until next time.

For Castleton knew there would be a next time. There always had been.

They can't resist it, he thought. Once they've done it, they always come back for more. It's like waiting for fruit to fall from the tree.

He laughed to himself and crossed the room to the fire burning brightly in a polished grate. The slip of white paper curled up, turned brown and burst into flames, the writing leaping up suddenly for a moment and then crumbling into ash with the paper.

As Castleton leaned comfortably on the mantelpiece above the fire, there was a tap at the door, so quiet that he could easily have missed it and was uncertain about it, but it came again. 'Come in,' he called, thrusting the wallet, which he still held in one hand, deep into his pocket.

The door opened slowly, and nervously a young woman in

a maid's uniform slipped into the room. 'Please, sir . . . please, Mr Castleton . . . You said we should come . . . if ever we 'ad anything to ask . . . or tell you about anything funny . . .'

He wondered with irritation how to get her words out of the girl. Still, no good showing any anger. That way, her kind clammed up altogether. What was her damned name? He'd seen her in the laundry-room at the end of the corridor . . . On which floor?

He spoke up encouragingly. 'That's right, my dear. That's exactly what we want here. You come and talk to me about any goings-on – it may be important for the hotel, you know – for the management. It's always worthwhile them knowing what's happening under their roof – and they've got a perfect right to know, after all.'

The girl stood in the middle of the room, and Jonathan waved his hand expansively. 'Come and sit down by the fire. Now, what's your name?'

'Ruby, sir. Ruby Copeland.'

'Well, now, Ruby.'

She sat down and stayed perched at the edge of the sofa as though frightened to sit back. 'You see, I'm frightened about getting blamed for it, sir.'

Well, this sounded less interesting than he had hoped. The women hotel servants occasionally needed coaxing to tell him what they had seen – or glimpsed, or overheard. It was sometimes necessary to persuade them that looking through keyholes or cracks in the doors was desirable, even praiseworthy, in order to preserve the high moral standards of the hotel, of course. And it was usually about sex, in which case they got all hot and embarrassed – wouldn't admit that they'd come on a bit excited themselves, watching some ladyship being shafted on the carpet, perhaps, the maid with her hot little eye glued to the door all the while. Sometimes they even got a bit worked up while they were telling him about it, after he'd persuaded them it was all right to say out loud what they'd seen. Sometimes they didn't know the proper words for any of it, and he laughed at them stumbling over the dirty things they might have picked up. And then a little session with Uncle Jonathan might follow – just to show them what exactly had been going on. Slipping a hand up . . . was it here? . . . or here?

But they didn't usually blame themselves – not at this stage.

'Come on, then, what's it all about?'

'Well, sir, you see, I does the linen for Five and Six.'

These were the respective floors, in hotel parlance.

'Yes, Ruby?'

'And of course they told me they'll need a lot of extra linen for Six – on account of the mess, and everything.'

'What is the difficulty, Ruby? Have any of the . . .' he hesitated, 'the guests on Five been bothering you?'

'No, sir, but you see, I 'as to count the sheets. Count them when we put them on the beds, May and me, and I 'as to count them again when we send 'em back to the laundry. Well, sir, some of them's being taken sometimes from the laundry-room on Six and I'm afraid of getting the blame. I set forty sheets out on Monday afternoon ready for the rooms and the next mornin' there was only thirty-nine.'

Oh, Christ, he thought. Missing sheets! What's become of your glittering future, Jonathan my lad? What the hell am I doing here?

Nevertheless, he was briefly amused and knew where she had come from, could see the kids all in one bed stinking of piss. The mother would have a belly like an old sow after God knows how many pregnancies. The daughter would cross back and forth on her day off from her job on the other side of the river, the posh side of the Thames, and slip into the damp-walled little hovel with a few things in her pockets or carefully wrapped in a bit of paper – maybe some curled sandwiches rescued from the bins or a few candle-ends from the servants' rooms. She would not dare to take more: there was a pecking order in these things, from the upper servant's tipple of fine Madeira down to the kitchen-maids' scrapings from the plates.

He was smiling with his knowledge, and she was encouraged.

'It's 'appened a couple of times over the last weeks, I should say. And towels. The big 'uns – the white bath towels. There's half a dozen of them gone.'

Ruby had her face turned towards him pleadingly. She was a bit on the thin side, he thought, looking at the outline of her breasts under the black uniform with the white muslin pinafore over it. Still, she was a docile-looking little thing.

'You did absolutely right to come to me, Ruby. Don't worry about this. Do you want me to speak to Mrs Hilton for you?'

Mrs Hilton was the housekeeper, dreaded throughout the hotel for her fierceness. In the immemorial custom of staff perks, scraps and leftovers were one thing, but linen was another. It was definitely outside the boundaries of permissible scrounging – it was hotel property. Every item handed out for the guests' rooms, every scrap of linen, every face-flannel, every pillowcase – all would have to be accounted for, and old Hilton would check them off religiously in her linen-book, he was sure of it. The slightest hint that the girl had been stealing the hotel sheets and Ruby would be back in that smelly hole on the other side of the river for good.

Ruby's face brightened. 'Oh, would you, sir? I think they've taken them out on a trolley.'

'What do you mean?'

'There was a trolley went down in the special lift – I'd swear I saw it, just as the doors were closing. And sheets on it – so I'll get the blame, sir!'

'Of course. Don't worry about it any more. I'll sort it out.'

He could save the girl from Old Mother Hilton if he felt like it, he supposed. If he could be bothered. He put a hand on her shoulder, squeezing her a little closer. She moved uneasily, but did not pull away.

'Which linen cupboard are they missing from, Ruby?'

'The one on Six, sir. The one next to that lift – the special lift.'

17

ROSA DARBY HAD FILLED THE ROOMS WITH WHITE AND GOLD flowers; their scent was sharp, cutting through the air. At twilight the old man drifted to sleep, his energy exhausted, breathing the perfume exhaled at dusk, his memory drifting on its currents.

Camille had once done the same, arranging greenhouse flowers against the London gloom, though they could scarcely afford them.

It had been in December, must have been thirty years ago. Paris was occupied by the Prussians – the Second Empire was as rotten as old worm-eaten timber, and the defeat of that ridiculous procession of pompous fools was really neither a surprise nor an occasion to mourn. But, like thousands of other refugees, the young Claude Monet had crossed to England from Le Havre. His wife had joined him, with their first child, still a baby.

Camille Monet removed the heavy tartan travelling cloak and

sank on to the sofa. Outside, the lights of carriages clopping towards Piccadilly occasionally sent their yellow rays through the muslin curtains and Claude gazed affectionately at his wife's strong, pale face.

'It's better here than I had hoped. There are quite a few of us French exiles in London. There's Pissarro, of course. And the dealer Monsieur Durand-Ruel. He's willing to put some of my work in an exhibition here.'

'Oh, Claude, what an oppotunity!'

'It's a piece of luck, isn't it? But I will do some painting while I'm here.' He paused, looking out of the window, and then turned again towards her. 'What's the news from Paris?'

She remained silent for a moment or two, then lifted her face upwards to him and he saw there were tears standing in her eyes. 'Claude, I'm sorry to have to tell you this. Our poor friend Bazille has been killed. He joined the Zouaves.' Camille managed a smile. 'He died only three months after he had volunteered. He was a good friend to us, wasn't he?'

Monet was sitting beside her now, staring into the fire. He reached out and put an arm round her. 'Yes. But he was a fool to enlist.'

She turned to look at him, with a startled expression, and he found he could say nothing in response to that look of shock, of disappointment perhaps.

There was a long silence. He finally, awkwardly, broke it. 'Come, we'll have dinner tonight at a tavern – they do good chops here at any rate. It's quite respectable for women to dine out in London!'

'I'm glad to hear it.' Now Camille had relaxed, was laughing with him.

'And tomorrow I meet Pissarro to go to the National Gallery. The Turners are said to be magnificent.' And then he added, without thinking, 'We're hard up as usual. And now Bazille's dead – well, I was going to ask him for another loan.'

There was another pause.

His wife stood up and regarded him, almost as if she were looking at a stranger. Yet it was a look he loved in her, that unfathomable space that her gaze could put between them, a bridge the artist could not cross, no matter how closely he looked at her, no matter what his skill. Her mind was hidden from him in such moods, always preoccupied, reflecting, reading. At that moment, he did not want to guess at her thoughts.

He painted Camille during that time in London, sitting on a chintz sofa in a gloomy room near Piccadilly, the winter light almost greenish. In the picture, her dress is purple and black. She holds a book, but she does not look at it, nor at her surroundings – what is there to look at, indeed? She gazes into a void, her hands neat and mildly laid upon the red cover of the book, and a long muslin curtain hangs at the window like a shroud. In those days, her husband did not look beyond the window: the fogs and the mists outside held no special promise.

That spring the Commune in Paris was defeated and the French government – not the Prussians, but their own government, which horrified the Monets and their friends – murdered its leaders. Treachery everywhere, it seemed to them, so insecure and uncertain, as they crowded with other French exiles into a cold and uncomprehending London – then, as always, a fine city for the rich. But they were poor – they had little enough to live off, though Monet would never have believed that his family would sink as low as they did. It amazed him as an old man, as he looked around the beautiful room in the most luxurious hotel in London, where he could command anything at the push of a bell, to think of their desperate plight.

Michel wouldn't comprehend his father's life, nor would he remember the poverty. The father longed for a better feeling between them, yet it did not come. Was it because Michel had no struggles in his life, or was it because he was Camille's son? She had always had that distance about her, too.

What did Camille see when she sat upon the couch and gazed into the future on that December day? The old man was haunted by her in this city where they had been together before Michel was even born. He had no photographs of her, and struggled to remember what she looked like, exactly. The two birthmarks, the black moles on her right cheek, the pale creamy skin. Her face was always partly turned away, seen in profile: he recalled the large and serious eyes, the puffs of soft hair, but he could never see the whole of her face. There was always something hidden, some shading, her cheek slanting away. She was never strong; there was frequently some illness, some delicacy needed, doctor's bills, a cask of Cognac. Those dresses in which he painted her, yellow, rose, dark green as the sea at Étretat, green satin like the glassy wave – they were hired or borrowed. They covered the frailty of her body, great billowing folds of stuff that held her inside them.

All he could seek now was what lay outside, the almost palpable envelope of this dark city, the membrane that held them all. Her face had gone into the past, and that penumbra of feeling was all that was left. Is it always like this with the dead?

18

A DREADFUL SENSE OF UNREALITY CAME OVER OLIVER AS HE sat on the stiff upright chair at Sir Howard's usual table in the Athenaeum, where he had been bidden to dine. Sir Howard had been a figure of dreaded authority since Oliver had first crossed the threshold of the Foreign Office and he induced a schoolboyish terror even outside its portals. The beginning of this conversation had not portended well.

'I understand, Craston, you've been mixing in artistic circles?'

Damn, it must have been Madigan! Oliver, perhaps wanting to boast a little, at any rate almost painfully aware that something exciting had happened in the monotonous routine of his life, had confided in his fellow-clerk something of the events near Waterloo Bridge and their aftermath. But he had not expected Madigan to pass it on to higher authority. Must be careful, he thought to himself.

Sir Howard had obviously spotted his unease. 'Just a bit of gossip – no harm done. Buck up, young fellow! You may even have a few dinners in the Savoy – with the government's blessing! Now, most young chaps would be throwing their caps in the air! No, you needn't bother to write things down. Keep a careful look-out. There's a political complication, y'know. Mustn't forget we've got a war on our hands – even if it is with a pack of dirt farmers in South Africa.'

Greatly daring, sailing as close to the wind as he could, Oliver asked, 'What connection do you see, sir? With what's going on in South Africa?'

'There's a strong pro-Boer sentiment in France. We want to know who we've got here, right under our noses, but it's much too delicate a task for some clumsy oaf of a policeman.'

'Do you expect Monsieur Monet to take me into his confidence?'

'So much the better if he does, but we'll need you to scrape more of an acquaintance, and we would like to know what political company he keeps. Apparently he was rather keen on those damned rebels in the Paris Commune. Uprising against their own government – nasty business, you know. Thirty years ago, but the leopard doesn't change its spots.'

'But, sir, when he's in London, isn't that a matter of concern for the Home Office?' Oliver was anxious not to be led into any territorial conflicts: it was his perfectly correct instinct that the most junior person available is always the most liable to emerge grievously wounded from such battles.

'No, no, we want to know what French politicians he is associating with here. It's actually far more difficult to keep an eye on him when he's in Paris – the French don't like that sort of thing on their own home ground. It's purely for our own information, you see.'

The mutton chops with caper sauce had arrived. Oliver took up his heavy silver cutlery, and set to. The knife seemed blunt.

'Tough again!' But there was almost an approbation in Sir Howard's tone. The world was unchanging. Canary pudding was also on the menu for that evening.

'There are one or two things you won't know about Monsieur Monet. He's always been a friend of Clemenceau – now, there's a well-known radical. Committed republicans, his whole circle. And worse – just recently our artist friend has been a keen supporter of Émile Zola. A well-known agitator. A pack of their intellectuals raised the roof over that business. Suited us down to the ground, mind you – looked very bad for the French. And there's no doubt that the Prince has a lot of friends of – shall we say – the Hebrew persuasion. Money talks, Craston, money talks.'

'But, sir . . . wasn't Dreyfus wrongly accused . . . ?'

'Oh, quite, quite.' Sir Howard wiped his moustache with his napkin. 'But the point is, Zola stirred up trouble, you see. Much better to have just kept the whole thing under wraps. Just quietly let Dreyfus go after a few years. That's what we'd have done.'

But he was innocent! Oliver wanted to shout.

Strangely, Sir Howard seemed to have caught some echo of the words going through his head, for he leaned forward and said in kindly fashion, 'You're still an innocent, my boy. Need to learn a thing or two.'

'Yes, sir.'

'Just keep quiet, listen, and tell us if you hear anything of interest. We simply want to know who calls on him, where he goes, does he get around London much – that sort of thing. But remember to show some discretion. He's a famous personage now, whatever some people may think of the daubs—'

Here Sir Howard had broken off and gazed directly at Oliver, daring him to so much as flicker an eye in sympathy, yet somehow contriving to leave him in no doubt as to Sir Howard's own view. It was a highly skilled facial expression.

They emerged on to the steps of the club. Sir Howard's carriage was waiting.

'Where d'you go, boy?'

'Oh, I'll walk, thank you, sir.'

'Very well. Cold night, though. Step in for a few minutes. I'll take you in the general direction.'

'To Waterloo Bridge, if you don't mind, sir.'

Sir Howard called instructions to his driver, climbed up into the carriage and settled himself in the leather upholstery. Oliver followed after.

'Oh, Craston, one more thing.' The fumes of Sir Howard's cigar and brandy hung on the freezing air. 'Mere police matter – not our affair at all, y'know. Those Home Office johnnies can get themselves in a lather if they want. But I've been asked to have a word – on behalf of the Government, as it were – with anyone on the staff who gets into an *imbroglio*.'

Oliver snapped to attention. That mysterious word 'Government' could mean only one thing, and that was the most powerful force of all, and the most discreet: the Prime Minister's office, no less.

'Lord Salisbury, sir . . .'

'The PM wants no further difficulties of any kind. It is the view of his private office, and this of course I tell you as a matter of the most absolute discretion, that the present war is placing quite enough stress on the Government.'

So it was not going that well after all, in spite of all the jingoistic headlines in the newspapers.

'It was naturally reported to my attention that you were involved in an unpleasant business – some woman found in the river?'

'Yes, sir. The police—'

Sir Howard interrupted. 'Yes, that's all right, Craston. The main point is no-one wants any agitation. And this was – it was the second death of that type. So you see … well, we don't want a panic, do we? There are some unpleasant memories in the poorer quarters of London.'

Oliver understood. Over any incident would now hang the terrible shadow of the creature who had never been captured. That was why such senior levels of Government were concerned.

'There could be riots at the mere possibility of another such sequence of murders. We don't want anyone from the FO involved in the remotest possible way. So if the police should require any further assistance … well, they must seek it elsewhere. No more interviews with you.'

'I understand, sir.'

'Good. Then I trust no more need be said. Of course, you had to report the, er, incident, but it is now closed, is it not?'

'Yes, sir.'

'Ah, we're at the Bridge now.'

The carriage stopped in the Strand.

There was no doubt about it. Oliver's future had been in the balance. It might again be so.

On the other hand, there was now every prospect of seeing Rosa again – and with official blessing.

19

ALINE GARRETY DID NOT TELL WILL EVERYTHING. THE EXTENT of her desperation to bear a child was not fully known even to her husband, though keeping it from him increased the sense of isolation she felt in London. In particular, she missed the company of her mother and sisters. The few women with whom she had become casually acquainted – their landlady, even the more respectable ladies among the congregation at St George's – tended to put up a barrier when she told them her husband was a policeman. It was surely not that they themselves were committing any wrongdoing – indeed, she almost laughed at the thought of it in connection with some of the older people who trotted up the aisle in their high-buttoned boots to take the Mass. No, it was more that the Lambeth side of the river was an area where the police were never particularly welcome at the best of times, and everyone knew of some incident where they had been obliged to turn a blind eye. Perhaps there was a sudden commotion at night, or some scuffle glimpsed down an alleyway. Or maybe they'd just been present at the wrong moment, walking into a room when a dirty pound note was being slipped across from palm to palm. 'Best not to be too friendly with a policeman's wife.'

So all those small social acts – the invitations to take tea after the service, to come up into the landlady's parlour – all those gestures and overtures of friendship, were rarely repeated once Aline had revealed her husband's occupation.

And as for confiding her grief in Will, she hated to add to his burdens. She could see in his eyes how tired and despondent the work sometimes made him, when he came home late at night and fell into the big bed beside her, stretching out a hand as if to reassure himself that she was there. So she felt she could say nothing to him about her plans. She rationalized this to herself when thinking about the step she was about to take. 'He needn't know about it, not yet anyway. If there's some treatment they can give me, some operation maybe, and it doesn't work, I just won't tell him. And if it does, why, then he'll be as happy as a pig in clover so there'll be no cause for him to worry about it.'

But she could not bring herself to go to the hospital that day, and when she emerged from the front door into the street she found that her footsteps seemed to be taking her in the opposite direction. Although she felt quite weak, and the morning was misty, she walked all the way as far as Waterloo Station, along streets parallel with the Thames, looking at the market stalls, purchasing little, only a length of cheap green lace that she didn't really want, just because the woman was pleasant. She went into a tea-shop, seeing some scones set out on a dish in the window, and the scent of them made her homesick for a moment, for the damp, bread-smelling Irish parlour and the big iron stove in the kitchen at the back. It was a brute, that stove, but now she remembered her mother stooping and pulling out a flat shovelful of hot cakes from its black interior.

'Are you feeling all right?' It was the assistant in the tea-shop, breaking into her thoughts. 'Only, you look so pale . . .' Her voice trailed off.

'It's all right – please don't worry.' But she felt faint all the same. 'I just came in to buy some scones.' But she felt herself swaying as she spoke and when the girl came out from behind the counter and fetched a chair from its place at a table further inside Aline sat down gratefully, suddenly, and somehow her head inclined on to the counter for a moment so the assistant thought she had fainted, though Aline did not think she had – only a moment's muzziness, that was all. 'It's just . . .'

The girl looked down, sympathy on her face. 'I'll fetch Mrs Leadbetter. She knows a thing or two to help, you'll see.'

Almost before she realized it, Aline was being helped into a parlour in another house at the back of the shop. Mrs Leadbetter had a strong voice and powerful arms: Aline did not really take note of what she looked like for a few minutes, because a small bottle of some sharp-smelling stuff was being held under her nose – like smelling-salts, only with a whiff of something else. Aline gasped, took a deep breath, and was able to open her eyes properly and look around her.

The room was lined with a dark-red flock wallpaper, and the walls were crowded with sepia pictures in thin gilt frames, a little fly-spotted. The air felt damp: Aline realized that the house must be close to the river, was probably overlooking it at the back. One of the pictures made Aline uncomfortable and anxious for a moment, for it showed a bare-breasted woman standing at an open door for anyone to see, though it looked as if there was nothing but woods outside. But then she turned her head and saw a woman putting the bottle of smelling-salts down on a table. The woman was solidly encased in black up to her neck, where a small white lace collar fell over the top of her dress, which was caught up at the back in a small bustle, and her grey hair was drawn back into a neat bun, with a few short curls around her forehead and temples. Although the room seemed sombre, she had a cheerful pink cheek and everything about her person looked immaculate.

'I'm so sorry,' said Aline, and felt overcome with embarrassment.

'It's all right, my dear, we're all women here. Is it the usual thing?'

It would have been simplest merely to nod, to let this woman think she was just having a bad time of the month, that there was really nothing out of the ordinary, and to get up, thank her rescuer, and leave, but the truth was that as she recovered from her fainting fit she was unwilling as yet to trust her legs to get her up out of the chair. And worse: she felt again a slow but unmistakable trickle of blood. It hadn't finished, then. There was a sharp pang in the pit of her stomach.

'You see, it's the disappointment again that pulls me down. I'm afraid there's something wrong with me. I've got an appointment at the hospital, but I, well, I've been putting it off . . . but we want a child so bad.'

It was a relief to have another woman to confide in. Back home, she had been able to speak of these things to her mother, who shared her pain and disappointment, but in London she had no friend close enough. A little while later she found she had told the woman all about the failed attempts and sad little expulsions, the heavy bleedings and sleepless nights. A plump hand took hers in a grip she did not entirely like, for some reason, yet the relief of telling was immense.

The assistant was despatched to fetch a cab to carry Aline home, though she protested she could walk. 'Really, I'm feeling much better. And I hope it may be treated – I will go to see the doctor at St Thomas's. To see if they can find anything wrong. If anything can be done.'

She saw the woman registering the nervousness that she was unable to keep out of her face. 'Oh, if it wasn't for Will, I wouldn't do it!' she cried out. 'I can't bear it – every time, he looks so wretched. But I would just . . . I would just accept it . . . not having a child – God would help me bear it. I don't want to go there and have them . . .'

The woman soothed her, putting a cup of tea into her hand almost as if Aline were a child. 'No, I quite understand, my dear. Those doctors are not very sympathetic to women's troubles, are they? Not decent, I call it! What they make you do.'

The girl dashed in breathlessly, her hair flying round her face. 'I had to go all the way to the rank at the station! Anyway, he's outside now. But I didn't know where he was to take you.'

'Oh, not far – to Lambeth, that's all. I could have walked it, really.'

But both of them were certain she could not, should not, attempt it.

As she left the shop door, Mrs Leadbetter came after her and laid a hand on her arm, murmuring into her ear, 'I believe, my dear, I know a doctor who might help you. He is such a pleasant, quiet gentleman – and he specializes in ladies' complaints. In difficulties, if I may put it that way. Maybe there's something he could do for you.'

Aline tried to understand what lay beneath the woman's words. There were back-street abortionists around Waterloo, so much was common gossip. But she was desperate to conceive. 'I do want to have a child, that's the nature of my trouble, you see, Mrs Leadbetter. Is he a proper doctor?'

'Oh, dear me, yes! Letters after his name and all. Maybe you've got some little problem down there, and he could help you. It would be so much nicer than going to the hospital – and perhaps being in a public ward. Call back here when you are feeling better and I can tell you some more about it – that's if you decide not to go to the hospital.'

The cabby flicked the horse with his whip and they drove off. Aline looked back out of the tiny window and saw Mrs Leadbetter gazing after the cab.

20

GARRETY CONSIDERED THE MAN SITTING OPPOSITE HIM IN THE tea-room of the Savoy. Between them on the low table were white cups and saucers gleaming in the light from the electric chandeliers, and the murmur of conversation filled the air around them, interspersed with soft sounds of chinking and stirring.

Garrety settled his feet comfortably, pressing them into the deep carpet, and took another sip of tea. 'Indian, I suppose,' Castleton had said when he ordered the tea, and Garrety had not quite understood the inflection in his voice. But he noticed that the waiter almost imperceptibly altered his demeanour when he served the house detective. The flourishes and deep bows he lavished on two beplumed women at a nearby table were entirely lacking when Castleton and Garrety came to be served, and the tea-things were plonked down on the table between the two men with as much lack of grace as was possible for a fully trained Savoy waiter.

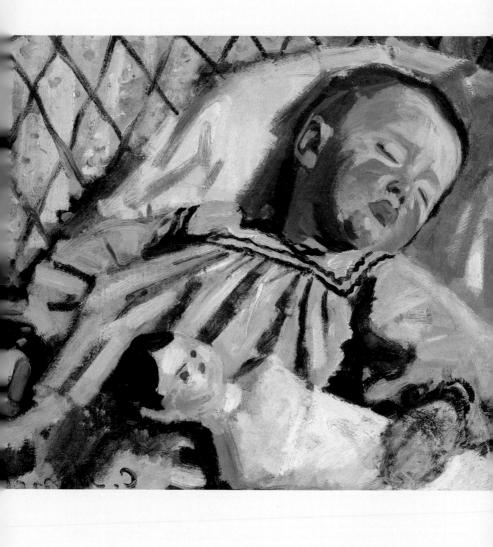

'Sorry about that,' said Castleton, as the black uniform swanned off. 'Fact is, the hotel detective's not a popular figure. All the little dodges, you know – oh, yes, all the fiddles, extra charge for lemon pencilled on the bill and then rubbed out, silver not counted back at night – I know their little secrets.'

It takes one to know one, thought Garrety.

'Fact is, it's not Craston I wanted to see you about. No, it's something on the sixth floor.' He leant over as he uttered the words 'sixth floor' as if they were some kind of code.

'Something you can't handle?' asked Garrety.

The fine nostrils snorted indignantly. 'Nothing I couldn't handle, I assure you! No, but that floor – it's something I don't want to talk about everywhere, if you get my meaning.' A handsome eye creased into a wink and Castleton's head nodded in the general direction of the phalanx of waiters in the hotel livery who stood at their posts ready to attend to the guests.

Doesn't want the hotel to know he's worried about this, thought Garrety. That's why he's called in an outsider, why he's even willing to be seen talking to someone who doesn't drink the right kind of tea – though God knows what's wrong with this. 'Do you want to go into details here?'

Castleton glanced at a slim fob-watch drawn from his striped silk waistcoat. 'Let's go outside'. He signed for a bill.

The day was mild and the two men moved out of the Savoy courtyard and turned right towards Charing Cross. On their left was a small garden beside the Savoy Chapel, and Castleton indicated it with a wave of his gloved hand. They turned into it and proceeded to move down the path.

'The sixth floor – you pick up things here and there, you know.'

Garrety had a sudden vision of that winking blue eye applied to a keyhole. That's how he sees the world, he thought. That's Castleton's natural way of looking at things – through a spyhole.

The other man went on. 'Sorry, I should explain something. There aren't individual guests. The suites have been given up to army wounded. It was arranged by Princess Louise as part of her charitable work for the soldiers. They've all been brought there – back from South Africa – and they're too badly injured to be looked after at home, so they have a doctor and nurses here with them. In fact, the place is fitted up as a hospital ward. No other guests are booked on to that floor – I don't think the Army exactly wants the world to know about it. Some of them are . . .' and he stumbled, as if remembering something, 'are in a bad way. Mutilated, and so on. Pretty nasty, you know. The other guests don't see much anyway – the service lifts are used to get them up and down – the wounded, I mean.'

Then he added quickly, as if to forestall any possible denigration of the Savoy, 'Of course, they're all officers. Some high-ranking gentlemen, I believe.'

'But there's something worrying you?'

'Yes. Not the usual sort of thing – I wouldn't be overly bothered about that. Like I said, anything goes here, if they can pay their way. So if it were just that some young spark was feeling a bit frisky – not missing everything in all departments, you might say – and wanted a girl or two fetched up, well, good luck to him, I'd say. Provided it was all as covered-up as the duchess's arse. Mind you, I'd expect a bob or two for keeping mum.'

Garrety pulled his tweed greatcoat closer round him. 'Then what? Boys?'

Castleton laughed. 'My, my, we don't have much faith in the military, do we? No, and I don't think it's the big, strapping lads, either. I don't think there's anyone slinking down Whitehall and slipping half a crown into a guardsman's boot, if that's what you mean. No, there's something going on from time to time. But not in the way you might think.'

They were walking along as the hotel detective was speaking, and had come to the street running down the side of the Savoy. Castleton jerked his thumb at a narrow door in the wall of the hotel. 'See that? Know what it's for?'

'Just a service entrance?'

Castleton laughed. 'Sort of, in a manner of speaking.' He plucked at Garrety's sleeve and pulled him back into the garden. It was getting dark now, and some small windows high up at the side of the hotel suddenly sprang alight. 'Aha,' said Castleton. 'Now, watch this.'

Somewhere in the Strand a clock struck five.

Looking about him, Garrety saw a plain, unmarked, covered vehicle appearing in the distance: it had nothing to distinguish it as it reached the end of the street, and the driver was hunched anonymously over his whip. The vehicle made its way up the fast-darkening street and halted at the small door in the wall, the driver remaining on his perch.

A low humming sound came across the road, through the gathering dusk, muffled yet familiar, and Garrety, straining his ears, thought he could hear the deep whirring sound of some heavy machinery. Then the light across the street flicked smoothly down by stages, and the policeman suddenly guessed what was happening.

The street door opened and a wheelchair appeared, attended by two men and hissing softly on rubberized wheels, a slumped figure sitting within outlined against the darker night. There was a light discreet clatter as a ramp appeared from the interior of the vehicle, the chair was wheeled up it and pulled inside by unseen hands. A nurse followed, carrying a bundle, and the doors at the back of the van were very quietly and carefully shut.

'You see?' said Castleton in a low voice as the door shut and the van made off down towards the river. 'That's where they bring 'em out. The invalids they want to get quietly out of the side of the hotel so as not to upset the guests. And the stiffs, I mean. If any of the guests die inconveniently, that is. Some of them, you see, they're not supposed to be here at all, and they pop off in unsuitable circumstances – like if they're on the job, and they're a bishop or something. Or a cabinet minister has a heart attack going up somewhere he shouldn't – that kind of thing. Then they have to get the party safely home, so they arrange for a carriage to be waiting here quietly at the side of the hotel. And there's a special service lift just inside that door – one that they can get a trolley into. So nothing goes through the front of the hotel, nothing to frighten the horses, if you take my meaning, and His Nibs can just be delivered nicely to his own residence where his ever-loving will start weeping and wailing and gnashing her teeth, and no-one will ever be the wiser.'

He turned towards Garrety and smiled. 'We make a few bob out of that, of course.'

I bet you do, thought Garrety. He said, 'What about the doctors, and don't you have to notify the coroner?'

'Cause of death and all that? Well, these society doctors can send in a hefty bill to the grieving widow, so they're likely to say the chap died peacefully in his own bed, which is want she wants to hear. Officially, that is. And, usually, you couldn't say it was unnatural causes – all too natural, if you ask me. So there's no harm done – it's just protecting someone's reputation, that's all.'

'But with invalided men . . .'

'Oh, I take your point, Mr Garrety. Of course, you'd expect a few more than usual to go, just around the present time, naturally. Died of wounds and so forth – not counting the ones who couldn't stand to think about it no more and topped themselves. No need for an inquest with army wounded, of course – hardly suspicious circumstances. They have a doctor up there, looking after them – he can sign the certificates. And the hotel wouldn't like an inquest anyway, of course – not that sort of publicity, thank you very much.'

'Whose job is it to do that?'

'The army doctor up there with them. I understand he was injured himself, but apparently they reckon he can cope, with a couple of orderlies and nurses. The agreed procedure is that he notifies the general manager of the hotel, who tells me so I know when a discreet removal is to take place. But sometimes it's a question of a patient who's still alive, and in a wheelchair, like just now. They want to be got out quietly themselves, often as not, without anyone staring at them.'

'But this time, why did you want me to come here?'

By now, they were walking down to the Victoria Embankment and looking out over the lights of the river. The van had disappeared.

'Just wanted you to see with your own eyes that there's a very quiet way out of this hotel. Plus, they don't always warn me, and I don't like that. They tell me, usually, you see, the management does. So I can help avoid any nasty publicity, keep a look-out for reporters – or policemen, if you must know. It all has to be kept in the family, if you see what I mean. But it only happens a couple of times a year – it's not a common event at all, you see, even with the wounded officers up there. After all, they've survived the worst – the field hospitals and the sea journey. And I think they're not telling me. Didn't take me into their confidence.'

His tone sounded injured, and Garrety wondered how much of Castleton's interest in what they had just witnessed was motivated by a blow to his professional pride as a hotel detective. He might have read the other man's thoughts correctly, for Castleton continued: 'They always make the same mistake, you see, in these places. They think the people at the bottom of the heap don't count – and they do, oh yes, they do. The laundry-maids, for instance – who cares about them? Well, I'm not saying any more, but there's always someone knows what's going on in a place like this, always a pair of eyes somewhere. That's it, you see. One of the maids told me she thought something wasn't right. And when I looked into it, it wasn't just the laundry. One of the maids, a girl called Ruby, saw something being brought down on a trolley, covered with sheets.'

The two men stopped and looked at each other. Castleton went on, aggrieved: 'They're supposed to tell me, if there's a death on the premises.'

Garrety looked up at the towering block of the hotel in the darkness behind them, its windows now streaming light, and pictured the endless doors and rooms and corridors. And moving along every corridor, turning down the bedspreads, running the baths, affecting never to have heard the conversation of their betters, almost members of a different species, a whole secret army. The servants, barely visible to the guests except when the bath was not run, the sheets not turned down. But they had ears, they had eyes.

2 1

IN THE DIVISIONAL POLICE STATION NEAR THE ELEPHANT AND Castle, Sergeant Hassblack was rubbing his big red hands over the coke-burning stove. Its metal chimney led up through the ceiling of the brown-panelled room, and it seemed to take all the heat up there too. Hassblack's mind was blazing with indignation, but his hands were still freezing. Put them on the stove and you burned them. Take them a few inches away and they were blocks of ice. He wanted to warm them up before he went into the inspector's office to make his report.

But he was delaying to give himself a few moments' grace before he had to go in and describe the treatment he had encountered in the coroner's office. The vagaries of the stove were merely adding to his bad temper. He had been insulted and treated almost as if he didn't exist. 'Who are you?' said in the most rude, most arrogant manner. And 'We can't give out information of that sort – certainly not to *you*, Sergeant. There's no question of allowing the police to speak to guests in the Savoy Hotel.' And 'Now, good day to you!' His face flushed as he recalled the humiliation of it.

And that wasn't even the coroner. That was just his clerk.

'It were no good, Mr Garrety. They wasn't going to say anything about it. Soon as I mentioned the word "Savoy", they went as close as clams.'

'Did you give them my note?'

'Yes, but it didn't make no difference.'

Hassblack did not repeat exactly what the coroner had said, an hour after the note had been passed through to him, during which time the sergeant was left uncomfortably standing in a cold corridor. 'I don't care who asks for this information, we cannot possibly divulge anything connected with the guests in the Savoy. It is a thoroughly impertinent request.' And, turning to his assistant, 'Who does this police inspector, this fellow Garrety, think he is? He'll have to learn his place!' The utter contempt with which the word 'fellow' had been pronounced still rung in Hassblack's mind.

'So they told you nothing?' said Garrety resignedly, looking at his sergeant's thin face. Hassblack was a tall fellow, with his eyes always slightly reddened by the London smoke, so that he had a chronically mournful appearance, even when he was reporting good news. The skin fell in bloodhound-like folds on his cheeks, but in spite of his cadaverous appearance he was reputed in the station to be a great performer with the female sex, though much devoted to the small, frail former dancer with whom he was presently living. She was always addressed as Mrs Hassblack: maybe they had got married after all, thought Garrety. Members of the Metropolitan Police Force were required to be 'of good character' and that meant, above all, no messing with sluts. Garrety, now looking at Hassblack's big, red, meaty hands and gangling limbs clad in blue serge, found himself wondering what Hassblack's body looked like stretched over a woman's.

He jerked his mind back to the question of what the coroner's office had told Hassblack.

'Not a word, sir.'

Garrety sighed. Hassblack looked at him hopefully, but he knew what would happen. Garrety wouldn't give up. However, he was preoccupied with something else at the moment – a report that lay on the desk before him.

'She got rid of it, Hassblack.'

'Sir?'

'The woman in the river – the one that was found first, at Bly's Wharf. She hadn't been in long, remember. The tissues were all well preserved by the cold, I gather, and Dr Gulliver's report says she'd just had an abortion. Not some back-street job with a knitting-needle, either. He thinks it was a termination by a professional man with the proper instruments – perhaps a doctor who's been struck off, or some such. And here's something else: "On removal of the lungs the distinctive odour of chloroform was apparent." That would be consistent with an abortion performed shortly before death.'

'So why . . . ?'

'Exactly, Sergeant.'

'She didn't stick that knife in herself, sir?'

'Oh, you've a grand elegance of expression, Hassblack! But that's it exactly. Who did? Was it the abortionist? Maybe she threatened to give him away for some reason. But that would be to broadcast her own sins to the world, as well as his. But if it wasn't him, then who stabbed her and tipped her into the river? There's something else as well. Those scratches on her thighs – the terrible gashes, and so on. They were inflicted before death, but Gulliver can't tell if it was before or after the abortion.'

'Were they connected with it?'

'God knows! How can you get into the mind of someone crazy enough to do that?'

The two men stared at each other for a moment in a mutual confirmation of their own normality.

Garrety continued. 'I can't see it, can you? Gulliver says they are the marks of a savage frenzy, whereas the abortion was a cool, professional job.'

'So we may have two criminals, sir? The person who carried out the abortion and the killer?'

'Makes it complicated, doesn't it? Gulliver says he can't tell us anything much about the second body – the one young Craston found. Seems likely she was actually killed before the other one, but it took longer to find her, so the state of the tissues was much worse. Anyway, he's still working on it. Get off home, now.'

Garrety rubbed his bristly head with his hands. Mercifully, he didn't demand anything further of Hassblack, who wanted nothing more than to get back to his woman.

'Ay, I was thinking my missis might have the fire built up, and maybe have bought a mutton chop or something similar on her way back. She's cleaning the waiting-rooms at the rail-way station now, sir.'

'Oh? She's given up—?'

'Yes, she's given up the music-hall, sir. I was always on at her about it. Singing and dancing – oh, there was no harm in her, sir, not a bit. But people don't think it's respectable, do they?'

'I suppose not.'

Alone in his office, after Hassblack had gone into the outer room to sign off duty, Garrety put his head in his hands for a moment. He was under no illusions about the social status of a policeman; indeed, every contact with the Savoy seemed to underline the bitter truth. A spurt of anger leapt up in him, but he held it back, pressing against his face with his hands for a moment as though physically to contain his feeling of rage.

There was a buzzing in the office outside.

'Sir!' It was Hassblack, who should have got off home, calling through the door.

Garrety welcomed the interruption.

'Telephone!' said Hassblack importantly. There was only one instrument in the station, mounted on the wall of the main office. 'It rang just as I was going out, sir.' The sergeant was deeply proud of the gadget, and never missed an opportunity to answer it whenever he could.

Walking into the outer office, Garrety saw that Benbow, Hassblack's replacement on the shift, had already arrived and was taking off his helmet and his greatcoat; on his uniform, the silver letter 'L' of their division gleamed in the light. There was a faint smell of burning hanging around Benbow, and Garrety saw that the inside of the regulation greatcoat looked curiously smoked – 'kippered', as they called it. Benbow had evidently been patrolling with his oil lantern held underneath his coat, like a miniature stove. It was a frequent practice, officially disapproved of, since it led inevitably to damage to police property and, what was almost regarded as the same thing, very often to policemen. Garrety, however, did not have the heart to reprimand the man; eight-hour beats in the freezing fog, with no official break even for a hot pie or a mug of tea, were an inhuman requirement.

Hassblack was holding the telephone. No doubt he had grabbed the receiver as soon as it had rung rather than let Benbow have the chance.

Garrety took the vulcanized receiver from Hassblack's

hand, which had left a sticky mark on the shiny black surface. The voice that came out of the pepper-pot holes was irascible, sounding even more so because the instrument imbued it with a kind of angry rasp. Garrety stared down for a moment as if he were holding a buzzing wasp, then reluctantly put it to his ear.

'This report of yours, on the woman who was found at Greet's Jetty, the one a certain young gentleman was unlucky enough to discover. I want to see you.'

'When, sir?'

'Straight away. Come to my house'.

Garrety had no time to reply. There was a loud click and the instrument started crackling meaninglessly. The superintendent did not believe in RSVP invitations to his staff.

It would take him at least half an hour to get to the super's house in Streatham, even assuming he could get a cab on a wet night like this, and he would be unable to let Aline know he would be late. Hassblack was just stepping outside.

'Hassblack?'

'Yes, sir?'

'You go past my house on your way, don't you?'

'Yes, sir.'

'Would you mind just calling in and leaving a note for my wife?'

Hassblack's face registered what had happened. He had recognized the chief's voice, barking out of the telephone almost as soon as he had lifted it off its stand.

'That's all right, sir. I'll be glad to.'

One thing taken care of, at any event. After he had scribbled a hasty note, Garrety donned his long overcoat and thick leather gloves and set out into the night. Damn all senior policemen, and why did they have to live in expensive villas in Streatham?

It was an impressive house, though. There must be some private money – the super couldn't afford this on police pay, surely. The inspector walked up a sweeping drive through dripping laurels and rose-bushes to a pillared porch. From the hallway, where the manservant who had opened the door proceeded to take his coat and gloves with due ceremony, Garrety caught a glimpse of a long room with a blazing fire, the chimneypiece adorned with heavy plasterwork, the floor covered with rugs. He could hear female voices: then came laughter, and a piano began to play as a soprano voice sweetly, if rather uncertainly, embarked on 'Plaisir d'amour'.

Thomas Worton appeared from the long room himself, rather than bidding a servant show Garrety into his study, an informality that actually indicated the seriousness of the matter.

They went into a small, solid room, the walls lined with shelves holding rows of law-books and bound runs of the *Police Gazette*. An ugly metal lamp with a green shade stood on the desk and Worton switched it on as he walked round to an upright chair. Garrety remained standing till the older man waved him into a seat.

Worton was an ugly man. Rolls of fat draped his chin and neck, and heavy pouches sagged under his eyes. Nevertheless, his eyes were sharp and clever, and Garrety found himself wondering if the superintendent was attractive to women, the idea perhaps implanted in his mind by the warmth of the female voices he heard in the hall. Was sexual attraction something that really had nothing to do with a man's social standing? he thought, and then wondered why that had never before crossed his mind as a way of looking at the relations between men and women. Was he so accustomed to the idea that the only sex between the rich and the poor would be paid for?

But Worton was speaking as he unlocked a drawer at the side of his desk and took out a buff-coloured binder. Garrety recognized his own notes on the discoveries of the bodies in the river. 'I asked you to come because there is something I want to emphasize to you – something you must take note of in the course of your investigation.'

Garrety assumed a receptive expression.

'You spoke to a young man, a Mr Craston.'

'Yes, sir. He found the woman at Lambeth. She was pulled out at a place called Greet's Jetty.'

'But you are intending to make further inquiries concerning this young man?'

Garrety detected an ominous note in Worton's tone. He felt obliged to explain himself. 'Sir, Mr Craston used to live in Barnes – that was the address he first gave us. But he recently moved to south of Waterloo Bridge – in fact, not far from the place where the body came to the surface. The river police think that the body and its rope and weight would have been disturbed by changes of current as the water became colder. So the chances are it didn't drift far before it was found. The pathologist's finding was that the rope had sunk deeply into the decomposed tissues, indicating that it had remained weighed down. And the mud – well, the mud deposited in the flesh and the garments is characteristic of that stretch of the river, not of cleaner water higher up. Impregnated with decaying matter and factory effluents.' He leaned forward. 'Oily. Greenish.'

That seemed enough to put Worton off that line of attack. But he continued: 'Very good, Inspector. But surely you did not suspect Mr Craston? He was merely an innocent passer-by who found the body.'

'With respect, we have someone who moved from a

populous household where he might be frequently observed to somewhere he could lead a solitary existence – near to the river, and to where the body might well have entered the water. Whoever killed the woman would have needed continual privacy, to put some of her clothing back on the body, as well as for the murder.'

'But the finding of the body, surely that was pure chance?'

'Oh, yes, sir. But why was Mr Craston there? Is it not possible that the murderer would have been anxious to see if . . . well, to see if he had done an adequate job of disposal? They do say that a killer will return to the scene of the crime, sir, don't they? So maybe the murderer here would haunt the river banks, waiting, watching to see . . .'

For a moment, Worton seemed mesmerized by the vision of a dark figure stalking the banks, peering into the muddy water, wondering whether his dreadful handiwork might somehow break loose from its bonds.

Have I got him? thought the policeman.

Then Worton pulled himself up with a start. 'But you know Mr Craston's occupation?'

Garrety knew what would happen now and he felt a deep sense of futility, and also a feeling of anger.

'You are not to make any further inquiries in that direction. Mr Craston – well, I am exceeding the boundaries of discretion by even telling you as much as this, Inspector, but I accept that you have some right to an explanation. Mr Craston works for an arm of our government, and no more need be said. I have it on the highest authority.'

'But why did . . . *how* did this, er, this *authority* come to know about Mr Craston's involvement with the affair?'

'I myself have made one or two inquiries. There are levels with which you need not concern yourself, Inspector – you can accept what you are told, and that is all. And in any case, Inspector, this matter requires . . . extraordinary discretion.'

'Yes, sir.' Pompous bastard, but what else could he say?

Worton was thrusting the buff file across the desk. 'There are aspects of this case that must not be given any publicity. It is possible – it is quite possible . . . This is the second body, is it not? Found with these injuries upon it?'

It was the name that could scarcely be spoken even now, so great was the damage done to the reputation of the Metropolitan Police.

'It is quite possibly that affair in Whitechapel—'

Garrety's thoughts continued to ricochet off Worton's statements, a silent counterpoint. The Ripper murders. But he daren't even say the words. Instead, he said aloud: 'But that was twenty years or so ago, sir. And these are quite different: those women were left where they died, not thrown into the river. Besides, the injuries are not the same, surely?'

'Yes, yes, but people haven't forgotten. They may well believe the man has come to life again – and the details won't signify to them. The last thing we want is another panic, with the press hounding at our heels and police accused of incompetence. If it's thought there's another of them on the loose in London . . . you see the agitation that might ensue, do you not, Inspector?'

Yes, he did. Of course, he hadn't directly experienced the Ripper frenzy that had seized London – he had been a boy in Belfast at the time – but he knew that the newspapers could hardly find column inches for anything else, that the politicians had berated the police for their failure to catch Spring-Heeled Jack even when they found the blood still running out of a trough where he had washed. A recurrence of that – the word spreading that women were once more being horribly killed and mutilated – it could in all probability lead to public panic, and an unwelcome push into the limelight for the police.

'So these two episodes – the women found in the river – are not to be linked, as if there might be another maniac on the loose. They are separate incidents, the result of the kind of life these ... unfortunates endured. In all probability, they brought their destruction on their own heads. There are to be no political repercussions, so that Mr Craston will receive no further attentions from the police. And you will write a new report, completely eliminating all references to the similarities between the two deaths. And you are to write it up yourself, in your own hand – your subordinates are to learn nothing of this business.'

As Garrety left the room, Worton called out, 'And steer clear of the Savoy.'

But the river flows past the Savoy, as it flows past the slums: he knows that as well as I, thought Garrety.

He was fuming inwardly as he strode past the long, dank front gardens of the road, which was lined with comfortable villas, where he could occasionally glimpse an interior through a looped-back curtain. Oliver Craston was not a serious suspect, but at present he seemed to be the only lead for any inquiries, and that avenue had been uncompromisingly closed.

A family was gathered round a table, a woman was writing in a pool of light, the sounds of a child practising a singing lesson echoed out into the street. All so safe, so comfortable.

And she is dead and rotting, that poor confounded creature at Greet's Jetty, he thought to himself. Pulled out of the river, and they don't care a damn how she went into the water, or at whose hands. Just as long as their damned silly plots and schemes, their comfortable lives, their reputations, aren't disturbed. It's the same story as with the coroner.

He hailed a cab with an angry jerk of his hand as he entered Streatham High Street. Within him the seeds of rage and frustration began to burgeon and he gnawed his fingers in a fury as the cab clattered back towards Lambeth, new determinations forming within him by the minute.

22

'I HAVE TO DO SOMETHING THAT I THINK IS RIGHT,' HE SAID TO
Aline, who had waited up for him after she had got Sergeant
Hassblack's message. 'But it might not be something that
brings me any advantage, my love. In fact, it might be the
opposite. So I wanted to ask you. I can't tell you what it's
about. But I can say, Aline, that I'm being stopped from pursuing some lines of an investigation for no good reason. And
I think I know a way to continue it. But it's a risk. If I mis-
judge, I may be out of a job because of it. You might have a
husband who has to go working on the railway or something
like that. I'm laying my career on the line.'

He thought longingly of Belfast: the easy acceptance, the
friendships. Until now, he had thought it was only Aline who
was homesick for the rolling green hills, the damp, clean air,
and the circle of faces round the hearth at home, the big, bony,
honest faces of men and women who meant what they said.

Aline looked up from the fireside chair. 'But you, William,
you think you must do this thing?'

'Yes. In my heart, I do. No matter what Worton says. There are people I'm not supposed to touch – and a place I'm not supposed to go.'

She frowned. 'Worton! If he's involved, then it's serious all right!'

He hesitated. 'All I can say is that it may be to do with something that happened to two women. It was something very . . .' He paused, knowing she had heard about the body pulled from the river at Greet's Jetty. He had said nothing since, but these things were always a matter of gossip and rumour alongside the Thames, travelling like capricious currents alongside the water.

Aline rescued him. 'That poor creature who was pulled out of the Thames? Yes, I heard it in the Lower Marsh. The woman on the oyster-stall was talking about it. I think she's got it from a bargeman who was drinking in a shanty nearby when they found the body. No need to tell me any more.'

They were silent for a while.

Involuntarily he recalled the scene in the mortuary, the muddy flow of river water from the woman's body, and tried to drive the recollection from his brain. Sometimes at night as they lay with their two heads on the same pillow, his skull pressed next to Aline's as she slept, he feared lest his mind should somehow, through the thin layers of bone that lay between their thoughts, transfer the sights he had seen that day to her mind, as if his waking horrors might enter her dreams.

She said slowly, 'I think you should do it, Will, if it is about something as terrible as that woman's death. I know you, and it will eat away at your heart if you neglect something you feel should have been done. And we have some savings, after all – we are not penniless.'

He longed for the comfortable networks, the automatic intimate knowledge of kinship and old history that bound him to Ireland. There he could always have bought the right fellow a drink, had a word in some quarter where it would go ringing round like a bright penny piece till it found a taker. There was no-one in this cruel antheap, especially not in that silently carpeted inner nest of the powerful, to whom he could go and say: 'I can't get some information I need to solve a killing, but you can, you with your connections and your position. They'll listen to you.' He, Garrety, knew no-one.

23

'WALK WITH ME, MR CRASTON, I BEG YOU!' OLIVER HAD called at the Savoy hoping to see Rosa Darby. Instead, he encountered the artist coming out of the hotel. 'My son and Miss Darby left some time ago. They have made up a skating party. Even though it's February, the ice is still quite thick in some places, I believe. Hampstead Pond, is that correct? I think that is what they mentioned. But I myself am bound for one of my great pleasures in London – the National Gallery.'

'Are there any British artists you admire, sir?' It was a question that was merely intended to establish a polite conversation. In default of a glimpse of his exciting new young friends, Oliver could at least perhaps glean something to please Sir Howard.

They fell into step.

'Ah, yes, your Turner! What a mastery of light! It is exactly what Impressionists are trying to do – to capture the effects of light and atmosphere. Do you know the pictures?'

'No, sir, I'm afraid not.'

'No! One of the greatest English artists? Then come with me, Mr Craston.'

Oliver did not want to decline such an opportunity of further acquaintance. In the long galleries, almost empty at that time of year, they stood together before 'Rain, Steam and Speed', and looked at what hurtled out of the mists towards them.

'It's like an eruption of lava, an incandescent outpouring! Not like a machine at all – something out of nature! The iridescence, the flamboyance of the sunlight. That's what I try to do, Mr Craston, to capture such things in paint. I take from it the renewal of courage. You may take from it what you will, but look well and you will feel the touch of a great experience. Just stand and look and say nothing. Let the picture do its work.'

Further instruction, in the sense with which Oliver was familiar, was not given. But he never forgot that precious chance that had been brought his way, and the opportunity he had taken then – all, he thought in later years, for the wrong reasons.

An hour or so later, Oliver sat in the small garden of the Barnes house. It had been a fine Sunday morning, but the weather was cold still, and Maggie had a thick shawl with a cream and blue dragon pattern wrapped round her shoulders. Her dark hair was loose – she would go in and put it up before lunch – and fell over the soft cream wool in loose curls and ringlets. Oliver wondered why his sister was sometimes accounted plain – had indeed been thought so by the few friends he had brought home from college and tried to interest in her, knowing their mother's expectations. But he himself always drew from her an automatic adoration, something that set off an answering affection within him, which a suitor would be unable to count upon.

Nevertheless, he had sensed a change in her lately. It was almost as if, he thought, she were in training for spinsterhood. Her face looked sometimes immobile and harsh, her eyes sinking into brown-skinned sockets; she never seemed to bother about new dresses, and her feet were always shod in stout little tanned boots. And though he loved her hair spread out on her shoulders as it was now, often it appeared tousled and uncombed, or else pulled back so tightly that there was nothing left to flutter round her face and soften her expression. Of late, too, she had argued constantly with their father, defiantly leaving the room when she pleased, as if she no longer wished to hear his side of a debate, which was usually about some bookish matter, such as literature and the morals of society. Mr Craston had been horrified when the novels of George Eliot were mentioned over dinner, but Maggie had boldly responded that she did not care if the lady were not really married to Mr Lewis or not, for how could that affect her sense? Father and daughter, both with the same intense expression, both with the same thin hunched shoulders, had confronted each other over the family dining-table.

On this particular Sunday, there was a more peaceable atmosphere. Mrs Craston, returned from church with Elinor, the youngest of her brood, was in the kitchen issuing instructions to Geraldine. Menander Craston, who did not accompany his wife to church, was reading in his study, unexasperated by either his offspring or his stomach. Maggie had cried off church, on the grounds that Oliver would probably arrive while they were out and she had so little chance to talk to him. It was not a particularly religious household, inclining to the intellectual rather than to the fervent, but even so Oliver had been surprised to find Maggie at home when he arrived.

Elinor's yellow dress was visible at the end of the garden as she gathered together a bunch of snowdrops and crocuses and Oliver could see the pale light shining on its buttery silk through the low branches of the old lilac tree. I never saw it before, he thought, the fine dappled light that comes through those tiny leaves.

Had he started to look at the world with new eyes?

Many thoughts seemed to be occurring to him that he had never before experienced. Intense sexual longings, imaginings, flashes of desire and pictures of lust, yet mingled with them glimpses of what he had seen in the waters of the Thames, occupied his dreams. Was his new-found vision part of that, the desire to open his eyes on the world? Now he began also to wonder about things that had not troubled him in the past.

Who is the strongest in our family? he thought, a question that had never before occurred to him. His father was the head of the household, and the older Craston was certainly deferred to, yet his mother made all the domestic decisions that affected their daily lives – choosing the furnishings, the menus, directing old Williams, the gardener who came every week, as to planting and lopping. But Maggie: take this business of church, for example. A year ago his mother would surely never have allowed her to stay at home, yet today it all seemed to have been taken as a matter of course; clearly, there had been no great family upheaval because of Maggie's rebellion. His sister seemed to have achieved a position where their mother did not try always to overrule her, allowing her to have her own way in certain matters.

'How have you been?' he said.

'Oh, Oliver! They still won't permit it. Father won't hear of it. He says the women studying at the university are positively unnatural creatures, and Mother backs him up. She thinks I'll turn into an old maid the moment I enrol, so what can I do against them both? After all, they would have to pay the fees and support me while I'm studying – though perhaps I should get a teaching position afterwards. But I shan't give up! I'll keep on reading and working on my own – and wear them away little by little till they agree! Mother will see I'm determined to be a spinster anyway!'

'Would you like me to speak to Father again?'

'No, it wouldn't do any good. It only led to a frightful row last time, didn't it? No, I'll just have to keep on trying to persuade them. Perhaps if Elinor gets married they won't worry so much about me.'

'Is she likely to?'

'There's a young man in the congregation who's paying her attention – a student of natural history, I believe, who will doubtless meet with Father's approval. But I shall manage it somehow, whatever happens with Elinor.'

'You are becoming a true suffragette!'

She laughed, for the first time in this conversation. 'No, I shan't join them, though I believe they are right. Of course women should be treated like adults. But what I want to do for myself, well, I am determined to study, you see. I'm like Father in that, at least.'

'Come for a walk, Mags. Let's go down to the river.'

'All right – I need some exercise.'

'Get a coat, then.'

Pausing on the grassy bank of the river, they looked down into the transparent brownish depths where mottled fish flicked lazily in the shadows. Yet this was the same water that, only a few miles downstream, had swallowed up that wretched creature. He tried to recall what the old man had said – something about looking into the depths, but he hadn't understood it.

'Oliver, sometimes I feel so trapped,' said Maggie suddenly. 'As if I can't escape from the house, and I'm standing still, yet just a short distance away the river is flowing past, life is flowing away from me. Do you remember, when we were children, you used to run out in the summer and bathe here, and I had to stay with Mother, all dressed up, and pass round all the little cakes and fruit-knives at tea-time? I hated it. I couldn't think of anything but this water and how free you were! But it seems that it's going to be like that all my life. I'll be just beyond the banks of the river, just beyond freedom.'

'No, Maggie! I'll get you away somehow!'

But the truth was that he wanted to talk about something else. He badly needed now to confide in someone about the business of the body in the river, but he could not visualize talking to either of his parents.

'Mags,' he said, using the old childish nickname, 'Mags, I want to talk to you.'

He told her about the discovery of the woman, carefully omitting the details of the drowned and battered remains he had seen beneath the surface of the water. The memory must have registered on his face, for he felt Maggie's eyes gazing anxiously at him.

A blackbird was singing, a ringing, insistent, alarmed note, like someone tapping on a metal pipe. Chink, chink, chink, over and over again.

'Oh, how terrible! What a dreadful end! That poor, poor

woman! And you, Oliver dearest, how horrifying for you to see something like that!'

Afterwards he thought that he shouldn't have told her, that he should have borne it alone and spared her. But he knew that she was the stronger.

24

THE TALL DOORMAN AT THE SAVOY WAS UNUSUALLY communicative. 'Yes, sir, it is an automobile, and it's waiting for you in the Strand. A Daimler, eight cylinders, I should say, sir; beautiful job. But young Mr Monny, he asked me to get a message to you, sir, because he's driving it himself. Hasn't got a chauffeur.' The doorman murmured these last words almost in a whisper and coughed, as though discreetly apologizing for mentioning such a shortcoming in the sacred precincts of the Savoy. 'So he doesn't want to stop the engine, sir, and begs you will hop in – er, that you will ascend into the vehicle, that is.'

Oliver, who had rushed along to the Savoy in answer to a message, dashed outside again and round into the street to find Michel Monet revving the engine of a huge motor car, with varnished coachwork, shining brass and a great horn mounted on the side. There seemed to be a vast expanse of leather seating. Michel was in the course of uttering a series of toots that were alarming the carriage horses waiting in the hotel courtyard into nervous skittering. A couple of elderly dowagers were expressing horror at the modern vulgarity of the scene. 'I really cannot imagine why anyone should wish to be transported in such an outrageous conveyance,' said one, skirting the bonnet and peering at the unnoticing Frenchman through a lorgnette. The other settled a long flurry of ostrich feathers round her shoulders before agreeing: 'Certainly they should not be allowed near the Savoy! We shall have to speak to someone about it!'

Michel was calling 'Jump in!', and Oliver sprang up on to the running board and thence into a leather-covered passenger seat. Suddenly there was a terrific rattling and knocking under the bonnet and the motor swept forward, rounded the Savoy courtyard and shot out into the Strand. 'Isn't she wonderful!' shouted Michel. 'I saw her in a newspaper.'

'What does your father think?' asked Oliver, expecting that the artist would be somewhat disapproving.

However, Michel yelled back, 'Oh, he adores motors! He has just bought one in France – a Panhard-Levassor!'

Michel seemed a different man, in a new mood altogether. 'You know, this motor car is supposed to seat eleven people. Imagine, the whole Monet family – we have lots of relatives, Mr Craston: our family is rather complicated. Splendid, isn't she?' he called to Oliver through the din, and proceeded to elaborate on the Daimler's virtues as they tore down to Trafalgar Square, while pedestrians scattered and cabs pulled frantically aside. 'I had to go to Norfolk to get this beauty!'

There was a pause. Oliver hadn't at first recognized the name from Michel's pronunciation, but it clicked into place.

'I saw an advertisement in *The Times*,' Michel continued enthusiastically. 'It turned out the owner doesn't have room to garage her. She was sitting in the stables with all the horse-muck piled up around, and I fell in love at first sight. I thought we'd give Rosa a spin as far as Richmond,' added Michel, whisking past Nelson in a magnificent curve. 'We might go for tea at some little place there.'

Oliver felt some trepidation at first, and his embarrassment at the public spectacle they made as the Daimler swept through the streets threatened to prevent his taking much pleasure in the novel experience. He had once or twice been in a motor car with friends from Oxford, but never anything as luxurious and powerful as this. After a few minutes, though, he began to feel a certain thrill in the way in which people turned and stared like so many sheep, small boys yelling and pointing as they passed. Indeed, he even began to manage a lordly sort of wave as they swept along, and donned the goggles that Michel passed him with a flourish. Young Monet seemed extraordinarily dashing, seated at the wheel in a cape and leather gauntlets. They proceeded west at a jerky pace, enlivened by plunging horses and swearing coachmen, and finally reached Bromfield Road, a long row of almost identical villas, where Michel brought the vehicle to a banging halt, but left the engine running.

'Don't want to stop her now she's going so well!' he shouted. 'You go and call Rosa.'

Oliver found himself in front of a white-painted door with a brass knocker in the shape of an angel, and, grasping the halo firmly, he banged it against the mount, and was answered in a moment or two by Rosaline Darby herself.

His heart took a sudden leap and he began stammering: the general fervent excitement created by the Daimler's progress was forgotten and he was taken aback again by Rosa's beauty, her large aquamarine eyes and long hair, which was held back by a red velvet ribbon and gleamed in the sun that fell through the doorway.

But Oliver didn't really need to say anything: she looked past him into the street and burst into laughter. 'Oh, he's got the motor car, then! Well, I do long to see what it's like! Will you wait a moment, Mr Craston, and I'll just get one or two things.'

He stepped into the hallway as she indicated. It was much lighter than the house at Barnes, and painted in shades of cream, with silvery curtains that were figured with some green leaf design that reminded him somehow of willows. The soothing effect of this was soon overtaken by shock, however, for hanging on the wall opposite the door, displayed with no reticence or warning, was a painting of a woman. Her arms were raised shamelessly above her head, and her heavy breasts were pushed forward. Between her fleshy thighs, which almost seemed to be opening towards him, was a dark triangle, and within it the shadowy trace of a cleft. But it was the expression on her pretty rounded face that most shocked him, for she was laughing and her whole skin glowed with a rosy radiance, as if she were revelling in her nakedness.

'Lovely, isn't it?' said Rosa, coming back, tying a veil across her hair and under her chin. 'It's a Renoir, of course. We're very lucky to have got it.'

'Oh, yes, of course.' Oliver held the door open for her, hoping that his hand would not shake visibly. He had never seen such a thing in his mother's house, nor even in the mildly pornographic etchings that had sometimes circulated on his staircase at Oxford. He tried hard to imagine the sort of household in which a painting of this kind would be openly on view.

'Of course, Monet doesn't paint nudes,' Rosa was saying. 'At least, he probably did in his youth, but I expect Alice doesn't let him any more.'

Fortunately for Oliver, who was conscious that his face was burning with a deep blush that had spread to his ears, they had reached the Daimler and the painting was forgotten, at least as a topic of conversation, though as they took their places side by side behind Michel he glanced down at Rosa's modestly clad lap and suddenly seemed to see through the chaste thick cotton of her dress to something that set his skin on fire again so that he was glad of the air as the Daimler started to move forward.

By the time they reached Richmond Park, in a rush of cold wind tugging at Rosa's veil, he had managed to put all these thoughts out of his mind, however. Michel pulled the snorting motor car to a halt. Steam seemed to be rising from the front of the engine.

'You two go on into the park – I must try to cool her down a bit. Don't go too far – I'll come and find you in a few minutes. There should be a smithy just along here where they'll let me have some water.' And before he could know it, Oliver found himself walking in Richmond Park side by side with Rosaline Darby. The chestnuts were just beginning to have tiny, barely visible purple-pink buds, and the yellow sun poured over the wintry grass.

'He's wanted one for ages – a motor car, I mean. I think old Monsieur Monet secretly likes the idea – at least, he's always wanting to know about them. Like skating, it's another of Michel's crazes.'

A terrible piercing thrust of jealousy, an emotion he had not experienced since his schooldays, took Oliver by surprise. He suddenly pictured the two of them, Rosa and Michel, laughing, their faces turned towards each other, as they slid over the ice.

He said, and managed to sound casual, for he was beginning to absorb some of the lessons of diplomacy, 'They seem an interesting family. I'd heard of him, of course, but I didn't know it was all so complicated.'

Rosa laughed. 'Oh, yes, though I don't think any of the children have inherited the artistic talent. But only two – well, possibly three of them – are Monet's own children. There are the two eldest boys, Jean and Michel, and then the youngest of the family. The children in between are Alice's by her first husband. Michel does sketch a little, but his lungs are weak, you know, and I think really that London in the winter does not do him much good. But he came here to stay with my family because they wanted him to learn English – old Monsieur Monet and Madame Alice.'

'Alice is Michel's mother?'

'No, no.' There was a pause, as if she were weighing up whether she could confide in him. 'She is his stepmother. His own mother died shortly after his birth, I believe, and Alice brought him up. There are eight children altogether – well, there were, but one of Alice's daughters, Suzanne, died recently, as you know. It is one of those huge families, but the eldest two, Jean and Michel, are the children of the first wife, Camille. Alice and her husband went to stay with the Monets when they were living in some little French village . . . Anyway, it ended up with Alice's husband walking out. Monet married Alice, eventually. But I think there was some talk about her after Camille . . . after Michel's mother died. In fact, it was quite scandalous, really, the circumstances. I do wonder if he ever – the old man – if he ever regrets . . . Well, perhaps some time I'll tell you more about it.' Her voice had suddenly dropped as she was speaking and Oliver saw that Michel was advancing towards them under the trees.

He waved in excitement, calling out, 'It's all right – I've left it at the smithy till we come back. They'll take care of everything. Shall we walk as far as the river?'

Rosa shook her head decisively. 'No, it'll be too cold. I can't stand the damp and fog coming from the water.'

The three young people walked abreast in the wintry sunshine. Rosa had tactfully changed the subject and started talking about her own family, telling them of the house in Ireland that was shut up for much of the year. 'Mother usually goes back for the summer. It seems so far away now!'

Later, after they had returned and left Rosa to dress for dinner, Oliver said cautiously to Michel as the car pulled up, 'That picture in their house . . .'

'Oh, that Renoir nude? Wonderful, isn't it? Though it shocks some people.'

Oliver was rather glad to hear this. To confront that painting and feel he was alone in the world in experiencing what he did – that would have been worse than mere embarrassment.

Michel seemed to take the sudden breath that his companion drew in as expressing surprise rather than relief, for he added, 'Oh, yes! It's the openness of it, you see. The way the woman is looking directly at you – and she's so unashamed. And her body is in bright light, not hiding in some veiled shadows.' He laughed, and then said, 'Let's go to a music-hall tonight!'

'I'm afraid I have some reading to do,' said Oliver, and rather mistrusted the way in which Michel laughed again.

25

THE PAINTER CONTEMPLATED A CANVAS.

Charing Cross Bridge loomed out of a fog, a sky feathered with light like the breast of a dove. In this sky, an orange sun had been scrubbed in with rough strokes. Around the sun was a nimbus of strange green, the sickly colour of moss, and in the water the sunlight was reflected in a long track of pinkish iridescence. In the foreground, that same shade of deliquescent green glimmered here and there on the surface of the river and just above it was the faint bluish outline of a boat, a flat, lumbering little craft making for the arches of the bridge. Had he caught the chilling nature of the fog of this river?

He found himself thinking of another river, in another country.

The winter when Camille died had been so cold.

He had already been living with Alice – the two families under the same roof, Camille sick, Alice at once her nurse-maid and his mistress, her strength looking after all the children, nursing, cleaning. It was at Vétheuil, he remembered suddenly, as it all flooded back, that little town on the Seine, and the village was cut off by blizzards. We were so poor we could scarcely afford firewood and the children were short of proper boots. Camille had even pawned her locket. Time after time, oblivious, he had gone out into the icy air and painted the light on the snow, the clearings in the woods flooded with white. And even after she died – yes, just after Camille died – he worked outside in those freezing short days, trying to capture that ice-bound river in paint.

There came now into his mind, sharp as sketches, images of those long-distant winter days in Vétheuil, the white and grey points of sharp frost on the bushes alongside the water, the drifting broken logs in those icy masses. And that iridescence and glitter, how it had at once seduced his eyes and eased his pain.

He leaned back from the desk and rubbed his hands, looking out of the window again. His present task, this painter's vigil, was in London, watching for a glimpse of light itself, light made almost solid and visible by refulgence and embodiment in the fumes and wraiths that floated over the city. And he studied the mists, too, that played opalescent tricks of distortion and reflection, outlines of deeper black in almost-black and indigo, the oily glistening of sheets of rose and pearl through which bridges and towers were distantly limned. To these capricious tricks of vision he had brought all his art, the technique of a lifetime, squinting with his poor and troubled eyesight into the sulphurous atmosphere.

And still to capture this on canvas tried all his skill, escaped his touch, escaped his sight, almost, as he peered into the shapes forming and re-forming in the water and its reflections. Now, as he looked out of the window, a thick patch of fog seemed to lift and disclosed the lineaments of a boat sculling madly downstream, and across the water came a soft splashing of oars.

We always had a boat at Giverny, he thought, even when we were poor.

In the distance he thought he saw the outline of the railway bridge, a long, metallic streak with the muddy water swirling round its pylons. There followed, in these few brief moments of vision through the gloom, a white plume of smoke and the long, thundering sound of a train passing over the bridge. Then the mist fell again, and the world went silent as the heavy grey cotton-like air descended on London.

His eyes felt old and tired: they had looked too intently at too much, and he rubbed them disconsolately as he sought to finish the letter to his wife, while at the same time glancing hopefully towards the balcony. Poor Alice: I should try to write every day.

There was a knock at the outer door of the hotel suite and Michel came in. 'Father, it is so dark in here! Surely you are not trying to write without any light!'

Michel reached towards the switch, but the old man said, 'No, leave it for a few moments more.'

Michel's face seemed so thin; the old man worried whether he and Alice had been too tender towards the others and perhaps not anxious enough about this child of Camille.

Perhaps the son, too, was feeling the burden of the past.

'Am I like her?' he suddenly said. 'Papa, am I like my mother?'

His father regarded him carefully.

'No, Papa, look at me as a man. Don't look at me as if I were something you are painting!'

The old man was startled. Then he was almost apologetic.

Michel felt deeply touched. He had never seen his father like this before, vulnerable, uncertain.

'Yes, you are like her,' he said at last. 'You have her strong features. The great eyebrows, the arches of the sockets. And also her frailty. She was not a powerful person, not like Alice. She could not have held the family together, as Alice has done.'

26

MONTGERON, 1876

THE SUN OF LATE SUMMER WAS FLOODING IN THROUGH THE
tall windows, illuminating the breakfast-table, on which lay
the scattered remains of croissants, bread, golden slabs of
butter, and great bunches of hothouse fruit.

'Come riding, Monsieur Monet! Or shall we go walking?'

The young man didn't wish to disappoint his hostess. After
all, Madame Hoschedé and her husband were among the most
influential collectors in Paris, but when they had invited him
to their house at Montgeron it had been understood that he
would be using the occasion to paint.

Argenteuil had got stale for him, somehow – too suburban,
perhaps, neither town nor country. There were more
factories, and though he had been happy for a while, leading
that peripheral life of the small town just outside the city, he
had been feeling a restlessness, the need for something of
greater intensity, greater isolation, perhaps.

Not that Montgeron could be said to be truly isolated: it
was still not far from Paris, some thirty-five kilometres, and

his hosts led such a lavish life-style that they could lay on a special train for their guests. Yet such was the size of the Hoschedé estate that the landscape stretched like vast expanses of countryside around the Château Rottembourg: one could bury oneself in it without disturbance. The grounds encompassed a lake and thick stretches of woodland. The Yerres river ran through the estate, and there was a fishing cabin where the artist, alone as if in a wilderness, could study the water, the reflections of sky and trees.

Camille remained at Argenteuil, since this was nominally a professional visit that Monet was paying to his patrons. He had actually been invited to paint some decorative panels for the interior of the house. The Hoschedés were modern rich, they prided themselves on their advanced taste, so they had invited the controversial young artist Claude Monet to design something that was in keeping with the theme of country life and yet had new perspectives on it. From the other side of the lake he had painted the château, and he also set himself to record the absurd flock of decorative white turkeys, of which his hostess was very proud, placing their foolish, scaly, gobbling wattles and trailing snowy pinions up close in the foreground, the house a mere cipher in the distance. If it was a comment, the Hoschedés did not seem to notice.

Alice, his hostess, seemed a restless woman. Always fashionably dressed, the mother of five small children, she nevertheless led a life that seemed taken up with the social round: when they were not in Paris, they often entertained artists, writers and musicians.

Alice had become acquainted with Claude Monet when she first appeared before him as a benevolent patroness, wife of a collector. She had the power of money, being a fashionable hostess able to invite struggling artists to stay at their country home. Indeed, the young man had been hired, like a decorator, to paint panelling.

Claude Monet had gone to stay at Rottembourg, disappearing early every morning into the woods and gardens to paint, usually setting his canvas up with a distant view of the house. Alice, often dressed for riding, inevitably came by to see the progress of the work.

After the third or fourth such occasion, it had become almost a regular custom and he sometimes got up from his work and walked with her in the grounds, rambling round the park, noticing how she pulled the veil of her riding-habit over her face as the morning breezes tugged her wiry hair loose.

There were parties that summer, attended by other artists – the Manets, Auguste Renoir. The lavish hospitality had included a masked ball, for which Monet and Renoir had designed their own masks.

But, when the others left and went back to Paris, Monet remained. He was fascinated by Alice. She was the first society woman he had ever known, and her trailing gowns from Paris couturiers, her generous gifts to charities, the odd mixture of religious fervour and defiance that he found in her, intrigued him. She had a kind of arrogance, yet he could not help but admire it and be fascinated by it.

'Oh, yes, she knows her own mind, Alice!' Ernest Hoschedé's mother, Honorine, commented one day, when she was paying them a visit. 'But she won't keep him steady, that's the trouble! Ernest runs off after everything new. He needs restraint, Monsieur Monet, restraint!' And she leaned forward and tapped the side of her old nose, just as she must have done when she had been a cashier and her husband a shop assistant, before they had made their fortune and had their own shop and their own assistants.

'Ernest should remember he's only a shopkeeper – even if Au Petit Gagne is a fashionable department store,' she said one day to Alice, who was wearing a new gown with trailing falls of blue panne velvet, and had dressed her children in miniature versions of the same outfit. As her daughter-in-law twirled her skirts for the benefit of the young artist, the old woman pinched up a fold of the skirt and rubbed it between finger and thumb, feeling the thickness. 'Forty francs a metre! You must be crazy! And no woman needs a lady's maid just to put her clothes on, for heaven's sake!'

Monet had felt rather embarrassed by this criticism of their hostess, but told himself that it was a family matter, and, besides, Alice seemed to take it in good part. In any case, the evidence of wealth was all around them: Venetian chandeliers, silk curtains, the gleam of polished satinwood and Boulle. He found that he enjoyed these things, liked looking at the lustres of fine material, enjoyed the feel of the best linen and the luxurious soaps and pomades that were always placed in the guests' rooms.

Although he set up his easel and spent most of the mornings, and often a good part of the afternoons, away from the house, he and Alice not infrequently passed evenings alone together, when there were no other guests, and Ernest was in Paris on business. She was a very anxious mother, fussing continually over small snuffles and rashes, unwilling to leave for Paris if any of the children were ill – and with four small ones, there was often some illness to be watched over. The children had maids, of course, who did all the washing and bathing and feeding, but Alice still liked to feel that she was a mother to her children. Sometimes, he felt, she went too far: it was rather foolish to dress up little Jacques like a girl, in velvet with a big silk sash, just so that he would look like his sisters. The child ought to be a little more boyish.

On this particular morning, when Alice invited Monet to go riding, he looked out of the window and thought of the light on the river near the fisherman's cabin, and the dragon-flies that would be darting over the surface, the shadows of the willows rippling in the water with the soft breeze.

'I thought I'd go down to the river,' he said. She laughed, brushing off the rejection, and moved quickly away, calling out some instruction to the maid. Her voice, like the rest of her, was strong: she was never disobeyed by her household.

But he was not surprised later on that morning when she appeared on the river-bank. There had been some nervous intensity that he had sensed. She was different now from her usual self; he could see the tension in the lines of her body beneath the riding-habit. As she came close, he saw her mouth was trembling and she looked as if she had been weeping.

'What's wrong?' he said, shocked by this sign of weakness, and as the tears spurted from her eyes, under the flickering sunshine of the willows, he put his arms round her and began kissing her mouth, tasting the salty tears on her cheeks.

On the day-bed in the cabin, the light filtered through the wattled walls. She had soft skin, velvety, glowing with health. Her naked body lay stretched out like a symphony in pinks and carmines and the folds of flesh and silver lines that bearing five children had left on her body were nothing ugly to him. 'I was lucky – I had them all easily,' she said, as he traced the lines with his hand, reaching up to her nipples with his mouth.

'Why were you weeping?' he said.

She sat upright and reached for her petticoat. She seemed to hesitate, then turned to face him. 'I can't talk about this to anyone else! We'll be bankrupt, or as good as. Apparently the other directors have forced Ernest out, and he's been spending like a madman since his father died. I'm afraid it will all have to go – the house, everything.'

'No, it's not possible, surely!'

He thought of the great house full of furniture, of the gilt clocks and Aubusson carpets, of the art collection – no, it was not possible it could all vanish, melting away like snow. 'There's the château,' he said. 'And your family would help.'

She gave a savage little laugh. 'Rottembourg was bought with my family's money. It was paid for with my inheritance from my father.'

'Well, there you are, then. That's safe.'

'Safe? Ernest has mortgaged it up to the hilt. It would have to go with the rest if anything happens.' She reached out towards him again. 'I'm afraid of it,' she said. 'I don't think we've got much longer.'

Neither of them thought the sexual passion that overtook them, something feverish, which involved frantic and hurried encounters, would lead to anything. He felt no guilt towards Camille. It was, in its way, almost a matter of form: the relationship between a talented young artist and a rich woman of pleasure, hostess of a sophisticated Bohemian circle. Though there were one or two things that gave him pause – the way she cried and prayed, for example. But some women did things like that.

Not Camille, of course. Camille never lost that remoteness which he loved, in her body and in her face. Alice was easily excited by his hands, easily weeping afterwards – guilty, she said, feeling so guilty.

Nevertheless, it appeared to him that summer at Montgeron that there was nothing to be taken seriously. The fears for Ernest's business receded, though Alice's anxieties continued, making her more tense and desiring than ever. But the future seemed clear enough. Monet would go back to Argenteuil, and Alice would doubtless find some other lover. The canvases he had yet to finish were more important than the affair with Alice. He had stayed on, as autumn came, and then the first frosts of winter. Camille was ill: problems of the womb; metritis, said the doctors at Argenteuil.

Disaster hadn't taken long to overcome them all. And soon would follow the terrible auction, in 1878.

The crowds on the pavement outside the Hôtel Drouot, the great Paris auction-house, were jostling and pushing in their efforts to crowd into the salon. Placards on the pavements announced the occasion of so much excitement: BANKRUPTCY SALE! JUNE 5TH–6TH.

Only two days, Monet thought, two days for Ernest Hoschedé, the talk of Paris, the most advanced and modern art patron of the day, to lose his lovingly acquired pictures. The Hoschedé town house in the Boulevard Haussmann was already emptied of furniture. Rottembourg had been inventoried. Now for the works of art.

Monet, back in Argenteuil with Camille, had come into Paris for the auction. Standing at the back, he was able to look over the heads of most of the crowd, trying not to see the avid faces, gluttonous for the humiliation of the ruined family. The summer heat was filling the building and already some of the people were perspiring. Red-faced men rubbed their whiskers with their pocket-handkerchiefs.

The auctioneer, Maître Dubourg, took his place at the stand and looked over the crowd. His face was impassive, professional, but he feared the worst: these were respectable bourgeois, their tastes in art running to stags, and ladies in crinolines. At some of the pictures about to fall under his hammer, he felt in his heart of hearts that they would only jeer. Nearly half the paintings were by Impressionists. The throng had come to see a spectacle, not to bid. Hoschedé had been far-sighted by some standards, a fool by most.

He looked to one side to check that the porters, with their baize aprons, were ready to carry the pictures into view, and was about to gesture to them to bring the first lot before the crowd, when there was a sudden buzz of excitement. The assembly parted at the back. Down to the very front of the auction-room moved a small plump figure, very upright, dressed in silks and carrying a ruffled parasol.

'It's Madame Hoschedé,' gasped someone.

Alice did not look round: she sat down on one of the little chairs with her back straight as a board, the deportment she had been taught at her expensive school for the daughters of the rich.

'Where is her husband?' asked Julie Pissarro.

'Dead drunk,' said a voice in the crowd, and there was a ripple of laughter. If Alice had heard it, she did not deign to turn round.

'Ladies and gentlemen, the sale is beginning.' Maître Dubourg flicked imaginary specks from his immaculate frock-coat, looked deliberately away from the direct gaze of Madame Hoschedé (as if to say, 'Really, the woman is positively unnerving!') and began proceedings. The lots moved fast: the humidity of Paris in June became positively unpleasant.

At the back, Julie was seated, with the artists standing beside her, and as affairs progressed the little group sank into a frozen and despairing silence.

'Number fifty-five,' announced Dubourg. ' "Impression –

Sunrise". Oil-painting by Monsieur Claude Monet. What am I bid for this fine view of Le Havre? Shown in the famous exhibition at Nadar's studios.'

'Five francs!' shouted a wag and another responded, 'View of what? Search me!'

'Oh God help you, you fools, it's the most important picture in the world! The one that gave Impressionism its name!' The voice came from Edmond Renoir, driven to fury at the triumph of philistinism he was witnessing.

Even that crowd, by now in the mood of a beer-garden rather than one appropriate to an auction-house, fell silent. The canvas, with its glowing ball of fire rising over indigo waters, was borne in by the porters. They supported it high over their heads, turning it this way and that to the public gaze, like a living creature condemned to shame.

There were a few hands raised. Eventually the bidding stopped and Dubourg pointed into the crowd. A dapper man, beautifully dressed with yellow doeskin gloves and pomaded hair, had been the purchaser.

'It's Monsieur de Bellio,' whispered Pissarro to Julie. 'He's already bought some of Claude's work – a train leaving St Lazare station was one of them, I remember. The Hoschedés sold it to him.'

'And he's got this one at a bargain price. Hoschedé paid me eight hundred for it.' Claude Monet's anger was barely restrained. The bidding had moved on.

'Lot fifty-seven.'

Lot 57 was one of the works Monet had painted at Rottembourg in that glorious autumn when all had still seemed outwardly well with the Hoschedé world and Ernest had been away attending to business in Paris. It showed a lane in the woods around the house, with no-one in sight.

It was the spot where he and Alice had first embraced.

The artist, the betrayer, was suddenly filled with an un-expected sensation of triumph and with it a powerful rush of sexual pleasure, even in the dusty surroundings of the auction-room. I can survive this, he thought. Even this public poverty, this disgrace. Alice will too. She and I – we don't break, we don't give in.

It was this thought, if the truth be told, that gave him the strength to stay and witness the apparent destruction of the Impressionist movement.

The next painting was also one of his works: the lake at Montgeron, with flowering rose-bushes reflected in the water.

He looked down to the front of the crowd, where Alice Hoschedé sat unmoving, upright. Impossible to imagine now, her abandonment. He hadn't seen her since they had returned separately to Paris, but at the side of that lake they had made the most intense, passionate love, on a bed of autumn leaves. Was she thinking of it, as the painting was raised, displayed for all to see, then lowered?

'One hundred and thirty francs.'

It was knocked down.

Each picture seemed to attract more gross laughter and a lower price than the one before. When one of Pissarro's canvases fetched seven francs, there was a cry of despair from Julie, and she rose and thrust her way out, tears spurting from her eyes. Finally, the last lot came and went for a song. The public ordeal was over.

The crowd seemed to pause a moment, like a child that suddenly doubts its cruelty, and parted to allow a small, deter-mined figure to make her way to the doors. There was a long silence as she walked through the room, and murmurs, whispers, that followed behind her.

Alice Hoschedé was forced to pass close to the artists, and stopped, her face a mask.

Pissarro bowed. 'Good day, madame. I am very sorry to see you in these straits.' He had the grace not to add, 'And all of us with you,' though he might well have.

She acknowledged Pissarro, and then turned to greet Monet formally, putting out her gloved hand towards him. It is not dead, he thought as he touched her hand and looked down into her face. Pity moved in him as a deep sexual longing.

27

SERGEANT HASSBLACK LOOKED UNCOMFORTABLY ABOUT HIM.
The little room at the morgue held nothing but wooden
shelves around the walls, and arrayed on the shelves were
pathetic bundles bearing labels written in cheap watery
official ink, which in some cases were fading, so that the
numbers and dates entered in a spidery hand could scarcely be
read.

A peculiar smell hung everywhere in the room: not so
much that of physical decay itself, but of strong carbolic overhanging a refractory, muddy, pervasive odour that could
never be abolished.

Spread out on the table in the middle of the room was a
jumble of garments.

'Take notes about everything,' Garrety had instructed him.
'Everything she was wearing. I want details – how much the
stuff might have cost, where she might have bought it,
whether it was old or new. Ask some woman if you have to.'

The remains of the clothing taken from the first body

found in the Thames had not been fumigated. They were still wet, having been sluiced of mud, but now emitting a disgusting odour, and Hassblack spread out the first item with reluctance. A tight-fitting dark blouse, in some thick stuff, colour now indeterminate. Hassblack held it up, turned it inside and out, and made a note of its appearance. There was a label still inside the collar, the name stitched in: 'Marshall & Co. Kensington'.

There was the corset from which the pathologist had cut her free at the last, but this held no clue as to its manufacture, though its stout material had survived the action of the water. The lower part of the corset was covered with dark stains, which seemed ingrained more deeply than the mud.

And lying on the table was a skirt, heavy and dark. It appeared to be patterned with a small flower design. Hassblack held it up. He saw that there seemed to be an extra fold of cloth on one side and felt reluctantly along the seams, his hands grasping at the slippery cloth, to which the slime still clung. His fingers felt a pocket, and within it some small, flat object. He pulled, but it was attached to the cloth, and, turning the pocket inside out like some monstrous jug-ear, he saw that there was a thin sliver of what looked like metal. It was bored, though the hole was solid with mud, to take a ring at one end, and fastened in place with a pin so that it could not be lost from the pocket – or stolen, either.

Hassblack unpinned the object and held it up to the light, rubbing it with his fingers. Through the blackened film appeared a silvery plaque bearing a number: '1st. No. 498'.

The police sergeant carefully noted down descriptions of the clothing, and then called for the attendant. 'I want to take this with me back to my inspector.' A receipt book was brought and the item carefully listed. Hassblack signed for the sliver of metal.

'This is good quality stuff,' said the attendant, indicating the pile of clothing. 'At least, it were, at one time. Usually we gets a load of old rags and rubbish off 'em.'

'You know about this sort of thing?'

'It's our perk, you might say. We sell 'em. If they're not claimed, of course, but even if they are the families often says they doesn't want 'em.'

Hassblack scratched his head. 'There's people who buys them? The clothes you get off the dead bodies?'

'The rag-merchants, yes. Buys 'em by the weight. But this jacket here, see this, it's good worsted, worth quite a bit more. Could be she was quite a classy piece, or a lady's maid or something of the sort, who got her lady's clothes second-hand. Don't know what that could be, though.' He gestured at the piece of metal, which Hassblack was holding in his hand. 'Pawn ticket, maybe. Never seen one like that before, though.' The voice cracked with a laugh. 'And I'm an expert on pawn tickets.'

'Maybe.' Hassblack had his own ideas about it, but he was keeping his thoughts to himself.

28

'I'LL SEE HIM NOW,' CALLED A VOICE, AND THE LADY TYPIST, dressed in neat grey with a modest bustle, rose from behind her desk and showed Hassblack into an office somewhere up in the neo-Gothic ramparts of Waterloo Station. Even here, well away from the platforms and the crowds, the smell of soot hung in the air. The cream and brown office was ventilated by a half-moon window, past which drifted sporadic clouds of steam. The sounds of whistles and shunting rose up from the depths below.

Behind the desk, which was covered with printed tables, sat a small, round-faced man rocking to and fro as he perused them. He stopped with a sudden start as Hassblack entered a few paces behind the bustle, and produced a large stop-watch from his pocket.

'Sergeant Hassblack, Mr Plumtree,' said the owner of the bustle.

'Ah, now, what is it you want to see me about, Sergeant? Mustn't waste any time, you know. Only way we can keep a great railway station like this running is to be absolutely accurate to the second.' He pressed the watch and an audible ticking began.

'I just want to ask if you can help me identify ... something, sir.' Hassblack produced the thin piece of metal found in the pocket of the woman pulled from the river.

'Good Lord, where did you get that? I presume it was stolen from its owner?'

'Possibly, sir.' Or possibly not, thought Hassblack, but now was not the moment to explain that its real owner would be fortunate if this had indeed been stolen. 'The point is, sir, can you help us identify it?'

'Oh, yes, the number is still quite legible.' Plumtree was rubbing the silver with his pocket-handkerchief now, and it was emerging with a bright glint under his busy fingers. He laid it down on the desk. 'Though it's in an appalling state, I must say. Fancy allowing a first-class railway token to fall into such a condition!'

'That's what it is, then, sir?'

'Oh, yes, Sergeant. They are issued only to the most respectable of personages, you know. I take it you wish to restore it to its rightful possessor. Where did you find it?'

'I'm afraid I can't tell you that, sir.'

'Can't tell me? Nonsense! Surely you can answer a civil question.'

Hassblack took an avenue of escape. It would mean telling a mild untruth, but he needed to get the information, not to aggravate Plumtree. 'I'm sorry, sir – I mean, I don't know where it was found.'

For a second, Hassblack had to close his eyes. He found the memory of that horrible water-soaked skirt pocket coming back to him – he could feel the rough wet material in his hand.

He rubbed his fingers together uncomfortably in an involuntary gesture.

Plumtree hadn't noticed his lapse in concentration. 'Oh, very well, Sergeant. I suppose policemen cannot be expected to execute more than the simplest errands. Just a moment,' he continued, reaching for a large leather-covered volume, one of several on the shelf behind his desk. 'Now, then, number four-nine-eight . . . Let me see.' Plumtree was running a fat finger at astonishing speed down a long page. It suddenly halted and stabbed at a line. 'Here we are, Sergeant.'

'Can I copy it down, sir?'

Plumtree handed the register over to Hassblack, who saw that the pages were ruled in lines and columns. Each line had a number, a name and an address, and a fourth column in which another name was sometimes inscribed. The entries were in a fair copperplate hand. At the top of the page was written 'August, 1898'. Halfway down appeared the number '498'.

'That is the lady to whom it was issued.'

'To a woman, then, sir?'

'Of course, man – why, can you not read there?' Plumtree sounded contemptuous: probably he believed that Hassblack could not read.

The sergeant took a certain satisfaction in pronouncing the words aloud, and slowly, engendering yet more impatience in Plumtree, who was positively drumming his fingers on the desk. '"Mrs Perdita Harston, 45, Holland Park Road". And then it says "Colonel Andrew Harston". And then there is the letter R, sir.'

'R for "Relict", Sergeant.'

'Relict, sir?'

'Widow, in common parlance. This is a kind of ticket,

Sergeant, a pass valid for life, which ensured free first-class travel to the widow of a very prominent railway official. Colonel Harston served on several Boards after he left the Indian Army, and was, if I remember rightly, a major shareholder. Clearly, Mrs Harston has had the misfortune to lose her pass and we must restore it to her with all speed. Will you undertake that duty, Sergeant, or will you allow me to do it for you?' The implication of his tone was that Hassblack could scarcely be trusted to restore a carrot to a donkey.

Nevertheless, the sergeant took no pleasure in removing the token from Plumtree's desk and pocketing it as he said, 'We will deal with the matter, thank you, sir.'

'Well, I hope you will do so with some efficiency.' Plumtree looked at his stop-watch. 'Seven minutes and forty-five seconds, Sergeant.'

'Beg pardon, sir – a moment more. This lady, did you say she was a widow?'

'Yes, indeed.'

'Would she have been an elderly lady, then, sir?'

'Why, as a matter of fact, Sergeant, in this particular case, no. I recollect the sad business: the colonel was killed in a carriage accident. I believe he was about fifty years of age and he had married a lady much younger than himself. Mrs Harston would not, I believe, be much above five-and-thirty, even now. Old Mrs Harston, the colonel's mother, is still alive, I believe – though I hope you will not go troubling her on such a trivial matter. She suffered a terrible loss, you know, in the death of her son.'

'Thank you, sir.'

The bustle showed Hassblack out. On the stairs, he stood for a moment or two, looking down at the rails running out beneath the blackened curving roofs into the distance, picturing for a moment a clean and wealthy suburb on the other side of the Thames.

And an old lady, waiting for news. No, it wouldn't be a pleasant job, going to Holland Park.

29

ALINE STOOD IRRESOLUTELY IN THE HALLWAY IN A WING OF St Thomas's Hospital. Through the archways and open doors she caught glimpses of long wards with narrow iron-framed beds, some with cot-like sides, where long shapes turned and twisted now and again under white covers. Sometimes a woman's voice called out. 'Ah, God, my Danny!' she heard, and 'Fetch my baby, nurse, fetch my baby!' followed by a long murmur and a sharp, shrill voice. And then sobbing.

These fragments played on her nerves more than anything else could have done. This was the second time she had come here, to the Women's and Infants' section, and she was still plucking up her courage to go in and keep her appointment.

A nurse with a cap stiffly starched and folded so that it stood out from her head like white wings came out of a side door. 'Come along, Doctor's waiting now!' she said importantly, and Aline moved reluctantly towards her. The nurse ushered her into a long room where a row of cubicles partitioned off with flimsy curtains awaited. 'In there, now,

Mrs Garrety. Get undressed and put your legs in the stirrups!'

The place smelled of some harsh carbolic disinfectant.

Aline began to take her clothes off, staring down at the green linoleum beneath her feet.

A young man poked his head through the curtains. 'I'm Dr Forbes,' he announced. He seemed terribly youthful, his hair almost downy around his neck. He wasted no time. 'Now, how long have you been married, Mrs Garrety?'

'Four years.'

'And you have never conceived?'

'No, Doctor, not in all that time.'

'It's not that long, you know. Some women try for much longer.'

Aline could think of nothing to say. How could this man begin to understand? It seemed a whole lifetime, decades measured out each month, yet galloping onwards nevertheless, towards a despairing, childless old age.

'You have consulted medical experts? Who attended you? One of my colleagues here?'

'It was in Belfast.'

As she took off her dress, he saw the crucifix on the chain round her neck.

'Catholic? Well, I suppose that's why you badly want to have children. That's what the priests tell you – bring more little RCs into the world. That's what they teach you, isn't it? London's full of the Irish; ten to a room and half the children dying at birth. They breed like rabbits.' He had the grace to add, 'Not that I was referring to you, of course. What is your husband's occupation? Builder, I suppose.'

'He's a policeman.'

'Now, that is unusual.'

Aline looked at Dr Forbes, who was standing confidently

in front of her holding the speculum, and then at her own white, stockingless legs, at the stirrups hanging over the narrow couch.

'Mrs Garrety, what are you doing?'

She couldn't go through with it, the humiliation and the doctor's scorn. Aline struggled back into her clothes and pushed past the doctor.

Out in the hall, the nurse called out: 'Mrs Garrety, wasting the doctor's time like that! Come back!'

The safe, comfortable feeling of her clothes back on again calmed her. And then there was the fresh cold air, reviving her. She ran along the embankment, buttoning up her jacket.

I can't, she thought. Not even for Will's sake. And the memory came back to her of old Finnegan in Belfast, bending over the bed. 'There's nothing wrong, Mrs Garrety – nothing physical that we can detect at all.'

So what might these clever London doctors find out that they couldn't tell her in Belfast? Nothing at all, surely.

She had scarcely noticed where she was going, but she had passed Charing Cross Bridge and was heading in the direction of Waterloo Station. Slowing her pace, she turned into Lower Marsh, and began to notice her surroundings again. She was passing a row of shops that seemed familiar. Yes, and there behind the counter of a pastry-shop was the girl who had been so helpful to her before, when she had fainted. They had both been so kind, the girl and the lady.

Aline came to a halt.

It was the pause in front of the window that really turned her footsteps, for in that brief space of time as her shadow fell across the glass the girl looked up and glimpsed her. She must have called out something to someone who was deeper inside the shop, because the woman who had spoken to Aline on the previous occasion emerged. Aline tried to recall her name. 'Mrs Leadbetter, isn't it?'

'It is indeed, my dear. How are you keeping now?'

It was said with such maternally enquiring tones that Aline felt a deep sense of relief, as though some dam had burst inside her and she was able to communicate again, as she had rarely felt, even with Will, since they had come to London. She realized how much she had missed her mother and sisters and their quick sympathies. She longed again to put her head on her mother's shoulder, against the black serge of her bosom, and to tell her all the troubles that had beset her.

It was hard to say why these thoughts and a vivid sense of her mother's presence should have gone through her mind as Mrs Leadbetter looked into her face. The woman did not really resemble Aline's mother: she was in truth younger and much less careworn, and dressed in far better clothes than Mrs O'Kernahan would ever have been able to afford. But Aline did not pause to try to work out any exact points of resemblance: the general impression of sympathy was enough to do the trick.

Before she knew it, Aline was through the door of the shop and again in the parlour she remembered from her last visit, and the girl was being summoned for tea and cakes. Mrs Leadbetter took out a small bottle and added a few drops from it to the tea, which was in a bone-china cup, as Aline gasped out her distress.

'Don't be upset, my dear. They treat us terrible there – I've heard all about it. Young doctors who don't know one end of a woman from the other – wet behind the ears, and telling us how to manage. You remember I mentioned a certain doctor to you? He could help you, quite privately.'

'Oh,' said Aline nervously. 'Well, that is, I don't think we could afford very much . . .'

'No need to worry – there's always some way of contriving!' Her hostess smiled, reaching forward and patting her knee. 'We'll manage it somehow, I'm sure. The doctor may be able to help you with a little operation. Why, it might be some small internal blockage that he could remove so easily that is stopping you having your babies. And there wouldn't be any need to say anything to your husband, if you find these things difficult to speak about. What did you say his occupation might be, my dear?'

Aline was recollecting herself a little. She wanted to keep this woman's friendship. She wanted her help. On other occasions, when she had mentioned that her husband was a policeman, people had shied away from friendship with her. 'Oh, he's . . . employed on the railway,' she said.

This was quite acceptable. After all, many of the men in the area worked at Waterloo, and it was quite natural for Mrs Leadbetter to assume the same.

'Works at the station, does he? I tell you what, my dear, I'll have a word with the doctor for you. I'm quite well known around here. I assure you I have many respected clients – oh, some very smart ladies, you know.' The woman was bridling with modest pride.

'Oh, I'd never doubt it,' said Aline faintly. Had it been laudanum in the tea? She never took it, but it was making her feel calmer, if a little dazed.

Mrs Leadbetter looked at her carefully, as if judging whether the other could be trusted with what she was about to say. She got up and closed the door, pulling it over the thick carpet, so that Aline felt the room was almost sealed. The windows were shut, of course, against the cold of the day, and heavy plush curtains partly drawn over them. An airlessness seemed to enter the parlour.

'It's not only ladies who want to have their babbies who come to me,' said Mrs Leadbetter in an undertone. 'If you take my meaning. I can help other little mamsies too. Though you, my dear, being Irish – I expect you're a Catholic, aren't you? So you'd never be wanting that sort of help. But if you know any as does – well, you could mention me.'

Aline stood up, holding on to the mantelpiece to steady herself. 'Thank you, Mrs Leadbetter. I think I'll be on my way.'

The other woman was evidently annoyed: perhaps she wished she had said less about her business, for she murmured quickly, 'Oh, don't misunderstand me! I would never do anything *wrong*! I'm a law-abiding woman – you may be sure of that!'

Aline pulled the door open and moved quickly into the hallway.

The woman followed her. 'Think about what I said, anyway, my dear. I'm sure you will. You'll come back to me, I know it! I'm sure the amount would not be excessive! A fee of not more than ten guineas, certainly!'

But Aline had opened the front door and stepped out into the street. She greeted the vulgar bustle of Lower Marsh market with relief, and, after breathing the outside air deeply, smoky as it was, for a few moments, set about selecting something for Will's tea.

30

THE CARRIAGES PASSING UP AND DOWN HOLLAND PARK ROAD splashed Hassblack and Garrety with water from the puddles of early spring rain. The two policemen were waiting to cross; on the opposite side was a tall, imposing house with white pillars at the gate and a good deal of elegant wrought-ironwork. Long windows looked out on to a garden with neatly clipped box hedges.

The front door of number 45 was opened by a maid with a little lace cap. She looked wary, and when Garrety asked for Mrs Harston and offered his card she glanced down at it and stared at him anxiously.

Garrety looked at the maid: over forty, he thought, a calm face, probably a sensible woman. 'How long have you been working here?' he asked.

'Oh, I've been here over twenty year, sir. With the family. But Colonel Harston, he's passed away, and young Mrs Harston is gone on a visit. So the old lady's all on her own just at present.'

Garrety made up his mind, and took the maid into his confidence. 'I have to tell you . . . What is your name?'

'Ellen, sir.'

'Well, Ellen, I have to tell you that there may be very bad news.'

The maid was turning pale, but she remained calm. He could see in her eyes that she understood what he was aiming at.

'The mistress has a bad heart, sir.'

'Who is her physician?'

'Dr Broome, sir, from Ladbroke Grove.'

'Then, Ellen, as soon as you have showed us in and told your mistress we are here, please send for Dr Broome immediately. And are there any other members of the family nearby who could be sent for?'

'There's no-one else, sir, only Master James and he's away at school. I'll go to the mistress straight away, sir.'

Ellen put her hand to her mouth, and hurried away. He heard her footsteps tapping towards the back of the house; there was a brief muttered conversation, and then a slow tapping shuffle, as a much older person moved through the house.

A voice carried through the hallway. 'You may tell them to come in now.'

Mrs Harston Senior was very small, but sitting bolt upright, in a chair at the side of the brightly burning fire, her white hair piled up on her head and a black band round her neck, with a large cameo brooch at her throat.

The room was a handsome one, freshly papered and painted in light colours, more modern in taste than might be expected, and a large china bowl planted with bulbs, with green shoots and buds thrusting out of it, stood on a polished side table. Beside the fireplace a miniature portrait of a young boy with golden curls was suspended on a blue silk ribbon: Master James, no doubt.

The old lady's grey eyes were still sharp, though they were sunk in a mass of wrinkles and there were long sad lines to the corners of her mouth. A dark-red shawl was flung about her shoulders, its long cream fringes trailing down over her black dress; it looked as if the shawl had been hastily arranged round her, perhaps by Ellen.

'Well, Mr . . . Garrety?'

The voice was creaking, but remarkably strong for a woman of such an age, and she looked steadily up into his face. She's strong enough to take it, he thought.

'Madam, I must ask you if you recognize this.' The policeman's palm extended before her, the silvery strip of metal lying across it.

Mrs Harston took it up, gazed at it, caressed it in her old fingers. 'It belongs to my daughter-in-law. It's a railway token – it entitles her to free travel. First-class, of course.'

'Naturally, madam.'

The old eyes looked up at them; she was aware something was wrong, but as yet only puzzlement showed in her face. 'I suppose she must have lost it somewhere, but how did you come by it, Inspector . . . er . . . ?'

'Garrety, ma'am. The lady . . . I understand she's not here. How long has she been . . . away?' He chose his words carefully.

The grey eyes looked away, then down to Hassblack's hand and the tiny streak of glinting metal. There was silence for a few moments.

'She is . . . visiting a cousin in Kent.'

'When did she go away?'

'About ten days ago.'

'And when did you last hear from her, ma'am?'

The old voice spoke very slowly now. 'I . . . have not heard from her.'

'Not since she left? Not even to let you know she had arrived safely – something of that sort?'

'No, Inspector, I have had no communication whatsoever from her. She did not write and we have no telephone.'

'When do you expect her return?'

Mrs Harston Senior's lips were dry and cracked; she swallowed uncomfortably. On the table beside her was a glass of water, covered with a small beaded lace cover. She reached towards it and Garrety removed the cover and handed her the glass.

'She had not arranged to return on any particular day?'

'No.' Very quiet, yet formal and frosty. Mrs Harston reached out and pressed a bell-push beside the fireplace. She shook her head fretfully. 'Where is Ellen? Why is she not answering the bell?'

Garrety said, 'Sergeant Hassblack, would you please go and see if you can find the maid?'

He produced his notebook as Hassblack left the room.

Mrs Harston's eyes followed his movements, fixed on the blank page as if in very fear of what he might inscribe upon it. 'It is a serious matter, then, Inspector.' It was a statement, not a question.

He did not answer her directly. 'Madam, would you give me the lady's full name, if you please?'

'Perdita. Rather a fanciful name – after one of Shakespeare's heroines. I'm afraid her parents were somewhat theatrical in their tastes. Her full name is Perdita Antonia Harston.'

Perdita – the lost one. Garrety's heart sank within him at

the thought of the poor creature in the morgue. Perdita indeed.

'And her age?'

The voice was finely balanced now, nervous with suspicion of loss to come, yet edged with remembered outrage. 'She is thirty-five years of age, Inspector. My son was fully twenty years her senior. I was astonished at his choice, I will admit. She seemed far too young and frivolous. But she had quite turned his head.' She stared, as if thinking of the past.

'Do you have any portraits or photographs of your daughter-in-law, Mrs Harston?' he said gently. This was an intelligent woman, her mind still functioning perfectly: she would know what that question implied.

There was a long sigh and the old woman pulled her red shawl tightly round her shoulders, as if against a sudden cold draught that had entered the room. 'You have not come about a missing railway token, have you, Inspector?'

Garrety took a step towards her. 'Mrs Harston . . . er, may I sit down?'

He wanted his face to be on the same level as hers, so that he could tell her quietly. And where was Ellen – had she managed to get hold of the doctor? It sounded as if there was no love lost between the widow and mother of Andrew Harston, but this news that he had to give her must come as a great shock, and to a woman who had already had to endure one with the death of Andrew himself. What was the information Hassblack had reported from Plumtree? That Harston had been killed in an accident.

There was a commotion at the doorway, and Ellen hurried into the room, closely followed by Hassblack.

'Madam,' said Garrety, 'I should like first to see a

photograph of Mrs Harston – Mrs Perdita Harston. If you would be so kind.'

'Ellen, the bureau.'

Ellen crossed to a small bureau of inlaid walnut that stood between the windows. On it was a silver-framed photograph of two men, one young and one, bristling with moustaches, a generation older. Both were in army uniform.

'On the right, Ellen.'

The maid had opened the front of the bureau, and now drew out another sepia photograph, in a matching frame, and passed it to Garrety at a nod from the older woman. It showed a young and pretty woman in an elaborate lace-trimmed blouse. Her hair, curling luxuriantly over her forehead, so like that of the boy in the miniature, was caught up at the top of her head with ribbons that cascaded down. The eyes were surprisingly deeply hollow-set. The photograph had been touched with colour: the cheeks tinged with pink, the lips carmined and the ribbon indicated with blue.

Garrety's eyes met those of Hassblack and saw a fractional movement of agreement. Of course, given the state of the body they had seen in the morgue, it was not positively identifiable from this photograph as Perdita Harston. But it fitted. Oh yes, thought Garrety, this could well be her.

'May I take this photograph away, Mrs Harston? You will get it back, of course. And I should like the address of the cousin.'

The old woman was nodding her consent, and murmuring to Ellen to pass her a leather-bound album, which proved to be an address book. As she turned the pages, there was the sound of the doorbell and Ellen went to answer it.

'Here is the address, Inspector. Our cousin lives in Deal –

you may copy down the details. And pray do not concern yourself about returning the photograph.'

A tall middle-aged gentleman holding a black bag had appeared in the doorway.

'I took the liberty of asking your maid to fetch a doctor.'

Mrs Harston turned enquiring eyes towards Garrety, but he felt that she was anticipating his next words. She did not seem startled: she sat absolutely still beside the fire. The doctor and Ellen crossed to her chair and took up positions beside it, like supporters to the marble statuary of an old tomb.

'Mrs Harston, I believe there is a strong possibility that your daughter-in-law may have been—'

The old voice interrupted him, startling, strong in spite of the years. 'She has been killed? In an accident?'

'No, I must tell you that, in all probability, it was not an accident.'

'Perdita would never have committed suicide, Inspector! I assure you, she was not the type – and, to do her justice, she loved James too much. She was a devoted mother – too indulgent, if anything. I do not believe she would have taken her own life. So what possibility does that leave, Inspector?'

'We know nothing of the ... the circumstances so far, madam. In any case, a positive identification has yet to be made of the lady. I'm afraid a body was found in the river, in the Thames.'

He looked at the faces before him. The old woman was keeping control of her features, twisting her hands together. There was a long pause. He expected her to ask more questions, but she did not.

'Very well, the police will inform me further, I take it?'

'Yes, of course, madam. Forgive me, Dr Broome, are you Mrs Perdita Harston's physician also?'

'Indeed, I was. I attended her in her confinement – I brought young James into the world.'

'Doctor, could I have a word with you?'

Broome followed them into the hallway. 'I don't want to ask the old lady to identify the body. Would you be able to help us there? The . . . er . . . remains are in the Lambeth morgue. Not very pleasant, I'm afraid.'

'Of course. I'll just see what I can do for Mrs Harston and then I'll be along.'

The door shut behind the policemen and they walked across Holland Park Road. We close the door on it, and to tell the truth we are mighty relieved to do so, thought Garrety. He did not enunciate this to Hassblack, but sensed the sergeant shared that guilty sensation of a weight lifting from their shoulders.

As though to echo his thoughts, Hassblack said, 'Glad the boy wasn't there, sir. Looked a nice little fellow. He'll have to know eventually, though. I suppose his grandmother will send for him from the school.'

'I expect so. We'll have to get a man down to Deal, to check up there. That was a good morning's work you did down at Waterloo, Hassblack. But tell me, what made you think it might be a railway token?'

Hassblack hesitated. If he told the truth the inspector would know he was blabbing at home about what went on at the station – and old Thorneycroft, Garrety's predecessor, had been a devil for pulling you up over every little thing. Might even have got the sack for something like that.

This new man was different. Hassblack took a chance. 'It was my lady-friend, sir. I happened to mention to her we had something might help us trace the poor soul in the river, only we didn't know what it was, just something a woman took good care of. I told her what it were like. And she said right enough she thought it were a railway pass. She cleans the ladies' waiting-rooms at Waterloo, you see, and sometimes they loses the things there.'

Garrety only laughed. 'Seems to me everyone in Lower Marsh is connected with Waterloo!' But without her help, would they have ever identified Perdita Harston? And Garrety's thoughts returned to Mrs Harston Senior, a chilly old creature indeed, even judged by English standards.

31

I SEE THE LORD MAYOR HAS OPENED A FUND FOR ARMY widows and orphans.

Not wives and children: widows and orphans.

Well, what do you expect from this damned war?

So clear, now, in my memory. Don't be weak now, don't pity her, I say to myself. She's still alive, I suppose, in that house where I grew up.

Sometimes you go on hearing them. No ghosts – of course, I don't mean that, stupid fantasies about phantasmagoria and all that foolish paraphernalia of conjuring tricks. No, not through some fat medium in an armchair pulling muslin out of her mouth and squawking away in the voices of the 'dear departed'. I mean just here, within the skull, privately.

Because I could not bear to contemplate it. The betrayal, I mean. How my mother betrayed me.

I don't feel guilty about the animals – in fact, not at all. Look at what so-called scientists do to them in laboratories. There is a surgeon who roasts stray dogs alive in his laboratory to find out the effects of heat on flesh and blood, or so he claims, and he walks respected through the London streets in his top hat, this king of torturers. For it is in the glorious cause of advancing human knowledge – that's what he claims. So I, too, can claim that what I did was in the name of science.

So I was sorry for the creatures, but I had to do it. Oh yes, I do have feelings.

We burned the Boer farms, that was policy, official policy. 'Scorched earth'. After we had stripped the homesteads of supplies, looted wagons, stoves, mattresses, we killed every creature we couldn't carry away.

But did we have to do what our soldiers did in the sheep-pens? They threw in dynamite, instead of expending a bullet on each animal. I can still hear those sounds, those weak cries, the bleating of the lambs left alive beside their dying mothers when the pens were filled with mangled animals. These sounds are outrages upon the world, they begin to turn one mad.

And then came the turn of the men themselves to suffer, lying wounded with only a blanket on the ground – no stretchers, no mattresses, no nurses. No room to step between them, so thick they lay on the ground.

'Don't think we can do much more, sir.'

That was the voice of the orderly.

That night I knelt down – not to pray, no, just to weep.

But there, upon my knees – oh yes, that's how it was. Only my face was pressed into the rough army blanket hanging down over the bed. The stink of paraffin from the lamp. There came the odd barks of command and night-challenges, the howling of a jackal on the veldt.

I was on my knees when she betrayed me.

I knew what was happening, though I could not articulate it even to myself at that age.

He made her his accomplice. He couldn't bear any kind of challenge, of course.

But why did she do it? Ah, that was what I screamed out, 'Why, Mother, why?' I found out later, of course.

She had never before been in the room while he did it. But that day he summoned me, and I saw the slithering whip in his hand, so I knew what was in store. It was just a question of how long he kept me waiting, dreading . . .

I wasn't expecting my mother to come in when he rang the bell, the one he used during surgery to summon the patients. It was evidently a pre-arranged signal. She opened the door and entered; I could sense her fear, too.

'Sit in that chair, if you please.'

I knew that if she obeyed him something terrible would happen. Silently, I willed her not to do so, yet somehow I knew that she would. I did have some simple God, some blue-robed Gentle Jesus of childhood, to pray to in those days. So I prayed inwardly as my mother crossed the room, stood there beside the big dark bookcase and looked down at me.

Her skirts rustled as she slowly settled into the chair.

32

GULLIVER REMOVED HIS APRON AND THREW IT INTO A BASKET. 'Butchery, Garrety, that's my trade! Let's go and have a chop!'

Though they had worked together for six months, they had never associated off-duty before. Back in Ireland, the first thing people usually did was go to the pub and have a stout; the unspoken assumption was that if you were going to work together, you needed to know what the other man was about. A few drinks – well, it just oiled the machinery, so to speak. Made the wheels go round and round. But the English didn't seem to operate on this principle, so at Gulliver's invitation Garrety felt some particular stage of probation had been passed.

The Hog's Head provided a quiet corner, good ale and a roaring fire. Seated at a table, they awaited their lunch with a fair degree of comfort. A smell of roast filled the air.

'I'll do the formalities later – send you the report on the second woman. I understand she was found by the young civil servant,' said Gulliver. 'But the essence of it is this: the first woman, who came out of the river at Bly's Wharf, had had an abortion.'

'We think we may know who she is. Her doctor is on his way down for formal identification.'

'I see. Well, it was a professional dilatation and curettage. That's to say, a surgical implement was inserted into the cervix, causing the foetus to be expelled. Then the womb itself was curetted – scraped out – so as to ensure there was no tissue left to become infected. The usual thing in amateur abortions is that, even if the cervical insertion is accurately performed – and of course it's usually not – women jab away with knitting-needles, enema syringes, and so on.'

'Yes, but this was not of that kind at all?'

'No. As I was saying, the scraping operation needs training and experience. Otherwise there's a very high chance of sepsis.'

'And then there's the administration of chloroform, which points to someone with medical training.'

'Yes, but my point is about the second woman pulled from the river. Come to the morgue with me after lunch. There are one or two things I want to show you.'

A waiter approached, napkin over one arm.

'You can't afford a sensitive stomach in my job,' said the pathologist, with satisfaction in his voice. 'Old Bill Vaughan had to give it up, you know. Couldn't eat a thing after a day's dissection.' He unfolded his napkin and laid it over his lap.

At his work, Gulliver always had an air of gravity, but here, in different surroundings, an impish expression seemed almost to alter his features, so that he shed his years and the muscles of the jaw relaxed. 'Ah, here's our lunch!' he said with pleasure.

*

An hour or so later, Garrety followed Gulliver into the morgue as the clopping of the cab-horse's hoofs died away.

They entered a side room, where glass slides and a microscope were set out on a table.

'They don't give me more than this wretched cupboard – how can I carry out any real scientific work! The point is this, I've taken some tissue samples from the body at Bly's Wharf – let's give the poor woman a name, call her Mrs Harston, on the assumption she'll be identified as such. Under the microscope, the sections confirm that she didn't die of drowning.'

'And this was different?'

'Yes, it was slightly abnormal, but that was probably accounted for by some loss of blood after the abortion. However, it was nothing like what one would expect after death by immersion. Anyway, come on, there's more.'

He pushed open the door into the next room.

Beneath a sheet lay the remains scooped from Greet's Jetty. Garrety deliberately forced himself not to gasp as he looked down. He had seen many of the drowned, yet for him they never lost their shocking pathos.

'The propeller lacerated the scalp and damaged the thorax – broke several ribs. This is the second body we found, but this lady went in the water earlier than poor Perdita Harston. She's been subject to much more decomposition, in spite of the winter temperatures – you can see the dark bronze tints, greenish in places. I'd say she's been in the water for three to four weeks. Look at this.'

A ghostly conjuring trick appeared to be happening, as if long, wrinkled grey gloves were sliding off the dead hands as the pathologist lifted them up. 'The skin becomes detached at this stage. Just slips off. Shuffling off the mortal coil, eh?

Dead man's gloves, they call it down on the wharfs. But something else had happened to this lady – I'll call her that, for the sake of decency. *Nil nisi bonum*, and so forth.'

'Meaning?'

Gulliver laughed. 'You're an honest man, Inspector! "Never speak ill of the dead." Have you not heard of it?'

'A good saying, sir, but not exactly helpful in our trade.'

Gulliver lifted a jar from a row arranged on a shelf above the drain in the corner. He handed it to Garrety, who took it and held it up to the light.

'It's her uterus,' said Gulliver.

The inspector felt the smooth, cold glass beneath his hands, looked at the liquid contents slowly swinging with the movement, and at the rounded greyish object floating inside, like a swollen fruit, cut open. Quite small, smaller than his two hands cupped together would encompass. The womb, the centre of life. He felt sick to his stomach – no, to his heart. Was this what that part of Aline looked like, the hidden and secret inside of her? Or would look like, one day, perhaps.

'She's had a hysterotomy, Inspector.'

'Sorry, sir. What happened to her?'

'An abortion usually performed in the more advanced stages of pregnancy, probably the fourth month in this case. You could call it an early Caesarean. Instead of performing the operation through the vagina, as was done with Perdita Harston, an incision is made over the uterus, which is opened up and the foetus – in fact, the whole foetal sac – is removed.'

Garrety was forcing his mind to function. 'But that must surely have meant a professional operation?'

'Yes, certainly. A rubber wrap had been fastened round her thighs and tied in place with twine. I had to remove it

before I took out the pelvic organs.'

'Good God above! Why should they have done that?'

'A rubber wrap is the kind of sheet that's used in gynaecological operations. It's put underneath a patient – to collect
any blood or discharges, you understand. And there was a
good reason why it was used here – as well as the abortion.'

'So why would they . . . ?'

'Her thighs, Inspector. They're covered in the same marks
as the other woman's, though it's not easy to tell. The
propeller that cut this woman free did quite a bit of damage –
lacerated the scalp, as well. That's why her head looks such a
mess. But these cuts would have bled quite a bit, if she was
still alive when they were inflicted. And from subsidiary
bruising around them, I'd say she was. The rubber was probably to stop blood leaking out as she was being carried from
the place where she was killed. Anyway, it was still largely in
place, so it had protected some of the tissues from the worst
of the river mud. The mud hastens decay.'

'But did the abortion kill her?'

'No. She died in the same way as the other victim. She too
had been stabbed, very neatly, in the heart. A *coup de grâce*, I
would say. But from the same hand that killed Perdita
Harston.'

33

ANOTHER BALCONY OVERLOOKING THE RIVER: BUT THIS TIME the old man is peering over the water like a sailor staring towards the horizon, shielding his narrowed eyes. Finally, he concedes victory to the damp and cold, and gets up to retire indoors, where he rubs his hands for a few minutes to warm them. Then he sits down at the desk and begins to write, chafing his fingers from time to time, for, warm though the room may be, his bones are chilled by what has gone before.

'My darling . . . In the early hours of the morning there was an extraordinary yellow fog . . .'

How to tell her? The heavy sulphurous tint that met his eyes at dawn, umber shading to a palest orange, almost the colour of spring aconites, where the faint aureole of the sun rose in the east. The taste, the feel, of the fog palpable on his lips and mouth when he stepped out into the air, pulling a cloak around him. In the room behind, the wet canvases, laboured and streaked with oily ochres and sienna, with flaming reds and oxide yellows, glistened in the electric light that held its own against the London morning. Each succeeding effect of nature filtered through the chemical haze lasted only a few minutes, so that he despaired, for the first time in his working life. This deep and violent palette of London was so far removed from the gentle lilac hazes that he pulled over the canvas with such skill, the veils of soft diffuse colours to which his hand and eye had become accustomed in France. How to paint the moment itself, the mystery of the fleeting instant of light before it changed and slipped away for ever, the endless succession of colours that were borne away on the tide of time?

He rubbed his eyelids with his hand and then worriedly desisted, fearful now of the effort of seeing, of peering through the mist and the fog at these dim outlines on the river.

He was still thinking about the problems of painting under an English sky, sipping at coffee after a waiter had brought him a silver pot and blue china cup, when the door opened and Michel burst in.

'Papa, what a morning! You haven't been outside on the balcony?'

'How else can I see it all? But you are the one whose health worries us. You will be ill again, and after your sister's death . . . Look at what your mother has suffered already!'

'My mother? My mother is dead. Perhaps it's time we acknowledged that!'

'But, Michel, Alice and I love all of you as if you were our own!'

Michel advanced into the room and the old man saw a tall figure behind that of his son. He checked himself. 'Oh, Mr Craston. I am so sorry to have troubled you with our family affairs. I did not realize you were accompanying my son!'

'Not at all, Monsieur Monet, and I assure you I have already tried to persuade him that we should not take a jaunt in the motor this morning. He has been coughing already, on the way here.'

'But, Oliver, we promised to take Rosa for a spin! Father, it's all arranged!'

'Michel, I forbid it! You are not to go for a drive today. You will worry us into the grave!'

Michel said nothing for a moment, but looked strangely cold and angry. Then he said, very intently, 'You forbid it, Papa?'

'Yes! For your own good. Your illness last year was quite enough anxiety ... Mr Craston, please stay! I know you English are very reticent, but please, add your voice to mine!'

'I say, Michel, your father is quite right—'

Old M. Monet broke in. 'In any case, Michel, I would like you to give me some help here this morning, if you do not mind. I need to get some canvases ready for despatch to Paris.'

'But what about Rosa, Papa – and her mother? They are expecting me to collect them in the motor, outside Liberty's. I can't let them down.'

Anger was very evidently replacing anxiety in the breast of the elder Monet, and he came forward to rebuke his son.

Oliver saw an opportunity to assist. He stepped in. 'I can go to meet the ladies and explain the situation—'

The painter seized the possibility. 'Yes, Mr Craston, that would be most kind! And why don't we all have lunch here, in the grill-room? Please ask them to be my guests – I'm sure they'll understand. Michel's lungs should not be exposed to the climate on a morning like this.'

Michel put up no more resistance. The father's word was

law, it appeared. And Oliver relished the fact that, although his own means were modest, having a salary of his own gave him an independence from paternal intervention that Michel was unable to enjoy. He felt a certain satisfaction a few minutes later as he walked briskly towards Bond Street on his way to meet the Darby ladies. This feeling was not merely that of having achieved a successful manoeuvre: he had seen a flash of feeling on Michel's face at the mention of Rosa's name that revealed a situation to him, something he had previously only suspected.

He knew little about sexual jealousy, other than the feelings of rejection he had experienced in the tribal rituals and favouritism of schoolboy life. But that he, Oliver, might be considered a threat by a young male such as Michel was both fearful and pleasurable. Oliver did not desire conflict, yet he felt waves of shivering anticipation wash through him.

34

ARRIVING AT LIBERTY'S AS THE CLOCK STRUCK MIDDAY, OLIVER walked in past the uniformed commissionaire and found himself in the wood-panelled vestibule of the shop, where Michel had arranged to meet the Darbys. He was nervous of the introduction to Rosa's mother, who had presumably been elsewhere in the house on the day when he and Michel had called for Rosa. Oliver remembered how he had been shocked by the painting of the naked woman that hung in the hall. He wondered again what sort of a family would have that picture on public display, and what on earth his own mother would have thought about Mrs Darby.

Beginning now to regret the precipitate arrangement to meet the Darby women, feeling an alarming yet pleasurable sexual arousal, he paced nervously round, examining some silk cravats in minute detail so that the tiny golden suns and frisky cockerels of the ornate design seemed burned into his brain. He would always associate them with that moment when Rosa descended the stairs from an upper floor of the shop, calling out his name as she did so.

'Oliver! How lovely to see you!'

Behind her down the stairs came a woman dressed in a positively theatrical way, with a great plumed hat in dusky pink and a coat of some thick silvery fur that reached right down to her tiny feet. Her face was plump, the flesh cushioning out over the bones, yet pleasing like a cherub's or a pretty cat's, and her skin was an exquisite flush of rosy red. Only as Oliver got closer could he see the patterns of veins within the delicate rubicund penumbra of rouge. As he bent over her hand, a delicious fragrance, perhaps of orchids, wafted over him.

Rosa followed her. Oliver was captivated again by the brilliance of her light-coloured eyes, the grace of her movements. The skin of her throat was soft, rose-flushed, above a white lace collar, and he longed to press his lips to it.

'Mr Craston! I'm so delighted to meet you. Rosa has been telling me all about you – a friend of the Monet family, I believe!'

He was surprised. Mrs Darby had a rich Irish accent, and, not only that, an openness of affection entirely un-English – at least, in the English circles known to him. It struck him that Rosa had not mentioned that her mother was from Ireland.

Oliver's explanations were received with cries of understanding. 'Of course! You know, he has been lodging with us, Mr Craston, and I must tell you in all confidence I have been concerned about his health. His father is quite right! Shall we take a cab to the Savoy? Lunch is a most delightful plan, in any case. How kind of dear Monsieur Monet.'

'I'll get the commissionaire to call us a cab.'

'Thank you, Mr Craston, and perhaps you young things would wait for just a few minutes more. I have a little business matter to see to, you know! I must settle my account here.'

The commissionaire was despatched, Mrs Darby swept towards the offices of Messrs Liberty, and Rosa and Oliver were left standing in the lobby. It was a quiet morning in the shop and only the occasional well-heeled customer bustled past.

Rosa laughed gently at him as he stood speechless. 'My mother is a somewhat powerful personality, I'm afraid!'

'Oh, no, not at all – very charming!' But a question did not stop spinning around in his head. Was this the woman in the painting he had seen at Rosa's? It could be: the face had that same rosy, uptilted appearance, and the artist had caught something about the way in which she held her head and the warmth that radiated from her. 'Does your mother have, er, any connection with the art world?'

'Oh, yes, she lived in Paris in her youth. She knew a lot of artists.'

He had the uncomfortable feeling that Rosa had read his mind, but then Mrs Darby came back. In a few minutes they were tucked into the hansom and on their way to the Savoy.

As they approached the hotel, Rosa saw a flower-seller in the Strand and called to the cabby to stop.

'Mother, I'll just get out and buy some of those. Look – early spring flowers! Daffodils and narcissi! They'll be perfect for the Monets' rooms – it seems so gloomy in there some-times. I'll join you in the foyer!'

In an instant she was gone, while Oliver was still protesting that he would get the flowers, but then Mrs Darby said, 'No, please, be my escort,' and he was left feeling that this would be the more gentlemanly course.

The cab-horse trotted into the forecourt of the Savoy and the commissionaire advanced to open the door and assist the occupants as they entered the foyer. Waiting there a few minutes for Rosa, Mrs Darby patted Oliver's arm and whispered confidentially: 'You know, Mr Craston, there are some rather strange things about the Monet family.'

Oliver looked down at her in some embarrassment; he was not accustomed to people who confided so quickly to strangers about their feelings. She seemed to have a complete trust in him, and was running on with her theme.

'Michel, for example, is not the son of the current Madame Monet.'

'Yes, I had some intimation of that.'

'No, indeed he's not!' Mrs Darby continued. 'His mother died shortly after he was born, when Alice, the present wife, was living in the same house. She nursed Camille, Michel's mother. It causes a certain amount of – how shall we say? – *tension* between them, though of course the family don't like to admit it out loud. They're a huge clan, you know. Michel always has to refer to Alice as his mother – and, to be fair, she brought up all the children together. But frankly, Mr Craston, I feel there is a *tendresse* there – I mean, between my daughter and Michel Monet – and I would not like that relationship to become deeper.'

'But surely . . .' This was difficult to put into words. How to tell a woman that her own moral standards did not appear to be of the highest. He tried again. 'Surely, you are accustomed to . . . to artistic circles?'

'Yes, of course, but the Monet family is one big group – a clan, you might say. Alice Monet is a very strong-minded woman. She quite dominates the children's lives, almost as if they were still in the nursery. And, more than that, Mr Craston, when she was here at the end of last year—'

'Madame Monet was in London?'

'Yes, last December. They both stayed at the Savoy. But he had to come alone this time, because one of Alice's daughters has died – one of her children by her first husband. So sad. But what I was going to say, Mr Craston, is that I didn't feel entirely comfortable about visiting their suite last year. She most certainly made me feel unwelcome. I think poor Alice – sure, she's really at heart a desperately respectable woman, if you know what I mean! She madly wants to be conventional! Poor Ernest was a shopkeeper – on a rather grand scale, it's true – till he lost everything, poor lamb. Well, obviously, I'm not very good at being conventional!'

Oliver was spared from trying to reply to this, because at that moment Rosa, with her arms full of flowers, came rushing into the foyer. 'Aren't they wonderful, Mama, Oliver? Like white stars! Do let's go up and put them in water.'

35

THAT EVENING, OLIVER ARRANGED A ROW OF BOOKS ON A
shelf: three matching green-bound volumes of Shakespeare's
plays, some collected volumes of *The Strand Magazine*, a
long, solid, brown and gilt set of Dickens given him by an
aunt. He added a few year-books and directories which he
might occasionally consult for his work. He would buy some
more decent books, he decided, stepping back to look at the
effect. The gold lettering on the bindings looked very well.
He had nailed up some neat strips of embossed green leather
which hung over the shelves and protected the tops of the
books from dust.

The process of settling in was quite similar to arranging his
rooms at Oxford, except that there chaps were really sometimes rather wilder in their tastes – and if any damage was
done, one could always settle up with the College.

He doubted whether it would be easy to settle up with Mrs
Rattern, landlady of the set of rooms he had taken in
Stamford Street, just south of Waterloo Bridge. Better ask her

permission before he had an extra picture-rail put up for his small collection of prints, which he had yet to unpack.

The landlady was rather harsh-faced, but the location of the rooms, so close to the river, the newness of the building and its fittings – the bathroom and bachelor kitchen, its gas fires and electric light – these had attracted him and the rent was very reasonable. That was because it was on the south side of the Thames, of course. But this was a perfectly respectable street, though it ran towards the network of alleyways around Waterloo station, beyond which lay Lambeth and its marshy slums.

But, no matter where his new abode was, he had the wonderful sensation of freedom, from the loving, badgering domesticity of his sisters, from his mother's Ladies' Circles. And from his father's remote coldness, felt throughout the Barnes residence as a damp, chilly cellar is always felt even on the topmost storeys, striking upwards through the house. He missed Maggie, remembering the sadness in her round brown eyes as she said goodbye. The trap had arrived to carry his boxes and small bags of books and odd utensils, the golf clubs he had bought at Oxford, though he had never played since, the new kettle and a very awkward cake-stand his mother had wished on him.

'Don't worry, Mags! I'll be back every weekend.'

'Yes, but you're going for good, aren't you, Oliver?'

It had to be admitted. He was, and the sensation of relief was still fresh and delightful as he stood before his mantel-piece and plunged the top of a tobacco humidifier up and down. He didn't smoke, of course, but it was a very hand-some object with a crest on the side and had not been at all expensive, not really, in the little antiques shop in York Place.

Oliver crossed the room and sat down on the edge of the

couch in his new surroundings. Though he leaned back on the cushions in an effort to relax, a guilt about Mags tugged at him. Still, he would do his best. His mother's expectations were social, and though he recognized that Maggie was really never going to fulfil Mrs Craston's hopes, Oliver thought that at least their mother might be won over more if her eldest daughter tried to comply with what the world wanted from a young woman. Mrs Craston had asked him several times to invite some young people to Barnes; by 'people' she meant young men, of course, suitable for her daughters. Very well. He would invite John Madigan.

For a brief moment he allowed himself to imagine inviting Michel and Rosa to that tall grey house in Barnes. What would his mother make of his new friends? He saw them through her eyes for a moment, birds of paradise in her grey wilderness of good taste.

He dismissed the thought with that instinctive sense of fitness which is the basis of diplomacy.

36

THE OLD MAN ROSE BEFORE IT WAS LIGHT. AT SEVEN O'CLOCK
in the morning he was like a stubborn peasant who gets up by
lamplight, and makes his way out to plough his land at day-
break. He had those same square shoulders, that same
determination of purpose, as he looked over the Thames.
There was a faint brownish-yellow glow coming from the east
where the sun was rising, and on the painting before the artist
this sulphur-ridden dawn was seen reflected in the view of the
river, in the shades of ochre and tobacco, of bracken, sienna
and russet, that had been dashed across the canvas.

There was just enough light to make out the roofs of houses
and factories across the water – streaked with white already,
for snow was falling. The ragged flakes whirled down to the
darkness of the water and melted into it; closer in, they
vanished on the surface of the embankment into a thick
compact of glimmering grey slush.

Snow fell on his shoulders and arms. The electric chandelier
within the room behind gleamed on the wet oils of a dozen

more canvases, set up on easels across the room, like a chain of windows, framing the view from the balcony at all times of the morning, over a spectrum that ranged from dark mauves and damsons to a pale gluey-grey luminosity.

The light rose in the sky, becoming more and more yellow till an incandescent brackish fog was swirling along the river, made dense by the snow, which formed a curtain that rendered invisible the opposite bank of the river. As the light changed, the old man switched from canvas to canvas, trying to capture the lurid shades that dawn was chasing across the palette of the London sky. The wind howled along the river and into the room. His utter concentration did not flicker.

Later that day, he took up his pen. The young people had left and he was alone once more with his thoughts – it was too dark for work now. 'It was a fearful struggle today,' he wrote to his wife. 'You lose sight of things, and in the beginning you always think you'll find an effect again and be able to finish the picture, but later it never seems possible. I already have something like sixty-five canvases covered with paint, and I'll be needing more.'

He sat back. The electric light had been on all day, so little natural daylight had penetrated through the clouds.

'How can I do it?' He laid down the pen and flexed the fingers of his hands. How could he go on with this, which was taxing his physical stamina to the utmost, making his eyes ache as he strained them from dawn to dusk into the London fog? For the first time in his life, his stout body was failing him. In this city he was beginning to feel his sixty years in this world. Age was descending on his joints, stiffening the fine musculature of the arm that directed the brush-strokes, right down to the tips of his fingers. He stroked the wood of the desk beneath the paper on which his letter lay and could no longer feel its delicate whorls and striations. Once his finger-tips had been as sensitive as spiders, skimming across textures, stroking along silk without catching. He remembered the slippery glides of satin and of flesh, and wondered if those sensations were now denied him for ever.

He could not write to Alice of this. Naturally not: she was too sad, too distressed by the death of Suzanne. The loss of a child was a terrible thing, even when that child herself was a mature woman.

He had always treated Suzanne as his own daughter. But now, perched in his eyrie over the Thames, he knew that flesh and blood had obscure and powerful claims that were not based on duty, nor derived even from love. Michel was his child, no matter what, whether he, his father, liked the way he lived, whether he spent his money foolishly on motor cars or girls. Somewhere within Michel's pale face, when his father peered into it wonderingly as he had found himself doing of late, could be seen an inheritance from his mother.

If this had been a man who thought in long and complex language, he might have reflected on the irony of Alice in France mourning her dead child, the daughter of her first husband, while he sat in London thinking of his first wife, Camille, lost to him long ago.

But he was direct, a man of reactions and feelings, of rules even, by which his life was guided. Impossible to speak of these London pictures to Alice, overwhelmed as she was by her own grief. But it was not only that. For the first time, he realized he could not write about them because Alice, too, was covered with that thick padding and armour of age which had overtaken her youth.

As he looked outside again, a storm was breaking. Lightning flashed over the river. Somewhere within the

thunderous air outside there flickered images: the white creases and folds of the linen of the dying, the cold penumbra of light that had surrounded Camille, a bony angel, as she lay dying, and as he had painted her.

The old man got up and walked across the darkening room.

There was a photograph of Alice on a side table. It was a recent one, and he recognized, sadly, that her dear face, under her thick, springing knot of white hair, had aged suddenly, prematurely. Alice's dress seemed a heavy mass of black crape, trimmed with a thin frill of white muslin at the neck, her body below it thickened and heavy. He picked up the photograph and tried to look at her face intently, but somehow it dissolved beneath his gaze.

London was playing its tricks. The dwindling light from outside seemed to vanish into the hangings of the room, swallowed up in the dense velvet curtains and long expanse of Venetian red carpet. As he set the photograph back, in the heavy mirror over the mantelpiece he thought he saw another face forming in thick and rapid strokes, almost as if a brush were dashing it on the gleaming surface: great eyes and strong black brows set over them. A trick of the light merely, distorted reflections of shadows given back by mercury and glass. But it resembled someone. He peered into the mirror again, as if into a lake, and saw beneath the glaucous surface the features of his first wife, Camille, dead these twenty years.

He had painted Camille on her deathbed, and now her face rose between him and the thought of Alice: Camille as she had been on that last day of her life, her head propped against the heaped-up pillows and surrounded in a spectral half-light by the bluish-white linen of the sick-bed.

He wanted to tell Michel about the bond between himself and Alice, to explain about their lives in Vétheuil, that winter when his wife was sick. 'We are strong, Alice and I,' he wanted to say. 'We were always alike in that. But Ernest had a nervous collapse when he went bankrupt – and Alice had to pick up the pieces, with five children to feed.' Ernest had tried, though, it had to be said. He had become a private tutor, miserable, bullied. Eventually, he had seen how it was between Monet and Alice, and left Vétheuil. Reduced to making wretched little business deals, the former owner of a Paris department store scraped a living as best he could. The sense of failure, that's what must have stuck in his throat, thought the old man. But we have this in common, Alice and I, we are survivors – as her husband and my wife were not. We can go down into the depths and come up and live.

Guilt pierced him suddenly as he remembered that winter: he had found himself detached from all emotion, absorbed in studying Camille as the inexorable processes overtook her, watching as the colours of her skin changed: blue, yellow, grey. In his rendering of her flesh he had painted death itself.

He crossed abruptly to his desk, on which lay the un-completed letter to Alice. What to tell her? The truth? 'I can't stay any longer in this dark country. It is destroying me – my mind is leaving you, Alice, and turning back to those sad old matters.' No, he could not write these things down. He laid the pen back on the desk.

37

JONATHAN CASTLETON REGARDED HIS VISITOR WITH SOME distaste.

Old cat! he thought. I suppose it's pure jealousy. The girl has got herself a young man, or maybe even an old one, and she's lighted out of here – and I don't blame her!

'I shouldn't mind so much, Mr Castleton,' the housekeeper was saying. 'After all, girls are so silly nowadays there's no training them up anyway, only I did think Ruby was a bit more sensible than most. Well, she needn't come here begging for her job back, I can tell you! There's only the most respectable of staff allowed in this hotel. Any suspicion that she's up to a bit of hanky-panky, and she's out of the door. But what else is one to think, I ask you?'

Oh, it was Ruby went missing. Pity, thought Castleton. I might have had a bit of that myself before she went chasing off. Aloud, he said, 'Did she have any followers?'

'Certainly not! I should never have allowed it!'

Castleton was a patient man in many ways. He forbore to

make the obvious comment; there was little point in provoking the woman. The thing was to get rid of her as fast as possible so that he could return to his modest plan of attending the operetta that evening. He was supposed to be off duty, after all. 'So she hasn't been seen since Tuesday night?'

'No, and Bella Jones says her bed hasn't been slept in. And I had all those rooms to turn out. Really, it was wicked of the girl!'

'What about her things?'

'Her things? Oh, goodness me, she had nothing to speak of. Just a few bits of rubbish and some old clothes. They don't have anything, those girls, Mr Castleton – so they're not going to care if they leave it behind. I suppose she's off with some young fellow, so why should she worry about taking her rags with her? I dare say she thinks he'll buy her some finery!'

'Well, I can't really see what I can do about it. She's free to go, of course, if she doesn't want the wages owing. She hasn't stolen anything, has she?'

The woman leaned nearer, her pointed nose sniffing the air a foot or two from Castleton's face. 'That's the point, Mr Castleton! We don't know, do we? We can't search the whole hotel – but something might come to light! There was some linen missing on the sixth floor, you know – Ruby reported it to me! Oh, she might be a cunning one – reporting missing sheets and towels and selling them off herself!'

'But all the hotel linen is marked, surely?'

Snort. 'You think where she comes from they care about things like that?' The housekeeper pursued her theme. 'Or, who knows, it might be something much worse. One of the guests might be missing something and not know it!'

Castleton was silent, considering. On the one hand, the

housekeeper was a vindictive creature, probably motivated by spite in her determination to find the girl guilty of something. In all probability, Ruby had simply met some young man and gone off with him. There were plenty of soldiers hanging round waiting for their transits to South Africa, crowding round the 'Dilly every night, and they were notorious for promising a girl the whole world just so they could get inside her drawers.

On the other hand, there was a possibility the errant chambermaid had stolen something, and very shortly some Lady FeatherArse would run shrieking from her suite because her sodding great Kimberley diamond ring had vanished from her jewel-case, or her ta-ra-ra was missing from her dressing-table. And that would require the extensive attentions of J. Castleton, hotel detective, whose duty it was to see that the aristocracy were unmolested by the lower orders . . . If he just looked into things now, it might well save him a lot of grief later on . . .

The girl had probably just vanished. Still, he had to start somewhere. 'All right, I'll see if I can do anything. Where do her family live?'

The nose twitched. 'Family? Oh, she gave an address when we employed her. In Lambeth. Some hovel, I suppose.'

She took out a little notebook: evidently, she had been preparing for this moment. Castleton took it from her and silently copied down the address.

After she had gone, he contemplated the scene from his room. She's got into trouble, that's the likeliest thing, I suppose, he thought as he gazed at the Thames flowing beside the hotel. It seemed quiet now, even peaceable. 'Covers all sins, the river,' said Castleton to himself.

He himself, like a cat, preferred not to get too close to the water. Going down there, seeing the rubbish that drifted on its surface, the oozing sewers that opened on to its muddy banks – these things, like Ruby, reminded him of something he had spent most of his lifetime trying to escape. When he went to get a coat from his wardrobe, he was uneasy that his route would take him towards the Thames. He reluctantly forced his footsteps in that direction.

38

ALINE GARRETY FELT NERVOUS, BUT STRONGER THAN HER
apprehension was the fear of going through the whole
wretched business again. She had endured it month after
month, year after year, and now she proposed to do something about it.

These were the thoughts that had led to her standing in
front of Mrs Leadbetter's door in Lower Marsh on a shiny
day when London suddenly seemed to have thrown off the
pall of smoke that had covered it for most of the winter, and
a blue sky and scudding clouds were visible above the glittering surface of the river. The bridges – Lambeth, Battersea –
could be seen by anyone looking along the embankments,
gleaming outlines with tiny black blobs hurrying across, and
an occasional train went rushing over at Charing Cross with
plumes of white smoke ascending as it roared over the water.

The young face, now familiar, opened the door. 'Please,
mum, to come in and wait. There's a gentleman here just
now.'

In the house, there was a strange smell, quite clean and
sweet, that seemed to seep into the parlour. Aline put her

hand to her throat. It reminded her obscurely of hospital wards, but the flock wallpaper, the gilt-framed pictures, reassured her, and when the girl returned with a tea-tray she felt at ease.

'Are you warm enough, mum? It's a fine, sunny day, but cold. I'll put some more coals on the fire.'

There was not long to wait. Aline found she was closing her eyes, the warmth of the room making her dozy. There was a gentle murmuring of voices that seemed to be in the next room. At one point, she woke with a start, thinking she had heard a faint cry, but it ceased immediately and she might have dreamed it, or perhaps it had been in the street outside.

Some time later, Mrs Leadbetter appeared. 'Are you comfortable, my dear? Oh, no, don't get up – you look so cosy there! Remember our discussion – and you are in luck!'

Aline was sitting up in her chair. Mrs Leadbetter was beaming down at her. She was wearing a floral dress with a big apron tied securely round her waist, and her sleeves were rolled up. She had a small lace cap on her head: it looked somehow incongruous, as though she had been setting briskly about some domestic task with frills perched on the top of her head.

'Yes – you remember the gentleman – the medical man of whom we spoke? Well, by chance, he is visiting today. In fact, he is in the next room! What do you think of that? Shall I ask him if he can see you now? You need not trouble to call on another occasion then, and it will all be settled as soon as may be! The quicker, the better, with these things, my dear. No time for nervousness!'

Aline was indeed murmuring and stuttering rather, taken by surprise, but felt she could not object. Having come this far, to a place where she never had expected to find herself, she surely must go through with it. I am so feeble – so lacking in determination, she thought.

And so she found herself assenting, and Mrs Leadbetter retreated, to come back a few minutes later with a gentleman in tow.

'I have explained the . . . er . . . the difficulty, my dear,' she said. 'I'll leave you alone now with Dr Bolitho. You'll want to talk privately, no doubt.'

The doctor smiled and sat down opposite Aline. He had a weather-beaten face, but was still not more than thirty: perhaps he had been in a harsh climate. He wore a comfortable jacket of brown tweed, his hair and whiskers were red and his eyes were a clear light brown. A pleasant expression, she thought, but tired-looking. As if confirming this thought, he rubbed his hands over his face. There was a faint smell – not the one she had first smelt in the house, though. She identified the new odour as carbolic, which was reassuring, since it was associated with cleanliness and well-scoured sick-rooms. She noticed that his hands were scrubbed white. That reassured her too.

'Now, my dear lady, I understand you have had some troubling times in relation to your desire to bear a child. Oh, do not fear – I shall not examine you on this occasion. It will be quite sufficient if you tell me about it. All in absolute confidence, of course – you have my word as a medical man. These problems are quite a speciality of mine. There are things that can be done to help you.'

It was all a lot easier than she had thought. He didn't seem to want to know a great deal – in fact, less than they had demanded at St Thomas's. How pleasant it is to be treated this way, she thought, as if I were a lady. He didn't ask her much about her husband – just whether they lived in the area.

He didn't seem to want to know what her husband did for a living, but of course Mrs Leadbetter might already have mentioned . . . Aline recalled she had told Mrs Leadbetter that her husband worked for the railway. Should she perhaps tell this man the truth? But it didn't seem to matter very much, and already the moment had passed.

'Now, I think I can do something for you, my dear lady. We have encountered cases such as yours – and treated them with every success, I assure you. Very often, you know, it is due to some nervous condition that makes the female organ unable quite to accept the introduction of the male effusion. That may well be the case here.'

He even talked about it in a way that made her feel more comfortable, as though it were impersonal, nothing to do with her and Will and their private world.

'Now, what I think we should do is to make an appointment for you to come and see me again, before too long. I have a course of treatment that I'm sure will assist you— Oh, my dear lady, do not weep, I beg you!'

Aline found tears coming to her eyes at the thought that someone could help her conceive at last, but she was smiling also. 'Oh, Dr Bolitho, I can't thank you enough!'

'Nonsense, my dear! The best thanks you can give me will be a happy, bouncing baby!'

He could see her again in a week's time. He had said nothing about a fee, Aline realized as she stepped out into the Lower Marsh, but doubtless that would be rectified by Mrs Leadbetter, who had bustled in at the end of the interview.

'And you will be the godfather, I dare say!' said the woman to him with a knowing smile as he took his leave. She turned to Aline. 'Such a nice gentleman, my love, and wounded, you know, in South Africa.'

39

DR BROOME STEPPED INTO THE MORGUE, SWEEPING OFF HIS glossy blue-black top hat, followed by Hassblack, who had accompanied him from Holland Park.

'This way, sir.'

Garrety and Gulliver were standing near the sheet which was pulled back from the face as Broome drew near. He had a handsome, well-fleshed face, in spite of his sixty-odd years.

He made no delay but went straight to the slab. 'Saw plenty of this sort of thing during my training at St Thomas's.' He peered down at the face and sighed reluctantly. 'Yes. It's Perdita Harston, poor thing. The usual difficulty, I imagine?'

'Did she come to consult you about it?'

'No. She would not have done so: I was the family physician and there was not much feeling between the old lady and young Mrs Harston. But she had had a child already, and the signs would have been unmistakable after a certain point. She must have been in no doubt, but it was the very fact she did not consult me that has made me assume she was with child. For anything else I think she would have consulted me. I attended her for influenza last December, for example.'

Gulliver gestured to the attendant and the sheet was drawn again over what remained of the features of Perdita Harston.

'Dr Broome, the child was taken away.'

'What, aborted?'

'Yes.'

Garrety's unfamiliarity with English life made him surprised when Broome said merely, 'Well, let us not be hypocritical. We impose the strictest penalties on this operation, yet we make it difficult for women to prevent pregnancy and we turn them into social outcasts if they don't have a baby when society deems respectable. My experience in Holland Park, gentlemen, has convinced me that wealthy women are no happier in this respect than their poorer sisters – merely better able to conceal the consequences. But of course she would have been unable to conceal it from old Mrs Harston.'

There was no need to elaborate on that. Garrety recalled his visit to the old lady, and her eyes: rheumy, yet sharp still, even in grief at the recollection of her son's death. They would miss nothing about her daughter-in-law.

Gulliver took up the story. 'Dr Broome, this death is apparently not the result of a botched abortion, nor of suicide.' He gestured to the attendant, who drew the covering back further, exposing the small gaping black mouth of the wound to the heart, over which the flesh had been stitched together after the post-mortem.

Broome bent down in silence for a moment or two and then stood up with an expression of shock. 'What a dreadful thing! Poor woman, how frightful to come to such an end!'

Gulliver sounded formal and impassive as he recited,

'Death was the result of a deep incision that penetrated to the heart and there were in addition many superficial pre-mortem grazes and minor wounds, which appear to be the result of a frenzied attack.'

There was a pause. Garrety added a contribution of his own. 'We are dealing with a very dangerous personality here, I would hazard.'

Broome started. 'Good Lord, so there is something extraordinary in every way here!'

'Do you know, Dr Broome, if there is any medical person she might have consulted instead of yourself – on such a delicate matter?'

'I cannot say I do, Inspector. But I think it unlikely she would have found assistance in the neighbourhood – she would have had to venture further afield.'

'Quite so, sir. And you have no idea as to whom—'

'The father? No, none whatsoever. I saw the older lady quite frequently, but Mrs Perdita was not always there when I called. Very often I was admitted to the house by Ellen. As I said, I saw Mrs Perdita Harston last December, for influenza. I do not recall seeing her since – at least, not more than to exchange pleasantries. I'm afraid you cannot apply to me for her circle of acquaintances.'

'Thank you, Doctor. You've been most helpful.'

'I'll let you know if anything comes to mind. Good day to you. Good day, Gulliver.'

'He's quite an eminent man,' said Gulliver, as they watched Broome stride away. 'Safe family practitioner – that sort of reputation. I wouldn't think there's anything untoward there.'

'Oh, well, we could be making some more inquiries in Holland Park.'

'If you're discreet about it. At least you're well away from the Savoy!' Gulliver was laughing. 'Don't look so astonished – news travels fast, if not along official channels. Yes, there's always an Irish housemaid somewhere in the neighbourhood – they'll surely stop for a gossip and a drop of whiskey. You'd be well in there. Oh, sorry, Garrety. No offence.'

'No, sir.' But he was deeply, obscurely, offended.

The following morning there was more news, an hour or two after he had received Hassblack's report on the criminal excitements of the previous evening. There had been half a dozen street fights, a circus juggler had thwacked a bricklayer over the head with an Indian club, several prostitutes were arrested for plying their trade with more than usual commercial vigour. All of these participants in their various dramas were now safely confined in the cells below, pending their appearance at the magistrates' court.

'And I called round at Holland Park, to the servants' entrance. Got some interesting information. Not straight away, but it came out gradually. Reckon she must have been turning it over in her mind, like.'

'Oh?'

'The housemaid, Ellen Boyce. Seems Mrs Perdita had an admirer. But it was kept very quiet.'

'The old lady objected to the ... friendship?'

'Yes, sir. Reckon she'd have objected to anyone who tried to take her son's place. But she didn't like this Major Burnaby one bit. His family were low people, that's what the maid heard. But he was in Harston's regiment.'

'Is that how she came to meet him?'

'Well, he was brought back after he was wounded at Bloemfontein, and it seems Mrs Perdita started doing a little charity work just then. Comforts for wounded officers. The maid reckons that's when she met him again and they sparked off.'

'Where did she meet him – did the woman say?'

'In the Savoy, sir. He was with the other wounded officers on the top floor.'

'D'you think the maid has talked about it?'

'I doubt it, sir. She's a sensible woman, I think.'

'Get round and tell her to keep quiet about this Major Burnaby, will you, Hassblack? No gossiping with the other servants in Holland Park – nothing of the kind! There's a dangerous customer out here on the loose.' He laughed, surprising Hassblack. 'Well, I shouldn't have suspected that milk-and-water boy Craston in the first place. No need to follow up in that direction, whatever officialdom says.'

40

THE LIFT-BOY WAS IN ATTENDANCE, RULING HIS TINY mirrored domain with an assurance beyond his years. 'What floor, sir?'

'Sixth.'

They ascended.

The rooms were like expensive antechambers of hell. Rich curtains hung at the windows, glossy side tables bore flower arrangements, cream and gold wall-lights cast a soft glow. Odours of polish and disinfectant mingled in Garrety's nostrils as he walked through, men glancing up at him as he passed, but each man with his own preoccupations. Here and there a desultory little group conversed around a table.

Beyond, Garrety could see through glass doors, were ranged long rows of beds, some empty with covers folded back. Here lay the badly wounded, men whose eyes turned to the door in hope as Garrety approached, avid for a visitor or some temporary distraction, some momentary interruption.

At the far end of the room was a nurse in a long white

uniform, the stiffly starched folds pleated round her head and unbecomingly pulled across her brows. Garrety could not help thinking that the nurse's uniform must make the patients feel worse – she was like a sheeted ghost starting up from her chair.

She walked down the ward towards him. 'Yes? Have you permission to come in here?' Her question was spoken in an important sort of whisper.

Garrety was startled. 'Permission? From whom?'

Her face was red, scrubbed and shiny. 'Doctor Newbold, of course. No-one is allowed in here without his permission.'

Garrety said, 'I'm a policeman.'

'A policeman can cause as much disturbance to the patients as anyone else – if not more,' she said mulishly.

Garrety felt the justice of her words, but he persisted. 'Well, there is an officer here I should like to have a word with. A Major Burnaby.'

They had moved back through the glass doors into the sitting-room area. It was a cold day, but outside on the balconies were invalid chairs and reclining couches, and a few muffled figures lay upon them, attempting to get a little fresh air into their lungs.

'Nurse, can we not have more coal on the fire?' The grate was huge and the chimney-piece elaborately wrought, but only a tiny fire burned within it, near which the speaker, a thin middle-aged man, was huddled.

'A cool temperature is more healthful, Captain Rogers!'

Rogers sighed. His eyebrows rose in a rueful expression as his eyes met Garrety's. 'You're a hard woman, Sister Lawrence. London's so damned cold after the Cape. Can't get used to it.'

'Well, needs must, Captain!' Sister Lawrence turned briskly

back to Garrety. 'Now, Doctor Newbold is not here at present and I cannot give you any information about our patients without his permission. He is most particular on that point, er, Sergeant—'

'Inspector. The name is Garrety, madam.' She would be a tough nut to crack, but Garrety knew that indirection was often the best way round such an obstacle. 'How long have you been working here, Sister? I am sure the ward is most admirably managed!'

She began, almost imperceptibly at first, to soften. 'A mere two weeks. Yes, I had a good deal to do here at first.'

'You are in charge here – during the doctor's absence, of course?'

'Yes – I have several nurses under me, to do the rough work. In these surroundings, of course, they must have a lady in charge. I fear that many nurses would not satisfy on that point. I have some very aristocratic gentlemen under my care.' Sister Lawrence gave a snobbish little sniff, her nose in the air.

'Yes, that is very true, I'm sure.'

Captain Rogers uttered a sound that was possibly a snort, covering it up hastily with a pocket-handkerchief held before his face. 'He's kissed the Blarney Stone all right, Sister!' he said.

'Captain Rogers, that is quite enough!'

'You see how strictly she treats us!'

But the little exchange had clearly improved Sister Lawrence's mood. She volunteered the information that Dr Newbold was expected to return that evening. 'He usually looks in on the patients before he retires. You could request the information then.'

Garrety gave it another try. 'Sister, this relates to a very important case. If you could give me the information now, it might save very valuable time.'

She considered, her lower lip pushed out.

'After all, I don't want to waste the doctor's time unnecessarily,' he added.

That did the trick. 'Oh, very well. Come into the office.'

This was a room furnished with wooden boxes of files and records, and a desk and chair. The patients' records were held on lined cards in the boxes.

'I'm afraid the person in charge of nursing records before I came was very careless ... What name did you say? Bradbury?'

'Burnaby.'

'Brain, Burdell ... Ah, yes. There was a Major Burnaby. He was discharged a week ago.'

'Did he rejoin his regiment?'

'No. His injuries had been quite severe, apparently. He was sent home to convalesce.'

'Do you have an address?' Come on, woman! He barely managed to keep his thoughts to himself as she slowly turned the card over between her fingers.

She had found a pencil on the desk and was writing an address down on a sheet of paper. 'His family are quite *ordinary* people, I would think. They live in Dulwich.'

Garrety supposed that most of her patients had their abodes in far-flung manors and castles, and in St James's or Park Lane. 'Number 57, Basserton Crescent, Dulwich' seemed very modest. Murmuring soothingly in response to Sister Lawrence's comments on the lowliness of this address, he took his leave. She returned to the ward, leaving him to find his own way out. As he passed the young captain, he bent and added some coals to the fire from the coal-bucket beside the grate. The fire was giving out a fierce heat now. But Captain Rogers was asleep.

41

CRASTON SENIOR HAD BEEN SITTING AT A PILE OF BOOKS, methodically opening them, locating pages, inserting slips of paper, and closing them again to form another pile, which towered up at his other elbow.

The light of Barnes filtered through the window. There was the occasional distant rumble of a trolley-bus, but on the whole this was a den secure and safe from the distractions of the world.

'Father, please listen to me!' Oliver was exasperated. This was the old difficulty he had always known with his parent. His father was by no means a cruel man – he had never struck his children and rarely raised his voice – but he ignored them and their wishes absolutely. He was not amenable to discussion or persuasion of any kind. There was a particular phrase which the children dreaded: 'Your father's made up his mind.'

Mrs Craston was often deputed to convey her spouse's decisions. The offspring grew up knowing those words were invincible. If he had made up his mind they were not to go to the zoo, then they would not go. If Oliver begged and pleaded not to be sent back to school, but Father had made up his mind, then back he would go. And these commands extended to his wife: the cousins of whom Mr Craston disapproved would not be allowed to stay, no matter how much his wife would have liked their company.

And now Maggie would not, on any account, be allowed to attend the university. His mind was made up. Women simply had brains that were inferior, that was all, and there was no point in educating them beyond their capacity.

Sometimes Oliver thought that if Maggie had wanted to study something else, something considered less demanding, more appropriate – literature, maybe – it might have been possible. Their mother might have approved of that.

But both parents were shocked and horrified when she revealed her ambition, though Menander Craston had observed his daughter looking through his old physiology books. This gave him few qualms, however: he had simply assumed that she could not understand them and would leave off, though he reprimanded her anyway since there were some very undesirable illustrations in certain sections.

For once, she did not fly up, and appeared content to lay the textbooks aside. Maggie's father was not party to the latest edition of *Gray's Anatomy*, purchased by Oliver at Maggie's behest and secretly studied in her room.

'Medicine! Not a subject for a lady, not at all!' gasped their mother.

Oliver, trying to reach a compromise that would allow his sister to realize at least something of her ambition, suggested nursing. In this, as peacemakers often do, he succeeded only in upsetting both sides.

'Certainly not!' said their mother. 'Nurses are simply not of our class, dear.'

'What about Florence Nightingale?' protested Oliver feebly.

'Miss Nightingale was an exception – and, besides, look what happened to her! She has lain on a sofa for the rest of her life and never got married!' said their mother, illogically but clearly expecting her daughter to understand the implications.

'In any case, I don't want to train as a nurse,' said Maggie. 'I don't want second-best. I want to do some real science. Also,' she added, 'nurses have no power. Doctors do.'

But she had no money to pay the fees and nowhere else to live but her father's house.

Oliver, however, was trying his wings. After he had taken the great step of moving out into his own quarters, he felt he had reached a position where he could have some say in family affairs, and offer Maggie more than moral support and smuggled copies of medical books. After he had set up in Stamford Street, he went again to his father, having found himself possessed of a new courage and resolution, perhaps derived from his independent living quarters, perhaps from the standing that his position at the Foreign Office had conferred on him.

'Father, have you seen how Maggie looks lately?'

'She looks very well.' Menander Craston glanced up with grey eyes magnified by his spectacles.

'You must see she is unhappy! She still has the same ambition – don't you think you might let her try it? After all, she is twenty-five years old now, and she has her heart set on this business of medical studies. Why not let her try?'

'I know medical students – they are a most disgraceful bunch – no young woman would be able to keep her reputation if she mixes with them! To say nothing of the things she must look at – the sights she must see! She will have to study such subjects as gynaecology – and other matters.'

Oliver knew perfectly well what was meant. 'But what on earth can be wrong with women studying gynaecology? And, if she gets married, there are . . . certain things she will have to know.'

'All in the proper time. Besides, I don't want any daughter of mine making a fool of herself! She is not at all quick enough for the examinations; it would be a great mistake for her to enter them.'

'Father, I assure you – you must know for yourself, Maggie has a very good brain—' Oliver stopped. He had seen a look in his father's face and understood what it was that really made him prevent his clever daughter from realizing her ambitions.

Not that she might fail, but that she might succeed.

His father had been the great mind of the family for so long, looked up to, deferred to. And a mere woman of the household might rival his achievements. Oliver remembered Maggie saying that doctors had power. They did indeed: the power of life and death. Even Mr Craston would have to acknowledge that if his daughter succeeded in her ambitions.

'Besides, think of the fees! I cannot possibly afford it!'

Oliver made another move into adulthood, so long delayed by the sheltered life of Barnes and Oxford. He took the plunge. 'I can, Father. And I shall.'

'What did you say?' The older Craston dropped his pen on to the table with a small clatter.

'I can. I don't earn much, but enough to pay Maggie's fees – and I'm sure some time she'll be able to repay me. I'll take the risk anyway.'

His father was standing up now, in a towering rage. Oliver had never seen him so angry.

'She lives in my house, beneath my roof! And I forbid it!'

Oliver was shaking, but he felt a kind of anger surging up in him, too. 'She can come and live beneath my roof! She can be my housekeeper. A lot of sisters keep house for their brothers. She's old enough to decide!'

Seeming unable to speak, through a kind of amazed anger, his father leaned his fists on the table and put his weight on them, so that the table shook. His teeth were clenched and Oliver noticed with the clarity of shock that his father had an old man's mouth, the teeth grinding mechanically together, the lips slack and grey.

'Get out! Get out!'

Oliver left the room but he knew that somehow between the two generations the tables had been turned. He walked out of the house and found Maggie in the garden, parting the grass to search for some snowdrops.

'Mags. You can do it if you want.'

She stood up. Her eyes opened wide, but it was as if she did not dare to guess at what he meant. 'How on earth . . . ? He would surely not even have me in the house!'

'You can apply to study medicine. I will pay the fees if he won't.' The look of delight on her face convinced him how right he had been to stand up to their father.

'How on earth . . ?'

'I told him you could come and live with me – as my house-keeper, if you wanted – while you studied. That would be perfectly proper and you are old enough to make up your own mind. Of course, I only thought of it while I was in there with him, or I'd have asked what you thought of it first.'

She burst out into peals of laughter that seemed to go winging out of the garden and all the way down to the river beyond.

Oliver had faced his father down.

42

BURNABY'S OUTSTRETCHED LEGS SEEMED TO OCCUPY HALF
the parlour of the schoolmaster's house in Dulwich. A crutch
was propped beside his chair.

Across the road came the high-pitched shouting of boys'
voices.

'A rugby match, Sergeant. One of my amusements is to
watch the little devils from the parlour window. Anyway, I get
out as much as I can now – need the fresh air and the exercise.
It's all so green out there. Used to be a rower, y'know.'

Hassblack noticed the broad athlete's shoulders and the
red jacket lying over a chair nearby. He had seen the crews
sculling up and down the Thames near Hammersmith.
He could see this man on the river, his powerful arms at
the oars.

'Yes, we took a hammering at Ladysmith. Damned glad
to be back in the parental home – and to have all my limbs
intact, I can tell you. God, it's hard now to imagine what
it was like . . . Sorry, Sergeant, what d'you want to ask me?'

'It's about a lady, sir.'

Burnaby stretched out and laughed, in an easy, good-tempered way, the casual laugh of a man who has often been chaffed on the subject of his attractiveness to women. 'Ah, well, best not let my mother or my sisters hear you, I dare say! What have I been up to? Something more interesting than my South African service, I'm sure!'

Hassblack sensed there was something superficial about the captain's reaction. But he had encountered this before, in soldiers like his brother-in-law, recently returned from Africa. It was as if they had come back from another world, not just another country, as though what they were seeing in England was not real at all. Blank stares, no interest in things that mattered a lot back home. Hassblack didn't understand it, but he recognized it.

'I believe it may be quite a serious matter, sir.'

Burnaby's face changed at that.

'A Mrs Harston. Mrs Perdita Harston, sir.'

'I know her, yes. Through army circles, of course.'

'Yes, but Mrs Harston . . . I'm sorry, sir.'

'What is it?' Burnaby was sitting up now.

'Mrs Harston is dead.'

The man's face, weather-beaten and ruddy, was suddenly drained of blood, so that the South African suntan looked like a mask, with two bright blue eyes staring out of it, round with shock.

'Oh God, no!'

Burnaby's right hand was gripping the arm of his chair; and Hassblack was conscious of how much power there still was in this big lean body.

Then Burnaby muttered under his breath like a curse: 'He botched it, the bastard! I'll kill him—'

'Who? Who "botched it"?'

The man leant back. Something seemed at last to have got through the mask of joking indifference with which he greeted the stuffy little world of Dulwich and policemen. There was genuine pain in his voice now. 'I thought we could trust him.'

'Who, sir?'

'I knew of him in Bloemfontein – I'd been transferred from the hospital in Ladysmith and the men there thought highly of him. There were plenty of butchers out there masquerading as doctors, but he was reckoned a good 'un. And he'd been wounded himself, so when I was sent to the Savoy for recuperation I thought it was all right to tell him about Perry – Mrs Harston. He was a medico – I thought he might know somebody. He said he'd take care of it.'

Burnaby seemed willing to pour this out, but Hassblack was uncertain whether he would get any solid information.

'Who, sir? What is his name?'

Burnaby had seemed almost to have fancied himself alone. He was staring out of the window at the schoolboys on the rugger ground across the road.

'Newbold. Carter Newbold.' He added bitterly, '*Doctor* Carter Newbold,' and was silent for a moment. 'Anyway, it was settled. He said he'd . . . see about it himself – and there would be . . . no problem about money. I wrote to Perry, from the Savoy. Didn't dare say very much, in case that old harpy of a mother-in-law sneaked a look at it. Told her that a medical man would get in touch with her and she could trust him. God damn it! I'll kill him myself!'

There was a rap on the door and a startled maid appeared. 'Beg pardon, sir – is there anything wrong?'

Burnaby seemed to get control over himself, though

Hassblack could see his nails digging into the chair. 'No. Thank you, Ellis – it's all right. Just a . . . an attack of pain in my arm. The sergeant can help me.'

The maid disappeared.

'There's no-one else in the house. My father is teaching at the school.'

'And Mrs Burnaby?'

'My mother died some years ago, Sergeant. I don't know much about women, if the truth be known – though I never seemed to have any problems getting acquainted with one when the fancy took me. Only, Perry Harston – she was more than a fancy. Would have married her, if the circumstances had been different, but she wouldn't have . . .'

'Yes, sir?' But Hassblack thought he knew what was coming.

'There wouldn't be any . . . It was all tied up, you see, for the boy.'

Hassblack felt an urge to push him into saying it. The whole thing spoke for itself: a young man, not clever, but gifted with athleticism and a charm that must be devastating to women. The gold-tabbed jacket told its own story: a smart regiment, perhaps through some good connections, yet his father was a schoolmaster. A career to make, the expense of the mess bills, of wining and dining the right people – and damn all at home to pay for it. Yes, when this man married he would do so with an eye to the main chance. Some pretty young creature who would hang on an officer's arm – and definitely not Perdita Harston, burdened with a son, and easily separated from her allowance by a jealous mother-in-law.

'Yes, sir. What was tied up, exactly?'

'The . . . money. The trust fund for her and the boy.'

It was out at last. The bravado had evaporated.

Burnaby had some show of grace left. 'Poor boy – the poor lad! Only a child. Still, no good my calling round there, I don't suppose. The old bitch won't let me see him. But will you go after him, Sergeant? That bloody man Newbold, I mean.'

'Yes, sir. But it's not certain, not by any means certain, that she died as a result of . . .'

'You mean it wasn't the baby? The abortion? Then how did she . . . ?'

'It may have been connected with it. But her body was found in the river.'

Burnaby closed his eyes as if trying to shut out a vision that had suddenly shot before his mind. 'She took her own life? I would never have thought it, Sergeant. Never. She adored that boy of hers.'

'No. Sir, we're not at all sure how she came to be in the water. But it's pretty certain she didn't drown – she had had the . . . the operation already. So she had no reason to jump in the river, did she? No-one need have known she was expecting.'

The handsome eyes stared in puzzlement.

43

AS OLIVER WALKED ALONG THE STRAND, HE WAS AWARE OF A commotion at the entrance to Villiers Street, at the side of Charing Cross Station. A cordon of police blocked it off from the Strand at one end and the Embankment at the other.

As a group of men poured suddenly out of the side entrance to Charing Cross and up the street, the police ranks closed up and Oliver, trying to get along the pavement, found himself jostled by a burly sergeant.

'Sorry, sir.'

'What's going on?'

The sergeant eyed Oliver carefully, and observed a respectable young gentleman in pin-stripe jacket and trousers. 'It's them Irish, sir. Them Home Rulers.'

Beyond the solid blue-clad arms that barred the way to the side street, Oliver could see placards held above the knot of the crowd. 'HOME RULE NOW!' 'REMEMBER WOLF TONE!'

'They'll never get Home Rule, sir, will they, now Mr Gladstone's gone?'

'No, I suppose not. Are you going to block off the Embankment too?'

'No, we're not going to let them get that far. We're going to break it up right away. We've got orders to pick up any trouble-makers.'

Oliver was preoccupied with getting along. He didn't want to be delayed on his way to the Savoy. When the policeman moved aside to let him pass, he dashed off along the Strand, fearing he might be late.

But all was well, and shortly afterwards he was sitting round the dining-table in the suite at the Savoy, managing quite well to conceal his awe at the huge dining-room, the chandeliers and the hothouse flowers, and found a moment to look across at Rosa and smile. Menus were passed around, the merits of *timbales de filets de sole* and *coquilles au vin blanc* discussed.

Looking puzzled, he caught Rosa's eye and blushed, but she seemed to have divined his difficulty and mouthed across the table, so that he understood 'scallops' perfectly clearly, and was even delighted at the conspiratorial moment his ignorance had created. Nobody noticed, for the others – Mrs Darby, the Monets father and son – were engaged in a lively discussion in French about gardens and the problems of drainage. He was able to follow it quite well, though he was not particularly interested in the topic of their conversation.

'A water-garden is a lovely thing, yes.' Mrs Darby had a charming voice, long, lazy, graceful vowels. Some time, Oliver thought, he would ask Rosa more about her family history. 'But the difficulties, dear Monsieur Monet – the ground can become so easily waterlogged, can it not? And then there are all the problems of insects in hot weather – I think it is not very healthful, if the water stagnates. Of course, in England, mosquitoes are not much of a hazard, but they're a danger in hot weather, even in County Cork, where there is boggy ground.'

The head waiter stood at M. Monet's side, awaiting the rest of the order, and Oliver followed Michel in choosing *noisettes de mouton à la chasseur* to follow the scallops.

'Escoffier has left, unfortunately – he's with César Ritz in Paris – but I believe Thouraud was chef to the Duc de la Rochefoucauld.'

Rosa smiled back at Oliver as Michel spoke. Oliver took courage.

After dinner, the group went up to M. Monet's sitting-room, where cigars, coffee and liqueurs were brought. Mrs Darby and M. Monet reverted to the universal middle-aged topic of gardening, telling the young people to amuse themselves. Oliver, his head flown with a brandy whose age he could not possibly have guessed and one dusty bottle of which probably cost more than Craston Senior's entire annual expenditure on wine, somehow found a moment to look at Rosa and gesture across towards the long windows. She nodded, with a charming smile that again gave him that moment of private delight, and the two young people pushed back their chairs. Michel rose too and followed them. It was not possible to make any objection.

'Rosa darling, take your wrap if you go out on to the balcony,' called Mrs Darby.

'Very well, Mother.'

Oliver found that though he had longed to be alone with Rosa, the truth was that he was afraid of what lay beneath his feelings. Sometimes he wanted to go back and talk to Maggie, to confide in her, but he feared that he could not – that she would never understand what had happened to him. Their worlds were already becoming too different. His sister could never have felt this, he thought, this physical longing and need, sensations that became interfused with what he thought of as a kind of worship. He would do anything for Rosa – and yet he wanted her, too, wanted her mouth and her body. Perhaps Maggie is more like Father in this, he thought, unable to remember his sister ever displaying loves or passions, even the innocent ones of childhood.

He couldn't have Rosa to himself, which was what he desired. Very well, he wanted to leave, to walk out into the cold air. Perhaps the meal, the surroundings, were too rich for him.

He went back to his host, began to take his leave, and rather to his surprise Mrs Darby stood up.

'Mr Craston, I think we should all make a move! It is much later than I thought! Was that not eleven o'clock chiming?'

'Indeed it was.'

'Then I think we should all go down and take a hansom – they will be waiting still, I am sure.'

Yes, thought Oliver, there would be a rank of freezing horses, and chilled men hunched over them, stretching round the courtyard of the Savoy, their breath steaming in the freezing night air, waiting till all hours lest some wealthy occupant should emerge from the cocooned and gilded fug with a fancy to travel. And he was simultaneously aware that he would never have had such a thought in the past, before the jetty, before the shack.

He was jolted from his thoughts by Mrs Darby's protestations.

'Oh no! Michel dear, it is far too cold for me to go spinning across London in your motor car! But, Rosa, if you wish to go, I shall not object – provided you wrap up well. Michel may drive you home. Only do not oblige me to share your discomforts!'

To add to Oliver's discontent, he now felt obliged to accompany Mrs Darby and, out of politeness, escort her home. He longed to be near Rosa and yet did not relish travelling in Michel's motor car, an uncomfortable third.

But surely Mrs Darby would not let her daughter travel alone? His own mother would never have let her daughters go about unchaperoned at night with a young man in any form of transport, let alone a motor, in which they could go where they pleased, and quite unaccompanied if they desired.

Mrs Darby, however, consented to permit it. Oliver caught a strange look on her face, almost calculating, as she made an effusive good-night. It occurred to him that though he had always thought of artists as bohemian and raffish, Claude Monet was really a very famous figure in French society. He recollected his mother returning from an evening party at which some literary lion had been the guest of honour. 'And Fanny Dunlop was positively *throwing* Amy at him! Poor man!' It was the kind of thing he had never noticed for himself.

'Come, Mr Craston. Let us two sensible creatures go down and ask the doorman to call a cab. I am sure we will cause no gossip – you need not fear anyone will remark on your being seen with an old lady like me!'

He stammered appropriate demurrals and helped Mrs Darby into her down-lined cloak, feeling the thick pile of the velvet under his hands as he held it out and helped her to pull it round her shoulders.

Michel, who had been looking quite weary, was suddenly full of life. 'Why, yes, I'll ask the hotel garage to bring the motor round. You must not wait outside, Rosa. Stay here till it is brought.'

He crossed to the telephone and made some arrangements with the porter downstairs. Rosa looked across at Oliver and shrugged her shoulders. The old man rose from the table and said simply, 'And I must get up at dawn. I never miss it – the light is so extraordinary.'

Thus encouraged on their way, Oliver and Mrs Darby found themselves in the lift. Remembering the flowers that Rosa had brought, Oliver suddenly saw an opportunity.

'Have you ever been to the gardens at Kew, Mrs Darby? Would you allow me to escort you – you and Rosa? Of course, it is rather cold for walking outside, but the hothouses will be open.'

Mrs Darby smiled in a sideways, cat-like way. 'Mr Craston, that would be delightful. I am sure we will be free next Sunday, if that would be convenient.'

Hastily, the young man agreed that it would be perfectly so, adding that he would arrange for a cab to take the ladies to the gardens. He had no doubts about Rosa. In Oliver's world, young ladies' social engagements were decided by their mothers.

He sensed that he had been unable to keep a great smile from appearing on his face, for Mrs Darby was almost laughing at him as she said, 'Michel is a perfectly charming young man. Don't you find so? You young men are good judges of one another, I fancy.'

Oliver was about to muster a reply, though he had no particular desire to sing Michel's praises, and still less to take what seemed to be a hint to include Michel in their party, when the lift stopped at the next floor down and a man got in. He was dressed in respectable tweeds, trailing a curious odour.

'Evening, Doctor,' said the lift-boy. The newcomer nodded.

Mrs Darby looked at him curiously, with an eye for interesting strangers. He didn't look like the usual run of Savoy guests – his clothes were workaday. His eyes were quick, observant, darting almost.

At the ground floor, the three passengers got out. In the lobby of the hotel was a comfortable-looking couch beside a banked-up fire. There was no-one behind the night desk.

'Do wait inside, Mrs Darby,' said Oliver. 'I'll just go and ask the commissionaire to call the hansom.'

'Thank you, dear boy.' Mrs Darby sank on to the couch. 'Do you know, I feel just a little faint. I expect the fresh air will do me good.'

The night air was so cold it hit Oliver like a physical blow, but, as he had surmised, there was a row of carriages, the jingling sound of champing bits, ready waiting for passengers. The commissionaire was stamping up and down, talking to a driver.

Just as Oliver was about to speak to him, there was a roaring sound and Michel's motor car came sweeping round into the courtyard. It had been brought round by a chauffeur, who called out to Oliver, thinking it was he who had summoned the car. Oliver went over and explained. 'I'll get them to call young Monsieur Monet. They'll be down in a few minutes.'

'Thank you kindly, sir.'

Oliver retreated into the foyer and found that Mrs Darby was no longer alone. She was still on the couch where he had left her, but she had been joined by the man in tweeds who had travelled down with them in the lift, a small weather-beaten man, who was leaning over her very intently and feeling her wrist.

'Oh, my dear Oliver! This is Doctor . . . Newbold – Doctor Newbold, is it? I'm so sorry, I'm not good at names. The doctor saw me here and thought I needed . . .'

'I thought the lady needed some assistance.' The man had remarkably bright eyes, wet-looking, watery. He seemed anxious to leave, now that Oliver had appeared on the scene. 'I thought I should offer ... Your pulse is a trifle irregular, madam. I do recommend you to consult your physician without delay.' Bowing hastily like a jerky marionette, Dr Newbold made off through the doors into the outside world.

'Odd little man,' said Mrs Darby. 'But he was trying to help.'

Oliver felt a vague sense of apprehension, though he could not say exactly what had generated it. The doctor's eyes, perhaps, that seemed to have fixed so brightly on Mrs Darby. Or the finger-nails on the hand that had held Mrs Darby's plump wrist: they were rather unacceptably long for a man, and odd for a doctor. Medical men usually had their nails cut very short, surely. Brisk scrubbed hands with close-clipped finger-nails were the custom.

The clerk had returned to the reception desk.

'Did you see that gentleman?'

'Yes, sir. It's Dr Newbold. He looks after the wounded officers. A pleasant gentleman, sir.'

Ah, well, there was plainly nothing odd. A physician had seen a lady who perhaps required his professional attention and had kindly stopped to offer it. That was all.

Oliver damped down the feeling of unease that persisted like the faint, sharp smell that hung in the air.

Mrs Darby commented as Oliver was signalling to the cab. 'He gave me something – I think it was sal volatile – to put on my handkerchief,' she said, and laughed. 'I hope it doesn't ruin it – it's Liberty silk!'

44

OLIVER FOUND THE THREE DAYS THAT MUST ELAPSE BEFORE the visit to Kew passed with painful slowness. His hopes were briefly aroused in the interlude by an unexpected message from Michel asking if he could join the Monets for dinner at the Café Royal, but his excited expectation that Rosa might be there was not to be fulfilled.

The restaurant seemed suddenly full of army uniforms. Michel said casually as Oliver joined the Monet table, where a small and sharp-eyed stranger was seated, 'The ladies can't be with us this evening – we are just a masculine party! Allow me to present Monsieur Clemenceau. I'm afraid there may be a lot of discussion of French politics. I do hope it's not too tedious for you.' And then he whispered, so that the elders could not overhear, 'Frankly, I need the company of someone of my own age! I'm so grateful to you for accepting the invitation at such short notice!'

Oliver, conscious of his instructions from Sir Howard, made mental notes of the conversation, but much of the talk was about art, which did not square with his understanding of what might interest his superiors. When they did touch on politics, it was prompted by M. Monet looking at the sea of military serge and braid around them. 'All volunteers for South Africa, I suppose! Poor devils, London is full of them.'

The mingled pity and contempt in his voice startled Oliver.

'Mr Craston, I must tell you the truth as I see it,' continued the painter. 'These young men are going in all probability to disaster – but it's fashionable to enlist: they are wined and dined like heroes already. They have no notion of what awaits them.'

Clemenceau looked across the table at Oliver. 'Perhaps we should not speak of this war. Mr Craston will feel embarrassed, no doubt.'

Oliver stammered a little to indicate suitably patriotic dissent with his host, but he secretly felt an exhilaration. He had heard the lone voice in the crowd.

Michel intervened to change the subject. 'Papa, would you object if Oliver and I left you and Monsieur Clemenceau to talk? We still have time to take in a show, I think. Would that be to your liking, Oliver?'

'Oh, well, yes – that is, if you will excuse us . . .'

There was a place under Hungerford Arches on the Embankment where a raucous sound of voices spilled out into the frosty night.

'A music-hall?'

'Don't sound so shocked! You wouldn't come, last time.'

'But does your father—?'

'Does he know? Yes, he does. In fact, he loves the music-hall himself. Though perhaps isn't aware of the place I have in mind. Alice is as jealous as a cat.'

Inside, there was a thick fug of cigar-smoke and flaring

gaslight, a bluish haze that hung in between the audience and a stage draped with gold and crimson. The crowd seemed mostly drunk, red-faced. A woman near Oliver, dressed neatly in black with a small flower-trimmed bonnet perched on top of her head, fumbled in a bag and produced a bottle of gin.

Michel seemed perfectly at his ease. 'Ah, what luck – Florrie is singing tonight! I adore Florrie!'

They had to wait a while, however, while a conjuror and then a young soubrette with a pretty face entertained them, enduring occasional catcalls. Oliver looked sideways at his companion, who was laughing with the crowd.

Suddenly there was a rustle of anticipation in the audience and a roll of drums. A sulphurous yellow circle of light shone upon the stage.

'Here she comes!' whispered Michel, and an extraordinary figure strode on, a woman whose hourglass body was contained in male evening dress. She was wielding a silver-topped cane. Brunette locks hung down beneath a top hat, and her mouth was a slash of scarlet rouge. She twirled in the centre of the stage, showing the prominent swell of her hips and buttocks beneath the tight black cloth.

'Hold your hand out, you naughty boy!' she sang in an immensely powerful voice and the crowd roared the line back at her.

The big gyrating body, the cane as it thrashed through the air, were riveting. The woman was in total command of this unruly, drunken audience. After the first song, which everyone evidently knew, she made some remarks about 'our brave heroes in Africa' and led them in patriotic songs. They all stood and bawled them out, and Oliver felt impelled to rise to his feet along with the rest. He was glad that Michel stood up at his side: this was no time for dissent.

After 'God Save the Queen' had been sung several times, they got up to leave.

'There are some pretty women in here – and they look quite clean, too.' Michel said it so casually that Oliver thought at first he had misheard.

He saw a group of women, young, well groomed, wearing dresses of white and pink. 'Are they . . . are they really?'

Michel was still in great good humour, laughing as he said, 'Oh, yes, my friend, my good English friend, I assure you they are.'

One of the girls had turned round, eyeing the two young men as if she knew what was under discussion, and Oliver felt a tidal wave of embarrassment. 'I think I should call a cab.'

He marched out alone into the icy air.

45

IT WAS A CLEAR MORNING, FOR WHICH OLIVER GAVE THANKS, as the cab bowled them upriver towards Kew on Sunday, Rosa and Mrs Darby with a rug across their knees.

'It's a beautiful morning!' exclaimed Mrs Darby, but Rosa rubbed her gloved hands together and did not reply. 'Did you not bring your muff?' asked her mother. 'Do have mine – I'm not cold!' She held out her hands to show them her fingers, pink and glowing.

'So kind of you to invite us, Mr Craston,' she said. 'It's not easy for a widow and a fatherless daughter, without a gentleman to attend them, when they want to see something of the world. We don't like sitting in the parlour, I assure you – no, we were never bred to that!'

Rosa seemed to be in better spirits as they entered the Gardens and drove towards the greenhouses, which glittered frostily amid white-fringed lawns and rimed tree branches. Oliver having settled the cab and the entrance fee, they passed through the sets of doors into the steamy heat of the first conservatory. Palm trees rose above them, and the warm dampness invaded their throats and lungs. Beneath the palms were small plants, some ordinary-looking but with exotic labels in Latin and in ordinary English: pineapple, tamarind, *Mimosa pudica*. A tunnel led through into the next green-house, and as they passed through Oliver smelt a mushroomy damp odour that he did not like.

'Do you know Kew well, Mr Craston?' enquired Mrs Darby.

Oliver had learned enough to resist the temptation to pretend to knowledge and contented himself by saying, 'My family lives nearby – at Barnes, near the river.'

'How charming!'

In this glasshouse, green tendrils twined up around stakes.'Are those orchid plants?' exclaimed Mrs Darby. 'I do adore orchids!'

'Yes, ma'am, but they won't flower a while yet.' It was a uniformed attendant, who was conducting another small group through the hothouses, two elderly ladies and a small girl, who was exclaiming at the heat. Oliver himself could feel perspiration breaking out, between his shoulder-blades and on his forehead. Looking at Mrs Darby, he could see a soft sheen of sweat on her cheeks. Rosa seemed as cool and fresh as ever. A great wave of nervousness seemed to sweep up from his stomach to his throat.

They moved on, from latticed glass bubble to glass bubble, the winter chill held at bay, heavy scents wafting out as inner doors opened and closed upon dark greenery. The other party was close behind, so they could hear the attendant's ex-planations of the boilers, the degrees needed for the various species. Suddenly there was a tall feathered expanse of thickly growing bamboo, as if they had been transported to the other side of the world, to a land only glimpsed in pictures. It seemed much hotter here. Even Rosa took out a handkerchief and dabbed her forehead. 'We might imagine we were in China!' she exclaimed, and Oliver thought he sensed approval at last.

A path led through the giant thicket, and they made their way along it in single file, Oliver leading, Rosa between him and her mother. Beyond the bamboo house, a tunnel led to a door marked 'Tropical Lily House'.

As they were about to enter, one of the elderly ladies in the other party called out, 'Oh dear, the heat is just too much for me!' causing a flurry along the jungle path they had just traversed. There was a bench in the tunnel, where the temperature was much cooler, and the other party made their way towards it.

Mrs Darby turned back and hurried up to them. 'Do let me help – I believe I have some salts with me.'

Oliver and Rosa were in the lily house, walking round a water tank in the centre, where wide tangles of nymphae lilies spread out over the surface. They were not yet properly in bloom, but there was a blossom just starting to open, a bud with a delicate sheen of mauve-blue on the outside of the petals. A huge papyrus plant feathered above their heads. Drips of water fell into the tank from the roof as the steam condensed on the glass over their heads. The water was dark but clear and they could see down into its depths, where minute red goldfish darted about, to shoot to the surface occasionally and then fall back like tiny comets into the shadows of the plants. The sound of voices drifted from the direction of the tunnel.

'My mother seems to fall into conversation with everyone she meets. It can be a little difficult sometimes.' Rosa looked embarrassed. An awkwardness he had not expected seemed to have overcome her.

'I didn't think you would feel that.'

She looked up, and said, 'For a mother and daughter alone, life is often so insecure. And we rush about, between Paris and London and Dublin. Sometimes I feel that I need . . .'

'Need what?'

He was afraid she wouldn't answer, but she said reluctantly, 'Something solid under my feet. A rock beneath the flow, if that makes sense.'

She looked as if she were about to weep. He had not seen her in this light before, and it was a touch of pity as much as the plans he had formed in his fantasies that propelled Oliver forward to put his arms round her and press his lips down to hers. He could feel the heat of her cheeks. Her lips seemed unbelievably soft, but they were responsive beneath his own and he tightened his arms round her. Her body felt frail and thin.

When he drew back, he was afraid that he had been mistaken about her response, that she would be offended, distressed, perhaps even call out. But she was looking up at him, and her green-blue eyes were slanted by a smile.

'I've never met anyone as beautiful as you!' He was aware that he sounded like a schoolboy, and her gentle smile seemed even more remarkable. She put up a gloved hand and touched his cheek. She was about to say something when they heard footsteps behind them and her mother came to join them beside the lily ponds. He longed to be alone with Rosa, not just to make love to her, he told himself, but to talk to her, to find out what went on inside the head of this enigmatic creature.

Mrs Darby suggested they make their way out of the

extreme heat and he was obliged to escort them from the glasshouse, reluctantly, but consoling himself with the thought that he would see Rosa with the Monets the following evening.

46

AT FIRST, I THOUGHT THE WOMAN IN THE HOTEL WAS JUST THE type I like, a mature creature. But she wasn't entirely right: there has to be some weakness, some desperation. That's the thing – when they are weakened by something, maybe their bodies, maybe a husband or a lover has betrayed them; they are like a creature trailing through the veldt with a broken leg or wing. Something that keeps them out of the herd, a sign to predators that they are vulnerable, already wounded.

It's not just that it's easier to catch them but you can observe them suffering from the injuries already inflicted by someone else. Before you go on to deal with them yourself, of course. I've got a place to do it, now. That Leadbetter woman was ready enough to let a couple of rooms at the back of her house. She couldn't refuse me, because I saw her at Waterloo Station. You could say it was one vulture knowing another. I saw them in Africa, flapping over the bodies.

She was looking for them, too. A red-eyed girl getting off a train, run away, looking round her in desperation for help, and she ready with her doses of ergot for those who were in trouble. Oh, yes, I knew what she was at. We are a partnership, you might say. I have put up a brass plate over her side door. Dr Bolitho, I call myself. Poor Bolitho died at Spion Kop, ministering to the wounded, still under fire. I read his obituary.

But I don't want to trust Leadbetter too far. Don't want to trust anyone too far. I'll get another girl to clean my rooms – that maid of Leadbetter's will run tattling to her mistress, I can see. Damned gossips.

I should have been a woman's doctor, though, because I have a natural tenderness for them, for that soft area of their bodies. I'm very gentle always, taking care to dissipate their embarrassment, to warm the speculum ... My hands slip and probe gently, and I watch their faces for the blush that always comes.

What an irony that I, of all people, should end up doctoring male patients only! I get sick of them, their coarseness, their great stinking bushes, the lack of strangeness, of mystery. Nothing veiled, hidden, as it is with women.

During the long night hours when the wounded men are dreaming, if they're lucky enough to sleep, and crying out about their battlefields, I put in some study. There's no likelihood I'd get a job in a women's hospital – not in London, at any rate, where I'd need testimonials – but I can go into private practice on my own account. And that lady, poor little bird, desperate to fill her nest – now, there's a good subject for a little experimentation. I want to keep her a secret from *him*, if I can, or he'll take over. I struggle to keep him away when I am on the long watches of the night, reading papers, studying diagrams, as the lamps in the ward are turned low and the coals in my fire shift and sink down to ashes with small sighs and crackles.

Her head is filled with some medieval superstitions and she's convinced she's barren. She thought it must be all the woman's fault. I've had a word in her ear and persuaded her that may not be the case. Perhaps, after all, he is to blame. Now, that's a novel idea for her. These women with devout religious upbringings are the victims of their own shame. They will not do what is necessary to conceive and are made to suffer if they are barren . . . It is always the woman's fault, never the man's, no matter what the scientific facts. Nowadays we can see that a man is a different creature under the microscope – in fact, if we are to say in what maleness consists, we know it is not the ability to get up a stiff rod and spurt out fluid. That's no evidence of the capacity to father brats, though often men will shout and threaten when they're told the truth. 'But I can do it!' they cry. 'I've done it to her, Doctor! I've done it to her!'

And he's done it too. He's capable of the act, from what she says, or, rather, what I can prompt her to admit. But that proves nothing.

I have lately had some remission of my malady, and been able to consult the literature on the treatment of infertility. Percy, in 1861, found living sperm in post-coital mucus taken from the woman. Haussmann has shown the sperm are mobile as long as five days after intercourse, lazy, swimming, swinging from side to side as they died within the fluid. But I want her to come here as freshly from the husband as possible. The Americans have done most work on this and they say – the two Sims, father and son – that the seminal fluid lives no longer than twelve hours in the vaginal mucus. I have it in my notes. 'A drop or two of the semen taken from the vagina, or from the cervical canal, soon after coition and placed under the microscope will show the presence of zoosperms in great abundance if the semen is normal and fit for procreation. But if these are wanting, then fecundation is impossible.'

This is the course I will adopt. Chloric ether to be administered beforehand to ensure the patient is relaxed.

I have to control my drinking if I'm to achieve this goal. No more blotting it all out with brandy; no more drunken nights behind the locked door of my study, trying to keep him at bay. I have a purpose in life, at least in the part of it remaining to me, and that is to ensure I continue living by one means or another. In short, that he does not destroy me and write me out of all existence, as if I had never been.

That's what it is, of course, a disease. There are times when I am free of it and so far it has always been confined to attacks when I could not be betrayed. But it is growing in strength and possesses me more frequently than I would have thought possible. I look out of the windows of the Savoy, and whereas others turn their heads this way and that, praising the 'magnificent views', and seeing the river stretching away towards the sea, I think of it only as a means of escape, of oblivion.

Sometimes I have walked along the towpaths at night contemplating the muddy depths. I have stood on Westminster Bridge at an icy midnight, looking at the great tower and hearing the chimes of Big Ben, and known that in a moment I could end it all.

But then he came into my head, that other, and spoke softly so that I moved on from that moment. I know that he wants to save me for his own purposes, so that I am his creature, his instrument. He will not let me vanish beneath the surface of the water until he has accomplished his task. Sometimes I have a sensation of falling through time, that things are tumbling fast towards their conclusion. In a way, it will be a relief. My life seems to have passed in a tiny space between that time and this.

That time? When I was held there in her lap, between her legs, which I could feel through the folds of her dress, could smell, even, as I buried my face there, begging her to stop him, screaming for the pain to stop, believing any second she must save me. Every time, I believed that. How trusting children are!

She didn't save me, of course. I knew she was frightened too. Her hands were trembling, yet they always held me down. As I screamed, she pressed my face deeper and deeper so that I was afraid of being smothered, I couldn't breathe. But she still didn't stop him. When I reached up threshing about with my puny little arms to try to wriggle free, she held my hands down on her lap. Her stomach felt soft and rounded, a plump cushion beneath me.

It was only when my father's arm was tired that he fell still, panting for breath. She let me up from her lap. The first time, I was silenced in astonishment at the next thing she did. My mother, who had never allowed me to enter her room, even when I was tiny, except when she was fully dressed, whom I had never even glimpsed without shoes on her feet and stockinged ankles, lifted up her skirt then and there, and the petticoats underneath it. I saw the rounded swelling of her belly, and below on her thigh a ring of little bluish dents round a red oval, on the white place where her stocking stopped, and beside it a fan of scratches made by my papery little nails into which the blood was rushing.

'He bit me!'

Their voices were very low then.

My father, exhausted: 'He's a monster. An unnatural little monster. And he must be treated as such.'

I thought he would have struck at me again if his arm had not been so tired. But he no longer seemed to notice I was present. I looked at my mother and her eyes had a brightness in them that I can still remember and her lips were curved in a slight smile. There was an odd, harsh smell in the room.

They did it again, of course.

Sometimes they hardly waited till I got out of the room before they turned the key in the lock behind me.

It stopped when I was sent away to school. I was eleven years old then. Looking back, I wonder if they perhaps thought I would tell a master, or maybe the parents of one of the other boys, with whom I occasionally stayed during the holidays. A formal paternal beating would not, of course, raise any eyebrows whatsoever, but certain things about the way my parents did it, what they did together afterwards, for example, might have given too much away.

I've been forced to do it several times now. I had bad luck twice.

Usually, it didn't cause any problems. I gave a few whiffs of chloroform, so they didn't feel anything, just went under as gently as death. It's him then, he comes in as I am performing the surgery . . . the bloody forceps . . . the shining bowl with the cloth over the foetus . . . And – how can I put it? – I lose control. He *leaps* into me, that's it, and knocks me out of the way, and then goes down between her legs . . . all the while her unconscious breathing . . .

Usually, he is satisfied quite quickly and then suddenly I know he has gone, and the room just has the two of us in it again. And she may not have felt very much – or may have been unaware ... They see some blood afterwards, and a few lacerations ... well, they don't really know what to expect anyway. They're innocent creatures, you see. Mostly. So I mop them up, make them use the bidet, and give them some veronal, or laudanum drops. Warn them they'll feel some pain. They expect it. Sometimes they pray, and often they're weeping – you wouldn't believe it, the sobbing. Riddled with guilt, the poor things. And they would never go to the police. There's another advantage to picking respectable women: they need to hide things.

But he has got more and more savage with them, and the last two occasions ... The stranger I met at Waterloo. I never found out her name, but she was quite willing to come back to the hotel for a consultation. After I performed the abortion, I couldn't risk leaving her in the state she was, such a dreadful, bloody, spongy mess he had turned it into. So the best thing, really the only thing, was just to finish her quickly, very swiftly, with one blow straight into the heart.

And Perdita, too, the lost one. So pretty and charming, poor little thing. But he did the same thing to her, though he held back till I'd finished, in that case. Perhaps he pitied her, so he delayed a while. But in the end it was as bad, if not worse. And I had to – what shall I say? – dispatch her.

I saw the newspaper headlines. A police inspector – Garnet or Garret, or some such name – was carrying out investigations. Yes, it was Burnaby's woman, all right. Poor Perdita. They've traced her somehow, though I took care to remove everything from her body that might lead back to me.

They found the first one, too. I weighted her down and got her to the side entrance and ran her to the Embankment on one of the trolleys with silent rubber wheels. Didn't think she'd come up again, but it doesn't really matter.

Perdita's a different case – much greater danger for me, because if the police get on to that fool Burnaby there's a direct link. It was much harder to get her to the water. There was no easy way. I had to wait till the early hours of the morning, when the streets of Lambeth had finally gone quiet, and then have my arm round her and try to 'walk' her to the bridge, holding her up at the same time. Dead weight. It reminded me of the amputations in the surgical tents on the veldt: the heaviness of lifeless human limbs. There was a group of late-night drunks coming along towards us, so I turned down along a wharf towards the water . . . They jeered after . . . I lay down with her and they passed along the riverside.

All I could do was tie a few bricks in her scarf and knot it around her waist. I didn't think it would last long.

I keep going back over it, over the details, over my life. I get feverish, sometimes.

My mother didn't save me, as children should be saved. I recognize now that when I knelt and pressed my body into her skirts, certain physical tendencies were beginning to be aroused within me. And they can't be satisfied. That's why *he* comes. He can complete it, finish it. I have to make way for him.

47

OLIVER CAME INTO THE ROOM AND FLICKED THE LIGHT
switch and could not at first make sense of what he saw. He
began to stutter an apology without thinking, words
trembling and pouring from his mouth, absurdly, as if they
could ease the pain that had gripped him somewhere inside
his chest.

They moved apart.

'I – was just coming back for my scarf.' He said these stupid
childish words miserably, as things that he had hoped for, love
and, yes, friendship itself, shattered and fell away from him
with the sight of Rosa and Michel in the tangle of white
sheets. The harsh light was cruel to their bodies – triangles of
hair, yellow-shadowed naked thighs exposed without pity.

'Oliver . . .' It was Rosa, sitting up with a sheet clutched
across her body, her lips open, staring at him, with almost a
playing expression, but he backed out and stood shuddering
for a few moments, trying to steady himself. He was
desperate to get out, to get away.

Oliver, stepping out of the room, barely knowing where he was going, his mind in a state of flight, his limbs behaving with some trained mechanical response, saw that the windows on to the freezing balcony were wide open, though dusk was falling.

On the balcony itself there was visible the unmistakable outline of an artist's easel with a painting propped on it, protected by a flimsy awning. There was a stream of cold air pouring over the chair and its occupant, and Oliver saw the few first flicks of rain coming down outside and the storm bursting over the river.

He stepped out on to the balcony. The canvas was so strange, so utterly unlike any picture he had ever seen before, or even imagined. It stopped him, thrust itself into his vision, to obliterate everything else.

It seemed covered with a sea of virulent green, reminding him almost of a bottle of absinthe, and then again it was different, something in nature, bright but with a kind of softness, like the feathers of a parrot. The sky above it and the water itself, the factory chimneys in the distance: all shared that watery light that drew you down into its depths. Slamming across the centre of the canvas were the dark arches of Waterloo Bridge. Oliver recognized it, though it looked so strange, with tiny blossoms of white and lilac light strung along it.

He looked back into the room, fearing he had woken the old man, and then drew closer to the picture, staring at the canvas and then out at the river, and he saw it, saw that extraordinary emerald light reflected in the water and the stormy sky.

Michel Monet, dressed and tying a cravat, appeared in the room. He looked towards the windows, saw Oliver struggling with the canvas against the growing gale, and went out on to the balcony.

The rain was soaking them now, threatening the painting.

Without a word, Michel and Oliver lifted the canvas, carried it indoors and propped it up against the wall with the others. The two young men enacted this in absolute silence, as if it were a ritual moment that compelled a truce, by some unspoken mutual consent, not looking each other in the face. The picture was a live thing between them, the viridian surface glistening in the dim light.

Oliver shut the balcony doors behind him. He crossed the room and saw the green picture glowing almost with phosphorescent light as he walked out. He did not, could not, speak.

The old man dozed on his bed, dreaming of a garden emerging from winter to spring. Care must be taken to ensure that it grew as he had planned. Before he left Giverny, he had given instructions for sowing poppies and sweet-peas in pots for planting out later, the poppies against a western wall where they would get the light of the dying sun and return it, intensified to scarlet.

It would soon be March and the chrysanthemum buds should have been forced – and they should have put up supports for climbers, the roses and the clematis. A feeling of anxiety disturbed his dreamlike visions – had these things been done? That was the trouble with a garden: you must not miss doing things at the right season, or there would be another whole year's delay. Then there were the dahlias and the agrimony, white and yellow, which he had ordered in January. And the iris. Iris and the blue lilies for the water-garden, for that live and vibrant water, as teeming below the surface as the Thames was dead, the pool as rich as butter in the sunshine, the stalks and fish and insects moving and growing, snapping out into the clear air above. There, instead of these harsh girders of iron and steel that drove remorselessly across the river that flowed outside his window in London, would be that gentle curve of the Japanese bridge, and beneath its reflection the life of spring starting to move beneath the surface of the water. Within the mists above the Thames suffering and betrayal seemed to be swirling in this filthy air. His consciousness of the wounded men who lay above him, fear for the young Englishman who loved Rosa, horror of the body found rolling in the water of the river – these were draining his strength.

He would tell Michel that he wanted to go home. Back to Giverny.

48

HASSBLACK RUBBED HIS HANDS IN FRONT OF THE FIRE glowing in the black grate. Outside, the rain lashed on their window. There was only the one, high up and difficult to close because the casement didn't fit properly and the land-lady wouldn't replace the swollen wood, but the Hassblacks didn't mind the cosy fug that filled the room off Joanna Street, behind the Spanish Patriot.

Cora came in with a plate of sardines, then returned with a folding wire grill, pulling out the handle.

'Here, see to the sardines, will you, Harry? I got them from the fish-stall in the Marsh. I'll just make the tea and cut the bread and butter.'

He crouched there contentedly, holding out the fish to the coals, where the skin sizzled and blistered in the heat. 'Got any horseradish?' he asked.

Cora called back, 'Got some today. From the market.' She came in again, carrying a tray. 'She's a caution!'

'Who?'

'Old Lolo. The woman on the stall. I knew you'd fancy it.'

'Lolo?'

'She says it's short for Loretta. Reckon she was on the game – must have been a good-looking woman in her youth. She sells all kinds of stuff – mustard and spices, and so on. Some funny-looking things.'

Cora was pouring the tea out into big cups, the steam mingling with smoke from the fire that blew back into the room when a gust of wind occasionally twisted down the chimney. Hassblack enjoyed the warm, sooty smell, though it irritated Cora because sometimes a black layer of dust was deposited in the room. She hated cleaning and dust-ing – she got quite enough of that at the station.

'I've heard a few rumours about her, though.'

'Oh?'

Cora sprinkled some vinegar on to her fish and settled her feet on a little stool. 'Don't know if I should tell you.'

He was aware there were things she kept from him, that were better for him not to know, because he was a policeman and he might feel obliged to do something about them. It was part of the way they lived together, that was all. He knew it wasn't always easy for a policeman's family. He never pressed her.

'Women's things, that's all,' she went on.

'Pass the horseradish.'

'I was saying downstairs young Evvie looked a bit – that way, you know. Sick in the mornings.'

'What's that got to do with old Lolo?'

'Evvie's mother said maybe old Lolo could help her out. 'Course, it's better than gin or knitting-needles.'

Hassblack winced. How could women be so down-to-earth?

'Well, I don't want to hear anything about it.' He didn't want to get involved in all this back-street business – not unless someone died or something. It was against the law, but what did they expect women to do? It took two to make one, after all. Probably nothing much to it anyway – just a handful of herbs and a hot bath.

'But then ... there's something new going on. There's a doctor involved. Anyway, that's what she says.'

He began to take an interest. A bunch of women helping one another out was one thing. But a doctor involved – well, that was quite another. A proper professional man ... taking money for abortions ... Sounded like police business.

'Who ... What do you mean?'

She was eating a piece of bread and butter sprinkled with salt. 'Evvie's mother, she said old Lolo would be out of business soon. Said there was a doctor doing it. He's got a surgery and all, but that's just a front.'

Hassblack piled the remains of his sardines on the side of his plate. 'Whereabouts?'

'He's rented rooms from that Mrs Leadbetter. She's a funny sort anyway ...' She had sensed his interest, for she said anxiously, 'Look, you won't say anything, will you? There's quite a few women round here she's helped ... I wish I hadn't said anything now.' She came over and sat on the arm of his chair and he put a hand on her waist, feeling the warm stuff of the dress and her body underneath it. 'Promise me you won't say anything about it.' She really was anxious.

'I promise,' he said, and began to pull the lacing at the back of her dress.

She pushed his hand away. 'No, listen, Harry! I am serious!'

'I promise,' he said again.

49

'AH, COME IN, INSPECTOR. WE SPOKE ON THE TELEPHONE THIS morning?' The superintendent of St Thomas's Hospital had finished his morning rounds, had lunched comfortably and was inclined to view affably the visitor to his residence in the hospital buildings stretching along the river.

'Yes, very good of you to see me, sir.' Garrety looked round the room and was thankful to see that a blazing fire burned steadily in a grate, where the hood had been burnished to a mirror-like quality. Outside, snow had begun to fall again, and he was glad to get indoors.

'I had the required records brought up from our basement. They have been in storage for some time, of course, but we never destroy them. Of course, I cannot let you read the documents for yourself – that would be a breach of confidentiality – and I confess, until I consulted them myself, I was unwilling to respond at all to your request.' The superintendent eased his heavy bulk into a chair next to a table laden with papers. In his fifties, he was a handsome man still, with thick white hair. 'Usually, of course, requests for information contained in our records concern former patients.'

'Yes, sir, I do appreciate that. I believe that during the period of the ... the Whitechapel murders all the London teaching hospitals were asked to scrutinize their records for any likely suspects among the medical students or staff.'

'That was so, I understand. It did set a precedent,' the superintendent acknowledged. Clearly, he was the kind of doctor who proceeded with legalistic caution. The natural-born administrator, Garrety decided, ruling his small empire here with the aid of complex knots of red tape.

A brown folder was opened on the shining surface of the table. The head of St Thomas's lifted it and tipped it discreetly sideways so that it would be impossible for his visitor to obtain a glimpse of the contents. 'Yes ... Newbold – here we are. He qualified in 1890. As a student, he trained here, and then was employed for a brief period of time afterwards.'

'How brief, sir?' asked Garrety quietly.

'Three months.'

There was a pause, as Garrety was taken by surprise. 'Surely that is a remarkably short period?'

'And you will want to know why, Inspector. He was considered unsuitable for hospital duties.' The superintendent sighed, and then said, 'You want to know more, and you are right to do so. At first, I think there was no more than a feeling of unease and some rumours of what had happened during his training. I myself was not superintendent at the time, of course – I had a comparatively junior post. There is a statement here that was taken from the night nurse in a gynae-cological ward. Dr Newbold was not on duty that night – at least, not officially. But he was seen leaving the ward – it seems he passed the nurse in a corridor. She described him as staring in a fixed and terrifying way – the woman was probably inclined to hysteria – and talking aloud, but also muttering and whimpering.'

Garrety involuntarily looked upwards at the ceiling, imagined the long, dark corridor, the solitary nurse encountering the jabbering figure.

There was more. 'But not absent-mindedly. "As if he were conversing, though there was no-one else present." I am quoting from her description, Inspector. Then she entered the ward and found that one of the patients was haemorrhaging. There were lacerations to the sexual parts and scratches on her thighs. Of course, someone else could have been responsible – some attacker from outside or even another patient with whom the woman had some quarrel: such things are not unknown. We deal with a very hard class of woman sometimes, Inspector – but you will know that, operating as you do in Lambeth.'

'Was the woman able to give any information as to her attacker?'

'No. She had recently been returned from the operating theatre and was still under the influence of chloroform. It seems she had an abortion at the hands of some ignorant back-street practitioner and was brought to us suffering from septicaemia. She subsequently died, in any case. Newbold was asked if he knew anything about the matter and he claimed that he had been called to help in an emergency. No record was found of any member of the night staff summoning his assistance. And he said he had seen a figure slipping on to a fire-escape outside the windows near the injured woman's bed. He claimed he hadn't had an opportunity to report it.'

Garrety walked across the room, closer to the fire. Had the

snow stopped? It felt colder than ever. He began to say something, but the superintendent pre-empted him.

'You do not believe in the shadowy figure, I would surmise, Inspector. And neither did my predecessor.'

'You said something about Newbold as a student, sir?'

'Oh, yes, he was intellectually quite brilliant, there was no doubt about that. His father had been a very gifted medical man. The son specialized in the microscopic analysis of human blood and tissue. Among his medical interests was the study of human infertility and its treatment – quite unusual for a young man. There are specialists in the subject, of course, especially in America. But young Newbold showed unusual interest – quite fervent, it appears. Unfortunately, two young women made complaints which they sub-sequently withdrew. Of course, that happens quite often where intimate matters are concerned. Women do not care for these matters to be made public.'

The heat from the fire suddenly seemed to be making the sweat run at Garrety's throat. He stared at the flames and the velvety black coals. 'Does it say exactly what they com-plained of, sir?'

'No. If a complaint is withdrawn, all details are removed from the records. That is only just, is it not, Inspector?'

'Oh, yes, of course, sir. So all we know about are these: the incident in the night ward and the complaints that came to nothing?'

'He passed all his examinations with flying colours. But a note was made upon the record that he was not suited for gynaecological work. Of course, there would have been no objection if he worked with male patients only, and I heard he did go to South Africa with an army medical unit.'

'Sir, about what the nurse encountered . . . her description

of Newbold's manner as he came away from the ward ...'
Garrety moved forward urgently.

'Yes, what of it?'

'Would you mind telling me whether, in your opinion, his
behaviour implies a serious medical condition?'

The other man rubbed a forefinger along his chin, as if trying to make a decision. The fire crackled in the grate. Garrety
stood, scarcely moving, sensing that an interruption might
precipitate a decision to end the interview.

At last, the answer came, slowly and cautiously. 'Of course,
young men working under great stress, as is quite usual in our
profession, do sometimes have nervous collapses, Inspector.
But this was apparently something rather different.
Conversing with an imaginary person – that is a delusion of
insanity. It suggests hallucination, and possibly – well, that
would be an extreme development!' The superintendent had
closed the file with a snap.

He feels he's gone far enough, thought Garrety. But one
more answer, just one! 'What development would that be?'

At first, he thought he would get no answer. But it came,
reluctantly.

'Oh, very well, Inspector, but please remember this is a rare
condition, and it is extremely unlikely that any physician
trained in this hospital could suffer from it undetected.'

'Of course not, sir.'

'There is a disease of the mind known as dementia praecox,
Inspector. It degenerates into total insanity: delusions, raving,
aggression. There are abnormal fears, intense preoccupation
with one idea. The patient may feel he ceases to have any real
existence. He may imagine another personality taking control
of him. Its worst form is paranoia – that is, the patient feels
persecuted, under attack. You will recollect that the nurse said

she heard him babbling as well as holding an imaginary conversation. It is a very terrifying disease.' His voice had become slow and serious, losing something of its official brusqueness. He stood up, as though wanting to shake off his thoughts.'I have seen a good many patients with it, from all classes of society. There is, in the end, no cure.'

'What causes it?'

'We cannot tell. Sometimes it appears to be inherited. Very often the onset is associated with some shocking or frightful experience.'

'And Dr Newbold – he might have suffered from this? Suffer still, I suppose. Is it a long time-span with this disease?'

'*Praecox* means "early maturing". It is a rapidly progressive disease, though of course the actual course of the illness varies from patient to patient. As for Newbold, I would be loath to make such a diagnosis of a fellow medical man, Inspector. That is all I can say.'

'So you would not be prepared to say that he has some serious mental disorder?'

'No, I would certainly not do so.'

No evidence, thought Garrety, nothing that would give us grounds for any further action. Without the detailed inform- ation in the file – possibly even with it – what did all this amount to but gossip? Well-informed medical gossip, but nothing more.

The bell was duly rung for the servant, to show the police- man out.

As Garrety left, he heard the superintendent calling out an order. 'I'll take tea now. And take some up to the gentleman on the balcony. He must be frozen!'

50

ON AN UPPER FLOOR, THE SUPERINTENDENT'S HOUSEKEEPER
was bearing a round silver tray of tea-things through a door.
She gasped at the cold that filled the room. 'Sir, you'll catch
your death!'

But he seemed oblivious, sitting out on the balcony in the
near-freezing air as he did every afternoon. It bewildered her
that a man should leave the comfort of the Savoy Hotel, cross
the river and spend half the day here at St Thomas's. The housekeeper put the tray on a table and hurriedly began to build up
the fire, which had died down to a slumbering bed of grey. She
called to him again, and this time he turned round, leaning
back, and she saw the canvas on which he had been working.

A dark outline, a burning tower of shiny dark-red and blue,
the colours all dashed on and glistening, and, below, its
swirling reflection. The Houses of Parliament, gothic, spiky,
and their ghostly reflections in the river. The picture made her
feel mad, sick, yet it was impossible to look away. She
stopped, frightened.

He got up, putting aside the rugs and blankets with which he had been covered. He looked more ordinary now, and the shock the painting had given her began to subside. Why, he was like a countryman, really, a big, stocky man, with a weather-beaten face above a square grizzled beard. He thanked her in a few words of English as he came back into the room from the balcony. Like a man who has come back from a long journey, he seemed to be slowly recognizing his surroundings again, and he stood in front of the fire rubbing his hands. She poured out the tea.

'I'll tell the girl to bring more coals.'

She shut the picture out, shut the tall windows that gave on to the balcony where the superintendent's family enjoyed the summer breezes.

After she had gone, he sat down, holding the cup and saucer high in front of his mouth, like an old man afraid to spill it. The day had been fine. There would be an incandescent nightfall in a little while, as the sun died over the filthy river. The reds, alizarin crimson, madder lake, the orange notes hidden deep in carmine, the bluish cochineal, purpurin – this water would briefly be their kingdom, flowing from the sky to the surface of the river in a final ecstatic burst. Colours of passion and warmth, colours of blood, of the membranes hanging in butchers' shops, the underside of the tongue, madder violet, black violet.

Flakes of snow were beginning to fall, white against the red-streaked sky. Strange, there had always been reds in his paintings of pale-faced Camille. In the garden at Argenteuil, with the masses of roses behind her, or her face at the window, where pots of fuchsias outside carried their brave splashes.

Had she been forced out in the end, just as the housekeeper

had shut out the freezing world outside this room? He had painted her once standing in the snow, poor Camille, not as a face inside the house, looking out on the garden, but standing outside and looking in, a deep, rich scarlet hood over her head and shoulders.

She was going away from him then, he thought. Or he was putting her away. But he understood it only through the picture. Just as he understood Camille was already dying inside, because he had painted two women in the cornfield, one at the top of the slope, one further down, descending the hillside to walk straight past him in a trance. They were the one who was to come, a distant figure at the top, and the one who was leaving him, with that great swathe of poppies between them. He could not see their faces. But in the painting he knew that Camille was going away, and there would be another to take her place, to walk through the fields again. That is life, that is the course of nature. Blood, death, mourning – and then the summer fields again. She was so gentle, Camille – no strength to fight. She glides for ever down that poppy-filled slope, her head held back beneath the straw brim, her grey dress floating and insubstantial, feet invisible in the soft long grass. And at the top, remorseless, the other, in black, awaits her turn. His lover. His second wife. Alice.

He set down his cup suddenly. There was no time to lose. Soon he would be leaving this city, this river-kingdom that suited him so ill, made him melancholy, revived old memories and fears. Below the balcony, tiny specks were hurrying fast along the embankment to reach home. The sky had filled with a lurid dusky light and the buildings of Westminster on the opposite bank of the Thames were so dark they were visible only in outline. He flung back the windows and seized his palette.

51

ALINE GARRETY WAS ONE OF THE TINY FIGURES HURRYING along beneath a darkening sky. There were long red streaks in the west, and the spires and towers of the Houses of Parliament on the other side of the river were bathed in a lurid light, so they seemed strange colours, not natural, yellow or maroon in the twilight. The street-lights were just coming on, strung out along the bridges across the river, but somehow they didn't make it easier to see any further. Their brownish lamps seemed to be reflected back by the thickness of the deepening fog, not to penetrate it, so that anything might lie invisible beyond the edges. She moved quickly, wanting to hurry to Lower Marsh.

The river lay to her right. She glanced at the gleams in the darkness that represented that brooding presence, the reflections of light on the water, where it was impossible to see down into the murky depths. Will wouldn't ask me about this sort of thing, she suddenly thought. Not about doctors and so on. He doesn't want to know about it. He doesn't want to look beneath the surface, not where this is concerned. He doesn't want to see some things – not at all.

The house seemed to have been rearranged. She had thought Dr Bolitho would have Mrs Leadbetter's parlour, the room where she had been before, which looked out on to the street. But there was his name on a brass plate at the side entrance and there was no need to knock. The door itself was open. It was all very discreetly arranged. She went into a room which overlooked a yard surrounded with a high fence. There were blinds at the window, and a big desk with a green-shaded enamelled lamp on it. No instruments in sight, though there was a cabinet with several shelves of medical books behind the glass, and a folding screen in the corner with some pleated white fabric across the frames.

It was really quite a nice room, she thought, for a doctor's surgery, without much to upset you, if you were a nervous patient. Warm, too. The fire was lit, the grate evidently recently swept, with a small mesh screen placed neatly in front of it.

Dr Bolitho must be somewhere else in the house.

She took off her cloak, put it over the back of a chintz arm-chair that stood in front of the desk and waited indecisively for a moment. She was sure about the date and time of the appointment – she had written it down carefully and, good-ness knows, she had checked the piece of paper enough times.

The room seemed less and less like a doctor's surgery as she looked round. Her premonitions eased and she sat down in the chair and stretched out her hands to the fire. Outside, the evening skies of early March teemed with snow, but within this room was a small warm world that held the season at bay.

Aline closed her eyes. She had been up since the early hours of the morning, unable to sleep, perhaps because of the

stormy weather, which always seemed to find strange corres-
pondences within her. It was a great relief when the storm
actually broke. Looking at the little carriage clock they kept
beside the bed, she saw it was about four o'clock. She got up
quietly, pulling on a dressing-gown, so as not to wake Will,
who lay sleeping heavily beneath the counterpane. He hadn't
got home till after midnight.

She sat by the window in the dark watching the rain thrash-
ing down over the city, distorting the street-lights into yellow
streaks and smears. Somewhere close at hand there came the
long mournful hooting of a train bound out of a railway
station – whether Waterloo or Charing Cross she was not
sure; the storm muffled sound and made distance indeterminate. It was a long, dark, cold night, but the dawn had
come eventually.

All day, as she worked in their draughty lodgings and when
she wrapped herself up and went out to the market, she had
been cold. It was only now, as she closed her eyes in front of
Dr Bolitho's fire, that she felt warm and her body relaxed.

So she was half-asleep when he came into the room, and she
jumped up in a state of mild confusion.

'My dear lady, please stay where you are! I must apologize
most profusely for being late – I'm afraid I was delayed . . .
No, please, I'll ring for some tea.'

She had never expected to be offered tea when she went to
the doctor, but looking at him she saw that his face seemed
to have been reddened by the storm. He probably needed it as
much as she did. His hair and face were wet, and his outer
coat was steaming with damp as he took it off and placed it on
a coat-stand in the corner of the room, near the desk, with a
practised movement. He returned and pressed the bell-push
next to the fireplace.

Evidently, he had given instructions in advance, for within a few minutes a girl came in bearing a tray and tea-things.

It was a different maid from the usual one – the girl who had let Aline into the house that time when she had met Mrs Leadbetter. Perhaps the doctor had a servant of his own. Aline decided this might be very likely, someone who knew how to clean the surgery and . . . She did not know what else might be needed and her mind seemed to shy away from it. He was pouring the tea, which was steaming gently and had a pleasant smoky taste. He passed the cream and sugar to her.

'Now, there's nothing in this world to worry about. Nothing at all.'

Nothing to worry about and no need to say anything to Will. The doctor sounded almost like one of the comforting voices from her childhood, resonant and deep, bidding a child to fear nothing, no evil.

52

ON THE OTHER SIDE OF THE RIVER TO THE HUMBLE LITTLE house where Aline Garrety was almost drifting into sleep, a light shone high in the Palace of Westminster, in a room where the trappings of power – the crests, frescos, deep chairs and thick-piled rugs – were swathed in shadows.

Under a green-shaded lamp, Lord Sanderson contemplated a list of names that his principal assistant had just handed him. They were assessing the new entry of junior clerks, a tedious task which his lordship preferred to conduct after dinner in the comfort of his rooms in the House of Lords.

'Hmm, that one will do well.'

'Not over-bright,' responded the assistant. 'Hasn't put a foot wrong, though.'

'All right, we'll keep him. And him? No, he's a blabber-mouth. I knew his father at Eton and he was just the same. Didn't know when to keep mum.'

'The dowager will kick up a fuss – the boy's the apple of her eye.'

'Well, we can ride out that storm. Family's a bit bohemian, in any case. The mother dabbles in poetry, I'm told.' Lord Sanderson reached for his pen, dipped it in a highly polished silver inkwell shaped like the Great Sphinx and made a note against the name of the poetry-lover's offspring.

The man standing on the other side of the vast mahogany desk swished his coat-tails approvingly. Above his head, a portrait of Lord Palmerston surveyed the scene belligerently. 'Young Madigan?' asked the assistant.

'Yes, we'll probably put him up pretty soon. Not much of a diplomat, no connections, but a looker – the women adore him. Might even try him in a posting next year. He's got charm, and that's as rare as hen's teeth. The Comtesse de Paris was bowled over like a rabbit at the reception.'

'A very plump rabbit.'

Sanderson gave his peculiar laugh of acknowledgement, somewhere between a grunt and a chuckle. 'Clean-bowled, though. Yes, we can use his sort.'

The assistant crossed to the window overlooking the Thames and gazed downriver at the Embankment lights that stretched like glittering laces alongside the black depths. ' "Sweet Thames, run softly . . ." Well, you can't see the filth at night.'

His Lordship had made another tick beside a name. 'Now, what about this?' He sounded somewhat irritable. 'Young Craston.' He was peering across the room, over his half-moon spectacles. 'Mmm, I'm in considerable doubt here,' he continued. 'Wasn't this the young fellow who got himself involved in some affair of a body in your "Sweet Thames"? Some woman who'd drowned herself?'

The assistant felt obliged to be even-handed. He said judiciously, his shiny cheeks flushing with the heat from the blazing fire in the grate, 'Well, in all fairness, he merely found the body. I suppose he looked down and saw it in the water.'

'And then spoke to the police?'

'Well, yes, I suppose he was obliged to – he had seen it.'

'Obliged!' Lord Sanderson barked sharply. 'You may look at things in the water, but you don't need to *see* them. In fact, there may be many occasions on which it is positively unwise to do so. The boy got himself involved in a bad business there.'

'Still, he may be useful to us; he's in with this French artist at the Savoy, who had a lot of turbulent friends in Paris – he's managed to get close to some republican rabble-rousers. Doesn't seem to have had anything much to report yet. But Monsieur Monet seems to be quite well connected in this country.'

'Yes, I believe he attended a reception held by the Asquiths. But as for Craston, I have doubts, serious doubts, that the young fellow is real FO material.'

'And as I think we've said before, sir, there are no family connections worth mentioning. In fact, there is apparently someone in the family background who might be positively to his disadvantage . . .'

Lord Sanderson sat upright in his chair.

'His sister, sir,' continued the other. 'The elder sister. Of course, this is merely unverified information, but the source is well known to me . . .'

It was. It had, in fact, been one of the Misses Elcho, whispering genteelly in the background.

'Yes, well, what is it, man?'

'I believe, sir, his sister intends to become a lady doctor. She's the kind of woman who supports female suffrage. And is defying her father's wishes in order to study.'

There was a deep sigh from the other side of the desk. 'Oh, one of those new women, I suppose, all educated minds and plain serge skirts. Well, that is a bit of a disadvantage, no doubt. Can a man with someone like that in the family – someone unusual, one might say, original – can he be considered for posts that demand the utmost discretion? I suppose she'll go on to want the vote – it has been suggested in some quarters, even for unmarried women.'

'Not at St James's! Not under my charge!' the assistant was protesting, almost as if he had been accused of a serious dereliction of duty. He grew pinker still. 'But we must face the future, you know. Take the long view. Young Craston may be saddled for life with an unsuitable family connection, but there is a new century upon us and we must admit, between ourselves, there has been a decline in the health of Her Imperial Majesty. "The old order changeth...", you know, "The old order changeth".'

The two men looked up instinctively at the portrait facing Palmerston: the elderly Victoria, upon whose bosom gleamed the silky blue sash and diamonds of the Order of the Garter.

'Yes, new men, new ideas, may be coming in. And new women too, I fear. Then, of course, this young man may marry well. Or, at least, appropriately. A suitable spouse is always a help to a young fellow in his position – in fact, you might drop a discreet hint to that effect, when you feel the time is ripe. Outline what the FO expects of a diplomatic wife, and so forth. Yes, very well, we'll give young Craston a chance. He may even pick up some social polish from his contacts with our French friends, since they evidently are bon viveurs. But any hint of scandal and he's out, mind. He's been warned, after all. Now, who's next?'

53

OLIVER WALKED OUT OF THE HOTEL AND INTO THE FREEZING night air in a daze, oblivious of the cold. In his mind there were only the same words, echoing over and over again, 'Rosa' and 'No!', but yet he knew it must be borne, and he walked mechanically towards Waterloo Bridge and soon was crossing over the river.

The shack at the top of Greet's Jetty gave out a reddish smoky light through its one window. Oliver found himself pushing open the door without hesitation and stared inside.

For a moment he was transported out of his shock and into the real world. He had been a fool to think that he could come here and they would know him – that somehow he could sit there as he had done after the woman . . . the woman in the river . . .

There was a ring of faces in the gloom, near the door, and they looked up as he hovered at the entrance, but then the wind slammed the door behind him. The men seemed flushed and angry and he didn't recognize any of their faces. They

were gathered in a semicircle round the fire as before, but now he felt they were a wall of hostility.

Anger was seizing him too now, rage at Rosa and Michel, which he recognized as both useless and stupid, but it was fuelling him on, so that he suddenly had no fear or caution and almost flung himself across the room to the bar. The woman there was different; this one was older, with her hair in a crimped fringe and a band round her neck. But there was something that reminded him of the younger one who had served brandy on that earlier occasion, and now he saw that same girl push her way through the group of men round the fire and come to stand beside him.

'He drinks brandy, Ma.'

Oliver felt a tremendous wave of relief. Someone knew him, someone picked him out of the mass of humanity drifting across London that night. No matter that it was a ragged girl in a flimsy drinking shack. The woman poured out a glass, and he tipped it down his throat. Then he looked at the girl.

'Er . . . what will you . . . ?'

'I'll have a gin and cordial.'

A long reddish drink was set before her, the edges purplish-brown where it tipped in the thick glass of the tumbler. She chinked it heavily against his own glass.

'You was here before, when they found that poor soul?'

He nodded.

'Don't mind them,' she said, gesturing towards the group round the fire. 'They don't mean to be hard, like. 'Spect they thought you was a copper. There was a copper wiv you, though, when you was here?'

'Yes, but I just . . . it was just because of the . . . the body . . .'

'Yeah, I understand. You've come by yourself now, all alone, for a bit of company.'

She did seem to understand. The group of men appeared to relax.

Oliver's eyes were adjusting to the gloom of the shack. A battered storm-lantern hung above the bar, and the only other light in the room was the dull glow of the coals. The fire was ventilated by a mere gap in the roof, through which the smoke stirred sluggishly up and out into the night, sometimes billowing back into the room when there was a stormy gust outside. The men had gone back to their conversation, a wary eye in a ruddy flame-lit face occasionally turned in Oliver's direction. Oliver saw that in a corner beyond the bar, at the bottom of a rickety staircase, there was another group – a woman and a couple of men seated round a table.

'Come on over,' said the girl who was standing next to Oliver, and she led the way towards the table in the corner. 'Them's my mates,' she added, 'so come and sit you down wiv us.'

When he reached the table, Oliver saw that one of the men at any rate was someone who had been in the bar when he and Garrety had been there, a young man with black tangled hair and a dirt-smudged face, his rough shirt open to the waist in spite of the season. He greeted Oliver and pushed his chair to one side to make room for the newcomers.

'This is Dickie,' said the girl, indicating the young man, 'and these here is Sal and Lionel.'

'Oliver,' said Oliver. Now that he was seated with them he knew that it would be awkward to get out of the place, but it didn't seem to matter much.

'Ollie,' said the girl. 'That's nice! Lot of Catholics called that. After a Blessed or something. You a Catholic, then?'

'The Blessed Oliver Plunkett? No, I'm not a Catholic.'

'There's lots of 'em round here. Working on the railways and the roads and all that.'

There'd been a lot of agitation about Home Rule and Fenians in the papers. He thought of the placards he had seen down by Charing Cross Station, and the crowds of police. He wanted to keep clear of any entanglements.

'What's your name?' he asked the girl.

'Regina.' She laughed. Her teeth were small and neat, the mouth rounded and red. 'My old mam called me that – closest she'd ever get to royalty, that's what she said! It means "Queen". Like in Victoria Regina. Oh, I know you gents think we're as ignorant as muck down here, but my mam had a bit of schooling before she come to London. Anyway, they call me Reggie. Bit of a man's name, but some of the gentlemen likes it. The funny ones!'

Oliver laughed, though at what he was not sure.

The man Dickie got up and went to the bar and came back with drinks. He set down a glass in front of Oliver. 'Knock it down yer! It were a right nasty thing, that woman in the wa'er.'

Oliver drank, and Reggie shifted her chair slightly so that she was sitting closer. He noticed, as the storm-lantern swayed overhead and the shadows came and went, that when she leaned forward the front of her dress fell away from her body and he could glimpse her breasts. The nipples had big soft circles round them. He was shocked and excited to see how different they were from the boys' nipples at school, which was all he had to compare them with.

A smell of piss wafted in from the direction of a door under the staircase and Oliver after a while excused himself and made in that direction, where, out in the open but screened by a fence, he found a steaming heap and a pot. The moonlight poured down; as Oliver looked up he felt a moment of elation, as though the whole beautiful London night was his own possession.

When he got back inside, Dickie laughed and said, 'Freeze it enough to drop off, then?' This seemed amazingly funny, and Oliver laughed too.

Something new had developed since Oliver went out for his poetic moonlight piss. Sal was sitting with a grubby piece of paper in front of her, wielding a stub of pencil as the others called out names and what he supposed to be stakes.

'Silver Swan.'

'Two bob, I reckon.'

'Cory's Lightning.'

'Naah, niver worth a sixpence.'

But Sal had trouble keeping up, and Dickie leaned across and snatched the pencil and paper from her.

'Here, Ollie, you do it. Write 'em down.'

Oliver obliged.

'Jammie Lady.'

'Hound of Spring.'

'Naah,' said someone. 'Wide on the bends.'

'Ain't he writing nice!' said Sal, peering over Oliver's shoulder. 'Gennlemen always writes different.'

A snuffling boy appeared at Oliver's elbow and was sent off with the piece of paper and some coins.

Some time later the child reappeared with what seemed like a fistful of money, which he threw on the table.

'Ollie's brung us luck,' shouted Dickie, and clapped his arm round Oliver's shoulder.

Someone went and got more drinks and Oliver's head began to swim.

Reggie was leaning closer than ever. Oliver found his eyes drawn again to her dark-pink nipples. He couldn't seem to look anywhere else. She had tugged her skirt up a little so that he could see the white skin above her boots and had moved her legs apart. He hadn't thought a girl like this would have such white skin.

The next moments became a blur and only afterwards did he remember the sound of their feet clattering on the wooden staircase. At the top was an alcove with a truckle bed and a curtain that partitioned it off. A few moments later, and Reggie had pulled her dress off and was lying on the bed. Drunkenly, but still with a kind of ecstasy, Oliver saw her thin, pale body stretched out in one long moment when time seemed to stand still. Tearing off his shirt and trousers, Oliver fell on top of her and their limbs moved wildly for a few moments, until he felt himself sliding into a long, exquisite, wet, piercing heat. He rolled over on his back and lay beside her. The spunk came shooting out of him as she pulled away towards the wall and he smelt the acrid odour. He saw the thick white trickle on her thighs.

He awoke and had no idea what time it was. There were no sounds from the bar downstairs, and the air seemed chill and full of stale smoke. The girl lay beside him: she was sleeping, too. Oliver made to pull the sheet up over her, and it was only then that his eyes focused and he saw the man, Dickie.

Dickie had pulled back the curtain and extracted Oliver's trousers from the heap on the floor. He was holding them up with one hand. The other was dipping into one of the pockets. The rough floorboards were creaking beneath his feet as he swayed a little in his concentration. Oliver supposed that was what had woken him. His own reactions now seemed needle-sharp. His senses had sprung awake.

He leapt from the bed and made a grab at the trousers, but Dickie pulled away and waved them mockingly.

'Want to take 'em off, do we? His Lordship's come here after a fuck-hole – well, Mr Scratch-my-Arse, you pays for it in this house. Doesn't yer know that?'

The trousers were flapping out of Oliver's reach.

All of a sudden, there was a movement from the bed and Reggie, who had curled herself up and drawn the single grubby sheet over her body, leapt at Dickie, naked as she was, and bit his hand.

He swore and knocked her off. She fell down the stairs, screaming, and Dickie threw Oliver's trousers down after her.

The next few minutes seemed forever blotted out of his consciousness by a merciful shame. He must somehow have dived down the stairs, struggled into his trousers and out through the silent bar, where a figure appeared to be sleeping in a heap of rags. Years later, he would sometimes remember Dickie's mocking laughter that seemed to reach to the roof-tops as he ran out into the street.

The cold air sobered him. It was freezing now, and there was a brittle skin of ice forming over the river into a flat viscous surface that seemed barely to move beneath the moonlight. The sky was clear, the stars high and bluish. Looking upriver, he saw a London of innocence and beauty, its dirt hidden till daytime should return.

The sight calmed him: he stopped his headlong flight and was entranced by the sight before him. Perhaps he was still drunk, perhaps exhausted and in some sense cleansed. Nothing stirred. He stepped out on to Waterloo Bridge and looked upriver to the Houses of Parliament, their distinctive jagged Gothic outline looming against the moonlit sky. Along the partly frozen river echoed the chimes of Big

Ben striking the hour: three o'clock in the morning.

The chill struck him and he moved back and started to make his way off the bridge and towards the network of streets on the southern bank. Remembering his new home meant that a sense of freedom ran through him, so that he almost forgot about his shameful encounter. He need account for himself to no-one.

But there was some movement across the bridge: as he stepped into the shadows near the station, he saw that there was a figure, stooped, but moving rapidly, coming towards him.

Instinctively, Oliver stood still. He felt the night air freezing around his skin, felt his body trembling with the cold, yet did not dare to move. The fellow – he was sure now it was a man – was bearing down on him very fast. Across the bridge he came, on the opposite side from Oliver, so that the moonlight was full upon him for a moment and Oliver saw him, drained of all colour, yet etched out in silver and black, the features absolutely clear.

The strangest thing. It was the doctor who had spoken to Mrs Darby in the lobby of the Savoy.

His coat fell open. He was wearing an apron of some sort.

There was a long, mournful hoot from the railway tracks near the station, and then the weary sound of an engine hauling along into the early morning.

54

GARRETY STARED AT THE PICTURE. IN THE FOREGROUND THE water rippled with burnished gold, yet the sky was subdued, darker than the river, which had a curious shining wind-ruffled surface, almost frozen in movement, like chopped jelly. Dark prows intruded into the lower right-hand corner. He could almost see the boats swaying and bobbing with the breeze. Across the water was the long streak of a bridge. Garrety supposed that, judging by the trails of pinkish steam above, it was a railway bridge and the tall grey shapes in the distance looked like the bank of the Thames at Westminster. Charing Cross Bridge, probably, but it seemed to be swirling before his eyes, its outlines blurred and shadowy. There were flecks and stretches of pale yellow, like sunshine, but they were in the water as well as the sky.

It made his eyes ache, to look like this, from far away. He moved back and forth in the room, trying to focus on something, but there was nothing that he could see close up, nothing definite, and it made him feel uneasy. Though not as uneasy as the picture hanging in the hall, that great pink naked woman: he found he couldn't think of anything but sex while he was looking at that. He knew instinctively that the artist – well, the picture damned near told you so.

He turned to the young woman at his side. 'I'm sorry, miss – I don't really understand these things . . .'

'It's how Monsieur Monet sees it. The air, not so much the things themselves.' There was a pause. They stood side by side, looking into the watery depths. 'The picture's just on loan to us, of course. Monsieur Monet is planning to return to France and all his other canvases have been packed up, but my mother loved this one, and she hopes to buy it. But that's not what you came to see. Just a moment, Inspector, I'll ask my mother to come and talk to you. She is resting just now.'

'Yes, of course, miss. It's just that we had an anonymous call about an encounter I believe your mother had with a certain gentleman.'

She laughed. 'How mysterious and interesting.'

Garrety moved back as Rosa Darby went out of the room, and stared again at the painting that stood against the opposite wall. It was like looking through water at sunlight, but there were dark shapes here, in which you could see something, but not clearly, all smudged and half-lit, as though London were suddenly a different city and all its solid shapes were dissolving. These purplish marks in the foreground that he thought were the prows of little boats, they could even be raised arms, bent, just in the act of stretching in the strange half-light. The bridge itself was insubstantial, not just one colour, he realized, but all sorts of blues and greys and greenish shades – colours like roof slates or wet metal.

The woman came into the room and stood beside him, so that he could smell a heavy perfume, sweet, like lilies.

'Do you like the picture, Inspector? How does it make you feel?' she asked.

He knew instantly that she was an Irishwoman, and not only from her accent but from the way she asked him what he felt about the painting. But the truth was that as he stared at it he scarcely knew, any more than an Englishman, how to answer her. 'I don't know, madam. Is it . . . is it the bridge – the railway bridge?'

'Yes, Charing Cross Bridge. You can see the steam from the engines going across.'

So he could now, pinkish and white plumes drifting south over the water, and there the jagged outline of funnels and coaches, tiny in the distance – or was he imagining that?

'Going to be a fine day, madam. Only it's overcast just now.'

It was the gold in the picture had made him say that – knowing that there was sunshine somewhere in the sky, looking west upriver beyond the bridge, towards the Abbey. He stared at the picture. How strange; it seemed to be changing something deep inside him, but what that was, he could not tell. With an effort, he concentrated on Mrs Darby's conversation.

'You've come about the doctor I talked to in the Savoy? I don't think I have any more to tell you, Inspector. He didn't *do* anything, if you see what I mean. You see, he went to the reception desk and asked if there were any letters for him, and the man said, "No, sorry, Dr Newbold," so I knew he was a doctor. He turned round to leave and saw that I had sat down on the couch. I was feeling a little faint and he came up to me and said something like "I'm a doctor – can I help you?" And he had a little bottle of something in his pocket and put some on a handkerchief and gave it to me to smell.'

'Did anyone see him do that?'

'No, I don't think so. He held it quite low down as he did so, and there was no-one nearby. Well, of course, I knew that he was a doctor – the hotel staff called him so – and he was obviously a guest in the hotel, so I thought he must be trustworthy. It never entered my head to doubt it all.'

'And later, what did he do?'

'Why, nothing. Mr Craston came back to tell me he had got us a cab.'

There's no real evidence to be had. But what do I want, after all? Garrety asked himself. That this poor woman should have actually been in danger? 'Do you want to make a complaint, madam?' he said.

Mrs Darby smiled. 'What would I complain about, Inspector? He did nothing at all. I don't even know that what he put on the handkerchief was anything more than sal volatile.'

As a last chance, Garrety asked, 'Did you keep the handkerchief, by any chance?'

'Yes, but it's been washed and ironed. It was my own silk handkerchief and I was rather anxious it shouldn't be spoilt.'

'Ah, well, there's no help there, then. So Mr Craston came in and that was the end of it?'

'Yes, Inspector. Oh, there was one thing – he did say he was opening a surgery on the other side of the river.'

Garrety found he was sitting up, like a fox scenting the wind. 'Did he give you an address?'

'Not exactly. He said it was in Lambeth. I was surprised, I must say. I mean, it's quite a different area from the Savoy, isn't it? Although I'm not absolutely certain of where it is. But one thing I can tell, Inspector – you're Irish! From the North, by your voice.' She was smiling now, in a friendly way.

'Yes, ma'am. From Belfast. From the Shankill. But my wife is from Cork.'

'Ah, well, Inspector, then she married out of her religion, I expect, did she? It can't have been easy for either of you. Is that why you came to London?'

He wanted to talk to this woman, to tell her how lonely Aline had felt, was still feeling, maybe to have one of those long conversations where they would discover that there was a second cousin twice removed in County Kildare who was a mutual relation, and it didn't matter that Mrs Darby owned a grand house, she would be just the same, like any ordinary person. But it wasn't possible, not here, not while he was doing this job.

'Well, ma'am, London makes a different person out of you. That's what I'm finding.'

'That's only too true, I'm afraid. I wish I could go back more often. I have a house near Cork, you know, but it's shut up most of the year. Rosa was brought up in Paris and London, and I find myself year by year getting further and further from the old country. Do you know Cork, Inspector?'

'No, I'm afraid not, madam, but my wife misses it, that I can say.'

'She should come one day and talk to me. London can make people so lonely, Inspector, and I expect a policeman's wife will be on her own a great deal. Do you have any children?'

The question direct. He had to answer it. 'No, madam.'

'Ah, that will come, I expect, and fill up her days. In the mean time, tell your wife she will be made very welcome here, if she misses the old country.'

'Thank you, ma'am. That's very generous-hearted of you.'

But he knew he wouldn't. 'Don't mix business with pleasure.' That was the rule, this side of the Irish Sea. 'Ma'am, if you could recall to yourself any little detail of the appearance of this man, please tell me.'

She looked up at him blankly, and then a thought seemed to cross her mind. 'Did I mention, Inspector, that he had red hair? But not like yours.'

'Oh?' For a moment he thought she was going to reach up and touch his own scrubby red-grey thatch. She was just the sort of woman who might have done that. Her hand moved in a tentative gesture, and then fell away.

'No, it was real dark red – yours is a lighter colour. And his was all straight and floppy – not springy, like yours.'

He shuffled with embarrassment and yet maybe a tiny regret, if he was to be honest. Her skin looked so creamy and plumped out, like fruit.

'But that is really all I can remember.'

55

'MAGS,' SAID OLIVER. 'MAGS, I HAVE A PROBLEM.'

His sister looked up from the sofa in the little sitting-room. She had come to visit Oliver's new rooms, as they had arranged several days previously, and had found him very subdued. He was glad to see her, she had no doubt of that, but he was pale and stiff as he welcomed her when she first arrived.

She began to unpack a basket. 'Of course, Mother insisted on sending you some chutney – and here is a box of medical supplies! Goodness me – arnica for bruises, and what's this blue packet here? Oh, cotton wool. And a thermometer, and some plasters . . . What does she think is going to happen to you?'

He had managed to laugh with her and made the tea, and they had taken it together into the sitting-room, where a bright little fire danced away in the grate. It was only then that he said, 'Mags, I have a problem.'

'Tell me.'

'It's connected with that awful business – where I met a policeman – you remember—'

Maggie jumped immediately to the answer, as he had known she would, had relied on her to do. 'Is it to do with that poor woman in the river?' Her face was turned up towards his, very serious above the deep brown velvet of her cape.

'Yes. I'm sorry to talk about it, but, you see, something has happened.'

Maggie leaned over and put her hand on Oliver's arm. 'As a matter of fact, I'm glad you wish to speak about it.'

'What do you mean?'

'It hadn't escaped my notice how elated you seemed recently since you met your new friends. And then, this last week, you were so changed. I thought perhaps you had formed an attachment and that your feelings were troubled and distressed.'

'You thought I was in love?' He felt better now the words were out of his mouth. And he might as well continue: there was only one candidate after all. 'With Rosa Darby?'

'Yes, Oliver, I did. Was I wrong?'

'No. But she . . .'

'You don't need to say.'

Thank God for Maggie, he thought.

'But what about the case – the murder of that woman?'

'You see, Maggie, there's something . . . someone I saw by chance, and that person might, just might, have something to do with it. And I informed the police anonymously. I think I should give them my name, otherwise they won't treat it seriously. But there were, well, I'll say there were other circumstances they may want to know about.'

Maggie paused, thinking, the furrows that he remembered appearing between her eyebrows. 'Could you not give the police the information without revealing them? Would that not be possible? They needn't know everything, surely.'

He hung his head. 'I wish you were right. But they may feel that my account needs some support.'

He knew what Garrety would say. 'And you, Mr Craston, what were you doing at that hour of the morning when you saw the doctor from the Savoy making his way over Waterloo Bridge?'

Oliver had revolved the possibilities in his mind. Just going for a walk to clear my mind. 'At that hour of the morning on a freezing winter night? Come, come, sir – you'll have to think of something better than that.'

No, he would have to admit going to the shack on Greet's Jetty. It would be easy enough anyway for Garrety to put two and two together – the drinking den near the foot of the bridge would have been open still at that hour. It was so damned obvious.

And then more questions from Garrety. 'A common drinking den? Well, it was one thing to enter such a place in broad daylight in the company of a police officer when you were in urgent need of a restorative. But to return at night, alone . . . that is very strange, is it not? Did you remain at Greet's Jetty all the time? Is there anyone who can support your account?'

There was, of course. A whore called Regina.

Oliver put his head between his hands at the very thought of what would happen. He pictured himself in the witness box . . . He pictured Regina . . . the scenes that had happened that evening. It would mean the end of his career as a diplomat. No-one could afford such a scandal – at least, not while he still had the ladder to climb. When you got to the top you could have your lapses, could flaunt your mistresses even, and no-one would admit to seeing them. But at the bottom of the heap . . . no!

'Oliver, of course you must help the police!' Maggie was in absolute earnest. Her round eyes, a blackberry-brown in the warm light, gazed into his face. 'Even if it has some fearful repercussions. After all, if this knowledge that you have might bring a murderer to justice – well, punishment is a matter for the law, but the point is, he might do it . . .'

'He might kill again?'

'Yes. So if you know something that would save some other woman's life perhaps, you must go to the police. It is the right thing, is it not?'

But he still didn't want to listen to her, wished desperately to pretend the whole episode had never happened. Besides, there was another factor that had to be taken into account, something that would affect Maggie directly, something that might never come about if he 'did the right thing'. It would be the wrong thing for her, all right. Let her first think of that, and then make up her mind whether he should proceed.

'Maggie, something else may depend on it.'

As Oliver contemplated the possibility of disgrace in the eyes of his employers, he realized that Maggie's future was also in jeopardy as well as his own. Upon Oliver's shoulders rested the responsibility of paying her university fees. The leverage he had been able to bring to bear on Craston Senior depended on Oliver's employment at the Foreign Office. Without that the older man could do exactly what he pleased as far as his daughter's future was concerned, for she would be entirely dependent upon their father.

'Maggie,' Oliver said, as they stood opposite each other in his sitting-room in Stamford Street. 'Maggie, you do realize that if they find out about it, if they know at the FO what I'm involved in, then, well, there were plenty of candidates for the examinations. They wouldn't have any difficulty in getting another pen-pusher like me. And even if they let me stay, there'll be no advancement, almost certainly.'

Was she taking it all in? She looked stunned. For the first time, Oliver felt Maggie's mind hadn't got to the end of the chain ahead of him.

'And if I do lose my employment, I shan't be able to meet the fees.' There, it was said, the last logical consequence of what she was urging him to do.

She took his hands in hers. There was a long delay. She seemed to be holding her breath. Then she said simply, looking down, 'Well, but you must do it, all the same. You must go to the police.'

Her voice was steady, but when he lifted her chin up and gazed into her face he saw there were tears in her eyes.

56

THE FLUID OF LIFE ITSELF — THE WHITE STICKY STUBBORNNESS of it, that mysterious river of creamy lakes and islands seen under the microscope, and within it, wriggling ridiculously about like tadpoles, the very sources of our creation — how could one not be moved to witness this? There are times when I feel it is a great privilege to be able to look down through a microscope and understand what I see.

She came in the morning as I had arranged, and I had got over from the other side of the river and was all ready. She was nervous, but determined to go through with it.

'Will it be painful at all, Doctor?'

'Oh no, not in the slightest. I'll give you a light anaesthetic to ensure you feel absolutely no discomfort. Afterwards, there may be a little bleeding, no more.'

I took it from her with great care, first giving her some ether to ensure she did not become tense as I inserted the bivalve speculum. I had placed her in the supine position with her hips elevated by cushions. Then the mucus was taken with a platinum loop on a glass rod and a specimen immediately placed on a glass slide so that I could examine it. She felt nothing, and was fully awake within a few minutes. As I was placing the slide under the microscope, she was stirring, pulling down her dress with sleepy hands before she even knew her surroundings. It had not been necessary even to ask her to remove it.

'No need for haste. Take your time.'

She was moving gently, realizing where she was. Her face was flushed, as they usually are when such a procedure is performed and recognition was evidently occurring to her.

'Is it all right, Doctor?'

'Perfectly. I have exactly what I wanted.' I went over to her and poured her a glass of water. 'You see, it was all very quick, was it not?'

'Oh, yes. Thank you so much, Doctor. You made it all very . . . easy for me.'

'Shall I ring for Mrs Leadbetter? She can bring you some tea.'

'No, thank you.' She rose to her feet, went behind the screen where she had left her drawers, and emerged smoothing her hair.

I had felt not the slightest impulse to do her any harm. Though I could smell the acrid scent of his spunk and it excited me, I admit, the backs of my hands against her pubic hair, which was all sticky and beaded. I had to tell her not to wash beforehand, of course – she is the kind of woman who would have done that immediately: she probably leaps out of his bed and sluices herself with soap. I did cause some local excitement by gentle massage to make sure the muscles were relaxed and she moved and moaned a little. But even that did not make the devil come stirring out in me. So I was practically a model doctor – and she was a model patient.

'When shall I return, Doctor?'

'Oh, I shall know the results very quickly. You could come tomorrow, if you wish. Say, early in the morning? That would ensure discretion, would it not? No-one is likely to be about at that hour.'

'You will have had time enough?'

All I had to do was to examine it under the microscope.

'Yes, that will be excellent. Mrs Leadbetter will show you out.' I reached for the bell.

'Don't trouble yourself, Doctor. I can see myself out.'

I fancy she does not care for the Leadbetter woman. Well, I myself do not, either. A nosy, intrusive creature, full of genteel pretensions and really as bad as any old dame who goes to it with a knitting-needle or a catheter.

All the same, I shall continue to need these rooms in her house for the next stage of my plans. Ah, I can still make plans and execute them. Is that not a proof of my continuing sanity?

I look at myself in the mirror.

'So do you conclude, Dr Newbold, that I am still sane?'

'Oh yes, Dr Newbold, you are!'

When she returns for her next appointment, I, still in the guise of that reputable sawbones and baby-merchant, Dr Cavendish Bolitho, will explain to her about insufflation. That the likeliest cause of her infertility is a blockage in the Fallopian tubes. Doubtless, I must describe to her what the Fallopian tubes are, so innocent is this creature come to live among the dirty streets of London. Air can be introduced into these tubes and forced through them so that they may be opened and operate according to the laws that nature intended. This discovery was made a half-century ago, yet I am sure she will know nothing of it.

That is the version of events I will outline for her. In reality, it will of course be very different. As far as I know, there is nothing obstructing her Fallopians and no need whatsoever to puff air or anything else through them.

For when I looked down into the microscope upon his ejaculate, what did I see? Did I see motile spermatozoa swimming and struggling towards their destiny? Did I see, in that very source of life, the vital movements of life itself?

I did not. There was nothing there. The man is sterile. That creamy river has no fish. There will be no child from him.

I will not tell her this, of course, when she returns. No, I have quite another plan in mind to resolve the problem of her failure to conceive. My difficulty will be not in persuading her to co-operate but in preparing myself for my part. Although I feel arousal in the appropriate member when I am handling her soft parts as she lies anaesthetized before me, they no longer have the effect they would once have had, namely to conclude arousal with ejaculation.

My appetite has been coarsened. I need other sensations.

57

ELIZABETH BELFRAGE STOOD IRRESOLUTELY BEFORE THE engraved glass doors of the station tea-room. From within came a lively hum of voices and the clinking of cups and glasses. Occasionally, a red-faced porter struggled past with a great load, but there were few passengers about at this time of the evening. The clerks who made their way by train to their villas in far-flung outer suburbs, the ladies who had been in town shopping for the day – these had dispersed, gratefully, making for their firesides.

How stupid of her to have missed it! How could she have done anything so silly! She had made sure that the Margate train departed at seven o'clock sharp, and then when she had got to Waterloo, rather flustered because of having left Dottie so late, it had pulled out a few minutes previously. To add to her embarrassment, when she had remonstrated with one of the officials, he merely looked at her and pointed to the timetable pasted up on the central board, which clearly indicated 6.55 p.m. She had to apologize for her accusation that the train had departed earlier than advertised. So it was entirely her own fault, which made it all worse, and now there were two hours to wait on this draughty station, with no book to pass the time.

Still, she hadn't liked to leave Dottie, and had stayed with her till the last possible moment.

Alistair would be anxious. Should she send a telegram? 'Missed train – on next.' No, it probably wouldn't be worth it. She would be home by the time Mrs Dunstan's boy had taken the telegram up the hill to Fourways. Really, the telephone was a wondrous invention! Perhaps they should consider the expense of having one installed, especially since Dottie really had not looked too good. There might well be an emergency . . .

Elizabeth found that her feet had strayed towards the tearoom, but she went first into the ladies' waiting-room, where a fire burned nicely, but the room was empty apart from a nervous-looking young girl sitting with a trunk at her feet and an old woman in the corner of one of the padded benches. A yellow electric light bulb hung from the ceiling, with a marbled shade that cast an uneven and mottled light which seemed to be swallowed up by the wooden panelling with its varnished grain.

The general atmosphere of gloom was such that she barely spent a few moments tidying her hair in the mirror over the fireplace. Her face looked small and, she felt, quite frail in the big glass: her hair had come down and needed pinning up again. She rolled it carefully under at the sides, so that the small streaks of grey were hidden. It was something to be blonde, after all, because the grey showed much less, and she fancied she still had a lot of the natural bright colouring of her youth, which had so taken Alistair. She smiled, and repinned

her little mauve hat, patting the long glistening feathers that
perked up at the back, pulling the veil down over her face.
Reflected in a corner of the mirror, she saw the old woman in
the corner take a small bottle out of her muff and tilt it up to
her lips. The smell of gin filled the room.

Hastily, Elizabeth made her way back towards the tea-
room. Of course, the place was not entirely respectable – you
could not guarantee that in a railway station – but it would
surely be preferable to that ladies' waiting-room with its
suggestions of wasted lives. She felt sorry for the girl and the
way she had stared into space, a picture of loneliness.

The smell of soot hung in the air under the great roof, and
Elizabeth wiped her mouth with her handkerchief. She felt
like a tiny island, and to comfort herself she thought of her
resources: the morocco leather purse with three sovereigns
and several florins as well as coppers, the piece of chocolate in
her coat pocket, the solid thick pasteboard oblong of her
ticket home. First class – Alistair had insisted. She felt his
affection still around her like a warm cloak as she walked into
the tea-room.

There were small circles of white table-cloths in the gloom
and a smell of toasted bread and cake and warm tea. Only two
or three tables were empty. Further along was a bar with long
rows of green and brown bottles and glasses set on runners. A
couple of men were standing talking quietly, soberly dressed,
one with his foot up on the brass rail.

Elizabeth was relieved. The atmosphere was cheerful, but
seemed quite temperate. She veered towards the tables and a
waitress emerged, wearing a white apron. The tea menu
featured muffins, scones, crumpets, bloaters, Gentleman's
Relish . . . Elizabeth ordered a pot of Indian tea and a plate of
scones.

She realized how hungry she had become – no wonder she looked rather pale, she had really not had very much to eat all day. At Dottie's she had just had a little omelette, and it had all been rather a strain. When the girl set the tea-things on the table, Elizabeth poured herself a cup with relief.

She was still absorbed in her thoughts when she became aware of someone hovering over her.

'I said, would you mind if I . . . ?' The man gestured to an empty chair.

58

ELIZABETH LOOKED UP AND WAS IMMEDIATELY ANXIOUS. THE newcomer was a gaunt-looking man, respectable enough, with an old-fashioned cravat round his throat, but the clothes were not very clean: she saw the folds of the cravat were dirty, and as he put his hands on the back of the chair the black moons of grime at the tips of his finger-nails were apparent. He was looking at her face in an odd and interested way, not at all the sort of attitude that would reassure a woman sitting on her own. But she would have found it difficult to object, not liking to make a scene in the waiting-room, though look-ing round she saw that there were in fact two empty tables, where he could perfectly well have seated himself. The man was already pulling a chair out, taking her consent for granted. She was on the verge of picking up her bag, ready to flee; but then the voice of sense and reason told her to calm down. She could not possibly come to harm here in a station waiting-room, surrounded by a most mundane group of people.

At the same time, her inner self was full of a mounting anxiety. There was a powerful smell of drink as the stranger leaned over her and mumbled things that she could not make out.

So it was with immense relief that she saw a most respectable-looking personage approach and say firmly, 'This lady is with me!'

The grimy fellow shuffled off, mumbling something again and dragging a leg.

'I trust you did not object, madam. I saw that you might be in difficulties!'

A gentleman of her own class, she could tell by the voice.

'May I assure you, I am a professional man . . . Oh, here is my card!'

She did not look at it immediately, being so relieved that Grimy had been driven off, and occupied with trying to assess the newcomer, a clean-shaven gentleman whose eyes were nice and bright and twinkling, and who smelt reassuringly of some bay-leaf hair Cologne such as Alistair favoured.

'May I observe, madam, as a medical man, that you look somewhat fatigued?'

Looking round the room, rather flustered, she saw the barmaid talking to Grimy as he limped his way to the bar beyond the tea-room. He hastened his dragging progress and vanished out of the door. It looked as though the woman had recognized him as an undesirable.

Elizabeth felt a wave of gratitude to the stranger.

'Of course, a lady would be nervous in such circumstances,' he was saying, 'and travelling is in any case so fatiguing. Do you have a long wait for your train?'

'Yes, I'm afraid so,' acknowledged Elizabeth. 'Two hours or so!'

'How scandalous! The organization of the railways leaves much to be desired! But I'm afraid you will be quite faint if you are obliged to remain that long in these circumstances. Permit me to fetch you a small Cognac – yes – you need something to act as a restorative, madam, on such a night as this!'

Before she could decline, he had stood up and fetched her a small glass. 'Now, drink it down!'

It was like being a child again with the comfort of a doctor telling her what to do. She did indeed feel much better as she drank it down.

'Really, I should diagnose anaemia,' he was saying. 'A lack of iron, perhaps. I shouldn't wonder if you have suffered from chlorosis at some time. What does your own doctor advise?'

Elizabeth had been feeling rather weary of late, but she had not bothered to trouble Dr Carew with what might just be female imaginings. Now she wondered if perhaps she shouldn't consult a younger man. They had always gone to Carew, of course, but the old man was getting frail, there was no doubt about it. All he recommended, for every ill, seemed to be cascara! She shuddered at the memory of humiliating hours spent in the water-closet.

The stranger had very clean linen, she noticed, and had placed a leather bag at the side of the table – a reassuring sight, for it was clearly and recognizably a doctor's case. He had been saying something more about anaemia and the lack of red blood cells, but she hadn't been paying attention, and now, as she tried to, she felt so very drowsy. In fact, she felt herself almost sliding a little to one side: her head seemed too heavy to hold upright and her eyesight slightly blurred. The long day and the anxiety over Dottie had taken their toll. Perhaps he could help Dottie too.

'My dear lady,' he was saying now, and she saw his small red mouth very wet and clear as he spoke, 'you must allow me to assist you! My surgery is very close by the station. It's a mere step away from here.'

The tea-room seemed so stuffy and she was quite dizzy now. If he would just perhaps help her outside for a few moments so that she could get some fresh air . . . An arm was slipped beneath her shoulder. He was saying something to a woman at a neighbouring table, who had looked round with concern, something about his being a doctor and taking care of her . . . 'But I'm not his patient!' she tried to say. It was so much easier just to get up from the table and walk to the door, still with the aid of his supportive arm.

59

'I HAVE A CALL FOR YOU. KINDLY WAIT A MOMENT!' THE refined accents of Miss Elcho had chirped out of the telephone.

Then came a nervous male voice, speaking rather quietly. 'Hello, hello, I want to speak to Inspector Garrety.'

'He's not here at the moment, sir.'

'Oh, er . . . well, I suppose . . . When will he be there?'

Hassblack sensed the voice was fading away. Whatever had prompted this young man to call Lambeth nick was losing its original impetus. Hassblack diagnosed a bad case of conscience, and he had known such to fizzle out like a damp squib. 'I'm not sure, sir. Would you like him to call on you?' That would put him on the spot.

'Ah, er, that is—'

'What is the address, sir?'

'Well, perhaps Inspector Garrety could call this evening. The name is Craston, Oliver Craston. I live in Stamford Road.'

'Aah, yes, Mr Craston, I believe he has your details.'

There was a pause at the other end. Then Craston said, sounding very subdued, 'Very well. Shall we say about seven o'clock?'

'I dare say the inspector can manage that. Sir.' Best not to frighten him off.

When Garrety returned, Hassblack was elated. Garrety came in, pulled off his leather gauntlets and rubbed his hands. Hassblack had instructed his latest recruit, an anxious lad of fourteen, to put the kettle on the gas the moment the inspector came through the door, and they heard the familiar chinking and hissing sounds from the back of the building as Garrety stamped his feet on the doormat. Glistening splinters of ice fell off his boots.

'Anything in the Occurrence Book?'

'Couple of Irish navvies got themselves in a punch-up down at the Whittington.' This was the great glass-and-mahogany pub near St George's Cathedral. Garrety braced himself for some comments about sod-busters and spud-eaters, but they didn't come. 'We got them both in the bag. And some clever little grafter tried to pinch a set of candle-sticks from Lambeth Palace, but the old bishop nabbed him.'

'The bishop himself?'

'Not in person. His housekeeper caught the kid in the act and she and some visiting vicar locked him up in a cellar. Right old battle-axe, that one looks. Anyway, I bunged him up and she'll give evidence.'

'She's willing to do so?'

'Willing? Just try to keep her out of the court – she'll be grabbing the judge by the lughole.'

'Just so long as the clergy don't start taking the bread out of our mouths and feeling the collars of all the villains in

Lambeth. But as far as the serious stuff goes, we're getting somewhere with those women in the river – at least, I think there's something afoot. We now have two different leads, Hassblack, that bring us close to our army-doctor friend. He attempted to get a lady called Mrs Darby into conversation, put some dubious substance that might have been ether on to her handkerchief and hinted she should come to see him privately. And there was a chambermaid at the Savoy, girl called Ruby. She told Castleton a few weeks ago that there was some linen missing on that floor.'

'What floor is that, sir?'

'At the Savoy – the one that's been taken over for wounded officers. Anyway, now the girl's disappeared herself. It's my intention to apply for a search warrant.'

'For the Savoy Hotel, sir?'

'For the sixth floor. Yes, Sergeant. Is that so shocking?'

'It'll ruffle some feathers, sir.'

'That it may well do, but I cannot rely on getting all my information from Castleton. The hotel won't let him have the run of the premises, there's no doubt about that. He may be the hotel detective, but he's got to play by house rules and not upset the inmates. No, we've got to do the next bit ourselves.'

'And Mr Craston, sir? He telephoned while you was out. There's something he wants to see you about. He said, could you call round about seven this evening? It sounded to me . . .'

'Yes, Hassblack?'

'It sounded as if he were real bothered, sir. But it might wear off, if you know what I mean.'

Garrety did know what Hassblack meant: every policeman worth his salt could sense when a witness was bursting to bare his soul, and when he was going off the boil.

'I'll go round there now.' Garrety was looking up at the

charge-room clock, which struck six in its melodious voice, a booming small-scale imitation of Big Ben, which Authority must have felt would command imperial respect even in these unpromising surroundings.

The temperature was well below freezing as he made his way along the riverside. He could sense it on his skin, feeling his face go numb, and the folds of his coat were stiff and crackling with cold. Above the crowded roofs of Lambeth the starlight skittered brightly, swamped by the yellow glow of the street-lights closer to the embankment. As Garrety walked past St Thomas's Hospital, a figure came lurching out of the darkness. Under a street-lamp, the policeman saw a long gash on the man's cheek, with the neat handiwork of some surgeon that had stitched the edges together.

'Tell me, for the love of God, is there a Catholic church near here. I need a priest!'

The man clutched Garrety's lapel, oblivious to everything but some inner demon. His clothes and hair were disordered and he stank oddly of rum with a strong whiff of Lister's or some such disinfectant, with which presumably they had swabbed his cheek in the hospital.

'You've got a bad injury. You ought to go home.'

'Fuck that, mister, I can't feel a thing. Where's the church? I got to see him now – the priest.'

'Turn left at the next bridge and carry straight on down the main road. The Cathedral's on your right.'

'God bless you.' He stumbled off.

Gone to confess? wondered Garrety. What makes it so urgent for them?

He turned away to the right and found himself a few minutes later in Stamford Street. The light was on in young

Craston's rooms and Oliver clattered down the stairs and answered the door himself.

The room seemed disordered, with books lying about and several dirty cups and glasses on the tables. A fern set in a brass planter on top of a tall stand looked dismally dry and withered at the edges. Garrety pulled off his gloves and, without waiting for an invitation, took off his greatcoat and put it over the back of an upright chair.

Craston did not offer Garrety any refreshment. He did not look at him. He sat down and began to speak in an absolutely colourless and flat voice that seemed so distant and artificial that Garrety was somehow reminded of a phonograph. 'I have some information to give you.'

'Just a moment, sir. I'd like to take notes.'

'Very well.' The young fellow sounded truculent, but made no difficulties. 'I suppose now I've got this far . . .' he said, and broke off.

There was a pause. As Garrety fished out his notebook, rubbing his still-frozen hands together, Oliver looked up, and the policeman was reminded irrelevantly of the lurching drunk who had wanted a priest – the same haggard eyes, the same inner compulsion driving him – to do what? Clear his conscience?

'As I reported to your man on the telephone, when I was going home I saw a man – a doctor – from the Savoy Hotel. It's the doctor looking after the wounded officers on the sixth floor. The one whom I encountered speaking to a lady by the name of Mrs Darby.'

'Where did you see him, sir?'

'At this end of Waterloo Bridge. He had his coat unbuttoned . . . and he was wearing something strange beneath it. It looked like an apron.'

'Describe it.'

'Like a butcher's apron. But not striped. And, Inspector, it was very stained. The marks looked blackish in the light.'

'In the street-lights, sir? What time was this?'

Craston answered very slowly and reluctantly, twisting his hands together as he spoke. 'Three o'clock in the morning.'

Garrety couldn't help himself exclaiming, 'Three o'clock, sir?'

Craston's face looked up in total misery. 'Yes, Inspector. I was on my way back to my rooms.'

'When was this, sir?'

'Two nights ago.'

'Were you alone?'

'Yes.'

'Where had you been?'

The young man took a long breath. 'Can you promise me it won't go any further?'

'No,' said Garrety unfeelingly. 'I can't promise you that. You have to tell me, nevertheless. I'll need some corroboration of the time. We'll search the area for more witnesses, of course, so there may be someone who saw you—'

'Greet's Jetty.' Oliver blurted it out.

'You mean to the shack near where we found the woman in the river?' Garrety was astonished for a moment, though afterwards when he reflected he thought he should not have been. Decent young men like Craston did it all the time – went to places like that a couple of times and were caught out by fate before they had time to clean the puke off their trousers.

Craston nodded.

'You were alone at the bridge, but was there anyone at the Jetty who knew you?'

Again, Craston nodded. He hung his head, and Garrety saw that the back of his neck was very thin and bony. Then he looked up.

He's not going to answer, thought Garrety. Not if he went down there with a pal of his. English public schoolboys – they don't tell tales. That's where they draw the line and confession stops.

But Craston did go on. 'A woman.'

Because women in places like that don't count, Garrety added silently to himself. Aloud, he asked, 'Did she give you a name?'

Craston gave a small, unhappy laugh. 'Regina. It means —'

' "Victoria Regina" and all that. Think she was a joker?'

'Might have been. But she seemed quite proud of it, so maybe it was her real name after all.'

'Maybe. How long were you with her?'

'All the time, practically. At first there was a group of people, and they were putting bets on greyhounds.'

'Did you give them any money?'

'No, I just wrote down the names of the dogs for them. Then a boy brought a lot of money back and they bought me more drinks. And then she and I – well, we went upstairs, just the two of us.' Craston was silent for a few minutes, his face very white.

Garrety said nothing, waiting for the physical memories to subside and the public story to be resumed. No good asking for the details right now. Craston would be too embarrassed – or ashamed, or both.

'And then, after a time, a man came in.'

Garrety closed his notebook and sighed. 'Get your cash, did he?'

'Everything I had on me.'

'Watch – anything like that? Anything that could connect you to the place?' Garrety's voice was normal, routine.

'No, just the money.'

'And then?'

'Then I left.' Craston slumped like a marionette that has had its strings pulled. 'Inspector, I needn't tell you that if I have to give evidence in court, the scandal would ruin everything for me. I would be finished. They can't take risks like that.' No need to spell out who 'They' might be.

'I understand that, sir. But you'll have to face the possibility, I'm afraid. We'll need you to make a full statement later on.'

'Would it have to come out . . . about the woman? Will you be speaking to her?'

'Well, she could testify you were in that area at that time, though of course the evidence of a prostitute's not worth much. Yes, I'll get one of my men to speak to her.'

'Yes, I understand.'

Garrety picked up his coat and gloves.

'Inspector, the woman, Regina – well, she didn't have anything to do with the money.'

'Come on, sir. We're all grown up now, aren't we?'

'Yes, but she tried to stop him. And he hit her. Gave her a damned hard knock.'

'Ah, sure, she'll be pure as the driven snow, Mr Craston!' Garrety knew he'd gone too far and now the boy would clam up.

Craston gave him an angry look and compressed his lips. 'Well, in any case, that's all I have to say.'

Garrety was almost out of the door when he was called back. Craston was on the staircase, holding on to the banister as if it were the last thing left in the world.

'There is something more, Inspector, on another matter. Not connected with that business.'

They took only a minute or so, but it was interesting, what Craston had to say, and he'd have to pass a note on elsewhere. It was rightfully the business of another department altogether. But there was no doubt – he couldn't dodge his duty. They'd be grateful.

All the same, thought Garrety as he went out into the freezing night, placing his notebook once more in his pocket, the boy had blabbed that out. He wouldn't have thought him capable of it.

CASTLETON WALKED FROM THE SAVOY IN A DIRECTION HE had not taken for a long while. He disliked crossing the river at the best of times, but did so from time to time when it was necessary to act as escort to one of the guests or make enquiries on behalf of some exalted personage. It was hardly possible always to avoid the major railway junctions of Waterloo or London Bridge, or the expanse of smart villas that stretched from Streatham to Balham. Occasionally a message must be delivered, an enquiry must be made in these outposts, but Castleton did not linger in the realms that lay close in to the river. As fast as he could, he passed through, in a hansom or a railway carriage, staring from a window at the mean alleys that congregated like thick black charcoal streaks close to the docks and jetties.

It was with reluctance, therefore, that he picked his way down from the embankment. Ufford Row lay a little further south still, towards the Elephant and Castle. It was an uncovered drain a few feet wide rather than a street: uneven slabs and cobbles, stepping-stones rather than paving, sloped towards a gutter. Feet slipped and slithered on their icy surfaces, as well as on the nameless scraps embedded in the ice.

Not that there were many of these. Precious little was cast away. Potatoes were not peeled in Ufford Row; bones were sold to the rag-and-bone man. Human shit was freely parted with, though Ufford Row denizens valued the equine variety, which was collected from those nicer streets wide enough to allow the passage of a horse, and sold for manure. The communal privies in the basements were always overflowing, but the dogs and rats were excellent scavengers. The house walls were a single skin of porous brick in thickness, and that so rotted through, so penetrated by soot and wet, that it was often possible to put a fist into the very fabric.

Castleton did not need directions. His feet quickly found a balance, toes pointed in towards the gutter, that kept him from sliding downwards. Urchins had crowded round him at first, one or two jeering and others begging. The weather kept women from sitting on their doorsteps, as they did in summer, but it did not prevent the children from running up and down. Most of them had the necks of their vests and jerseys sewn up tightly for the winter, so they could not take them off. He clipped the nearest – a grubby boy with solidified rivulets of Chartreuse-green snot between nostrils and upper lip – a mighty stroke round the ear, and followed it up with a torrent of abuse.

The children troubled him no longer. Wrapped in his long waterproof, he moved on.

There had been no number in the address Ruby had given. The very bottom of society, like the very top, has no need of numbering its houses. The families are sufficiently widely known in the district.

It was thus, after one or two enquiries only, that Castleton stopped outside a rotting wooden door, which might have given entry to a shed. He called out and banged his fist cautiously.

After a few moments, the door was pulled open. The woman was gross, her skin whitish-yellow, walrus-like, oddly smooth, as if it were so bloated from the inside that the wrinkles were reduced to shallow lines. She was short of breath; her long dress was of an indescribable colour now, washed to a felted grey, with a deep flounce of dirt round the hem.

'I've come about Ruby.'

Now he could see that this woman had eyes that must once have resembled Ruby's, but were now sunk in little fatty nests and cushions, and reddened with years of smoke and grime.

'She ain't 'ere, mister.'

Castleton could practically have seen this for himself, so small was the space beyond the fat shoulder. One room, with a shallow stone sink in the corner and an open drain that doubtless poured into the gutter outside. The floor was earth: the splintered remains of floorboards round the edges of the room showed where they had been torn out, for sale or to burn as firewood.

There was a movement in the corner and a bundle of rags reared up, dividing surprisingly into two children, who stared at him out of dirty faces.

'Gi' us summat.'

He ignored them, and they subsided as the woman raised a hand towards them.

'I want to know about Ruby. What did she bring you?'

The woman looked terrified. 'She never stole nothing, mister. I 'asn't seen her for two week or more.'

'I know she brought stuff here – now, what was it?'

'Nothin', honest. It were only some food, sometimes. Just scraps, sir, trash, like. Else it would have gone to the pigswill. There's pigs eat a damn sight better than what we do.'

There was a snorting noise from the floor, and Castleton looked down. There was a man, lying in straw, thin, like the children, shaking a fist uselessly. 'Too drunk to stand on his legs, I suppose.'

'He'll be all right. Takes it for the pain. When he can get it.'

'Did she leave anything with you?'

'What do you mean, leave anything?'

'What did she bring besides food? Stolen stuff?'

He leaned down and grabbed the ear of one of the youngsters. 'Ruby ever give you anything to sell? Any sheets, towels . . . rings – anything like that?'

But he thought he knew the answer already. This was a level of poverty below even that of the thief or the pawnshop: there had probably been nothing to sell in this house for a very long time. If the woman was fat, she was so from disease.

The woman rushed at him like a toothless bear defending her cub, and knocked his arm away, an exertion that left her panting for breath and wheezing as she held the child behind her back. He laughed, remembering something.

'Look, Ruby's gone missing. I don't want to accuse her of anything, but there's folk that will – they'll say she's been pinching stuff and run away. So tell me if you know where she is, will you, you stupid cow?'

'Run away?'

The man seemed to understand something. From the floor, he called out, 'She wouldn't do that! Our Rube!'

'Well, it looks like she's gone and done it. Did she have any blokes round here?'

347

'Naw, not Ruby. She was a good, quiet girl. Our Arthur leathered 'er if she weren't, didn't yer?'

'Yeh, leathered 'er.' The thin arm made a feeble beating movement in the nest of straw and there was a thin laugh that echoed Castleton's own.

Castleton was too canny to retreat yet. 'Where did he get it?'

The woman pretended not to know what he meant.

'The grog. Come on, where did he get the money for it? He's had a right session, hasn't he? Must have been so drunk he was pissing through his neck. Look at him – he can hardly crawl now. And don't tell me he'd get anything on the slate – so where did he get the brass?'

Backing away from the door, frightened but with a sort of anger, she said, 'He didn't steal nothing, if that's what you're meaning!'

'Then how? Oh, for God's sake! You're not on the game at your age?'

The woman suddenly bowed her head. 'I can't, no longer, 'cept sometimes at night.' Then she looked up again. 'But Ruby did give us a bit. She said some doctor give her summat to clean his place. On this side of the river.'

Castleton dug his fist into his pocket and the children started to clamour like geese seeing a handful of corn. He pushed a few coins into the woman's hand. 'Don't let him have that, you daft bitch.'

The inside of the room was no warmer than outside in the street.

It was not far to Lambeth Police Station, where he found Garrety arraigning a couple of young fellows caught an hour or two ago with intent to rob a wine shop. He watched, expressionless, as they were charged and taken to the cells, and Hassblack clanged the metal door shut behind them. One of them started blubbering and there came the sound of an abrupt blow and then a wail, worse than ever. Garrety turned to Castleton and led him into his office, with the frosted glass panel in the door and the desk piled high with record books and charge sheets. There was a strange smell of ink and urine and disinfectant. An immaculately clean pen-wiper of red felt embroidered with marigolds sat on the desk, beside the photograph of a pretty, sad-eyed woman with her dark hair piled up and a cross on a chain round her neck.

Castleton didn't waste time, though he took out a small silver cigar-case, offered it to Garrety, who declined, and took and lit one for himself.

'There's a girl, one of the chambermaids, who's run off – at least, that's what it might be. She came to me because some sheets had disappeared.'

Garrety raised his eyebrows.

'Oh, I haven't come here over some stolen sheets. It's where they went missing. From the sixth floor. Where our pal the doctor is in charge of the wounded heroes, and it seems he got our Ruby cleaning his surgery. 'Course, the girl might have run off by herself – afraid of being blamed.'

'Do you think she ran away?'

There was an odd alliance between the two men, as though they trusted each other's judgement.

'No. Poor little bitch, I don't think she did.'

'I suppose she didn't go back to her family?'

'No, I checked. Don't know why I bothered going there in the first place. There's nothing there.'

Pulling his muffler round his neck, he threw the butt of his little cigar into the street outside the police station and it hissed on the ground and melted a small spreading pool in the frost. Castleton began walking, but somehow not in the direction he had expected to take. He walked back the way he had come, to a spot a few streets north of Ufford Row. He turned into a road that was just a little better than Ruby's home, as though the inhabitants were fighting to keep their distance from the slippery edges of the pit. Windows were cleaner, on the whole the panes were uncracked, some effort had been made here and there to paint the woodwork. The occasional house boasted an iron boot-scraper at the side.

He moved slowly along, his blond hair shining in the cold morning light, not acknowledging the occasional greeting or jeer. After a while he stepped up and pushed without hesitation at a door, which swung open. A woman turned round with surprise. Her hair grew over her forehead in the same deep wave as his own.

61

'NO, NO, ABSOLUTELY OUT OF THE QUESTION!' THOMAS
Worton slammed his fist down on the desk to illustrate his
point. His office in Scotland Yard seemed to resound with the
thud. 'Do you realize who those people are? Army officers,
Garrety, and all well connected. Members of prominent
families. War heroes to boot!'

'I don't think any of them are involved in this business. It's
just that we might find out something.'

'And what evidence do you have to suggest that? Some
taradiddle about this man Newbold running over Waterloo
Bridge at night – and a missing chambermaid! And for that
you expect to disturb the privacy of these gentlemen in the
Savoy Hotel! Really, Garrety, we cannot have such disorderly
Irish notions here! You must learn to adapt to the way in
which things are conducted in London – it's good advice! You
may question the servants and the medical staff, and that is as
much as will be permitted.'

There was a long pause and then he heard footsteps. A

uniformed man opened the door without knocking and announced: 'Sir Edward Bradford.'

The man who came into the room was one of the few people in London who would have required no introduction. The left sleeve of his frock-coat was pinned emptily across his breast, and the beaten maroon cheeks betrayed his long service in an altogether different climate. He had in fact seen long service in India, and was notorious and beloved among the Metropolitan Police, whose Commissioner he now was, for having lost an arm to a tiger.

He was evidently expected, and Worton suddenly was standing upright and greeting the visitor deferentially, offering a chair, a whisky. Both were refused. Only then was Garrety introduced.

'Ah, yes,' said Sir Edward. 'You've got involved in something on the other side of the river. Strictly speaking, it's out of your divisional territory in any case.'

Garrety was surprised that Sir Edward seemed to know about the Savoy affair, but something told him that there were repercussions at higher levels.

He found Worton was nodding at him in dismissal.

'I'll see you get the credit for this other business.' Cold, unfeeling, just. There was more warmth in the commissioner than in his underling, thought Garrety, more of a man you could have enjoyed the crack with.

The senior man said, as Garrety was leaving, 'Mr Craston deserves some sort of a reward – oh, nothing material, of course. He is a gentleman, after all, and in any case you could say it was his patriotic duty. Acknowledging his part in the matter will have to be very discreetly done, of course. I'll make sure it's passed on to the right quarter.'

'No warrant,' Garrety said to Hassblack later.

'Damme, that's a facer, sir! We can't just go arresting him. We haven't got nothing that'll stand up in court!'

'No, and we likely won't get it if we go ballet-dancing round. But he's not killing for convenience, or because he's botched his abortion job. He likes hurting women – and then he finishes them off. So he'll do it again.'

'Because he enjoys it.'

'Yes, exactly.'

'This Ruby girl—'

'Yes, I know. She doesn't fit. The others were older, ladies from well-to-do backgrounds. But it doesn't mean she's safe – not if she knew something that would give him away.'

62

I LIKE THIS ONE. I LIKED HER FROM THE MOMENT I SAW HER IN the tea-room: she was lifting her cup to her mouth, sipping it, slightly nervous. It's so easy to pick them out, the women who aren't used to being on their own in a public place, unless it's to patronize the stores in Knightsbridge. Women like Elizabeth usually have a husband in tow, or a daughter, a sister . . . That's why it's good to find them at railway stations. The normal rhythm of their lives has been interrupted for some reason. There's been a family emergency, something out of the ordinary, a special shopping trip . . . or perhaps some private reason which she doesn't want to confide to anyone, least of all her own family doctor, some whiskery bore who plays golf with her husband. If they find themselves pregnant at that age, they're often desperate not to go through with it. A woman of forty doesn't want to find herself landed again with all the pain and noise and screaming, just when her other children are grown up. And if the husband has been amusing himself somewhere else, well, so perhaps has she . . . and the lover will vanish faster than a rat diving down a rathole when she starts letting out her corset.

Yes, very fruitful hunting grounds, the London railway stations, if you have a slight nose for women in trouble. Or even for ones who are slightly anxious, as was Elizabeth.

In her case, of course, it wasn't that she was pregnant. That would have been rather ironic, really, given the circumstances. No, it was a cousin living on her own, and this person, Dottie, God bless her, had developed an illness that necessitated Elizabeth's attentions. So she had travelled up to London from her safe little home in the suburbs, and then she was delayed in getting away from the aforesaid Dottie. So she had missed her train. And there she was, alone, pulling her good fur tippet round her shoulders, taking off her best kid gloves, looking about anxiously as she sat sipping her tea rather uncomfortably at the wrought-iron table. Anaemic, I should say, and probably feeling a little faint, to judge from the way she put her hand suddenly to her head.

I have become an expert at observing these details. No-one notices the casual, well-dressed passenger idling along a platform, peering here and there as one does to pass the time, at railway timetables, at public notices. And through the frosted glass of doors and windows. Sometimes I feel hugely powerful there, my eyes are so sharp, my senses quivering with excitement, waiting like a cat at a mousehole.

I could see with Elizabeth it would be quite difficult. Fortunately, old Jack was outside the station, and in just the right state – sober enough to understand what I wanted him to do, drunk enough to frighten the lady. So, for a platform ticket and half a crown, he went in and tried to speak to her, and she was duly horrified. God, he does stink, old Jack! I don't know where he sleeps – he must roll in the gutters to get himself into that state.

Anyway, he got to the lady before the barmaid could throw him out and I could see she was panicking. Never had anything like that to cope with on her own – now she was in the big city and some drunk was shoving his unwashed bristles in her face and upsetting her nice little tea-party.

I had taken care to dress as respectably as possible, making sure there were no tell-tale stains, best white starched shirt, regimental cuff-links. Of course, she was glad to see me! A brisk professional man coming to her rescue.

Bait the trap!

The next bit took some work, but I am very determined. Oh yes, and, of course, I don't have to mislead them on the first point. I am a doctor, after all. I have the jargon, the training. I can take a pulse in the authentic, unhesitating cold-fingered manner. And once they are convinced of that, the rest is easy. Very often ladies of a certain age have little problems anyway – perhaps they are flushing too brightly, or their husbands have too much interest . . . or too little . . . and they have headaches . . . Oh yes, they often want to speak to a medical man. Anyway, she allowed me to buy her a 'pick-me-up' – how I like my small jokes! – and that was my first success. I don't usually have to use that subterfuge: very often I can persuade them to come with me anyway. But she was quite cautious.

The wretched Dottie unknowingly assisted me; I was able to listen to the account of her symptoms, and to agree with the diagnosis made by some fellow who had always attended her. Then I suggested that her life could be made more comfortable, even prolonged. Elizabeth was of course now deeply involved with the possibilities: I was in fact providing a second medical opinion and she leaned earnestly over the white table-cloth towards me. I could see that the pupils of her eyes were contracting and she was getting drowsy. She had to prop her cheek on her hand. All was going remarkably well.

So I was able to assist her away from the tea-room. There was a nasty moment when she said that she would just go into the ladies' waiting-room until her train came, but I suggested I could give her something that would relieve her faintness, and promised to put her on the train when the time came.

She believed me.

And by the time I got her away out of the back of the station and along the Lower Marsh, she really was quite woolly. Her legs were almost giving way and I was a little concerned that I had overdone the dose. It was dark, of course, and there were not many people about, and there would be nothing unusual in that area in seeing a woman having to be supported along the pavement, but, even so, I didn't want to actually carry her. That would have been noticed, even in Lambeth.

We made it to the house and I managed to open the door myself, holding her with my other arm. Once inside, I took her into the consulting-room and sat her down in the chair . . . and that is always what starts it for me.

She was exactly right. I took off her outer garments, the absurd tippet and a thick coat underneath. Then I unpinned her hat, which was trimmed with ribbon and a bunch of silk. Her hair was still quite blonde, though with a little grey at the temples.

What delighted me especially was that underneath the coat she had on a dress in a deep lilac colour, a smoky pink-grey. Ah, now that colour reminds me of my childhood: of the lilac trees in our garden, which formed great overhanging, curving tents with their weighty sprays. My mother loved to sit under them when they were in bloom.

There was no fear of being disturbed; the Leadbetter woman and her servant are well paid not to attend to any noises emanating from my rooms. My usual business in Leadbetter's house, of course, does sometimes involve the patients in some crying and weeping: it is inevitable. But that was not likely on this occasion. And Elizabeth was getting sleepier minute by minute. I lit the gas-fire to make her comfortable and so that the warmth would encourage torpor. She tried to apologize, struggling a few times to get up out of the chair, but I gently pushed her down again, and when I brought her a glass of warm milk and told her to drink it all, she did so without a word. I tipped the chain of the gaslight so that it dimmed. She fell asleep and still, when I looked at my watch at ten o'clock, was in deep slumber.

The rest took only a few minutes. I lifted up her eyelid and felt her pulse. Then I took her next door. I wanted to keep her in the chair, but the consulting-room would be needed again very shortly.

The dress was of some silky stuff, so that the lilac skirts gleamed with bluish tints as I lifted her and spread her on the table. Then I pushed up the skirts, and the white and pink petticoats underneath, and it all looked like the trumpet of a flower with her black-stockinged legs as the stamens.

I had intended to wait for a few more hours, but she was plump and the flesh still firm and rounded; there was a dusting of talcum powder on her thighs. She smelt of it, and of that faint smoky smell of urine as I knelt down, and that was all I wanted to start me off. I buried my face down between her legs and opened my mouth, pulling at my clothes, reaching for what I needed at the same time.

I think she tried to cry out, but I reached up easily enough and put one hand over her face, pressing the pad down on her mouth till she was silent. The blood from my bites was running down her legs now, soaking the stockings, but everything in here could be easily cleaned. Deeper and deeper I went, the teeth sharp and gnawing, my head tossing from side to side, the harsh net of pubic hair rubbing against my mouth. Maybe I was making sounds then, too ... I lost myself. That other presence came leaping into me. I was two people, one bent frantically over the still-living body, the other watching clinically from a distance.

But she gave me what I wanted. Blood and saliva were dripping from my mouth when I sank down on the floor beneath her. I had what was needed. I gasped for breath for a few moments and looked up at the still white face. There was no movement.

Hastily, I carried out the procedure I had planned.

My sweet Mrs Aline will call round early in the morning – as I had suggested, so that she can avoid the danger of prying eyes. I am in no anxiety about the lapse of time: all the scientific papers I had read demonstrated that I was well within the time limit.

53

AN ANGRY VOICE WAS RAISED, YELLING ABOVE THE TUMULT.
'Where the hell do you think you are?'

Garrety said, 'Go on, Hassblack. Get inside. Now!' He saw
his sergeant's stout serge back disappearing into the room.
'Through the ward – all the cupboards, under the beds.'

The two constables went through the doors ahead, beyond
which Garrety caught a glimpse of astonished men peering
from their beds or stopping in mid-hop on their crutches.
'For God's sake, what's going on?' called out one man, sitting
in pyjamas on the end of his bed. It was the authentic officer's
voice, but deprived of its certainty of command, and given no
answer.

'Sorry, sir.' A tall wardrobe door swung open and a blue-
uniformed arm riffled through the khakis and the gold-braided
jackets, revealed a pile of topees and long drawers. Another
policeman had already reached the matron's office at the far
end of the ward and pushed at the long navy cloak that hung
emptily on the back of the door.

His fellow pulled open a large canvas bag lying on the floor and turned his head aside, wrinkling up his face like a monkey's muzzle in disgust. 'God, the stink! It's the dirty linen, sir.'

Garrety had come up behind them. 'Tip it out. Go on, man.'

The sack was heavy, tied with a string that ran through slots in the neck. The big rough hands pulled them loose and tipped up the bag.

A tangle of stained sheets, some bloody and some with the greenish slime of diarrhoea flux, fell in a heap on the matron's carpet.

Garrety turned to the enraged commissionaire, who had pounded up the stairs, the lift being in use for the benefit of a marchioness on the floor below, returning from taking her dachshunds for their early-morning walk. She would not entrust this to a maid, insisting on observing for herself the state of their motions.

The man was sweating heavily inside his uniform. Behind him, less sweaty but equally enraged, came a man in a frock-coat and pin-stripe trousers. I suppose, thought Garrety, this is no less a person than the hotel manager. He braced himself. This was the really dangerous opposition. The commission-aire he could override; maybe even the angry nurse who was rushing along the corridor towards them. But this man would know a lot of people – he had enough pull to really cause trouble.

'Who gave you orders to do this? Where's your warrant?'

The throng was now increased by the nurse, who had been rolling a bandage at a bedside. 'Stop this! It's an absolute dis-grace – we have patients here to think about!' Her headdress bobbed with her rage.

'Sorry, madam.' Garrety signalled, and the sheets were shovelled back into their container.

'Your career will be finished!'

They went on. Wash-rooms, shouts, lavatories, apologies. A surgical trolley sent flying as a sergeant stumbled. Chemical smells as a bottle overturned.

Nothing.

Back through the ward, enraged faces, reddened permanently by sun and temporarily by anger.

Newbold's office, where Hassblack had already pulled open the cupboard doors.

Wooden boxes for filing cards. Stethoscope, cases of instruments.

Green baize screen.

Washbasin, commode.

Hassblack's voice. 'Sir, it's no good.'

The manager writing down the numbers on the sergeants' uniforms, taking their names, apologizing on behalf of the hotel to some moustachioed hero on crutches.

'I'm so sorry, Sir Edward. I assure you the Savoy is in no way to blame ... Yes, we will be taking action ... most definitely, I assure you! Yes, the commissioner, quite!'

His own face, reflected in the glass of the windows overlooking the river as he went along the corridor.

Fool. Gambler. Disobeying orders. Bloody idiotic Irishman, charging in, ignoring all the rules these people lived by.

He could say it all about himself.

Castleton's pale face in the corridor, staring at him.

Well, he needn't worry. Garrety wasn't going to give him away. It was a trivial point in all this – why had the man helped him anyway? It was something the policeman didn't understand. Irrelevantly, Garrety noticed the pale sunlight on the man's smooth blond head. Did he never look rumpled or sprawling? A man with a perfect varnish on him. But he had taken the risk of coming to the police over Ruby. The hotel might never forgive one of its employees whose actions had contributed to a police raid.

The police were retreating, their tails between their legs.

Castleton was jerking his head slightly to one side.

Looking in that direction, Garrety saw that a passageway led across the corridor – to the service lift, if Garrety had his bearings correct, the one that led down to that discreet side entrance.

Striding down the passage, he ignored the shouts of the hotel manager, feeling the clumsy width of his shoulders in the narrow space, as he saw the plain unmarked door.

Locked.

But flimsily: no bonds or tiaras to protect in here.

Wrenching at the small brass handle with desperation, not betrayed on his face, only in the surge of rage within his body. His shoulder thudding against the door.

The silent, muffled room. The shelves piled high with white linen, with deeply folded towels.

Taking a step, slowly now. Pulling at the linen.

'For God's sake, man, are you mad? The police are going to pay for every penny of the damage!'

And then the voice stopping suddenly, and only the sound of the man breathing as he looked over his shoulder in the narrow confine of the linen-room.

And, as Garrety pushed the heap of bath towels to one side, more and more of that thin red-elbowed arm coming into view, flopping down quite suddenly and swinging back and forth. Until it stopped still.

There was a pillowcase under the body, with brown stains that had leaked through from something inside.

Garrety carefully reached inside and pulled it out.

A rubberized apron, with a dreadful kind of practicality about it.

64

'THE BLOOD ON THE PILLOWCASE DIDN'T COME FROM HER. She was strangled.' Gulliver indicated the body of Ruby, lying on the pathologist's table in the morgue. 'You can see the pressure of his hands – look, there are the thumb-marks.'

'The doctor was seen on Waterloo Bridge with a stained apron.'

'Well, wherever that apron is now, it was stained with another's blood, not Ruby's.'

Castleton, who was waiting in the background to say his formal piece, came nearer and looked with Garrety at the two deep impressions dug into her throat.

'And she was a good girl, poor Ruby, if that's who she is,' the pathologist continued. 'Not a candidate for his special medical services.'

Castleton made his statement of identification. 'I suppose the hotel's name must appear on the death certificate,' he added, turning away.

Gulliver looked up sharply. 'I shall object most strongly if the coroner's certificate does not accurately describe the place of death! And that in itself would ensure the matter receives the attention of the newspapers!'

Castleton sighed. 'Just thought it was worth a try.' He smoothed his immaculate lapels, and added, 'I'll go and inform her mother, before she gets an official visit from you bluebottles. I'm not a complete bastard, you know.'

'You could have fooled me.' Gulliver turned back to the body.

'The question is,' said Garrety, 'where is Newbold now? This wasn't his usual method. Ruby must have stumbled into this, caught him unawares. Maybe he was disposing of the linen, or even one of the bodies. He must have thought she would give him away – if he was hiding stuff in the linen cupboard, or used the sheets to wrap the bodies in. Poor Perdita Harston, and the other woman pulled out of the river. There may have been more – we might never know. But, from what he said to Mrs Darby, he's found somewhere else, somewhere safer.'

'She doesn't know where?'

Garrety moved away from the table.

'Can you put the sheet back over her?' Gulliver called to his assistant. Ruby's white sculptured face vanished from their view.

'No,' Garrety said. 'Except that it was in Lambeth.'

Gulliver gave a grim laugh. 'Like finding a needle in a haystack!'

'Not quite. My sergeant's on to something. Men who prey on lonely women: now, where would they find a respectable lady, a nice middle-class person, as you might say, alone at night? Hassblack's wife picked up a bit of gossip, from the tea-room girl at Waterloo Station. A man who regularly goes there, perfectly respectable, and scrapes acquaintance with strange women. I'll lay a small wager his new "surgery" is near a station – and one of the biggest is right on this patch, and right opposite the Savoy.'

'It's just tittle-tattle, though, isn't it? You might likely end up with nothing!'

'It's all we can try.'

65

THE MARKET STALLS WERE BEING SET UP IN THE CHILL OF THE early morning, and it would be difficult to get a hansom any-where near the house. Aline Garrety set off to walk.

Will was working an early shift today: he had set off in the dark, and she had watched his dark shape depart as he went down the street, his breath a misty cloud in the dim light of the lamps. Then she had slipped out of bed, and down to the kitchen, where the frying-pan was still hot from the bacon and eggs he had cooked for himself. She felt no pain after the visit to Dr Bolitho the previous day, though he had warned her there might be some. 'But come as early as you can tomorrow morning,' he had said. 'I have a lot of work ahead of me with my war patients, I'm afraid.'

She slipped into the side entrance and found him waiting. 'It's so good of you, Doctor, to make time to see me like this.'

'Ah, well, infertility is a special medical interest of mine. There's not been much work done on it in this country, you know. The leading medical men are American. It will be quite a feather in our caps if we can do something about it here!'

She undressed behind a screen, but there was a loose gown waiting for her to put on, and she didn't feel embarrassed with him.

'Now, I'm going to ask you to breathe this – just for a few minutes. It will relax you, you understand? I'll keep talking to you as you go to sleep, so you can hear my voice. I'll ask you a few questions, just to see if you can still hear me ... Think about something ordinary, just your life every day ... like drinking tea, meal-times ... When do you usually take your dinner, Mrs Garrety?'

She said drowsily, 'Oh, when he comes off his shift.'

'Oh? And what is his employment?'

She was just managing to answer him, hearing the sleepiness in her own voice.

Aline felt that something enormous was happening in her life. If this worked ... but she would never tell Will. He would have hated the idea that she had gone to some place that was a bit hole-in-the-corner. 'Only, it's the opposite of a back-street abortionist! This doctor helps you get that way!' It was a good joke she had made to herself and she broke into laughter.

She was still laughing happily as she breathed in through the mask. The rubber smelled nasty, but the sensation was really quite pleasant ... warm and buzzing. There was that cook who had called it champagne chloric – what was the story? – the doctors had made a fizzy drink of ether with aerated water and the cook had tried it out ... It seemed hilariously funny now, so nice of Dr Bolitho to tell her about it. 'And the cook said, "Oh, sir, can I have some more of that champagne chlory!"'

Aline was smiling now and it crossed her mind that this was

a lovely way of having this operation. It was going to be a success, she was sure of it, and she and Will would be laughing with their baby . . . She could see a little baby face, smiling and gurgling, the pink mouth opening . . . and then she had a whirling, giddy feeling so that the world went black and was spinning round and round and she was nearly falling off the edge . . . the edge of what?

There was a moment of truth before she went off, so that she recognized something to do with Will. He hated the thought of another man looking at her: it was a feeling she always sensed running beneath the surface of their long discussions, late at night, when she cried so often and he put his arm round her and stroked her tangled hair, combing it with his fingers. She would spare him the knowledge. Now and always, Will! No confessions. Ever!

Smiling, promising, she went off into a velvety darkness; she was just aware of Dr Bolitho going out of the room, which seemed odd, but then she fell asleep.

When she awoke, she was feeling a bit sick and she had an ache in her stomach, just a sort of scraping pain, nothing bad.

Dr Bolitho was bending over her. 'That's all right; you're doing fine.' He was holding a glass to her lips. 'Just take a sip of water. Now, you stay here for an hour or so, with your feet up . . . There, I'll just put a blanket over you, to keep you warm. Then you can go home – but take it easy for the rest of the day!'

How tender he is, she thought. No-one could be kinder!

MRS CRASTON LOOKED OUT OF THE WINDOW AT THE RIVER, chilly in the early evening. She did not really like living so close to it, fearing it might flood, and at this time of year she watched its level anxiously, as if it were a creeping menace threatening her household. But the house had belonged to her husband's parents and he had always lived here; there was no question of moving.

On this particular evening, Menander Craston was attending a Royal Society lecture, and would then take dinner with some of his colleagues. It was a good evening for her son to come to see her, avoiding the conflict that had recently erupted in the Craston family between the two older children and their father.

'So are you and Maggie truly intending to carry out this mad plan of yours?'

Oliver hesitated. 'We hope to do so still, Mother. I am determined to help her with her studies as much as I can. At present I am still very junior, though, and I may need a little advancement in the department before I can quite afford the expense of the fees.'

He saw a look of triumph on his mother's face, and felt a flash of anger, but there was nothing he could do. In any case, he thought, she does not see very far ahead – she never did. She lives for these little moments of success in her own schemes for us. But it may be that my career will not be broken apart altogether, that I have managed to save myself and Mags as well. That remains to be seen.

Since what he thought of as the loss of Rosa, Oliver had been alternately tormented and numbed. Each morning he washed, ate something – he didn't care what – climbed into his clothes, did up his cuff-links, knotted his tie, pulled on his waistcoat and moved down the stairs. He went to work, set about his daily routine like a machine and then returned to the emptiness of his rooms.

Unable to sleep, he would get up to peer out of the window at the empty freezing pavements. Those were the times when the memory of what he had seen in the Savoy came to torment him, no less vivid as the nights went by. He relived again and again the moment when he opened the door and saw their bodies entwined.

Smelling disgustedly his own rising lust, he would pound the pillow with his fists, imagining now Michel, now Rosa, beneath his blows. Eventually he would pull open the window to the winter night, his dreams and fantasies subsiding as the air blew in. I never knew I could feel like this, he thought, in an agony, and I don't know how to feel it and go on living. Someone tell me what to do, how to bear it.

There was no-one.

Once or twice in the following week Madigan made an approach: perhaps he suspected something was wrong. Oliver knew that he was looking strange, even after he had dressed and brushed his hair and done everything he thought was normal. There were grey hollows under his eyes, and already he looked thinner: the waistband of his trousers hung loosely. Madigan noticed this. 'You're looking a bit knocked, old man. Fancy an evening in the West End? We could go to a show, that sort of thing.'

But Oliver rebuffed his colleague, as he had done his mother, who of course had immediately blamed his new domestic circumstances, now that he no longer lived under her roof. 'I've had flu,' he said. 'Don't fuss, Mother!'

Maggie, he knew, had guessed his wretchedness, but was always too tactful, so that even her sensitivity was un-welcome, as if she were deliberately avoiding something that lay like an invisible obstacle between them. He could hardly bear to face her, though she never mentioned the fear of dis-appointment that must be eating away inside her, the fear that Oliver might never be able to help her.

He called round sometimes at Barnes, but only when, as now, his father would be out. He feared that his mother would scrutinize his face again, in that detailed, intimate way that he hated. But with relief he realized that her thoughts had turned towards another of her children. He was safe for the moment. Her loving devotion, her determination, was focused elsewhere.

'If your plans for Maggie don't come off, and she is not to be a lady doctor after all' – this was said with a rising note of satisfaction – 'then we will have to think of what she is to do.'

He hadn't given this any attention. It had never occurred to him that Maggie would do anything other than what she did at present, which was to read and study on her own as much as she could.

'She's been looking very drawn of late and she spends far too much time alone. We must give her some society, a little company, to take her out of herself. My interests – my Reading Ladies and so on – they are not enough for her. Now, your father goes to France next month for a conference in Paris and, since he hates social entertainment, that would be an ideal opportunity to give a dinner-party without annoying him. You could take his place. You are quite old enough to do so.'

Oliver visualized sitting in his father's chair, carving the meat, raising his glass. The vision condemned him, made a prisoner of his life, a nonsense of his escape from Barnes. 'Oh, Mother, I wouldn't want to . . .'

'For your sister's sake, Oliver. You must do it for Maggie. Now, who do we know . . .? We must invite people outside our normal circle of acquaintances – some new blood, yes. Now, who do you know . . . ? Isn't there someone in the ministry – perhaps a colleague in your office? Some young man?'

So that was what she was driving at! He should have foreseen it.

'Or perhaps one or two of the senior people there – after all, your father is quite well known in scientific circles. It's not as if we were nobodies.'

Oliver had dreadful visions of his mother issuing invitations to sundry Foreign Office dignitaries. He racked his brain for a diversion. 'No, no, there's a younger man – chap called Madigan. I work with him.'

'Perfect!' said his mother. 'Now, tell me about his family.'

67

THE DOORBELL RANG AGAIN. OLIVER PUT DOWN *PROTOCOL and Placing*, looking at the clock as the hands reached eleven, and wondered if by any chance it could be for him. He didn't have any friends who would call at this time of night, which made him feel fearful, because the only person he could think of was the policeman, Garrety.

He heard the landlady's footsteps. The door was opened on the chain and a low murmuring followed. Then the door swung open, there were voices in the hall, and Mrs Rattern called up the staircase, 'Mr Craston, there's a young lady here!'

The disapproval was evident in her voice, even before Oliver got downstairs and saw Mrs Rattern's face at the bottom of the stairs, peering upwards, mouth tightly pressed.

The lamp hung in the middle of the brown-painted hallway. There was a shape in the darkness just inside the door, the long outline of a woman's cape or coat, and he assumed at first that it was Maggie, come perhaps about some emergency in

Barnes. In fact, he had begun to say, 'It's all right, Mrs Rattern,' when he was cut off sharply.

'It is not all right, Mr Craston. I cannot have you receiving young women in your rooms late at night. What will people think?'

The woman had moved forward into the light and he saw with a shock that went right to his very heart that it was Rosa.

'Mrs Rattern, this is Miss Darby.'

'I'm so sorry,' she was saying. 'I do need to speak to Mr Craston for just a few minutes.'

The landlady looked her up and down, eaten up with curiosity. Rosa was wearing a heavy black wrap, trimmed at the neck with some white fur, and a tiny black velvet bonnet, beneath which her lemon-yellow hair gleamed, looking as exotic as ever.

'Oh, very well. But I don't think it would be at all suitable if you went up to Mr Craston's rooms. You can use my parlour if you want to talk.'

She ushered Rosa through a curtain and then through the door behind it, at the back of the hallway. Oliver followed. Mrs Rattern evidently did not quite have the nerve to leave the parlour door ostentatiously ajar, but she added, 'I'll be in the next room.' There was no mistaking the warning.

In another minute, they were in a small stuffy space, with the harsh light switched on, casting a ring from above that sharpened the bones of Rosa's face with shadows from underneath. They sat down at a little circular table covered with a green plush cloth with polished brass studs round the edges. The grate was full of dead coals and ashes and the room had a chill, smoky smell.

Rosa took her gloves off and put her outstretched hands on the table. Oliver looked across, and found himself staring directly at her aquamarine eyes. Tears were forming.

'What is it?' he asked. He found he didn't want to say to her any of the hurtful things he had rehearsed in those long nights. Because he didn't feel any of those things. Not any longer.

Her mouth was very soft and quivering. She said, almost in a whisper, 'Oliver, I'm so ashamed of . . . of the way you found us.'

Naked, he thought, but it no longer aroused him. 'I . . . I had no claim on you,' he said. 'I can't judge you.'

'But it's not why I'm here. It hasn't got anything to do with that,' she hurried on. 'Not with what happened that night. It's about my mother.'

He seemed unable to say much more than 'Tell me', which sounded like a croak.

But Rosa didn't seem to notice anything wrong with his voice. 'Oliver, she's been arrested! This morning.'

'Good Lord!'

'They've taken her to Holloway Prison!'

'Why, Rosa? On what grounds?'

'They didn't give any grounds. Two men with uniforms, and two others. They had special cards. They said they were within their rights to take her away for questioning! Oh, Oliver, I don't know what I'm going to do!'

'Why? Why did they take her away?'

'I don't know. They searched the house – everything! All our clothes, letters.'

Oliver gave a silent prayer of thanks that he had never committed his feelings for Rosa to paper. 'And they didn't give a reason?'

'No, but I think I might be able to guess.'

She leaned backwards a little, holding a handkerchief up,

patting at her eyes, but partly perhaps to hide her face as she spoke. Her face looked beautiful still, even in the harsh light of the little parlour, where the electric light hung gloomily above them. He thought absurdly of some spiritualist's seance illustrated in a magazine: the ectoplasmic wraith floating above a round table.

'It may be partly that we lead very unconventional lives. My mother knew a great many artists and Michel lodged with us for a time.' She looked across at Oliver and must have seen something in his face that made her move on quickly, for she continued, 'Mother paints a little herself, you know. She has a studio on the top floor of the house and sometimes other artists would come there to work. And some people might think that we are a little, well, Bohemian, in our life-style.'

'I understand,' said Oliver, thinking of the picture, the flamboyant nude he had seen in Rosa's house. Hung right inside the hallway, where everyone, any busybody merely on a social call, could not fail to see it.

'And we have had one or two arguments with the neighbours – they are very narrow people, I'm afraid. I think my mother was just too much for them. They made . . . unkind remarks, sometimes. Yes, you see, she has lots of foreign visitors – and, of course, she doesn't fit in as any ordinary kind of English person. But I think there's something more.'

'What do you mean?'

'She couldn't understand it! Mother has never really taken any interest in politics, but they asked her about Ireland. About a new party that's being formed to fight for independence. Anyway, the policemen who came – they weren't the usual kind – seem convinced anyone Irish is automatically under suspicion. Of course, she believes in Home Rule for Ireland – anybody with spirit does!'

'They arrested her because of that?'

'Yes, and that's why they've kept her in Holloway. She's in a dreadful state. I've just come from visiting her. She's refusing to eat. And she cries her heart out. Oh, Oliver, it's dreadful to see her. The cell is so dirty and tiny – you can't imagine! Her health is not good, in any case – she has trouble with her heart sometimes, you know. I want to get her out straight away. Prison will destroy her! If I can get her out, we'll go to France immediately. We have lots of friends there.'

'Well, I'm sure they'll give her bail.' Oliver wondered if he could, or should, contribute to the bail bond if necessary. Perhaps better not, if his name were to appear on it and the two women vanished off to France.

'No, apparently they won't!'

'But surely—'

'They haven't even charged her!'

'Look, Rosa, you have to get a lawyer.'

'Oh, Oliver, we have so little in the way of money. You wouldn't believe!'

'What about the Monets? Surely they could help.'

She got up and walked the few steps that the space of the room permitted. There was a view of Brighton on the wall. An odd choice for his landlady, thought Oliver, and wished that his brain would stop working on something so irrelevant. Rosa had turned away from him, and her voice was muffled as she said, 'I haven't heard from them recently.'

Had Michel left her? Oliver said aloud, 'But what do you think I can do?'

'I'm not asking for money. You know some important people – you work in government, Oliver. Can't you ask someone to intervene? Just to get her out? I promise you, Oliver, she's done nothing wrong. Only being – exceptional!

You know her; she doesn't dress or even talk like other women of her age.'

He stood up. 'Rosa, I'm desperately sorry to hear about this, but I don't think there's anything . . .'

She came close to him and put her hands on his shoulders, pulling him towards her a little. He could smell a scent of lilies and powder, just as he had always experienced when she entered a room at the Savoy. But there was something sharper underneath it tonight, something older, animal.

'Oliver, forgive me, but I know you felt something for me. You did, yes, I sensed it. I was right, wasn't I?'

He looked down into her face. What to say? I meant to, I wanted to, I was too scared? 'Rosa, I don't think there's any point now.'

'Oliver, please help me. Talk to someone important – someone who could get her out. I'll do anything if you will – anything you ask. Please!'

There was no doubt about the meaning. Her hands moved up round his neck, her mouth was tilted up to his, open, dark red, the lips wet. Her tongue flickered across her bottom lip. His face was very close to hers. He was afraid he would shake.

'Rosa, I'll try to help you. I really will. I'll think about what I can do, who I can speak to.'

'Oh, Oliver, thank you! I knew you would. Please get her out of there!' She kissed him softly.

He disengaged her arms. How to reject it all? How could he find words? He said slowly, 'No, no, I don't think this is wise. We should be discreet.'

She murmured something gratefully, but as his words fell into the void of the little room he heard himself speaking, and knew what had happened to him. The phrases might have come from any other of the hundred anxious youngsters running through the diplomatic hatcheries of Whitehall. The words had been learned from his elders and still felt strange in his mouth. Soon, they would become entirely his own tongue.

As soon as she had gone, he felt a terrible access of lust. 'But the thing is, she has gone,' he said to himself. 'She *has* gone.' And the whispered words held a note of triumph.

68

IT WAS THE MOST DIFFICULT THING, THOUGHT GARRETY, THE most humiliating, that he had ever gone through. Handing the little rubber bag over, one of a group of shamefaced men. At least they had a male orderly on duty, handing out the soap and towels. And there was a system here whereby you didn't have to give your name. You could just be a number if you wanted.

But the worst was over, and as he left St Thomas's men's ward and got out into the air, even the sooty London morning, he felt relieved. There was no-one else on earth but Aline for whom he would go through this.

He had tried to fend off the idea. It was not that he thought she must be to blame, that there was something wrong with her. It was just that he couldn't cope with the notion of having some other man, doctor or not, pronounce on whether he, Will Garrety, could father a child. Holding up some test-tube full of his fluid, his seed, and judging him.

But it had gnawed away in his head. What if there is

something wrong? What if you can't do it? The simplest thing, that any young lout in the street can manage – to father a child?

It had taken him some time to arrive at the decision, but when he did he knew that he had to do it as fast as possible and not tell her beforehand, in case he couldn't go through with it. Maybe it was the Savoy raid, the justification of the almighty risk he had taken, that gave him confidence. Though old Worton had been bloody angry, nevertheless. It might have saved Garrety's career, but it had done nothing to advance it. Still, he had felt a new strength since then. Maybe it was just that he was beginning to cope with London, to find that he had his own way of dealing with things.

However it was, he had to return in the evening for the results.

'I simply want to know if there's anything wrong – any reason my wife can't conceive a child.'

'Have we been treating her?'

'Yes. Mrs Garrety. Aline Garrety.'

The man made a note of it. 'It's better if you can come together, but of course many couples are too embarrassed. And the husbands are usually very reluctant. Well, we'll have the results later on today. When can you come back?' he asked.

'This evening, when I get off duty. About six?'

'Very well. We have a public surgery between five and seven in the evening here. Come along then. The doctor will tell you about it.'

Later that day, Garrety waited in the green-tiled hallway. After what seemed an infinity, his number was called and he entered a small panelled room where a young man sat with a drawer full of glass slides and a microscope in front of him.

'Ah, come in. Please sit down. You've given us your name, so I can call you Mr Garrety in the privacy of this room.'

'Yes, my wife was examined here – well, in this hospital.'

'I have a note of it. We took details of her medical history but she didn't stay for examination. Perhaps you could persuade her to return. In any case, I want you to know that I have made a very careful scrutiny of the sample you gave us. I took no fewer than four specimens in all to examine under the microscope.'

Garrety felt his anxiety increase. Was that normal? Why so many?

'I wanted to be sure. We'll arrange for you to have another series of tests to confirm it. And remember, the situation may always change at any time. There's no reason to think it is totally permanent and irreversible. Nevertheless, as things are at present, I am in no doubt.' The young man was looking very unhappy. His brown eyes were turned down at the corners. He sat back in his chair, as though unwilling to say it. 'I'm sorry, Mr Garrety.'

Funny, it was easier when he was actually stripped of his title. More anonymous, easier to bear.

Now he would have to tell Aline. But not yet. Perhaps not just yet.

69

I KNOW IT'S THE END. I EXPECTED IT, BUT NOT IN THIS WAY. OF course, in a sense, I am triumphing over everything, since I have a future even in the face of death.

I was devastated at first. Because I could see where it would end. I knew he would find me out. There was a young man at the end of the bridge that night. I'm almost certain it was the young fellow I saw in the Savoy, the one who called a carriage for that pretty woman I talked to in the foyer. Where had he been at that time of night? In some drinking-den near the mud-flats or the jetty, I suppose.

I stopped in Lower Marsh market and bought some old clothes from a woman called Lolo. I've seen her before. She trawls the streets at night, and is so far gone on the gin the chances are she'd never remember me. Then I went back to the hotel, slipping across the bridge wearing an old overcoat and with a workman's cloth cap on my head, and when I got to the side entrance the first thing I saw was a bobby standing there, arms folded, evidently detailed to guard the doorway.

Round at the front of the hotel, the whole entrance was in tumult – more policemen, and giving all the orders, coming out of the courtyard with a sergeant at his side, was a big red-headed fellow with a Belfast accent. Of course, I just stood in the street and watched, with a scarf pulled up round my jaws. I knew what had happened.

They'd found Ruby.

I was still thinking, you see, still working things out in the intervals, the spaces still allowed to me, between the times he leapt on my back.

There was a dog barking there, a little creature. But he may lurk in tiny things – in spiders, or insects even. I knew what it was. The devil, seeking out his own.

I was afraid the dog would come up to me. I stood absolutely still. I was within my clothes, even smelling those dirty old togs, yet seeing myself standing there.

The man standing there knows his danger. He is listening as the men pass, hearing the sergeant turning back, calling out to one of his men. And he hears, when some high-ranking fellow, all silver buttons and barking voice, leaps out of a hansom and calls out to the red-haired man, 'What the devil is going on, Garrety?'

'There's a body, sir. A girl.'

The blow, the devastating shock of the name. Garrety. It's got to be him.

I know what must be done. If they catch me, they'll find it all out, because the man's own wife will only have to see a picture in a paper or get a glimpse of me and she'll tell them, about my surgery, my special practice.

Not about the killings.

About the child. The child who will be borne by my special patient.

And then she'd get rid of it.

But maybe she'll be too ashamed to tell him and then they won't know what happened. The doctor who treated her can simply disappear, but his treatment worked, didn't it? They will be so excited at the prospect of parenthood after all this time, after all their feeble striving – ah, what joy! She will never tell him. Women know their husbands don't really want to be told about what another man has done to them, even a doctor.

It will succeed. I had given her precise instructions about gauging when she would be most likely to conceive, and I made her rest afterwards to encourage the upward motility of the spermatozoa. There was no difficulty: I syringed my sperm into her, wiping away all traces on her outer body. The fluid was taken as I was bent over the other woman in the next room, enabling me to complete the act of ejaculation. The other woman died for my child. Elizabeth was a martyr to my cause, you might say. I had nothing with which to reproach her, nothing whatsoever. I simply needed her in that way.

I have the rope. I'll wait for night. Get rid of all the evidence. That girl, Ruby, let me down. Thought I could trust her but she didn't understand about Dr Bolitho, even though I explained it to her. She didn't even struggle when I found her checking the linen.

There will shortly be no Dr Bolitho, no medical equipment, no chloral or chloroform. All in the river, like poor Elizabeth, weighed down with stones and bricks. Into the Thames. From these great buildings that loom over it, from the Savoy, from the railway station, from St Thomas's Hospital, goes all the effluent, the sewage, the waste, and from the tiny dark places also go their secrets. If the police come looking here, there'll be nothing to find. And the Leadbetter woman will say nothing: she has everything to fear from the police if they suspect there was an abortionist operating on the premises. She will clean up after me and keep quiet.

I know what the future will hold if I live, even if they don't find me. They are almost one now, poor Newbold and the creature that comes to him. A sentence of raving madness, and imprisonment in a hospital for the insane. It's either that or death by hanging if they find us.

It is dark, and the cabs are thundering over Waterloo Bridge, the carriage lamps reflected in the icy water. I don't want to go down there, down into the mud and the filth; and, besides, it's not a certain death. The body fights for life, even against the will, and I cannot trust myself in that regard. Will he come to save me this time? I can't bear this life any longer. He must let me go. I can't give him time.

No, it has to be quick and certain. I have the length of rope in my pocket. And the fog will come tonight. I can see it now, sweeping up along the river from the sea, rolling over the bridge like a deep blanket of peace.

But it's not the end. There's Newbold's legacy, a secret bequest to that impotent, uniformed ass. A posthumous child.

70

THE DOOR OPENED AND M. MONET GREETED OLIVER, BUT IN A distracted way. Oliver saw as he was ushered inside that the room had been stripped of everything personal. The decanters on the sideboard, the writing case, the silver-framed photographs and the pictures: all were gone. An aproned workman was nailing up wooden crates. A pile of luggage sat near the door, with a travelling rug strapped on the top case.

'Mr Craston, such a surprise! We are returning to France. But I must not forget my manners. It is a great pleasure to see you. I'm sorry that Michel didn't inform you of our departure.'

Oliver was in fact relieved that the suite was now so impersonal. This had reverted to being an ordinary hotel sitting-room, luxurious though it was. He had dreaded the moment of entering these rooms, forced himself to call round, fearful of enquiries from his superiors at the Foreign Office if he had no further contacts to report with the Monet family. Soon they would all be gone. His duty and his pain would both be over.

Yet at the same time he felt a deep sense of loss as he looked at the old man as he stood with his feet solidly planted on the Savoy carpet, looking intently into Oliver's face, as if he saw things there that he understood.

'Why, Mr Craston, you are distressed, I believe. Come, I have some Cognac next door.'

He came back in a moment and Oliver felt an arm round his shoulder, the strong flow of warmth and sympathy. He tried to explain what he had felt for Rosa, how he had admired Michel.

'I saw how it was, Mr Craston. Oh, of course, I am ignorant of the exact details of Michel's relationship with Mademoiselle Darby. But you need not say more. Come, my boy, drink this.' He steadied the younger man. 'There now, there. These things heal – you will not think so, but they do. My friend, you will forgive my intrusion. But she would not be right for you.'

'You knew . . . You saw it?'

'How you felt? Yes. I wondered how it would turn out with the three of you, I confess. But it is better for you to lose her. Don't you know that, really?'

Oliver Craston took a long, shuddering breath. 'Yes,' he said at last. 'I know it.'

He sat now, rigid, unmoving. Yet to the old man there seemed more to the boy's stillness. Was there something else, besides the normal-enough torments of young love?

Oliver stared across the room at the window. Outside, snowflakes fell thickly over the river. 'It's just that . . . I feel it inside . . . I feel frozen inside. Not in pain – just frozen.'

The young man is a survivor, thought the old one. Of a different type from myself, but still a survivor. That is my judgement, though I may be mistaken, of course. He leant forward and said, 'It will pass. You will learn that. Spring comes eventually, no matter how hard it is to believe. It will come for you.'

'My family . . .'

'You can't speak to them of this?'

'No. Impossible.'

'Speak to me, then. I have felt it too, this coldness, this chill of the heart. But the ice will break up, for you, as it did for me.'

'You felt it!' The young man looked incredulous. 'With my father – I can never talk of these things.'

'Nor I with my son. He likes worldly things, he doesn't reflect. Give him a pretty woman and a fast car – that's his life! I cannot speak to him of how it was with me after Camille, his mother, died. But it was not her loss alone that froze my heart. I was younger than you are now when I discovered something that gave me such a blow as you have suffered. It was my first experience of betrayal.'

'You were betrayed by a woman, sir?'

'Not exactly. I learned that my father had kept a mistress – I had a half-sister, even, of whom I knew nothing.'

'So he had been false to your mother?'

'To all of us, because we trusted him. But something worse can happen to the person who is betrayed.'

'What? What could possibly happen to me that is worse?'

The older man stared at the younger, and then said pityingly, 'You may learn treachery from it.'

Later, after the young Englishman had gone, the old man stared out upon another river. There was a flickering at the edges of his vision, and he thought for a few moments he was still at Argenteuil, on the day of the regatta, when the bright flags were fluttering wildly and the breezes ruffled the water. Little boats scudded back and forth, and Camille was laughing under a parasol. Then she looked towards him, taking his arm, as, with the movements of a dream, they floated up the hill towards the house and out into the garden between the frail curtains at the long windows. She sat on a bench, half-turning towards him, and her face was no longer laughing.

They had some money in those days, but then it had all gone, just as she became sick. The final blow had been delivered by the Hoschedé auction, which had made a laughing-stock of Impressionism. It had been almost impossible to sell a picture since then. It was a rare collector, such as de Bellio, who possessed the courage to buy according to the dictates of their own taste.

He opened his eyes and was looking now out of the window of their house at Vétheuil, from the casement that had been cut into the roof, giving a great, sweeping view of the loop of the Seine and the hills behind. The trees there held the grey mist long after it had all melted away from the valley.

Now he was looking left out of the window, towards the town, and he saw Camille in the distance, coming towards him, black-clad, the hem of her dress whipped about by the wind, walking along past the steep broken stone steps leading up to the church. Her pale, big-jawed face was turned upwards and she had a shawl pulled about her shoulders, like one of the village women. She moved slowly, and stopped for a few moments, with her hands pressed one over the other on her body, her head bowed.

Camille was still feeding her second son, Michel, though she herself was so weak, and her husband knew her health was weakening day by day.

The winter she died had been so cold. Alice and her

children lived with them – the two families under the same roof. Alice had become at once Camille's nursemaid and Monet's mistress. Alice's body then was thick, big-hipped, yet still supple, her movements casual and powerful, though the flesh of her belly was loosened by the birth of six children. Yet she was not weakened, possessing, indeed, the matriarchal confidence her experience had given her. Beside her, Camille seemed fainter still, a shadow merely. Though it was at Camille's side the children would sit, when they wanted someone to touch their hair, love them silently. Poor Alice, she had no gift for stillness. She did not understand it, even.

The Monets had arrived in Vétheuil after the Hoschedé auction, on the horse-drawn conveyance from Mantes, he and Camille and their two boys, almost penniless by then, because when Hoschedé had gone bankrupt his collection of Impressionists had been sold almost for nothing at that fateful auction. The budding worth of his pictures crashed as if it fell to the bottom of a pit.

Camille became increasingly weak. The doctors had diagnosed ulcerations of the womb even before Michel's birth. Alice made it clear that she did not think Camille should have had another child. 'In her condition!' she would say, looking at the baby as he struggled to get nourishment from his mother's breast. Michel's birth seemed to be causing the death of his mother. She began to have other, terrifying symptoms: fluxes, swollen body and legs; even her face seemed bloated. In that dreadful winter Vétheuil, remote from the rest of the world at the best of times, was cut off by blizzards. We were so poor we could scarcely afford firewood and the children were short of proper boots, the old man remembered later, in London, beside the wintry Thames. Time after time he had gone out into the icy air and painted the light on the snow, the clearings in the woods flooded with white.

In spring the grey and silver landscape, now churned with streaks of muddy brown, that lay before his window gave way at last to the brightest of green grass and blossom-bearing trees which flourished on a low-lying strip of land flanking the Seine. He loved the ever-changing spontaneity of the landscape around Vétheuil, which was set just at the tip of a mighty ox-bow loop of the Seine reflected in the aqueous skies, in a watery universe between heaven and earth. Dividing the sweep of the river into two channels was a long, low-lying island crowded with willows. On summer days he had crossed over to it and set up his easel there, the feathery grasses growing four or five feet deep around, surrounding him totally, enclosing him with their soft green and grey shivering. At the back of the house was a sheer chalk cliff, so close that dovecots and storage chambers were cut into it.

The people there were isolated, though it was only ten kilometres from Mantes, and that was a sizeable town, on the main railway line from Paris. At Vétheuil they mostly still lived off the land or the river, as their ancestors had done, except for a few shopkeepers, the *curé*, the doctor, and one or two well-off landowners, like the family who owned the house into which the Monets had moved.

It was a small house, much too small for the two families. After Ernest's bankruptcy, they had all announced to the world their intention to form a joint household. Ernest and Alice had lost everything: Rottembourg, the furniture, jewels, carriages – even Alice's gowns. The fiction that M. Hoschedé was living there too preserved appearances, though Ernest was actually hardly ever present. He was usually avoiding his creditors or dabbling in some new enterprise in Paris: already, he was on his drunken way to the gutter.

Monet, Camille and their two sons – the eldest, Jean, and the tiny Michel – were already installed when Alice arrived with her five children and the new-born baby. The little ones were all so small they didn't take up much room, she said. She didn't explain why she would not be staying with her sister in Biarritz, who was quite wealthy enough to keep them all comfortably.

He knew the answer. On the way to Biarritz, the child had been born – literally, at a railway station. And it was not Ernest's son. Alice knew it; Ernest knew it; the sister knew it.

It was the bastard child of the penniless artist Claude Monet.

They put it round the village that Alice had come to nurse Camille. No-one had been fooled. Some went along with the pretence; others pulled aside, turning their faces away when Alice went past, and spoke openly of 'poor Madame Monet'.

But Alice herself probably believed it, somewhere within her. She had that real strength that can always re-invent itself: from being a rich patroness of the arts, from being the mistress of an artist, she became in her own mind the devoted but impoverished nurse of a dying friend, albeit the artist's wife.

Alice came into the room at the top of the house, where Monet had set up his studio, one day not long before Camille died, a shawl pulled round her shoulders against the cold. Perhaps it was the same shawl that Monet had seen Camille wearing when she had last walked along the road – the two women had to share some of their clothes, so poor were they now. Camille rarely left the house, so she had little need of many garments. She had not set foot outside for three weeks now.

'I must talk to you about something,' said Alice.

'Not yet!' He knew what it would be about.

'When the time comes, you must let me do it! I would never forgive myself if I didn't.'

'Do what?'

'Send for the priest. For the last rites. She must receive the last sacrament.'

'No! We are not ... she is not a Catholic – not even a believer.'

'But I am – and it is my duty to make sure her soul is saved!'

For a moment he felt a terrible rage. How dare she speak of saving Camille's soul? 'If any creature on the face of this earth is virtuous, it is Camille.' He spoke angrily, and she sensed perhaps that she had gone too far. But she persisted.

'Yes, of course, but she must have the sacraments. That is the Church's teaching.'

'No, no!' This time he almost screamed it. 'She has never shown any interest in religion in her life – we had a civil marriage. I should know! Have you forgotten she is my wife?'

Alice had put her hands to her face as if the words had been blows. She turned and left the room.

But he knew how stubborn she was, and sighed, laying down the brush he had been holding as he looked out over the river. Alice would never give up, and perhaps when the time came he would not have the strength to oppose her on Camille's behalf.

She needs it for herself. He had suddenly understood. It was Alice who craved religion, longed for acceptance, reassurance, forgiveness. How deeply had it gone into her soul that it was Camille who was Mme Monet, not Alice? As long as her husband lived, in the eyes of her own church Mme Ernest

Hoschedé could never become Mme Claude Monet. All Alice could do was to get as close to Claude as she could, bear the insults and hope for the future. And ask of her religion that she be forgiven.

Perhaps Camille could have been saved if they had been able to afford better treatment. But it was the birth of the child that had so fatally weakened her.

Why? thought the old man years later, sitting in the hotel room overlooking another river in another country. Why did Camille want another child? She was sick, yet she wanted to conceive again. And then he knew the answer to a question he had never allowed himself to think about before these present days in London, as if the very distance and difference of place allowed questions of the past to be posed and answered.

Camille had become pregnant with her second child in the dreadful summer, the summer of 1877, of that terrible sale when Hoschedé went bankrupt. Had Camille anticipated what would happen and foreseen her rival, freed of the restraining presence of her husband, moving into her lover's household? Did Camille try to hold Monet thus, even though another child would almost certainly mean her death, only to suffer the indignity of having her husband's mistress become her indispensable nurse?

And he himself had thus been freed. To paint.

There came now into his mind, sharp as sketches, images of those long-distant winter days in Vétheuil, the white and grey points of sharp frost on the bushes alongside the water, the drifting broken logs in those icy masses. And that iridescence and glitter, how it had at once seduced his eyes and eased his pain. The canvases called 'Effects of Snow' – hadn't he told de Bellio to take what he wanted and give him anything he liked, any sum whatever? Even a few francs would buy something to ease Camille's suffering – some medicine, or a little Cognac, coals for the fire.

Camille was in such immense pain that she scarcely knew what was happening around her. Alice fetched the priest, and Monet did not drive him away. The last rites were punctuated by screams, which carried straight through the house to the upstairs room where the children were huddled, Monet's two boys by Camille and the six children borne by Alice.

'I want to get the locket back,' he said to Alice, and she was startled at the harshness in his voice. A woman from the village had come to lay out the thin and bony body. They were standing in the room next door, in the darkness, whispering and exhausted.

'What do you mean?'

'Camille pawned a locket in Paris. It was the only thing of value she had left.'

'Surely it doesn't matter now?'

'I want her to wear it.'

'To wear it to the grave?'

He was vicious in his response. 'There are some things that cannot be understood by a shopkeeper's wife!'

He pushed past her without a word.

He took pen and paper and wrote to de Bellio, begging for money to redeem the little ornament, so that Camille could be buried with it round her neck.

As he wrote that letter, he could almost hear her, gentle yet determined, as she had been that time in London when he had despaired at their poverty and spoken of giving up painting. He had asked her, 'How can I sacrifice you?' And her voice came echoing now within his mind, even as her body lay in the next room. 'You must do it. No matter what. You must!'

*

He was shut into his own world, a white prison of ice and snow. He barely spoke to Alice or the children. Now, all these years later, in the depths of a London winter, he knew what had held him in its grip: not just grief, but an isolating, numbing guilt that forbade him to turn even to Alice for comfort or human consolation. He had passed those days beside the frozen river like a man locked into a cave of ice. He slept alone.

The year inevitably took its course.

One night, he awoke with astonishment and fear to an ominous loud grating noise outside his window. The house itself seemed to be shaking. But this sound was inexplicable – the gushing sound of river water, yes, that he had expected, but this was far more sinister: it was as if something alien on the earth's surface had started to move. He reached out for the oil-lamp beside his bed and called to Alice. Outside, the savage grinding sounds were menacingly loud. Peering out into the moonlit night, he could see a terrifying sight: great grey-white shapes, sharp-edged and gleaming, moving irresistibly along as if pulled by some magnetic force, and to his horror he realized that they were pushing along the banks. The swollen river ice had broken into giant boulders, crushing everything in their path. Where the orchard and garden had lain flooded and frozen along the bank of the Seine, the floes were now crashing through, snapping off the thinner tree trunks as if they were matchsticks and carrying away logs and branches as they swept along. It was a picture of terrible destruction, yet there was something exhilarating in this release of the forces that had been locked into the ice all winter.

'It's the thaw. Alice, wake the children!'

They would have to get them out of the house if necessary.

Rubbing their sleepy eyes, the children emerged, asking, in a babble of frightened soft voices, what was happening.

Jean, a nervous child trying to conquer his fright, came running downstairs. 'Papa, Papa, what's going on?' The last time Jean had been awakened in the middle of the night was when his mother lay dying, and there was evident fear on his face that something terrible was again happening to his family.

His father put an arm round his shoulders. 'Don't be afraid, Jeannot. The ice is breaking up out there. It's natural – it's a force of life!'

The younger ones were put in the care of the three older girls, Marthe, Blanche and Suzanne. Monet came down carrying Michel and handed him to Blanche. And the smallest child, the tiny boy to whom Alice had given birth at a railway station, was cradled in his mother's arms. They were all in an assortment of old coats and shawls. Suzanne was limping and holding up the lamp so that all he could see were her feet in the flickering light. She was wearing boy's boots, and he recollected that Alice had told him Suzanne had grown out of her boots and they could not afford to buy her another pair. She must be wearing a handed-down pair belonging to Jean.

Lifting her up in his arms, he felt a rush of pity for the tiny feet dangling in their heavy boots. How little he had noticed what they needed! 'I will love this child as my own,' he swore to himself then. 'Love them all as if they were my own.'

'We'll all stay together and be ready to go along to the church, up on to the higher ground, if we have to,' he decreed. But they did not need to decamp to the hill on which stood the old, grim church, and as light dawned they were all gathered in the attic room at the top of the house, watching an extraordinary sunrise over the watery landscape, where a row of poplars at the edge of the river was half drowned beneath the torrent that had swirled out of the darkness as the ice broke up. The water had a strange, greenish light: it was still frozen here and there. On the banks were broken floes and spears of ice, swirled up out of the water. The air itself seemed glassy, and slow, icy ripples shuddered along the surface of the river. Frost-laden branches, sharply outlined by the dawning sun, were breaking and creaking, their burden sliding off into the waters beneath.

The children never forgot what happened that day. A cloaked figure, Monet disappeared in the direction of the town, and an hour or so later there was suddenly the jingling of a carriage. With their last few francs, he had succeeded in hiring a horse and cab, and insisted that all the older children pile in. 'No, it's crazy!' called Alice, peering out into the wilderness around them.

'Crazy! Let them use their eyes! It's something that will be with them all their lives!'

And he hauled them up, and insisted that Alice should get up beside him, and so they all drove wildly through the extraordinary landscape: a scene of immense destruction and yet enormous beauty. There was an orchard that was a sea of ice, the trees appearing out of frozen blocks which had piled up against the trunks and hedges. At La Roche-Guyon, the hillside was like something from a fairy-story, emerging at last from a kingdom where the Snow Queen had laid a curse on the castle. 'Look, look,' Monet kept shouting to the children. 'Use your eyes! Look! It's over. The winter is over!'

'You understand? That's why Alice and I are making a garden at our home, at Giverny,' he said patiently, many years later, to a sad young man. 'Because, you see, spring will come again, and one must be ready for it.'

71

THE SUNSHINE GLEAMED THROUGH THE TREES ON THE WHITE shirts and boaters. The young men, Oliver and John Madigan, were fooling about in a punt moored to the bank, where dappled shadows flickered over the water. 'Come on, Amelia,' called Madigan. 'Take you down the river! I love messing about in boats – even old pieces of lumber like this! Craston, keep her steady there!'

But Amelia called that she was unpacking the hamper, and they left the punt and scrambled up the bank. Oliver flung himself down, and, propped up on one elbow, felt that he had never seen such grass, jewel-bright green, each blade distinct with individual life, as was coming through the ground that spring, in Richmond Park.

Before him lay the snowy expanse of a starched table-cloth, and beyond it, between two sun-dappled oaks, he could see the shape of a deer moving in the distance, cropping at new shoots. He got up and joined the picnic group.

'Will you have some chicken, Mr Craston?' Amelia

Madigan, in a dress of some white striped muslin stuff that puffed out like a cloud around her, sitting on the other side of the cloth spread out on the grass, was holding out a dish towards him. Her brother, his handsome features framed by black sideburns and moustache, had sat down at her side. He was fiddling with a little silver spirit-stove.

'Yes, if I may. Thank you, Miss Madigan.'

Oliver soon felt drowsy. Perhaps the green bottles of Rhine wine, chilled in the river and beaded now with silvery moisture, had played their part in this. The glasses cast pleasantly glinting pale shadows as the sun struck across the cloth.

He had eaten his fill of the ham and truffle pie, the cold chicken fricassée, the mountain of salad. There were some dishes heaped with early fruit from the Madigans' green-house, which he had still to try, and small golden cheeses encrusted with powdery white at the rind.

The young Madigans and the Crastons had met several times that spring. Dinner at Barnes had been a stiff and rather uncomfortable occasion, and Oliver had been deeply grateful to John and Amelia. They had borne most of the brunt of making conversation with a cool charm that put their hosts at ease, even Maggie, who always found new company difficult.

Mrs Madigan, when it was her turn to extend hospitality, had looked out of her window at the spring flowers in her garden and determined on a picnic in Richmond Park. Mrs Craston declined, but decided it was perfectly proper for Oliver and Maggie to accept. Elinor was in Switzerland, at a finishing-school. The young Crastons sensed that their mother considered this Maggie's last chance. When Elinor came back, the younger sister would undoubtedly outdazzle the older.

Maggie was sitting carefully, opposite Amelia, her feet tucked up beneath her. Oliver wondered whether there was any attraction between her and John Madigan. He knew, and sometimes felt embarrassed, that his mother had been keenly fostering their relationship, but was unable to determine the feelings of the main participants. Madigan escorted Maggie on occasion, extending his arm to her sometimes when they walked, offering dishes to her at mealtimes, with perfect gentlemanliness. Madigan was, of course, extremely handsome, thought Oliver, but he was agreeably unaware of it.

As for Maggie, she had only said one or two things. 'He's very pleasant – yes, I like his company,' she had answered, when Oliver tried to probe.

Perhaps, he thought drowsily, she won't fall in love. Not ever. Perhaps she's just not like that.

If that was the case, she was fortunate in a way. He leaned against a tree in Richmond Park, closed his eyes and remembered a night not long after Rosa had come to see him, when he had walked the streets of London almost like a madman, striding mile after mile till at last he found himself in Chelsea, at a place which he suddenly realized that he had intended to come to.

The Darbys' house shone in the cold moonlight. Oliver stood there, in the road, with a terrible kind of howling inside, a scream of pain and jealousy that rose to his throat but was trapped there. He saw the white-painted front door, brass gleaming in the moonlight. So easy to climb the steps, put his hand to the doorbell, call to her urgently, speak to her.

He looked around. The road was empty; the silent houses ranged away on either side.

He walked into the garden, the frost rimming the gate and

the bushes, and stepped silently up to the house, not knowing what he wanted to do. He stood outside a window – surely that was the sitting-room? – and, peering in through the darkness, saw with a shock that it was empty. The walls were stripped of pictures. Bare wooden floors stretched away in the moonlight.

Oliver circled the house. Every window revealed an empty room.

They were gone. Like the Monet family. That whole world seemed to have vanished from him.

When he got to the end of the street, a hansom cab came clopping past, its driver hunched amid a pile of rugs, the horse's mane fringed with icicles, its gentle mouth and nostrils steaming in the freezing night. Oliver hailed the cab and climbed in, giving the driver instructions for Stamford Street.

They went alongside the silent river. He watched a man shuffling along a bridge, grotesque, solitary.

I never want to become one of them, he had thought, one of those night creatures who walk in the darkness, for whatever reason. Like the drunks, like the doctor from the Savoy, or the lone policeman clutching his lantern as he made his rounds in Lambeth Marsh.

Oliver shivered, and opened his eyes on the scene in Richmond Park. He felt a great surge of relief. It was all over, surely. The winter had gone.

Amelia Madigan was leaning forward, holding out a cup. 'Would you like some coffee, Mr Craston?' she was saying.

72

'WILL, I'M SO LONELY HERE,' SAID ALINE, TAKING HIS ARM AS they walked along on Sunday morning. 'They don't want to talk to me here – the women from the old country, I mean.'

Yes, of course, she would want women to talk to, especially at this time. He reached out and put an arm round her. 'Why don't you go home for a visit? See your mother and your sisters – why don't you do that?'

'Can't you come with me? Get a transfer or something of the sort? We could brave it out there, couldn't we? Eventually, surely, they'd accept us.'

He thought of their families, resolute in their mutual hatred. Of his next London promotion, looming in a few months. 'No, I can't do that.'

He heard a long sigh beside him.

'I know, really I do. But if only there was someone I could talk to when I feel like this!'

There might have been, he thought. That Darby woman had the gift of friendship, the knack of gathering waifs and strays round her. Of radiating something special, something warm and reassuring. Aline could have talked to her, could have been received as a friend. Mrs Darby would have eased Aline's path in this cruel city. She had offered friendship.

They stopped on Lambeth Bridge.

No, he thought. That was like thinking the river could flow in another direction. There were inexorable currents in their lives.

The sun was glittering on the Thames, and for some reason a picture appeared in his mind, a vision of obscure shapes that lay sketchily in the river, perhaps men, perhaps boats – who knew what? – and over this darkness a dazzling track of bright yellow and gold.

'You never went to that house where I saw the picture by Monsieur Monet.'

Aline was looking up at him in surprise.

'There was an Irish lady there, Mrs Darby. She went abroad, afterwards. Pity – you'd have liked her.'

'Wasn't she . . . ?'

'Yes. I regret it now. I felt I had to do it at the time.'

'It was your duty, Will. I know that's important to you.'

'Yes, Aline, it changed me. Seeing that picture and talking to that woman.' He struggled on for a moment. 'It altered something inside me.' He could say no more, but he took her hand as he remembered the gold of the painting. They walked on in silence.

Half an hour later, Garrety knelt uncomfortably in St George's Roman Catholic Cathedral. He felt awkward in his mind as well as in his body. He didn't know anything about Catholic ritual, had to try to overcome a dislike – fear would be a more honest word – of the mumbo-jumbo, and the gilt and bright colours glimpsed all around, the lacy white carvings and statuettes with blue and red robes. There were plaques around the wall and he deciphered the images as he waited. Christ carrying the cross, Christ being whipped. There was a tomb set into the wall nearby and he passed a few minutes studying the inscription. 'Thomas Provost Doyle. Founder of this church.' The name was Irish, familiar, comforting, like the Irish newspapers on sale at the entrance.

Perhaps he ought to try to say a prayer of some sort. He'd been brought up to believe it was wrong to pray for the dead, but he thought of them now, and with pity he also thought of the living, of the husband of Elizabeth Belfrage, waiting at home for a wife who never returned and had never been found. The last trace of her had been at Waterloo Station, where a woman answering to her description had been seen supported out of the tea-room by a thin, small, weather-beaten man in his thirties.

'I agree with you: probably the last of Newbold's victims.' Garrety remembered the commissioner, the tiger-chewed arm pinned uselessly across his chest, his strong voice echoing in the long panelled room at Scotland Yard. 'We have to face the truth, Worton. No good being mealy-mouthed about it. Anyway, it's all over now. Garrety, we can't give you a commendation – you understand? But the raid on the Savoy will not be recorded to your detriment.'

Garrety managed to decipher this sufficiently to thank the commissioner, even as Worton attempted to restrain his own angry exclamation. Thinking back on it, Garrety now had a moment of brief amusement, and felt better as he gazed around at the great arches of the cathedral.

The building was huge, bigger than he had expected. It had a cold, damp smell, in spite of the warm summer day. It must be freezing in winter: he remembered all the mornings Aline had got up to go to early Mass, and felt almost an anger that she should have thus subjected herself. He could see her now as she knelt before the rail, moving her lips, praying. Then she rose and went to the big stands burning on either side of the door, and fumbled in her purse. The sound of the coins slipping into a wooden box echoed down the nave.

Garrety got up and stood nearby as she picked out a candle, lit it from another, and set it on a great spiked gilded branch. He read the lettering on the box into which she had dropped her money. 'In thanks for answered prayers.'

Her face had a radiant flush of joy as she turned back to him and she slipped her hand under his arm.

Can I trust myself never to tell her? he wondered, looking down all the years of thoughts about this child, how exactly it would look, how he would feel about it. She would never betray me, he thought. I would stake my life on that.

They were walking down the steps now.

'I will love this child as my own,' he repeated to himself. 'Love it as my own,' and he clung to this phrase. 'Perhaps miracles do happen.' He knew that once he might have found such a thing impossible. When had he changed? A moment stood alone in time when he was talking to the Irish woman, looking at the painting of the river.

Epilogue

GIVERNY, 1927

'THE AIR IS VERY SOFT HERE, ISN'T IT?'

Oliver walked forward to the centre of the bridge. His wife followed him.

Amelia could be relied on to do the right thing; she was just like her brother. The Madigans had all possessed that knack.

The two of them stood side by side and contemplated the luminous blue water beneath them, the deeper indigo pools within the cornflower-tinted flow. The lilies gently shivered and drifted, casting slight lavender and lilac shadows on their great sharply frilled leaves of malachite green.

'I suppose it was very kind of them to drive us out from Paris after the exhibition opening,' said Amelia, 'but I really would have preferred us to come here alone.'

In the garden beyond, a middle-aged woman was walking, smoking a cigarette. 'She's quite an interesting person,' said Amelia. 'Did you say you knew her in London?'

'Yes, but it was years ago. It must have been – oh, twenty years before she opened the gallery.'

410

Amelia turned. 'I think I'll go back to the house. You go and talk to her.'

He was surprised. Amelia rarely allowed any note of dislike to creep into her voice, even when she and Oliver were alone.

He watched her neat figure traverse the paths between the massed bursts of flowers. What were the tints? Plum? Poppy? Ruby? Something more delicate?

The woman was coming towards him, her hair dyed a bright yellow and curled up fashionably. She was carrying a shiny yellow parasol, trimmed with lace, and her face was a powdered peachy colour beneath it, and the sun was filtering through. With a feeling of dread, as if some kind of absurd fate were walking on high heels towards him in the bright sunlight, he left the bridge and stopped in front of her.

'Do you want to go back to Paris?' she asked. 'Albert is waiting, whenever you want to leave. Perhaps Amelia is feeling a little tired?'

Her diamond-shaped eyes still had that extraordinary bright transparent look, though the skin was wrinkled, dusty with the powder, and the mouth looked bad-tempered, or perhaps tense. What happened to her, he thought, in all those years?

He said, 'Yes, I think we should go back. To Paris, I mean.'

Now she was laughing at him. 'Well, you have turned out just as I expected! Sir Oliver Craston, the famous diplomat. I'm not surprised at all. I thought you were a very proper person, Oliver! In the old days. Admit it, you were rather shocked. Do you remember that Renoir nude that hung in our hallway in London?'

'You're teasing me.'

She laughed. 'Yes, I am. You have become a noted connoisseur, after all – you must have seen the most shocking picture in Paris – Mademoiselle Olympia staring boldly out of her canvas! It was our Monsieur Monet who managed to procure her for the nation!'

'Yes.'

Oliver had stood before the Manet nude and it had indeed shocked him – not his outward conventionality, but deeper within his sexual being. The boldness of her face and body, the open nakedness, had reminded him of things in his life he preferred to forget, to remain buried, of pale limbs against stark sheets under a pitiless light.

Rosa continued with this relentless conversation. 'But really, admit it, you were rather interested at one time.'

'In art? Yes.'

'In me!' She already had an old woman's triumphal laugh. 'I did think that maybe ... but we had to leave London, of course. My mother was released in the end, so I owe you thanks for that, I expect. But I never saw you again, Oliver, though I did think you would try to see me. Oh well, women do get things wrong sometimes!'

He was being very careful now. 'When did you leave, Rosa?'

'In early spring. Do you remember, that beautiful spring, the first spring of the century? Not so lovely for us, after they arrested my mother!'

Anger was flaring up in her eyes and he could see how old she was, as the lines in her face contracted tightly. Yet what an inner strength seemed still to rage in her. Was that young man who drove the car her lover? It seemed absurd, yet she had such style, such drama.

'But she can only have been in prison for a short time? They can't have had any evidence against her.'

'Long enough!'

He wished he had never gone on with this conversation. There was a tear leaking out of the corner of her eye.

'It destroyed my mother – she couldn't bear being locked up.'

She's exaggerating, she's making such a fuss, it can't be true. Yet he knew it was.

'We came to Paris after she was released. She was frightened to stay in Britain in case they put her in prison again. And the house in County Cork – well, she had that shut up and it just rotted away really. You can't imagine what it was like, watching her go slowly downhill. There was a doctor who prescribed her something – I didn't know exactly what. Veronal, at first. Then it got worse. Because she had such bad nightmares about prison. The dirt, and the shame, and the feeling of being locked in.'

'Rosa – I'm so sorry!' He was quite sincere, but he wanted her to stop talking about it, stop that drop of gluey fluid slipping down her cheek, stop her ruining this perfect day.

'Oh, let's forget it! She died a long time ago. And the gallery was a great success, so now I can afford to face the world.' She closed the absurd little parasol with a snap. 'We never knew whether there was anything behind it.'

'What do you mean?'

'Whether someone reported her to the police as a Fenian sympathizer . . . There was a lot of alarm with the founding of Sinn Fein and so on. The police seemed to know a few things about us. Of course, when they saw the Renoir in the hall, it didn't help, though! Indecent, the commissioner called it, apparently. Not only was my mother a supporter of Irish independence, she owned an obscene picture! God knows what would have happened if they'd known she was the model for it!'

They turned and walked back towards the house. She put
her arm in his. 'Anyway, it's all in the past now, Oliver. All
flowed away, like water. If someone did go to the police about
her, I think I could even forgive him now. It was so long ago.
We never know the kinds of pressure people are under.'

Oliver remembered the police inspector, all those years ago.
The man had an Irish accent. That was why, really, he had the
idea of telling him about Mrs Darby. She mixed with dubious
French people who supported republicanism and were
actually against the Boer War. And she was Irish, and he,
Oliver, had reason to believe she supported Home Rule.
Surely the London police would want to know about
potential trouble-makers. He, Oliver, would make a statement, if required, about the political opinions he had heard
from Mrs Darby's own lips.

'Yes, that would be evidence enough, Mr Craston,' Garrety
had said. 'I should have to act on that. We would be in your
debt, of course.'

It was a bargain, and both parties had understood it.

A few days before the inquest on Newbold, Garrety had
come to Stamford Street.

'You will not be asked to give evidence, sir. It will not be
necessary. We have the body of the maid at the Savoy, and the
death by suicide of the prime suspect, who was also the prob-
able murderer of two other women. Possibly three. In any
event, the case can be closed.'

Oliver sat down with the light-headedness of relief. It had
worked.

There was something more. Garrety held out his hand.
Within the palm lay several grubby, crumpled pieces of paper.
'White Lady. Silver Dancer. 2/- . . .' The betting slips, in

Oliver's handwriting. The only tangible evidence that he had ever been anywhere near that grubby shack.

'We got them back from the bookie. Bit of pressure laid on there. And the girl, Regina, won't say anything, sir. And if she does, or one of the rest of them, well, it's just the word of a whore and a bunch of thieves. No need to worry, sir.'

The grubby strips of paper had flared up and turned to ashes in the fire.

Oliver had known Garrety would have to act on his information about Mrs Darby. Precisely because of his Irishness, the policeman had something to prove in London. He would never be able to afford to conceal information about Irish Republicans, even if he privately thought there was no truth in it. It was too dangerous for him. There had been no room for Garrety's private opinions. For the sake of his career, the man would take no risks.

Oliver had become an expert on saving careers, even at a tender age. He had saved his own, and Maggie's future with it.

He and Rosa walked now beside a long flower-bed and scents of small old-fashioned roses drifted up beside them.

'Did you see much of Michel after you went to Paris?' He said the name casually.

'Nothing at all then. Not for years. We were so poor and with Mother in the state she was in, well, to tell you the truth, I was ashamed to get in touch with the Monet family. It was a long, hard climb out of it, you know. But Michel and I are good friends now. He allows me to bring special visitors here, people who are interested in his father's paintings, though he's not really keeping things up.'

'How is Michel?' His question was a pure formality, but

the old feelings of rage and bitterness, to his amazement, came flooding back this time as he said the name.

Rosa must have realized something of his reactions, for she said, in a short and brusque way, 'He seems all right. He'll get married, I believe, quite soon. To an artist's model. They've been together for years, but he wouldn't dare to marry her till after the old man died. He'd never have given his approval.'

'Really?'

'Oh, no. He and Alice wanted their children to make good marriages. They had real French bourgeois notions at heart.'

Not only did she understand some of Oliver's feelings, she obviously shared some of his bitterness.

This was no good, this mulling over the past. He saw with relief the thin figure of Amelia, very correct in her English tweed two-piece, turning back to meet them.

'By the way,' Rosa was saying, 'how is your sister? I've read about her, of course.'

'Oh, Maggie's the most famous member of the family! She'll be principal of her college next year.'

'How splendid! She never married, I suppose?'

Malice, he thought. I never saw that in her. 'No.'

'Good afternoon,' Amelia said as she joined them, extending her gloved hand to Rosa. 'I believe we owe you our thanks. It was so kind of you to arrange this visit for us, Mrs, er . . . I'm so sorry, I can never remember names! So silly of me!'

'Miss Darby,' said Rosa, looking at Oliver. 'I did have opportunities – especially one in particular, I think, which would have turned into a deeper relationship – but I have never married. Of course, sometimes I regret it. One is bound to, isn't one?'

She turned back to Amelia. 'But there we are, life

sometimes pulls us in certain directions. Do you have children, Mrs Craston?'

'Yes: two boys and a girl. They are a great comfort, Miss Darby.'

Rosa smiled, but quite slowly, as though there was now something in the situation she was enjoying. 'Tell me, Mrs Craston, where did you and dear Oliver meet?'

'Oh, my brother and he were colleagues.'

'Ah, yes, of course. Both in the Foreign Office. Well, you obviously had a great deal in common, then, didn't you?'

She likes to know things, thought Oliver suddenly. Things that other people don't. And so do I. He suddenly felt protective towards Amelia and took her arm. 'Bury the past,' he said to himself. 'It's all over.'

'Yes, we had – and we still do! This has been a wonderful visit,' Amelia was saying, 'but I think we should really be getting along. We don't want to miss the boat-train tonight.'

'It's a good place to forget things,' he said, and the two women looked at him in surprise, so irrelevant his remark seemed to them. 'Old things, I meant,' he said, 'old, painful things,' and gestured around them, at the burning colours of the garden.

Historical Note

I HAVE FOLLOWED HISTORICAL FACT IN DESCRIBING THE LIVES of the Monet family, except for Michel's relationship with Rosa, which I have imagined (though he did stay in London with a family called Darby). Biographers are uncertain about the exact date when Monet and Alice became lovers, though Alice's youngest child, Jean-Pierre, born in 1877, himself implied that he was the artist's son. Camille Monet's correspondence and almost all photographs of her were destroyed by Alice.

Monet's three visits to London between 1899 and 1901, when he stayed at the Savoy Hotel, appear to have been marked by suffering and it is a matter of record that he had extraordinary difficulty in finishing his 'London' paintings. On the first visit, in the winter of 1899, he was accompanied by Alice, but she had been badly affected by the recent unexpected death of her daughter Suzanne at the age of thirty, and remained in France when Monet arrived for a second painting campaign in the winter of 1900. He himself was unwell during this particularly cold winter, suffering from crises of depression and taking belladonna for minor ailments. When the fashionable artist John Singer Sargent visited him, he found Monet surrounded by no fewer than eighty canvases on which he was frantically attempting to capture the fast-changing effects of light and mist over the Thames.

Monet returned to London in January the following year and watched Queen Victoria's cortège passing through the streets on 2 February. In April he returned to Giverny and in the summer of 1901 he embarked on a series of lyrical views, canvases filled with warmth and colour, of the small town of Vétheuil, where Camille had died twenty-two years previously and where she is buried.

Surprising though it may seem, Claude Monet did visit the London music-halls. He and Michel also enjoyed fast driving. Indeed, Michel, last survivor of the family at Giverny, died as the result of a car accident in 1966. He had married an artist's model, Gabrielle Bonaventure, in 1931. They had no children.

Acknowledgements

The principal source for the life and works of Claude Monet is Daniel Wildenstein's magisterial four-volume *Biographie et catalogue raisonné*. I have found Carla Rachman's compact one-volume work on Monet in the Phaidon Press 'World Perspectives' series extremely useful. For Monet in London, the catalogue of an exhibition, *Monet in the Twentieth Century*, by Paul Hayes Tucker and other Monet scholars, is particularly valuable.

Thomas Pakenham's splendid volume, *The Boer War*, is an indispensable source. The medical horrors of that war were described by two notable contemporaries, Sir Arthur Conan Doyle in his *Memories and Adventures* and the celebrated surgeon Sir Frederick Treves in *Tales of a Field Hospital*, as well as in reports in *The Times*, notably on 28 April 1900. Rooms on the floor above Monet's suite at the Savoy were actually given up to wounded officers, thanks to an appeal by Princess Louise, daughter of Queen Victoria.

Acknowledgements

Grateful thanks to Nicola Gold of the Savoy Hotel, London, for practical assistance with research.

Claude Monet: Chronology

1840. Oscar-Claude Monet born in Paris, 14 November.

1845. His family move to Le Havre, major port in Normandy.

1858. His first oil-painting is exhibited in Le Havre.

1859. Leaves for Paris to study art.

1861. Goes to Algeria on military service, suffers from typhoid.

1862. Returns to Le Havre to convalesce, goes back to Paris, meets other artists such as Renoir, Sisley and Bazille.

1865. Paints Camille Doncieux among other figures in *Luncheon on the Grass (Déjeuner sur l'herbe)*.

1866. Paints Camille in *The Green Dress* and also in *Women in a Garden*. Camille has become his mistress and they are living together in Sèvres, near Paris.

1867. They are penniless. He returns to his parents' home, while Camille stays in Paris. Their first son, Jean, is born. Monet attempts suicide by leaping into the river, but survives. He writes to Bazille of his love for his son and paints *Jean Monet in His Cradle* and *Portrait of the Artist's Son Asleep*.

1868. Paints Camille sitting on a river-bank in *On the Bank of the Seine at Bennecourt*.

1870. Marries Camille. Prussia invades France and Paris is besieged. The Monets take refuge in London, where they rent rooms in Piccadilly.

Monet paints Camille in *Meditation: Mme Monet on the Sofa*. In London, he meets the influential French art dealer Durand-Ruel.

1871. The Monets return to France and settle at Argenteuil, on the Seine close to Paris.

1871–8. Paints many views of Argenteuil and its surroundings, including views of the river and the fields.

1873. Monet becomes a leading figure in a new society founded by young artists (Société Anonyme des Artistes Peintres, Sculpteurs, Graveurs).

1874. The Society has an exhibition where one of Monet's paintings, *Impression, Sunrise*, causes a great stir and the artists become known as the Impressionists.

1876. He stays at the Château Rottembourg belonging to the wealthy businessman and art patron Ernest Hoschedé and his wife Alice. Hoschedé owns a department store in Paris. They have five children: Marthe, Blanche, Suzanne, Jacques, Germaine.

1877. Ernest Hoschedé is bankrupted. Alice gives birth to Jean-Pierre, possibly Monet's son.

1878. Camille's second child, Michel Monet, born. Camille is very ill, probably suffering from cancer of the womb. The Monets move to the isolated village of Vétheuil. The Hoschedé family move in with them. Both families are extremely poor. Ernest goes back to Paris and tries to earn some money.

1879. Camille dies on 5 September. Monet paints *Camille on Her Deathbed*.

1879–80. A particularly cold winter and spring. The temperature drops to -25°C and the village is cut off for weeks. Monet paints the icy landscape.

1881. Monet and Alice, now taking care of eight children, move to Poissy, a larger town near Vétheuil.

1881–9. Monet travels round France on painting trips, to the Normandy coast, Brittany, the South of France and the Massif Central.

1883. Visits the Riviera with Renoir. Rents Le Pressoir (The Cider-House) at Giverny.

1889. Works in Paris with Rodin.

1890. Paints the first of the *Haystack* series.

1891. Ernest Hoschedé dies and is buried at Giverny.

1892. Begins the Rouen cathedral series. Marries Alice in July.

1897. His eldest son, Jean, marries Alice's daughter Blanche.

1899. Starts paintings of the Japanese bridge and the pools in his garden at Giverny. Goes to London with Alice in September–October, stays in the Savoy Hotel and paints views of the Thames. Alice's daughter Suzanne dies. Michel Monet goes to London to learn English.

1899–1902. Britain is fighting the Boer War in South Africa.

1900. Monet stays in the Savoy again, on his own, February–March. Rooms on the floor above have been given up to officers wounded in the Boer War.

1901. Queen Victoria dies, 22 January.

1901. Monet's final visit to London.

1903. Starts sequence of *Water-lilies* paintings at Giverny.

1908. He and Alice visit Venice.

1910. Works on enlarging water-garden at Giverny.

1911. Alice dies, 19 May.

1912. Monet is suffering from cataracts.

1914. His eldest son, Jean, dies. Blanche moves back to keep house.

1915. A new studio is built in the grounds at Giverny for work on the huge *Water-lilies* paintings.

1923. Monet has cataract operation, partly successful.

1926. Monet dies on 5 December, aged eighty-six, and is buried at Giverny.

1927. *Water-lilies* paintings (*Les Grandes Décorations*) installed in the Orangerie, Paris, and opened to the public.

1931. Michel Monet marries Gabrielle Bonaventure, an artist's model. Michel dies in 1966, leaving everything to the Musée Marmottan in Paris.

Picture Credits

1. *Waterloo Bridge*, 1904. Kunsthaus, Zürich. Photograph © Christie's Images Ltd 2002.
2. *On the Bank of the Seine, Bennecourt*, 1868, Potter Palmer Collection, 1922.427. Photograph © 2002, The Art Institute of Chicago, All Rights Reserved.
3. *The Artist's Son*, 1868. Ny Carlsberg Glyptotek, Copenhagen.
4. *Waterloo Bridge, Cloudy Day*, 1900. Hugh Lane Municipal Gallery of Modern Art, Dublin/Bridgeman Art Library.
5. *Meditation*, or *Madame Monet on the Sofa*, c. 1871. Musée d'Orsay, Paris/Bridgeman Art Library.
6. *Charing Cross Bridge, Fog*, 1902. Art Gallery of Ontario, Toronto/Bridgeman Art Library.
7. *The Thames at Waterloo Bridge*, 1903. Private Collection/Bridgeman Art Library.
8. *Camille on Her Deathbed*, 1879, oil on canvas. Musée d'Orsay, Paris. Photo RMN – Hervé Lewandowski.
9. *Waterloo Bridge, London, at Dusk*, 1904. Collection of Mr and Mrs Paul Mellon, Photograph © 2002 Board of Trustees, National Gallery of Art, Washington.

427

10. *Houses of Parliament, Sunset,* 1904. Kunsthaus Zürich. ©
    Kunsthaus Zürich. All rights reserved.
11. *The Thames at Charing Cross,* 1903. Musée des Beaux-
    Arts, Lyons/Bridgeman Art Library.
12. *Garden at Giverny,* 1923. Musée de Grenoble/
    Bridgeman Art Library.

The paintings are all by Claude Monet (1840–1926).
Photographic material was supplied by the owners unless
otherwise credited.